Murder by Proxy

By

Joe B. Parr

MURDER BY PROXY

My Girls Publishing Fort Worth, TX

Print ISBN: 978-0-9913947-8-4

eBook ISBN: 978-0-9913947-9-1

Also by Joe B Parr

Fiction

The Victim
Stolen Innocence
Unseen Carnage

Non Fiction

Share Your Story
While You Were Away (limited publication)

For Conway, Cosner and Calhoun.
Bupo loves you.

JOE B. PARR

Chapter 1

"Weston Caldwell, I'm gonna kill you!"

The screeching woman's voice froze him on the steps of his building. He squinted against the bright afternoon as his gaze rose to see the barrel of a gun bearing down on him. Behind the trembling white knuckles, the look in her eyes scared him more than the gun.

His hands reflexively raised in surrender. "Whoa. Hold on."

"Hold on? You son of a bitch. You ruined my life."

Caldwell's heartrate spiked, but he took a deep breath, trying to stay calm. He flashed his trademark smile hoping to diffuse the situation. This wasn't the first time he'd faced down a gun. He focused on her face, blotchy red, sweat dripping off her forehead. Not a good sign.

She stood just off the curb on 5th street, maybe five yards from him. Cars already honked as they swerved around her, seemingly oblivious to the fact that she was holding a gun and screaming.

He had his back to a closed door. The only thing separating them were a few paces and a thin brass rail.

Who is this nut?

A crowd, attracted by the commotion, gathered on the sidewalk to either side of him. A few appeared to be calling 911, most used their phones to record the situation. "Ma'am, I think you've got the wrong person. I don't even…"

"You're Weston Caldwell, aren't you?" She wagged the gun at him like a finger.

His eyes tracked the barrel. "I am, but…"

"From Othello Industries, right?"

"Yes, but…"

"That's all I need to know." She set her jaw, stepped forward two more paces onto the curb, and jerked the gun into firing position.

Caldwell ducked, and raised his hands over his head. "Wait.

Please. Wait." This was getting out of hand. His voice was almost a cry. "I didn't do… I don't even… Who the hell are you?"

"Who am I?" She paused, looking momentarily confused. Then her eyes bulged. "You son of a bitch." She swept her left hand across her brow. Drops of perspiration flew into the warm air. Her outstretched right hand shook, pushing the barrel of the gun in all directions as she started to cry. "You know who I am. Don't play dumb with me. I have the emails. I have the texts, the SnapChats."

"What are…"

"Shut up, you bastard. Just shut the fuck up." Saliva sprayed through her sobs. "You know what you did."

Keeping his hands in front of him as if they'd stop a bullet, Caldwell calmed his voice and talked slowly. "Lady, I really don't know who you are or what you're talking about. I'm happy to help you, but you've gotta put down the gun."

"Help me? Oh, you've done enough already."

The crowd had expanded. It was late afternoon and the early work departures had mixed with the Sundance Square tourists. The onlookers gave the two a wide berth. Traffic had begun to back up.

This was great theater, just another reality show. They were busy snapping pictures and filming the drama unfolding in front of them.

A faint siren cut through the murmur of traffic and downtown noise. Someone must have gotten through to the police. Caldwell relaxed at the sound. A weight lifted from his shoulders. For a moment, he felt a cool breeze wash across the sheen on his forehead.

Maybe the cops can calm her down.

He smiled internally at the irony of him looking forward to the police showing up.

The woman stiffened and her hand steadied. "They aren't going to save you. You tried to destroy everything I lived for."

The high pitched siren grew louder, echoing off the tall buildings. With it, the fury in her eyes swelled. She sneered. "You won't take away my husband. You won't take away my job."

"Lady, you've got the wrong guy." He heard the panic in his own voice. His heart tore at his chest.

Her voice roared. "If I'm going to lose my kids and my life, I'm going to take you with me."

8

Caldwell begged, his pulse pounding in his ears. He almost dropped to his knees. "Lady, please listen to me."

The crowd turned in unison at the squeal of tires. The patrol car hopped a curb and slammed to a stop on 5th Street.

For a breath, time stopped. The woman's head twitched toward the sound. Caldwell saw his opening. He reached toward the back of his waistline while he lunged toward the rail, and her. But his hand never reached its destination. Flashes exploded from her muzzle, each one ripped through his flesh and jerked his body backwards out of control.

Some people dived for the ground, others ran. The woman's rage squeezed into shot after shot. Caldwell's body danced in a death spiral before dropping to the concrete step and rolling down to the sidewalk.

*　　*　　*　　*

She convulsed as a sob racked through her. Her eyes stared for a moment at the bloody lump on the ground.

Car doors slammed. Footsteps shuffled as the crowd scattered. The officers swam through the crowd and drew their weapons. They approached from behind her.

"Police, freeze."

The command was muffled in her ears.

"Drop the weapon."

She slowly lowered her arm and her shoulders slumped as if all her energy, her life, had flushed from her. With the crowd quiet, the scrape of dry leaves being pushed by the breeze intruded on the moment.

One officer crept forward, his voice calm. "Put the gun on the ground and drop to your knees."

She looked down at Weston Caldwell, the final vestiges of his life oozing from his chest. Her eyes went flat and the corners of her mouth twitched up. She opened her hand and the pistol clanged to the ground as she complied with the order. The officers swarmed, shoved her to the ground and cuffed her.

Chapter 2

"Guess he's had better days." Detective Jake Hunter removed his sun glasses as he and his partner, Detective Billy Sanders, stepped under the decorative metal and glass canopy attached to The Towers Condominium building.

The Towers Condominium is a thirty-five-story building in the center of downtown Fort Worth. The first really tall building built in the city. When it opened in 1974, it was the centerpiece of the Fort Worth skyline.

The infamous F3 tornado in March of 2000 that struck downtown inflicted so much damage on the building that it was deemed uninhabitable and all the tenants dispersed throughout the city. Because of asbestos in the building, the costs to either demolish or rebuild the structure deemed the endeavor prohibitive.

The city boarded it up with plywood and it sat as an eyesore for years. It was nicknamed the birdhouse because of the vent circles cut in the plywood sheets.

When the demand for downtown condominiums reached a fevered pitch in 2010, the potential profits outweighed the costs and developers renovated the structure to be a high end residential community.

Hunter sighed, let his eyes close for a moment as they adjusted to the lighting. He ached all over as if he'd worked out really hard the day before, only he hadn't, and this soreness and stiffness had become the norm rather than the exception.

Never knew forty-five was so ancient. Damn, getting old sucks.

He looked down at the bullet riddled corpse and whistled low. "He sure pissed off somebody."

"You can say that again."

Hunter and Billy turned to the voice.

"Officer Delaney, sir, Rich Delaney." The young patrolman, tall, lean and ramrod straight, reached out and shook each detective's hand. "My partner and I were first on the scene. She emptied her magazine on him just as we pulled up."

Hunter smiled at his eagerness. "Well, Officer Delaney, do we know who he is?"

"Not yet, sir. We've only had time to tape off the scene. CSI should be here momentarily to start processing. We followed procedure and called an ambulance right before we called you, but…" He glanced over at the body. "We checked for a pulse, couldn't find one so we contacted the ME's office."

The officer spent another five minutes describing what they'd encountered upon their arrival and letting them know the suspect was secured in the back of their squad car. "We advised her of her rights, but she seems a bit out of it."

"Good work, son." Hunter suppressed a smile as he scribbled notes on a small pad he'd pulled from the inside pocket of his sport coat. He noted the crowd behind the police tape with their cameras filming every move. "Have we identified any witnesses?"

Delaney nodded. "There were plenty of people who saw the whole thing, most caught some amount on their phones. My partner is collecting names and making sure they stick around."

"Can you help him with that while Detective Sanders and I look around? Oh, and find me some of those recordings."

"Yes, sir." He stood up straight and almost saluted before he spun on his heels and hurried off.

Sanders eyed Delaney as he scurried off, then snickered. "Damn, Cowboy, he sure thinks you're someone important. Must be all that gray hair."

"It's called salt and pepper." Hunter shot him a sideways glance, bowed up with his shoulders back, stretched out his lean six-foot-two-inch frame. "At least I've got hair." He ran his hand through his short cropped hair making it spike just a little. His dress jeans, Hugo Boss Oxford shoes and his Brooks Brother's sport coat belied his Cowboy nickname and made him look slightly overdressed for a crime scene.

"Choice, my friend." Sanders rubbed his glistening dark brown scalp. "I have a beautiful head I choose to feature." Sanders was nearly fifteen years younger than Hunter. He was a couple of inches shorter, but had once been a Division I college football running back and looked like he could still play.

Both men smiled, enjoying the playful banter. While they had been partners for less than a year, that year represented Billy Sanders' career as a detective. What started as a temporary assignment had turned into a roller coaster of big cases and dangerous situations. Somewhere along the way, the assignment had become permanent and the resulting bond was intense.

Hunter pointed to the door of the luxury high rise condominium building. "According to Officer Eager Beaver, our victim was leaving the building when the suspect confronted him. They had a short but heated exchange, and she ended the discussion with a bunch of bullets."

"Yeah, doesn't sound like we'll have to spend too much time figuring out who did it."

"But we need to understand why. That starts with figuring out who these people are."

Hunter knelt down and reached toward the body.

"What do you think you're doing detective?" A strong, but melodic female voice cut through the ambient noise and stopped his hand mid-reach. "You touch that body without gloves and I'll keep your hand as a souvenir."

Unable to hide his smile, he looked up to see an auburn haired beauty wearing a CSI windbreaker and carrying an evidence collection kit.

"Why CSI Morgan, you know these hands are at your service anytime you request."

"Always with the promises." Stacy waved a dismissive hand at him. "Why don't you let my team start processing?" She nodded toward the crowd. "Looks like you've got plenty of witnesses to talk to, and lots of 'detecting' to do."

Hunter moved to stand up, but was surprised at the amount of effort he had to expend. He managed to get upright without touching the body. "As you wish."

Her green eyes sparkled at the reference to one of their favorite movies. When she smiled, the tiny scar beneath her left eye seemed to dance. What had started out a little less than a year earlier with Stacy welcoming Hunter back from his leave of absence, had blossomed into a not very well kept secret relationship. Now they tended to smile a lot and finish each other's sentences.

*   *   *   *

After a few more rounds of flirtatious banter, Stacy Morgan dispatched Hunter and Sanders and set to work on the scene. One of her assistants photographed the area while another began a grid search for evidence, marking each find with a small yellow cone. As the lead forensics investigator, Stacy performed the initial examination of the body before the medical examiner arrived.

The victim, Caucasian, well dressed and groomed, appeared to be in his early forties. His body lay crumpled in a bloody heap at the bottom of a step. Based on the time of day and his upscale casual clothing, he could've been heading to a business meeting or connecting with someone for late afternoon drinks.

Her gaze scanned a few feet further down the sidewalk and noted the spent shell casings scattered near the edge of the sidewalk and out into the street. She counted.

Thirteen. Damn, the shooter wasn't fooling around.

She turned back to the body and studied its position. He was crumpled on the sidewalk lying on his side in a large pool of his own blood. Without even stepping close, she could count five bullet holes, four in his torso and one in his leg. She felt sure that when she turned him over, there'd be several more.

At this range, even a complete psycho will hit most of their shots.

She followed the natural trajectory of the bullets past the body and saw two ricochet marks on the concrete. One bullet had embedded in the aluminum fascia surrounding the glass doors of the building's entrance, with one pane of glass splintered. Possibly the result of one of the ricochets.

Her attention moved back to the body. She reached around with her gloved hand to extract his wallet. When she lifted up his untucked shirttail to get to his pocket, she froze.

"Well, aren't you full of surprises?"

Tucked neatly into a holster inside his pants in the small of his back was a compact semi-automatic pistol. It was silver and black, and barely visible above his belt.

"Roy…" Stacy signaled for the CSI tech to come over. She left the shirttail flipped up and pointed. "Document this. Get several shots."

"You got it."

She stood as Roy clicked off images from multiple angles.

Being careful not to move the body, Stacy knelt and gingerly slid the holstered weapon from his waistline. She removed the pistol from its leather home and inspected it to make sure the safety was engaged. Once confirmed, she ejected the magazine, noted it was full and set it on the ground. Then she racked the slide to eject the cartridge that was in the chamber.

A fully loaded magazine with one in the chamber. He was ready for action.

She noted on the evidence bag that it was a Bersa Thunder .380. After she slid the pistol, the seven shot magazine and the loose cartridges into separate evidence bags, Stacy returned to her original objective of retrieving his wallet.

"Let's see who our lucky grand prize winner is today." She pulled it from his pocket and flipped it open. "Hmm. Mr. Weston Caldwell, looks like you've won a permanent vacation." She frowned down at him. "Wonder what you did to enter the contest."

Chapter 3

"Stop right there. Don't take another step."

Stacy had turned at the sound of one of the glass doors opening. A dapper looking man in a suit and bowtie flinched and stopped short. "What? But…" He composed himself, raised his head indignantly. "I'm Sebastian Calvert, General Manager of The Towers and…"

"I don't care if you're the Pope. If you take one more step into my crime scene, I'll have you arrested." She pointed to the crime scene tape stretched across the doors. "That yellow tape is there for a reason."

"But…"

"Go around."

His mouth carped for a moment before he huffed, spun and disappeared back into the building.

Hunter laughed. "Really? Not even the Pope?"

Stacy turned and cocked her eyebrow. "Well, maybe the Pope. But only because he wears those cute Pope shoes." She nodded down the sidewalk toward Throckmorton Street where the manager quickstepped toward them. "He moves fast. Your turn, Cowboy."

Hunter had earned the nickname, Cowboy, early in his career for none of the obvious reasons.

With an exasperated exhale, Hunter moved to intercept the man. They arrived simultaneously at the tape and Hunter flashed his badge. "I'm Detective Jake Hu—"

"Are you in charge of this mess?"

A number of inappropriate remarks flashed through Hunter's mind, but he resisted the urge. "Yes. How can I he—"

"When will this be cleaned up and when will your people be out of here?"

Hunter set his jaw. "Why don't we start with 'who are you'?"

A mixture of annoyance and insult flashed across the man's face.

"As I told your..." He waved his hand dismissively toward Stacy. "Crime Tech girl." He straightened. "I'm Sebastian Calvert and I manage The Tower. This mess is inconveniencing my clients." His hands flittered about anxiously. "This is the last thing I need right now. When will you be done?"

With a sarcastic bite to his voice, Hunter pointed at the body. "Considering that at least one of your clients has been permanently inconvenienced, it may take a bit to get this 'mess' cleaned up."

As if acknowledging the body for the first time, Calvert huffed. "Not surprising, considering."

"You knew this man?"

"Of course. I know all of my tenants. Even his type."

"And what type would that be?"

"You know... hoodlum, gangster, criminal."

Feeling certain the man would continue without prompting, Hunter let a momentary silence do the work for him.

Calvert rolled his eyes and folded his arms across his chest. "He and his associates came and went at all hours. Wearing jackets even in the heat. You couldn't miss the bulges. Clearly, they were all packing heat."

Hunter tried to hide his smirk at the term. "Packing heat, huh?"

"Obviously. I can assure you it wasn't just some sort of second amendment statement. They were bad guys."

"What can you tell me about Mr. Caldwell?"

The manager spent the next few minutes providing basic details he knew of Caldwell's life. It wasn't much more than his condo number, and confirmation his employer was listed as Othello Industries all interlaced with additional suspicion and innuendo.

When Hunter felt he'd gotten all the useful information from Calvert, he nodded back in the direction from which Calvert had approached. "Thank you very much for your time, Mr. Calvert. I assure you we want to get this mess cleaned up as quickly as you do."

He escorted him outside the tape and left him craning to see what was happening on the scene.

"Detective."

Hunter turned to see Officer Delaney approaching.

"As you requested, we have several witnesses lined up to speak with you and Detective Sanders. Almost all of them have some amount of the altercation recorded on their phones."

"Great." Hunter surveyed the scene, caught Billy's eye and signaled for him to come over. "Can you bring them over to our car one at a time? Ask the others to please not watch the video or discuss what they witnessed. I'd like to get their views of what happened without it being processed."

Delaney nodded. "I sure will, but most of them have already watched the video. Half of them have already posted on FaceBook."

Hunter swore under his breath. "Social media." He shook his head. "It's going to be the death of us all." He looked at Delaney. "Do what you can."

*　　*　　*　　*

"This ought to be interesting." Billy nodded toward the first witness Delaney escorted over. The   red-haired guy, mid-twenties in skinny jeans and a gray hoodie, had his head so buried in his phone that Delaney had to guide him by his elbow. He was grinning, typing and laughing to himself. "By the way he's bouncing around, you'd think he won the lotto."

Delaney squeezed his elbow and stopped him just before he ran into the side of Hunter's SUV. "Detectives, this is Carter Sandford. He saw the whole incident."

"Saw it?" The guy looked up, eyes so wide Hunter thought he might hurt himself. "Hell, I got the whole thing." He pushed the phone toward Hunter. "This is so fucking cool! I've never seen someone get shot before. I guess you guys see it all the time."

"Not really…"

"Man, she just blew his ass away. Here, let me show you."

"Mr. Sandford." Hunter held up his hand to try to calm him. "I need you to take a deep breath, slow down and tell me what happened from the very beginning. Then we'll watch the clip. Okay?"

He nodded. "Sure thing." He pointed toward the street. "I was walking down the sidewalk over there when all of a sudden I hear this lady scream this guy's name. When I looked up, I saw she had a gun pointed at him." He grinned. "Man, I didn't waste any time. I grabbed my phone and started filming."

Hunter had been taking notes since they arrived and continued as the man spoke. But now he looked at his notepad and could barely read what he'd written. He squinted at first thinking his eyes were failing him, but realized that it wasn't his eyes, it was his penmanship. He frowned, flipped to a new page and continued. "What else did she say to him?"

He shook his head. "She just kept screaming about how he ruined her life and he wasn't getting away with it."

"What was his response?"

The guy calmed a little. "Well, that was the weird part. He didn't seem to even know who she was. He kept telling her she had the wrong guy." He exhaled as if what happened was finally sinking in. "But when the cops pulled up, she started firing and firing." He blinked. "It was really loud. Scared me to death. My recording is kind of jumbled at that point because I was diving for the ground."

Hunter could see that the adrenaline of the moment was starting to drain from the witness. Based on his experience, he knew that Mr. Excited was about to come crashing down from his adrenaline high any minute.

"This might be a good time to see that video."

The man tapped on his phone screen and turned it toward the detectives. The scene, exactly as had been described, unfolded on the small display.

Even as a homicide detective, it's not every day he saw a murder played out in high definition. Hunter was taken aback by how quickly it unfolded. In a matter of minutes, the scene went from the initial encounter to the woman being handcuffed.

Hunter looked at Billy. "Notice the guy's reaction?"

Sanders nodded. "Yeah, he looks genuinely confused. Like he has no idea who she is."

The man bounced on his feet and started to speak, but Hunter held up his hand and shushed him before he looked back to Billy. "There's no doubt in her mind she's got the right guy."

"Yeah, but based on what she says, it's also clear she's never met him before."

"Hmm…" Hunter gazed out over the scene and watched as Doc

and the ME team inspected the body. "Interesting."

He turned to the witness. "Mr. Sandford, you see that very attractive lady over there wearing the CSI vest?"

The man nodded and gave Hunter a sly grin.

Hunter glared at him and waved for Delaney. "Officer Delaney's going to escort you over to her so that she can get a copy of your video." He handed him a business card. "If there's anything else you remember, please give me a call."

Hunter shook his head and looked at Billy as the man was led away. "It's a good thing this one won't have to go to trial. Can you imagine putting that dipshit on the stand as a witness?"

"By the time it's over today, we may consider him the smart one."

Chapter 4

"Please, make it stop. I can't take any more of these self-obsessed social media morons." Hunter rubbed his eyes.

"That's the way of the world now, Cowboy." Sanders smirked. "Get used to it."

Hunter put his pen in his pocket. "I've had enough. We've talked to ten different witnesses, each one more worried about how many views they're going to get than the fact that they'd just seen a man murdered in cold blood." He shook his head. "Have Delaney take the rest of the statements."

"That'll make his day."

"At least someone will get something out of this." Hunter nodded toward the patrol car. "Meet me at the car and let's see if we can get anything out of our shooter."

Billy headed off to find Delaney as Hunter surveyed the scene. While it was cut and dried on who shot the victim, the rest didn't make sense. A woman, who, based on every eye witness account, was unknown to the victim, just walked up, accused the guy of ruining her life and emptied a 9mm on him in broad daylight.

Never ceases to amaze me. Just when I think I've seen it all.

Hunter reached up with his left hand to put his notepad in his pocket, but dropped it halfway up. Like his hand just stopped working. As he looked down at the notebook on the ground, he rubbed his hand. His fingers were stiff and a little numb. He interlaced them with his right hand and stretched them out. This wasn't the first time this had happened.

Hunter picked up his notebook, shook his head to get refocused and ambled over to the patrol car to find the woman sitting in the back seat with her hands cuffed behind her back. She rocked front and back, stared at the headrest and muttered to herself. He noted the faraway look in her eyes and shook his head.

This ought to be fun.

Sanders stepped up just as Hunter reached for the door handle. "You getting in the back with her, Cowboy?"

"As long as you're in the front and ready to shoot her if she gets crazy on me."

Billy cut his eyes toward the car. "Get crazy? I think she's already there."

"Good point." Hunter pulled on the handle. "I think I'll just talk with her through the window. Hop in the front and roll it down."

Hunter's concerns dissipated quickly as the woman showed no indication that she even noticed him leaning into the open window. Sanders remained in the front seat. Even though both were turned directly facing her, she hadn't reacted at all. She continued to rock, stare and mutter.

"Ma'am, I'm Detective Jake Hunter. This is my partner Detective Billy Sanders. Can you tell us your name?"

No response.

"Ma'am." Hunter waved his hand in front of her face. "Can you hear me?"

He looked at Billy. "She's totally gone."

Sanders shrugged.

"We have no idea who she is?"

"None." Billy shook his head. "No ID on her, no cell phone and no car keys. Her prints aren't in the system, so she doesn't have a criminal record. Until she snaps out of it or until someone comes looking for her, we've got squat."

Hunter spent the next few minutes trying to coax the woman from her catatonic state with no success. He shrugged, and looked at Sanders. The woman continued to rock and mutter.

"When Delaney wraps up with the witnesses, have him take her to the station to book her as a Jane Doe." He looked at his watch. The afternoon had slipped away. "We can try to ID her again tomorrow."

Billy nodded. "You got it."

"I'm going to walk the scene one more time. Once you've got Delaney set, let's compare notes with Stacy."

"Sounds like a plan."

Hunter stepped away from the car into the late afternoon shadows of downtown. The buildings had emptied their daytime tenants onto the sidewalks and the streets were now full of people trying to make their way home.

He scanned the street and sidewalk taped off south of The Towers. Doc and his team had removed the body and were probably already back at the morgue. Stacy and the crime scene techs were wrapping up their activities. Even Delaney and his partner looked to be ready to call it a day.

Hunter smiled at Delaney's excitement. He remembered his first homicide as a patrolman.

That was a long time ago. Makes me feel old.

"Did you get anything from the shooter?"

"What?" Stacy's voice shook him from his reminiscence. "Uh, no. The woman was completely out of it. What did your team find?"

Stacy reviewed the details about the number of shots and the type of weapon. She highlighted the victim's identity and that he was armed and clearly ready for a fight.

Hunter nodded. "According to the building manager, he apparently lived outside the lines some."

Billy had rejoined them. "We'll figure out who the hell she is tomorrow and do a full background on Weston Caldwell. Between the two, hopefully we can figure out what set this off."

"Yeah, it's not every day you see a housewife gun down a gangster in the middle of downtown." Hunter raised an eyebrow. "Something tells me we've barely scratched the surface on this one."

Chapter 5

"Have we got anything on Weston Caldwell?" Hunter burst into the conference room Tuesday morning without even nodding. The sun streamed in from the large window on the opposite wall.

Sanders sat at one of the work tables that formed a U shape with the whiteboard at the front. He cocked an eyebrow as he looked up from his laptop. "Good morning to you too Cowboy."

"Good morning my ass." Hunter dropped his laptop on the table. "I didn't sleep for shit last night." He looked at his watch: 9:30 a.m. "Hell, half the day's gone. Traffic on 35 was completely stopped." He tossed his half full Starbucks cup in the trash. "On top of that, my coffee's cold."

What Hunter didn't say was that today, like more and more mornings, his normal routine had just taken longer. Over the past six months, he'd gone from needing thirty minutes to go from alarm to out the door, to now consistently fifty minutes and sometimes an hour. The frustrating part was that there didn't seem to be any specific reason. Every activity was just taking a little longer. It was like he was in slow motion.

Billy smiled. "Could be worse. Could be Weston Caldwell."

Hunter shook off his frustration and stopped his mini-tantrum. "Yeah." He smiled and shook his head. "You know what's bugging me the most?"

Sanders shrugged.

"It's the concept that someone with no criminal record and no obvious motive would gun somebody down in the middle of the day with countless witnesses, knowing full well they'd get caught." He paused and pursed his lips. "I know she's nuts but that's just full blown crazy."

"As a wise old detective once told me, every crime has a reason."

"Watch that old stuff." He smiled. "Now, what have you got on Caldwell?"

Sanders tapped a few keys. "Quite the checkered past. Weston Caldwell is a homegrown bad guy, born and raised on the west side in the Ridglea area."

"Ridglea?" Hunter smiled. "Not exactly the neighborhood that comes to mind when I hear the term bad guy."

"No doubt. Apparently in his late teens he traded in his silver spoon for a chrome semi. Had a number of run-ins with the law, a variety of charges. Everything from assault, to breaking and entering to stealing a car. Dad's money got him off each time." Billy scrolled down. "By the time he was in his early twenties, apparently his dad got tired of coming to his rescue and he served five years for robbing a jewelry store."

"Based on how he was dressed and where he was living, I'm guessing he graduated from robbing jewelry stores."

"He did indeed. During his stint in Huntsville, he shared a cell with one of the lieutenants in the Mazanti family. They're into just about everything, drugs, gambling, you name it. He must have impressed. When he was released, he worked for them as muscle. He's been a person of interest in a number of assaults, but nothing stuck. According to our organized crime unit, he'd climbed the ladder to the point where he ran their online prostitution business and a couple of their strip clubs."

"That would certainly explain the clothes and the digs." Hunter frowned. "Our shooter doesn't strike me as a high end call girl or a stripper. More like a frumpy housewife. Did you get anything on her?"

"We did, thanks to social media." Sanders smirked. "Once the video of the shooting went viral on FaceBook yesterday, we got several calls into dispatch. Our shooter is Lucy Stanton. Initial background check turned up no criminal record and no connection to the Mazanti clan. She's married with two young children and worked as an accountant for Endless Wind Industries. They manufacture electronics that run wind turbines."

"Any connection to Caldwell?"

"Nothing so far."

"There's got to be something. You mentioned she's married. What about the husband?"

Sanders flipped through his notepad. "Looked him up this morning. Robert Stanton seems to be as clean as his wife. I've got an address. They're down near Westcreek Park. We can go see him later today."

Hunter nodded, got up and started pacing, talking, more to himself than to Billy. "A suburban housewife and accountant, guns down a local mobster in broad daylight on a downtown sidewalk." He shook his head, stopped and turned to Sanders. "You said they had kids?"

"Two. A twelve year old boy and a ten year old girl." Billy furrowed his brow. "Other than ages, I didn't go deeper on the kids. I can, but…"

"No need." Hunter waived it off. "I was just thinking that maybe the daughter had gotten mixed up in Caldwell's business and Lucy Stanton went full blown 'momma bear' on him, but she's too young."

Sanders shook his head. "Doesn't seem likely."

Hunter looked up at the clock. It was a little after ten. "I know it's still early, but have we heard anything from Stacy's team? I know they were working late last night."

"We can check. I called Stacy shortly before eight to let her know the shooter's ID."

Hunter reached over and punched in an extension on the speaker phone.

Stacy's voice crackled on the line. "You know patience is a virtue."

"I've never been accused of being virtuous." Hunter smiled.

"Now that's for sure." She giggled. "Good morning, Cowboy. Missed you last night."

A sheepish grin washed across his face. "Hey, Stace. Ditto."

Sanders laughed and puckered his lips in fake kisses.

Hunter rolled his eyes at Sanders and refocused on the speaker phone. "Got anything new for us?"

"You must be living right. I sent one of my guys back to the scene first thing this morning to take a few more measurements. When Billy gave us the ID, we ran a DMV search to get a make and model for her car. We got lucky and found it around the corner from the scene."

Hunter shot a look at Sanders and spoke into the speaker. "Find anything in it?"

"My guy wasn't able to process the car there. We're having it towed into the garage. He did find her purse, ID and phone. Nothing out of the ordinary on the purse or ID, but the phone was a little strange."

Hunter stared at the speaker. "Strange how?"

"The guy I sent down there, Roy is one of my tech experts. Knows phones and laptops inside and out." She paused. "While he hasn't had a chance to do any real diagnostics on it, he said the phone was completely toast."

"Okay? So, her phone didn't work."

"Not didn't work or was just broken. Completely fried. The circuitry had been fried to where nothing on it works. It's got power but everything else was obliterated. He said it was like an EMP hit it."

"Alright, let's pretend for a moment I'm not a computer geek. What the hell is an EMP?"

"Electromagnetic pulse." Sanders chimed in. "It's like a bomb that only affects electronic circuitry. Renders it useless to the point that nothing would be able to be recovered from the device."

Stacy jumped back in. "Might not mean a thing, but it is strange. We'll dig a little deeper once Roy gets back in the lab, we'll see if there's anything that can be salvaged. Other than that, we're still just getting everything logged in. Going to be a long day."

"I'll buy you dinner tonight," Hunter added.

"I'll hold you to that, Cowboy. Gotta go." She clicked off.

Hunter was pacing before the sound from the speaker had died. Just hearing Stacy's voice had lifted his mood. The lack of sleep and the heavy traffic were now distant memories.

He stopped and turned to Billy. "Can you keep digging on Caldwell and Stanton between now and lunch? After we grab a bite, we can go see the husband to see what he can…"

Hunter was interrupted when his phone rang. He pulled it from his jacket pocket, looked at the caller ID and smiled. "I need to get this."

He stepped out of the conference and punched the accept button.

"Colt Barkley. How the hell are you?"

"Better than you. That's for damn sure, Cowboy." Colt laughed, and continued in his cocky, self assured style. "Tell me, is Stacy still wasting her time hanging around with you?"

"Hard to imagine, but she is. How's the Texas Ranger's office today?"

Hunter stood in the hall as the two men caught up on family and home life. Colt Barkley was a seasoned detective with the state investigative agency. He and Hunter worked a human trafficking case together about six months earlier, and had clicked immediately. At six foot five without his boots and Stetson, Barkley's intimidating physical presence matched his cocky, loud and aggressive nature.

After all the usual questions were asked and answered, Hunter's tone got serious. "So, what's up with you Colt?"

There was a momentary pause on the line. "I'm in Fort Worth and I need to meet with you."

"Billy and I are going to grab a bite around noon. You want to meet up with us?"

"Lunch sounds great, but it needs to be just you and me."

It was Hunter's turn to pause. "Okay… What's going on?"

"I'll tell you when I see you. Can you meet me at Risky's in the Stockyards?"

"Sure"

"Great. I'll see you at noon. Thanks, Cowboy."

JOE B. PARR

Chapter 6

The Stockyards area in North Fort Worth catered predominantly to the tourist trade. However, there were a number of long established homegrown restaurants that attracted the locals as well. Risky's BBQ was toward the top. For over seventy-five years, Risky's had served their version of hand rubbed Texas BBQ.

Even without his trademark white Stetson, Colt Barkley was easy to spot across the crowded restaurant. He stood a head taller than everyone in the room. Hunter caught his eye, nodded and swam through the sea of bodies to reach him.

The two shook hands, yelled some quick hello's and made their way to the counter to place their orders. As they pushed through the line, Barkley noticed that instead of his normal beef brisket and fried okra, Hunter ordered grilled chicken and vegetables.

"Look at you being all healthy."

Hunter frowned. "I'm not exactly a spring chicken anymore."

"You're mid-forties, not mid-sixties."

"Sometimes I feel like I'm late-seventies."

The conversation died as they paid. Once through the line, they got lucky and found a corner table where the crowd's volume was somewhat tolerable.

Hunter settled in and situated his plate and utensils. "How're those two women that run your life?"

At the thought of his wife and daughter, Barkley flashed a crooked smile. "You got that run-my-life part right. They're keeping me in line."

"Is that possible?"

Barkley laughed.

"Come on. Don't hold out on me. I need to see pictures."

Colt reached into his back pocket for his phone, punched up his photo gallery and slid it across the table.

Hunter swiped through the photos. "Chelsey's just as beautiful as ever. How's she doing?"

"She recently got promoted to the Lead ER Nurse at Dell Seton Medical Center at The University of Texas in downtown Austin. It's the only Level One Trauma Center in the city, so she's been more than a little busy."

"No kidding." A big grin broke out across Hunter's face as his eyes landed on Colt's only daughter. "How old is Cassie now?"

"Just turned eight."

"Good thing her Daddy carries a gun and a badge. Even without her front teeth, she's a cutie. I pity you when she hits her teens."

Barkley nodded with a knowing smile.

It wasn't until Hunter mentioned the gun and badge that he realized, instead of his standard Texas Ranger dark blue suit and starched white shirt, Barkley wore a pair of dark, creased, Wrangler jeans, black boots and a light blue button downed shirt. There was no sign of his gun or badge.

Hunter nodded toward Barkley. "You're dressed kind of casual today. Are you on vacation?"

"Technically, yes."

"Technically?"

The smile slid off Colt's face and his posture stiffened. "I'm on vacation from the Rangers, but I'm not in Fort Worth for pleasure. It's business."

"Okay?"

"I'm working a situation I can't pursue as a Ranger. I'm helping a friend."

Hunter stopped eating. "So, this is a business lunch?"

"Yeah, it is." Barkley pursed his lips. The serious tone settled over the table thick and heavy. "I'm working a case off the books and I may need some help along the way. It could be dangerous and it may require me to step really close to the line." He looked across the table at Hunter. "You don't have to get involved, but I wouldn't have asked you here if it wasn't important. And I can't stress enough that it's off the books. You'd have to leave your badge at home."

Hunter stared across the table, one eyebrow twitched up. "How can I help?"

A lopsided grin slid across Colt's face. "Thought that might be your response." He adjusted in his seat, leaning forward across the table. "Here's what I know. McKenzie Ann Cheek, she goes by Kenzi, has gone missing."

"Cheek?" Hunter's head cocked to the side. "Why does that name sound familiar?"

"Landry and Elizabeth Cheek's daughter. As in Congressman Landry Cheek. I know them from my church. They asked me for my help and they asked to keep it off the record."

Hunter let out a low whistle then frowned. "Wait. A congressman's daughter is kidnapped and there isn't an army of Feds scouring the countryside? What's wrong with this picture?"

"She wasn't kidnapped."

"Okay. She ran away?"

Barkley shook his head. "It's not that simple. It looks like she's a victim of human trafficking."

"I thought you just said she wasn't kidnapped."

Colt smiled and nodded like he was waiting for the light bulb to come on. "Here's the deal, Cowboy. The case you and I were involved with was an extreme version of human trafficking, the kind that makes the news. Human trafficking in its most common form doesn't involve kidnapping at all. It's all about coercion, intimidation, threats and brutality."

"I'm listening." Hunter sounded confused.

Barkley lowered his voice. "Think of your average teenage girl. She's a bundle of anxiety and hormones. Her self-image is warped by the media. She feels lost and alone. Her parents don't understand. Her friends are a pit of vipers and the boy she likes doesn't know she exists. I could go on, but you get the image."

Hunter nodded. "Yep. Teenage girls are an emotional train wreck."

"Exactly. And all they're craving is acceptance."

"Okay."

"That's when the sharks circle. The lowlifes are professionals at manipulation. They usually make the first contact on social media. Instagram is the worst, but FaceBook and Twitter aren't far behind.

"They insert themselves into the girl's life and in the beginning are all about understanding. They're supportive and reinforce the girl's feelings. A shoulder to cry on. In very short order, they convince her to meet in person. They lay it on so thick, she thinks it's love and it feels so good, she's willing to do anything to keep it going."

Hunter felt his stomach turn. He started to say something but shook his head in frustration.

"Yeah." Colt nodded. "You see where this is going. It starts with 'oh baby, you're so fine' compliments, to 'oh baby, do it just once for me.' Then with the snap of his fingers, it turns to, 'I've got video of you and I'm going to send to all your friends if you don't go in the back room with this dude.'"

"Sick bastards." Hunter's voice turned hoarse.

"Oh, it gets worse. Once the façade of caring for her gets removed, it's full on physical and mental abuse. They threaten her friends and family, and beat the crap out of her. To make it more bearable, they offer her drugs. Then it's really over because she's hooked, and she'll blow fifteen guys in a row just to get her next fix."

Hunter pushed his plate away. He'd lost his appetite. They both fell silent and let the ambient noise of the restaurant surround them.

After a few minutes, Hunter cleared his throat. He scrunched his face. "So, the parents want this to be kept quiet to avoid bad publicity?"

"It's not that simple Cowboy. Yeah, the publicity wouldn't be good for the Congressman, but the publicity could also be deadly for his daughter." He stared across the table. "These guys are evil. If they get a whiff of law enforcement or see this plastered on the news, they'd kill her in a heartbeat. Or worse, they'd sell her off to someone even more evil."

"Damn. Got it, this has to be under wraps. But what leads you to my neighborhood?"

"She's been off the grid for three days, but I was able to pull some strings with another buddy who traced her last cell phone calls to the west side of Fort Worth."

"Okay. Other than shooting these bastards between the eyes when we find them, how can I help?"

"I need your knowledge of the local landscape. I might need some searches run and basic intel. I can't do it on the Ranger's system. I'm supposed to be on vacation. And...at the end of the day, when I find these pricks, I'm going to need backup."

Hunter set his jaw and nodded. "I'm in. Just call."

Chapter 7

The opening lines of Sympathy for the Devil by The Rolling Stones blared through the speakers in the tightly packed work area.

The man rocked back in his chair and let out a cackle. He clapped his hands together in delight and smiled like a kid at a magic show.

"Oh, Lucy, what a beautiful show!"

He leaned forward, clicked the mouse several times and stared in anticipation as he reset the video. Small fans whirred and LED's blinked all around him. The air conditioning worked in the background, keeping the room at precisely sixty-eight degrees.

"Check out the look on Caldwell's face. Beautiful, just beautiful." He shook his head. "He's completely clueless." He pointed at the screen. "That didn't stop you, though, did it Lucy? You just marched right up and littered him with bullets. Good girl."

He raised his hand above his head and slapped it forward. "There's a virtual high five."

He laughed again. "Right on cue. Thank you, YouTube. I knew I could count on you to have absolutely no shame in broadcasting someone's murder. Oh, sure, you'll eventually take it down. If the media comes calling, some flunky spokesperson will express faux outrage and talk about your policies. In the meantime, you'll rake in millions in advertisement."

Folding his arms across his chest, he frowned at the screen. "As disgusting as you are, what would I do without you?"

He sat quietly as if contemplating something, absorbing the moment. Snapping out of his thoughts, his hands went to the keyboard and began clicking away feverishly. "Okay, Lucy, let's finish this show. I've already dealt with your phone. Now that you've served my purpose, let's wipe your laptop. Wouldn't want to leave any breadcrumbs, now would we?"

An image flashed up on his display. It appeared to be the desktop workspace of a laptop. "People are so predictable. So much of this could have been avoided with a better password. Your dog's name, Lucy? Really? You could have at least made it challenging."

His fingers flew across the keyboard. "Before I send this laptop back to the stone age, let's make sure you don't have any cloud backup." His eyes perused the screen until he found the cloud icon. He clicked away and found the backed up files.

"Cloud backup my ass. Watch this."

With a few quick strokes, he deleted every file associated with her account.

He glanced back at the frozen YouTube image of Lucy Stanton, gun outstretched, smoke drifting up from the barrel. "I don't know about you Lucy, but I feel better knowing there are no backups for your data. Now, let's move on to your hard drive."

A look of determination washed over his face and he chewed on the inside of his lip as he worked. "Time for my worm to come out and play." He clicked on a folder icon. "Although, you're more like a snake, or maybe even a nine-headed hydra."

He smiled as he double clicked on the executable. "Go do your thing, darling, and leave nothing but destruction in your wake."

His eyes glowed as he watched the destruction. Files were erased, folders disappeared, programs were deleted. Any hint of communication such as emails or instant messages were obliterated. Every social network account she'd ever created was disabled. The worm systematically made Lucy Stanton's entire online existence evaporate as if she'd never existed.

After several minutes of watching the carnage, it was complete. His worm deleted itself, leaving no trace behind. He then accessed the laptop's operating system. With a few quick moves, he reformatted the hard drive and then dropped an electronic bomb into the middle of the BIOS.

"My symphony is complete. That laptop just became a paper weight. No one will ever be able to boot it up again."

With a smile of complete satisfaction, he leaned back and turned to Lucy's image on the screen. "Lucy, my proxy enforcer, thanks for your service in taking a scumbag like Weston Caldwell off the streets. And you weren't exactly some innocent lamb, now were you? What's that they say? Two birds, one stone."

He leaned back in his chair, his hands interlocking behind his head. His gaze swept across an array of six flat screen displays. Each showed live footage of a different person going about their normal activities, the mundane inanities of their useless, everyday lives. All seemingly unaware that they were on camera.

"Who wants to play next?"

Chapter 8

Hunter struggled up the stairs to the station's second floor, making sure to hold onto the rail. Thoughts pinballed around his brain. The girl Colt told him about, her parents, the victims of trafficking that he'd encountered in the previous case, the torture these girls were subjected to. The level of pain human beings could inflict on each other was staggering.

Sometimes the murdered victims get the easy way out.

"Cowboy," Billy called as he came around the corner.

Hunter dropped his laptop on the table, slumped into a chair and started unpacking without response.

"Cowboy. Hey, you okay?"

"Huh?" He looked up to see Billy staring at him. "Sorry." He shook his head. "I'm fine. What do you have?"

Billy hesitated as if he was going to continue to probe, but then moved on. "I've worked on the backgrounds for both the victim and the shooter."

"Run me through them."

"Let's start with Weston Caldwell." Billy looked at his notes. "He wasn't married, so it took a little digging to find his next of kin. Turns out he has a sister who lives out in the Hulen area. Patrol was dispatched to her workplace this morning to make the official notification." He looked up. "She took the rest of the day off. I thought we could pay her a visit this afternoon."

"That works. What do we know about her?"

"Looks to be clean. She's an eighth grade math teacher at Monnig Middle School."

Hunter snorted a quick laugh. "If she's teaching eighth graders math, she's either a saint or completely insane."

"Add this to the list... She's got twin four-year-old boys." Sanders raised his eyebrows and shook his head.

"Then she won't have any issue dealing with us, will she?" Hunter chuckled to himself before continuing. He stood, grimaced and stretched, started to pace slowly.

Sanders cocked his head as he watched Hunter for a moment. "You okay?"

"I'm fine, why?"

"You're kind of limping."

Hunter stopped pacing, scrunched his face. "I am?"

What the hell?

"Hmm, getting old sucks." He resumed pacing, but focused to avoid limping.

"Yeah, remind me not to do it."

Hunter's phone buzzed in his pocket. He pulled it out, looked at the display, frowned and shoved it back. When he looked up and saw Sanders looking at him, he shook his head. "Andre Kipton looking for a story."

"And the media circus begins." Billy shook his head.

Hunter flashed a detached smile. "Where were we? What about Lucy Stanton? Did we get the search warrant for her house?"

"Yep. Came in right after you left." Sanders held up several printed pages. "We can stop by there after talking with the sister. They're both on the west side."

"What about the husband? Do we know anything about him?"

"Looks to be as clean as Lucy."

"Does that mean we can expect him to shoot up a sidewalk tomorrow?"

Billy smiled, ignored Hunter's comment and looked at his notes. "He travels a lot. Was out of town yesterday meeting with a client. Once the video went viral, his phone lit up."

"Hell of a reason to have a meeting interrupted."

"No shit." Sanders twirled his pen with his fingers.

"Do you know if he's back in town? I'd prefer to interview him at the same time we execute the warrant."

"I spoke with the family attorney right after you left for lunch and told him we needed to speak to Mr. Stanton. The lawyer said Stanton got in late last night and is home with the kids today."

"You didn't mention the warrant, did you?"

"Nope. Thought I'd save that for when we arrived."

Hunter's phone dinged indicating a voicemail. He held up a finger, pulled out his phone and listened. Andre Kipton's voice came on. "Hey Hunter, Andre here. Saw the viral videos of the crazy lady gunning down that guy in broad daylight. I hear through the grapevine, you're the lead on it. Give me a call. Looking for some information."

Hunter rolled his eyes, mouthed the word 'Kipton' to Billy. He shoved his phone in his pocket, and looked across the table. "Let's go interview these guys before the media gets to them."

*   *   *   *

The sounds of the downtown hustle filtered in through the open window of Hunter's SUV. He breathed in deep, adjusted his sunglasses and looked toward Sanders in the passenger seat. "Man, I love the fall in Texas. Not too hot, not too cold."

"Yeah, reminds me of football season. Afternoons are mild and sunny, nights are cool and crisp."

"You miss it?"

"This time of year... Yeah, a little." He nodded slowly and looked out the front windshield. "I never got to the real big leagues, but I got close enough for a taste of what's it's like to be on the sideline with tens of thousands of fans in the stands going crazy." He shook his head. "Now, that's a rush."

"I bet." Hunter's voice drifted.

They drove silently west on Seventh Street as the soft October sun reflected off the buildings.

When they hit the light at University, Billy cleared his throat. "So, what was up with our favorite Texas Ranger?"

Hunter pulled his cell phone from his pocket and set it on the console. He held up a finger. "Hold that thought for a minute."

Using the Bluetooth connection to his truck, he gave the

verbal command to call the Tarrant County Jail. When it connected, he asked for the deputy in charge.

"Deputy Jarvis, how can I help you?"

"This is Detective Jake Hunter, FWPD. I need to check on the status of a prisoner."

"If you're looking for booking status, let me—"

Hunter gently cut him off. "No. That's not what I meant. I know her booking status. I need to know how she's doing mentally."

There was a low, guttural chuckle on the line. "That's a new one. Since when did the FWPD give a rat's ass about the mental wellbeing of a prisoner?"

"Since her getting stable enough to talk will help me close out my investigation."

"Let me guess, you're talking about that whacked out, catatonic redhead that blew the guy away on the steps of that high rise, aren't you?"

Hunter cut his eyes over to see Billy smiling. "That'd be the one. Lucy Stanton. Has her condition changed since they brought her in yesterday?"

"Not much. Her lawyer visited her about an hour ago. We can't listen to their conversations, but based on the video feed, I don't think he got much out of her."

"Well, hell." Hunter frowned. "If you would, take down my number and have someone call me if she seems to come around."

They were on I-30 heading west by the time Hunter had given the deputy his number and hung up. He went straight to his next call.

"Doctor Murray here."

"Hey Doc, Jake Hunter here."

"Cowboy, good to hear from you." He paused. "Well, I hope anyway. Is everything okay? Do we need to schedule some time?"

"I'm doing fine." Hunter frowned. "No need to break out the appointment book." Having the doctor reference their past meetings made him squirm slightly, since Billy heard every word beside him.

Doctor Chapman Murray was the staff psychiatrist for the Fort Worth Police Department. Several months earlier, Hunter was required to complete several sessions with him after an on-the-job shooting. While Hunter rarely discussed it, the sessions had helped him through a very tough stretch.

"I need your help on a case." He continued.

"What's the situation?"

Hunter spent the next five minutes giving the psychiatrist the rundown of Lucy Stanton's situation.

"Perhaps you can sit down with her and get her to at least the point where she can communicate. Without her talking, we may have a tough time figuring out exactly why she popped her cork."

"I think I can make some time tomorrow. Let me get the paperwork rolling. Assuming I don't run into any bureaucracy, I'll give you a call tomorrow afternoon with an update."

"Good luck with that lack of bureaucracy."

As they drove south on Hulen Street past Chisolm Trail Parkway, Hunter clicked off the phone. Before he could speak, Billy chimed in. "You were saying about your lunch with Barkley? What was up with all the secrecy?"

"Secrecy?" Hunter scrunched his face. "No, it was nothing. He just wanted to catch up on family stuff." He shook his head. "It was nothing."

Sanders cut his gaze toward Hunter with a squint. He started to say something, but Hunter cut him off.

"I think we're here. This is the street, right?"

Chapter 9

"Nice place." He smirked. "But it doesn't exactly look like the house of a mobster's sister." Hunter slowed the Explorer and pulled to the curb in front of a white brick single story ranch with a two car side entry garage, an extended covered carport and a circular drive.

"Nope. Looks more high end soccer mom to me."

"Or maybe eighth grade math teacher with twins?"

"Yeah, but this is definitely dual income territory."

"Speaking of, what does hubby do?"

Sanders flipped through some pages in his notebook. "I reviewed his profile on LinkedIn. He's a consultant of some kind." He looked at the sheet. "Says here he specializes in Cyber Security Analysis, Cyber Intrusion Detection and System Vulnerability Testing."

"Okay." Hunter smirked as he opened his door. "Hope that means more to you than it does to me."

After taking a moment to walk up the sidewalk, they knocked on the door and reflexively stepped back and slightly to the side. To be clear of windows or shots through the door. Hunter realized what they had done and smiled to himself.

Habits.

In spite of her blood shot eyes and the veil of sadness that enveloped her, Karla Perkins was a striking woman. She wore her thirty-nine years well with an athletic build, hazel eyes and just enough freckles across the bridge of her nose to be interesting.

She folded her arms across her chest and her lips flattened. "Let me guess, cops?"

Both men flashed their identification. "Detectives, ma'am. I'm Detective Jake Hunter. This is my partner Detective Billy Sanders. May we come in and speak with you for a moment?"

After a slight hesitation, she opened the door wider and gestured for them to enter.

Hunter nodded as they stepped past her. "Thank you."

The two detectives followed her to a small breakfast nook. Hunter perused the family photos on the wall as he maneuvered around the toys in the floor. They pulled out chairs and sat at a round, wood stained table. They declined her offer of drinks and jumped right into the discussion when she sat.

"Ms. Perkins, we're sorry for your loss..."

"Really? I kind of thought you guys might be celebrating."

Her dry, sarcastic tone caught Hunter off guard. He broke eye contact for a moment and cleared his throat. "Ma'am, we're homicide detectives, and while your brother may have had a somewhat...colorful past, neither of us had ever crossed paths with him. We're here because he was the victim of a violent, and to this point, unexplained crime."

Her shoulders softened. She looked down at her hands and fought back more tears. "I'm sorry. That was rude of me."

Hunter dropped his eyes and watched her hands as they gripped each other. He noted the slight tremble, how her skin went white as the fingers pressed on each other. He'd seen this pain too many times during his career.

"No problem. It's clear that you and your brother were close."

She laughed abruptly and wiped her eyes. "At one time, I guess. The truth is, as adults we lived very different lives." She absentmindedly picked up a napkin and wiped away some crumbs from the table.

"What can you tell us that might shine some light on why this happened?"

"Probably not much." She shrugged. "Mom and Dad have both been gone for years. Weston calls occasionally. We connect for dinner now and then. You know, birthdays and holidays."

"What about his work or his personal life? Does he have a girlfriend?"

She shook her head. "I'm sorry I'm not more help. Because of Weston's lifestyle, he and my husband weren't exactly buddies so we kept a distance."

Hunter nodded, reached into his pocket and pulled out a picture of Lucy Stanton. "Have you ever seen this woman?"

"Is this her?"

Neither Hunter or Sanders responded.

"No. I've never seen her." She pushed the picture away.

"Does the name Lucy Stanton mean anything to you?"

She shook her head and blinked several times. After a beat, she looked up at Hunter. "I'm under no disillusions. My brother wasn't a saint. The truth is, down deep, the phone call this morning wasn't a surprise." Her eyes focused. "But that doesn't mean he deserved to get gunned down in the street like a rabid animal."

*   *   *   *

"What the hell is a packaging designer for a corrugated company?" Hunter drove from Karla Perkins house to the Stanton's along I-20. As they turned south on McCart Ave toward Edgecliff Village, Sanders caught Hunter up on Robert Stanton.

"You know. The guys that design the boxes and inserts that display and protect products in shipment." Billy shrugged. "If you think about it, that stuff can get fairly complex. You've got tooling and die cuts, intricate folds, different cardboard gauges, strengths and types. Then there's all the graphics, barcodes and product information printed."

"Yeah, well, all I know is that half the time I need a chainsaw just to get whatever I ordered out of the box."

Sanders shook his head. "You sure you're not in your sixties instead of your forties?"

They took a left on Duringer Road and drove a few blocks before pulling to the curb in front of a house that backed up to Westcreek Park. The home was small, with white brick, a green roof and a large cement birdbath in the front yard.

They had to knock on the door twice before they detected movement on the other side. After another long moment, the door opened a crack and a man with a shaved head and a close cropped beard stared out at them. He frowned. "If you're reporters, get the hell off my property. I've got nothing to say."

Hunter and Billy reflexively flashed their badges. "Mr. Stanton, we're with the Fort Worth Police Department. I'm Detective Hunter and this is Detective Sanders."

His facial expression remained flat. "I guess I can't tell you to get the hell off my property, but I still have nothing to say."

"Mr. Stanton, we're just trying to figure out what happened. Do you mind if we step inside for a moment?"

Stanton stood frozen for a long moment, finally sighed and opened the door. He motioned for them to come in and directed them to the family room.

Billy took a seat on the couch while Hunter purposely sat in a chair on the opposite side of the coffee table. This meant that when Stanton sat down, he'd have to split his attention in two different directions. A calculated move.

Hunter scanned the room. Nothing out of the ordinary. When he looked back at Stanton, all he saw was confusion.

"Detectives, I'm not sure what I can tell you. I saw the video footage. I have no idea how that could have happened." He looked down at his hands laying in his lap and swallowed hard. "The woman I'm married to couldn't have done what I saw on that screen."

"Mr. Stanton, this seems to have taken everyone by surprise. We just need to ask you some questions. But before we do, for your protection, we're going to read you your rights."

The man went rigid. "What the hell do you mean?"

"It's merely a formality."

"My wife is in jail. My kids are in shock, and you think I had something to do with it?"

"No, sir. Again, it's just a formality."

He waved his hands in disgust. "Whatever."

Hunter nodded to Sanders. Billy cleared his throat, pulled out his card and read out the Miranda rights.

After he finished, Hunter leaned forward in his chair, looked past the man. "Mr. Stanton, are your kids at home?"

"No. They're at a neighbors."

"Before yesterday, did you know Weston Caldwell?"

"Never heard of him. Ever."

"Were you aware that your wife owned a gun?"

"No." An exasperated smile washed across his face. "She's always been anti-gun. To the point that she once protested the NRA."

Hunter nodded. "Was there any indication that something was wrong?"

Stanton leaned back, seemingly letting his shoulders relax. "Look, she's just a mom and an accountant. I mean. We've had our struggles for a while, but... None of this makes sense." He shrugged, looked up at Hunter, his eyes glistening. "She's not a violent person. Over the past two weeks, she seemed more tense than usual. When I asked about it, she just blamed work."

Hunter had heard this story before. A spouse gets so used to a person's behavior that it always seems normal to them. They don't see the rage seething underneath the surface.

The doorbell rang and Stanton started to stand.

Hunter motioned for him to stay seated. "That's probably for me."

Hunter had called in and requested a patrol car to assist with the execution of the search warrant, but had timed it so that he and Billy could interview Robert Stanton before they searched the house.

He walked over, opened the door and let the two officers step inside.

Stanton stood to protest, but Billy got his attention. "Mr. Stanton." The man turned to face Billy, who handed him a folded piece of paper. "That's a search warrant for the premises. It covers any weapons, computers, correspondence or records that might be pertinent. The officers are here to assist."

Stanton snatched the paper out of Billy's hand, stared at it for a moment, then fidgeted for a moment, and then growled at Sanders. "You son of a... You came in here acting all concerned. The whole time you've got a search warrant in your pocket? I can't believe..."

Billy interrupted him. "Officer." He signaled one of them over. "Can you sit with Mr. Stanton while we execute the warrant?"

"Will do." The officer motioned for Stanton to sit and when he did, the officer took the opposite chair.

For the next hour, Hunter, Sanders and the second officer

searched room by room, ultimately collecting a few items. They brought a box into the living room and went through the contents with Robert Stanton.

When they came to a laptop, Stanton snorted. "Good luck with that. I tried booting it up this morning and it just spun in circles."

Hunter looked up and stared at Stanton for a moment.

How convenient.

"We've got some pretty good techies. Maybe they can figure it out."

Hunter pulled out the last item, a box of ammunition.

"Are these yours?"

Stanton's face paled. "No. I've never seen those before." He hung his head. His voice barely more than a whisper as his eyes filled with tears. "My God Lucy, what the hell happened to you?"

Chapter 10

The smell of burgers, fries and the best chicken fried steak around permeated the air as Hunter and Stacy walked to their table in the back of the bar. The original location of Fred's Texas Café on Currie Street was surrounded by new buildings in the recently gentrified neighborhood just west of the Trinity River off West 7th Street.

Terry Chandler, the Outlaw Chef, was the owner of Fred's and the one responsible for all the interesting twists and flavors. The building with its worn exterior, looked like it ought to be condemned, but the food they served inside these walls was so good, the health inspectors looked the other way.

Once they settled into their booth, Hunter took in the crowded little bar. Even on a Tuesday evening, they were lucky to have gotten a table without a wait. As a regular to Fred's, he didn't need to look at the menu.

Stacy spent a few minutes perusing, with the occasional frown.

"What's wrong? I thought you liked this place."

"Like it? I love it. I just won't be able to fit in my pants if I eat what I want."

Hunter grinned and cocked an eyebrow. "I wouldn't worry. Last time I checked, your pants looked pretty amazing to me."

She swatted the menu at him. "You're biased. Your opinion doesn't count."

He reached over, pulled her hand to his lips and kissed her knuckles. "I'm hoping my opinion is the only one that counts."

A smiled washed across her face. "You win. Cheeseburger it is."

It had been almost a year since they reconnected at the scene of two murdered gangbangers. Since then, they'd settled into a really nice groove. The time they spent together during the week was mostly work related. Because of the crazy hours, they didn't have much free time. Like tonight, they managed to get out to dinner usually once a week and then, assuming they didn't catch a hot case, they were inseparable on the weekends. Those times he cherished.

"Did your team finish processing the car?"

As they waited for their food, they caught up on the day. Stacy insisted they get that part over with before the food arrived.

"They did, but there wasn't anything enlightening." She twiddled with her fork while she spoke.

"Was your tech guy ever able to get anything off her phone?"

Stacy shook her head. "No. He said it was fried."

"We'll have to get her phone records from her carrier." Hunter paused, a thoughtful frown washed across his face.

"What?"

He shook his head. "Probably nothing, but when we executed the search warrant, we collected her laptop and her husband commented that he hadn't been able to get it to work."

Stacy paused. "Do you think he did something to it?"

Hunter shrugged. "The thought crossed my mind."

She shrugged. "I'll have Roy check it out in the morning."

"Like I said, probably nothing." He dismissed the thought with a wave.

They compared notes on a few more evidentiary items, but neither seemed overly enthusiastic. By the time their burgers arrived, they were on to other topics.

Stacy took a bite and smiled as she chewed. "Mmm, this is so good. I won't be able to eat for the rest of the week." She reached for a fry. "Hey, what's the latest with Jess? How is she doing?"

Jessica Hunter was Jake's niece and had been involved with a case they had worked a few months previously. She'd been held at gunpoint in a life threatening moment. Recovering from the trauma had been a long road.

"The shrink recommended by Dr. Murray has been great. No more nightmares. She's back at work full time and back to organizing drug awareness events."

Stacy smiled. "That's great. She's such a sweet kid."

"She might take offense at the kid part, but…" He smirked and chomped down on his burger.

"Speaking of taking offense…" Stacy paused as a look of concern washed across her face. "I've got a question for you, but I don't want you to get testy."

"Who me?" He mumbled with his mouth full, swallowed hard and grinned. "Never."

"Right. Is there something I should know? Is everything okay with you?"

"What are you talking about?" Hunter smiled to mask his real concern.

"Lately, you've seemed a little distracted. And you're moving like you're in pain. Last Saturday when you mowed the lawn, you looked completely worn out." She furrowed her brow. "That's not normal for you."

Hunter shrugged. "Nothing more than my odometer getting up there."

"You're not that old and…" She smiled. "I know you're in great shape."

"Everything's fine…" Before he could add anymore, his phone buzzed and he saw it was Colt. He looked at Stacy, made an apologetic face and punched his finger at the phone. "I've got to take this."

"Colt. What's up?" His voice muffled with hamburger.

"Cowboy, hate to interrupt your evening, but I need some information."

"Hang on." He looked at Stacy. "You got a pen?"

She rolled her eyes, reached into her bag and provided him with both a pen and a small note pad.

He nodded his thanks and cradled the phone on his shoulder. "Shoot."

"I need all the information you can give me on Harley Lundsford."

"Okay. Who is he?"

Barkley hesitated for a moment as if contemplating whether to answer. "I was able to get some phone records and his number came up several times on Kenzi's phone."

"You think he's the guy who has her?"

"Good possibility. I'll know more when I track him down."

"Right now, I'm at dinner with Stacy. Can I get this back to you in the morning?"

Barkley cut in. "Oh man, I didn't mean to interrupt. I just figured on a Tuesday night, you'd be at home with Panther reviewing case files."

Panther was Hunter's abnormally large, pure black cat.

Hunter frowned. "Am I really that boring?"

"If you have to ask..." Barkley laughed. "Tell Stacy hi for me and ping me back when you have something."

Hunter clicked off and looked over at Stacy. "Sorry about that. Colt says hi."

He reached for his burger, but Stacy stopped his hand. "Okay Cowboy, spill the beans. What was that all about?"

He shrugged. "It's nothing. He just needed a little help on a case. He wanted some background on a guy."

Narrowing her eyes, she pretended to sniff. "Does it smell like bullshit in here? You want me to believe that the famous Detective Colt Barkley of the Texas Rangers needs the help of the FWPD to get background on a guy?" She leaned back and folded her arms. "I didn't just fall off the truck yesterday. What's going on?"

Hunter leaned back and sighed. "Okay. Here's the scoop."

For the next twenty minutes, in between juicy bites of his loaded bacon cheeseburger, he told her about Colt's case and how he had agreed to assist.

"Cowboy, you'd better be careful. I commend you for helping, but working off the books like that can cost you your badge."

Hunter waved her off. "I'm just researching for him."

"Yeah, and the next thing you know, you'll be kicking down a door in a sleazy hotel with God knows who on the other side of it."

"Glad to see you care." He smirked.

She raised an eyebrow and frowned at him. Her face softened. "That poor girl, though. She needs some help."

"Yeah. Sounds like she got herself into some trouble." His tone was casual.

Stacy bowed up. "What does that mean? You act like this is her fault."

He held up his hands in surrender. "That's not what I meant, but it's not exactly like they kidnapped her."

"Jake Hunter, I can't believe you just said that. This girl is the victim of professional manipulators. These guys are predators."

"I'm sorry. I didn't mean—"

"Didn't mean? You mean you didn't think." She leaned forward and poked at the air as she built a head of steam. "Do you have any idea what it's like to be a sixteen year old girl?" She shook her head as she realized what she'd said. "Of course you don't, but think back to when you were a teenager. Think about how everything seemed bigger than it was, how every day felt like it was a matter of life or death."

Hunter's six-foot-two frame seemed to shrink by the second.

"From the time I was fourteen until I was in my early twenties, every day seemed like stepping onto a battlefield where one wrong step would be the end of the world. Who were your friends? Who were your enemies? What would people think about your hair, your clothes, your shoes? It didn't matter if you were the prom queen or the science geek, all you wanted was to be accepted.

"These men... These professional conmen prey on those emotions and lure these unsuspecting girls in like a hunter. By the time they realize they've been conned, it's too late. These men now have pictures or videos of them doing stuff. They've gotten the girls hooked on drugs." She huffed back in her seat. "It's simply tragic."

After a moment of uncomfortable silence, during which it seemed like the whole bar had gone quiet, Hunter finally cleared his throat. "I'm sorry. I did promise to help."

"You need to do more than help." She clenched her jaw. "You need to nail these bastards."

Chapter 11

"Can you tell me your name?"

The dull, off white interrogation room remained silent except for the light rattle of handcuffs, and the low muttering the woman had been doing since Dr. Chapman Murray entered.

Lucy Stanton sat in a wooden chair at a metal table which was bolted to the floor. Her hands were cuffed to the table. As she rocked and twitched, her eyes seemed to dance aimlessly.

Dr. Murray, as was his usual habit, was dressed casually in faded jeans, a golf shirt and running shoes. His reasoning was that it helped patients to relax. It could also have been that he couldn't stand dress shoes.

He'd rearranged his Wednesday morning schedule in order to evaluate Lucy Stanton. Based on his first few minutes, it appeared this might be a one-sided conversation.

His voice was as calm as he could make it. "You're safe with me. I'm a doctor. My name is Chapman. Can you tell me your name?"

"He deserved what he got." Her words blurted out falling on top of each other.

I guess that's progress.

He looked at her chart and noted that she'd been given a mild sedative earlier in the day. It appeared to have only a minimal effect.

"According to your chart, your name is Lucy. Mind if I call you Lucy?"

No response. She rocked back and forth, her eyes vacillated between bouncing around the room and staring off into space.

"Lucy, who deserved what he got?"

"Sorry b-b-bastard… d-d-deserved it."

Dr. Chapman notated something on his pad. "Lucy, do you

remember what happened on Monday?"

"He tried to ruin my life." She shook her head erratically. "No. No. Won't let him."

"Lucy, do you know where you are, and why you're here?"

Her response was indecipherable muttering.

"Lucy, did you know Weston Caldwell before Monday?"

She stopped rocking and for the first time seemed to acknowledge his presence. Her eyes glistened and her face contorted slowly as she began to cry.

"Lucy, it's okay. You're safe with me. No one's going to hurt you." Dr. Murray leaned forward, reached out and took her hand. Her face relaxed and she stopped crying, but then went back to rocking and muttering.

This pattern went on for the next hour. She went from rocking and muttering to occasionally blurting out varying versions of, "I caught him," to "I figured it out," to "I stopped him."

Dr. Murray probed several avenues. He asked about her family, how she was being treated, and if she needed anything to help her sleep. Her demeanor and responses remained consistent. Finally, he brought it to a close. "Lucy, I'm going to go now. Can I visit you again soon?"

There was no response. She'd withdrawn completely and stared off into space, her body slowly moving back and forth.

*　　*　　*　　*

"Have a good one, Cowboy. Go catch some bad guys." Bernard, the goth looking, longtime barista at Hunter's regular Starbucks, waved, highlighting his black fingernail polish.

"Working on it." Hunter nodded as he turned to leave the Starbucks in downtown Fort Worth. He started to make a comment, but his phone buzzed.

"Hunter."

"Detective, this is Chapman Murray. How are you this morning?"

Hunter smiled. "Are you asking in a professional capacity or are you just being nice?"

"How should I be asking?"

"Typical shrink. Answer a question with a question."

"I was just following your lead."

"Touché." Hunter laughed as he walked down the sidewalk. "Doc, I'm doing great. Did you have a chance to check out our nutbag?"

"Nice to see that sensitivity training is working." The smile in Murray's voice was evident. "I did get a chance to visit with Lucy Stanton this morning. At least I tried. She was not very responsive."

"Based on how she was Monday, that's not a surprise."

Dr. Murray paused as if checking his notes. "During a full evaluation with her this morning, I did manage to get her to speak a little. She clearly knows she did something, but in her mind, whatever she did was justified."

"How's that?"

"She repeatedly made references to him deserving it and doing what she had to, etc. She really wasn't there."

Hunter breathed in the crisp morning air and let his eyes skip along the eastern horizon. "Is she going to be able to help us?"

"Not anytime soon. She's in the middle of a complete psychotic break. She is not mentally in this world at the moment." He paused. "Who knows? Given time and a calm environment, she may come around at some point."

"I'm guessing by 'calm environment,' you're probably not thinking of the Tarrant County Jail."

"Definitely not."

"What about a trial?"

"In her current condition, she barely knows her name much less right from wrong. Even a first year public defender could get her declared too incompetent to stand trial."

Hunter sipped his black coffee, but didn't reply, just let out a heavy sigh.

"My recommendation will be to move her to a psychiatric facility where she can get some real therapy. Hopefully, she can recover enough for her to possibly stand trial...eventually."

"Yeah, we need to nurse her back to health so we can lock her up the rest of her life."

"Cowboy, you're quite the cynic."

"I've been called worse, Doc. Thanks for your help."

*   *   *   *

Hunter stopped outside the back doors of the station, pulled up his speed dial for Colt and punched the button.

"Barkley." Colt's voice was curt.

"Did I catch you at a bad time?" Hunter let the sarcasm soak his words.

"Sorry. Cowboy." Barkley cleared his voice. "No. I've just been surveilling a sleazy hotel for too many hours with nothing to show for it yet."

"Maybe my news can brighten your morning."

"You got something on Harley Lundsford?"

"If that's who you're watching at the sleazy hotel, then he should fit right in. What a turd. He's got a sheet a mile long."

"Give me the highlights."

"Let's start with assault, domestic abuse, larceny, drugs...even a weapons charge."

There was a short pause on the line before Colt responded. "Let me ask the age old question. Why isn't he in jail?"

Hunter chuckled. "I'll give you the age old answers. A combination of plea bargains, lack of evidence and a surprising number of people unwilling to press charges." His tone shifted. "My sense is this guy's a bad dude."

"Yeah, I managed to get a glimpse of him last night and he certainly looks the part."

"I can email you the details when I get to my laptop. Should be about twenty minutes."

"Perfect. I'm about to take a break and get back to my hotel. I can spend some quality time getting to know Mr. Lundsford. Make sure to send it from your personal account to my personal account and delete everything afterwards. I want to keep your involvement as invisible as possible."

"Sounds like a plan. Call me if you need me."

JOE B. PARR

Chapter 12

"Dean… Dean, where are you? You can't hide from me forever."

A sing-song quality sounded in his voice as his fingers danced across the keyboard. He stared at the monitor and frowned. He pulled out a cell phone and tapped out a text message.

I have the evidence. I'm going to the police.

"That ought to get a response."

His fingers tapped on the table as he inhaled deeply a few times. He tilted his head and arched an eyebrow.

"Maybe…" He pulled up a GPS application. "Dean, did you already go after Marcus?" He smiled. "After all, I can't believe Marcus was so cruel as to threaten you. And he didn't even have the curtesy to blackmail you. All he did was taunt you, and poke at you until you couldn't take it anymore."

He smiled as a green dot appeared on the map on his screen.

"There you are. Now, let me get some eyes on you."

The next application he opened gave him access to all the traffic cameras throughout the city. He found the closest set of cameras near where the dot had appeared and popped the live feeds onto the array of displays hung in tight formation on his wall.

His eyes darted from screen to screen as he scanned the landscape. The earlier frown reappeared. He didn't see his prey.

"Damnit, Dean, are you in that parking garage? If I find out you're hiding from me, there's going to be hell to pay. You don't want to piss me off."

*   *   *   *

"Geez, I hate headshots. They're always so messy." Detective

Blaine Parker scrunched up his nose as he looked at the first victim lying face down near the parking garage stairwell. Parker, a tall, thin veteran detective in his mid-forties had seen his fair share of murder victims.

"You hate all murder scenes." His longtime partner Jimmy Reyes, a shorter, pudgier mid-forties Hispanic, paused. "Come to think of it, why the hell are you a homicide detective anyway?"

"The chicks."

"Parker, you're a pig." Stacy's voice echoed slightly as it bounced off the concrete walls. She had just walked up the incline from where she'd parked the crime scene van. A cool, October breeze drifted through the garage. "What do we have?"

"Good to see you too, CSI Morgan." Parker grinned as he turned to see her duck under the yellow tape carrying her analysis kit. He pointed to the two bodies, stood overly straight, puffed out his chest and pumped up the sarcasm. "Well, based on my years of homicide detecting experience and my incredibly fine-tuned deductive reasoning skills, I'd say headshot number two shot headshot number one in the back of the head. Then it appears, and I'm just guessing here, that headshot number two shot himself under the chin."

Stacy rolled her eyes and looked at Reyes. "How have you put up with his crap for so many years without strangling him?"

"I'm tempted every day."

She looked down at the two bodies. Parker may be a pain in the ass, but he was right about the headshots. Stacy looked at the first victim. A well-dressed white male in his mid-forties. The hole in the back of his head at the base of the skull was tight and tiny with some noticeable stippling and powder burns around the edges.

Very close range.

The upward trajectory of the bullet meant it exited where the middle of the forehead used to be. All that was there now was a gaping, ragged hole the size of a small grapefruit. What had been there before the encounter was sprayed all over the concrete wall beside the stairwell door.

Bullet disintegrated on impact. Probably frangible.

Parker's voice encroached on her thoughts. This time his

sarcasm was gone. "Based on the direction he's facing, looks like victim number one was about to enter the stairwell when victim number two came up behind him."

"Kind of interesting since there's no place around here to hide." Jimmy waved his hands around highlighting the area where the two bodies were very exposed. There weren't even any cars parked close by. "The first guy had to have known the other guy was there."

Stacy nodded as she continued to peruse the scene. She shifted her focus to the second victim. He was also white, also mid-forties, shorter and casually dressed. He'd been wearing sunglasses and a baseball cap at the time of the shooting. The glasses laid close to his head but the cap had been blown straight up with the blast and had impacted the ceiling of the garage before falling back down a few feet away from the body.

She noted similar size, powder burns and stippling on the entry wound under his chin. The exit wound in the very top of his skull showed similar destruction. Much of his brain matter, blood and skull fragments were literally stuck to the low ceiling. The rest had rained down in a chunky mist and covered a large area of the scene.

* * * *

He checked the GPS again. Based on the green dot's location, Dean appeared to be in the parking garage. Furthermore, the dot hadn't moved since he last checked.

Something else caught his eyes. He wasn't sure, but red and blue flashing lights seemed to radiate from the second floor of the parking garage. It was hard to be sure in the bright sunlight. Because of the angle of the street cam, he wasn't able to see into the structure. He scanned back through the camera feeds trying to find a better angle, but none gave him the visual he needed.

After a moment, his eyes widened and he smiled.

"There we go. There's always more than one way to catch a coyote."

He took control of one of the cameras and zoomed in on the sign attached to the adjoining building.

"Walker Industries? Hmm..." He squinted. "Dean, you're making me work today. How inconsiderate. But if you've already taken out Marcus, I just might forgive you."

His mind raced almost as fast as his fingers tapped. First stop was a brief perusal of the company website. He probed around the site to find a backdoor. Nothing was obvious.

He changed course, clicked on the Investor Relations tab, and found the company's annual report and the 10Q. Downloaded and scanned until he found the information he needed. They banked at Wells Fargo.

"How convenient."

The manic smile widened as he transitioned out of Internet Explorer and pulled up Tor, the notorious dark web browser. Within minutes, he exploited a previously planted breach in the firewall for Wells Fargo.

Once in their systems, finding the account information for Walker Industries was a snap. He scanned their monthly payables check register until he spotted a name he recognized.

"Boom. Gotcha." He shook his head. "Damn, I'm good. The least you could have done was make it a little more challenging."

With the name of their Internet Service Provider in hand, he went back to work. This time, it was almost child's play. With the number of open ports in their firewall, tapping into the ISP's system took mere minutes.

Just a few more steps and he was into the security systems for Walker Industries. Using some common sense, it didn't take him long to identify the video feeds for the four cameras listed as Parking Garage Cameras One through Four.

He pulled them up one at a time. On Camera Three, he struck gold, pushed back in his chair and bit his lip. He actually let out a little squeal like a child at a birthday party.

"Oh my, Dean. You're such a good puppet."

He watched the live crime scene as two detectives spoke with an attractive woman in a CSI jacket. Behind them, two bodies lay on the ground with puddles of blood pooling around their heads.

"Not only did you take out that asshole Marcus, but you saved me the trouble of figuring out what to do with you. Bravo!"

As he looked closer at the scene, he noticed a cell phone on the ground next to Dean.

"Oh, we need to take care of that ASAP." Moving quickly, he picked up his phone and punched in a series of commands. When he got a green light response, he smiled. "There. Good luck getting anything from that phone."

As he leaned back in his chair and watched the crime scene activity, his mind raced. His eyes reflected the movements on the display as he stared intently for a few moments. After several minutes, he relaxed, smiled and clicked on his MP3 player. The opening riff of Dire Straights' Money for Nothing blared from his speakers.

*　　*　　*　　*

Moving gingerly around the two bodies, Stacy carefully reached into the back pocket of the first victim, extracted his wallet, deposited it into an evidence bag and made some notes on it. She repeated that process with the second victim.

"Don't you two have some detecting to do?" She gave a sarcastic glance to both detectives as she handed the wallets to Jimmy Reyes. "My team has work to finish."

"I'll get the ID information." Reyes nodded to Stacy. "Call us if you need us. We'll circle back in a bit."

Blaine Parker smiled and pointed to a security camera mounted on the ceiling about thirty feet away, pointed directly at the scene. "I think I'll go find the security office and check out the movie version."

*　　*　　*　　*

He broke off his trance when the lady CSI tech stepped away from the bodies after extracting both men's wallets. She handed them to the Hispanic detective and the three conferred for a moment before she went back to work and the detectives went off in different directions.

"You people are so clueless. I'm watching every move you make and you have no idea I'm even here."

Leaning back momentarily, he started humming the tune, 'Another One Bites The Dust.' Finally, he reached down, opened a file drawer and retrieved a notebook. He held it with both hands, laid it gently on the desk in a caressing manner.

With a hint of formality, he opened the book to the first page. The cream colored paper contained a list of names impeccably written in black ink. The first, Weston Caldwell, had a single, neat line drawn through it. He picked up his pen and with one, deliberate stroke, marked through the name, Marcus Howell.

He looked at the next name on the list. His eyes narrowed slightly as his mouth curved into a slow smile. "Nicholas Briggs, I guess three's a charm for you." Setting down the pen, he closed the notebook and replaced it in the drawer.

He turned back to his bank of monitors and reached for his keyboard. "Now that we have our next target, let's see if we can find a not so willing executioner."

*   *   *   *

Something is off about these two bodies.

The photographer shot more photos documenting the scene from multiple angles as Stacy continued to make observations.

Two white males. Both in their forties. Both well-dressed but not the same. One in business clothes. The other casual. They're similar but very different.

She looked around the garage remembering Jimmy's earlier comment.

The victim saw the shooter but didn't recognize him, but the shooter clearly targeted the victim. Strange.

Once her photographer finished, she moved back into the area to begin processing the scene. The only obvious pieces of evidence other than the bodies were a cell phone and a pistol on the ground near the shooter.

Stacy picked up the gun, engaged the safety before ejecting the magazine. She then racked the slide and caught the shell as it popped out. Satisfied that the gun was secure, she bagged it as evidence.

Following her methodical process, she picked up the cell phone, punched a few buttons. No response. The phone appeared to be dead but didn't show any obvious damage.

It's a bad week for electronics.

After an hour of collecting evidence and documenting the scene, she smiled at the sound of Dr. Benjamin Grimes' voice.

"Good afternoon, Ms. Morgan. You're looking as lovely as ever."

"Considering the surroundings, Doc, anyone would look good."

Doc's rotund middle shook with laughter at the comment. "Yes, well, the setting is a bit nasty." He adjusted his wire rimmed glasses and surveyed the carnage.

Stacy took off her latex gloves and started packing up her supplies. "They're all yours, Doc."

He nodded. "Already a busy week and it's only Wednesday." He and his assistant began the task of removing the bodies as Stacy walked over to the CSI van.

"You won't believe this." Blaine's voice reverberated and stopped her in her tracks. She turned to see him holding up a USB drive. "Caught the whole thing. You got a laptop?"

"Sure do."

After putting her kit away, she propped up her laptop, plugged in the drive and clicked rapidly on the keyboard. The media program opened to a black and white, slightly grainy image moving across the screen.

The shooter stood near the stairwell door and appeared to be talking on his cell phone. The victim entered the frame from the right and walked past the shooter toward the stairwell. The victim made no acknowledgement of the suspect standing there.

In one swift movement, the shooter pulled his weapon and stepped forward. Without hesitation, he placed the barrel directly behind the victim's head and pulled the trigger. Stacy jumped. Even in black and white, the grizzly sight of brain matter and blood exploding from the front of the man's head knotted her stomach.

The body fell as if its skeleton disintegrated.

The shooter blankly stared down at the body for a brief moment. Then he shoved the gun under his own chin and pulled the trigger. Stacy jumped again and turned her head as the man's baseball cap and the top of his head flew upward in a wet blob.

"I guess we don't have to ponder what happened." Even Parker sounded unusually subdued.

I knew something was off about these two.

Stacy nodded. "Now, we just need to know why."

Chapter 13

Stacy inhaled the aroma from her Starbucks coffee deeply and smiled. It was just another Thursday morning as far as she knew, but Jake had made it wonderful by driving well out of his way to deliver her special blend. The gesture warmed her even more than the coffee.

Before Hunter made his surprise delivery, she'd distributed the various pieces of evidence from the Marcus Howell and Dean Fritz murder / suicide crime scene to her team members. They were each busily working their specialties.

She settled in and started to review the crime scene reports and evidence logs from the Weston Caldwell murder. Nothing new jumped out at her. In essence, everyone knew the 'who,' but because Lucy Stanton had so completely melted down, no one had any idea on the 'why'.

Based on conversations over the past few days, she knew her frustration, while certainly high, was mild in comparison to Hunter's. They'd hit a wall and the case was at risk of stalling completely. Hunter never handled stalls well.

She worried about him working to complete exhaustion, and hoped she'd be able to find something, anything, that would help them figure it out.

Someone knocked on the side of her cubicle.

She looked up to see Roy standing there. "What's up?"

"I'm not sure." He frowned and stepped into her workspace. "Take a look at this." He handed her the evidence bag containing the cell phone found next to the body of Dean Fritz at the scene from yesterday's shooting.

"What about it?" She looked at it without really knowing why.

"This may be just one of those crazy coincidences, but this cell phone has been fried in the same way as Lucy Stanton's."

Stacy scrunched her eyes. "But this is from yesterday's scene, right?"

"Right."

She thought for a moment. "So, both cell phones don't work?" Her voice turned the statement into a question.

"It's not so much that both of them don't work. It's more about 'how' they don't work. Neither show signs of physical damage. Based on phone records, both were clearly working within minutes of the crimes, and now it's as if their basic operating systems were completely torched."

When she didn't immediately respond, he continued. "I'm not an expert, but I've worked with a ton of cell phones and laptops from crime scenes. I've never seen one this completely fried before." He paused, raised his eyebrows. "And now we've got two that look almost identical in a matter of a few days." He shrugged. "I'm just saying that's really strange."

"Hmm. Got to agree with you there." She examined the phone more closely as if looking at it would make any difference. "Who is our cell phone expert?"

Roy stood for a moment, tilted his head. "A smart phone is basically a miniature computer. The best guy I know with computers is Sean Jackson over at Central Division."

Stacy smiled at that thought. *Central Division.* "Tell you what. I owe someone over there a surprise visit. Can you write something up explaining what you've observed and pack up both phones? I'll take them over there later this morning."

"You got it." Roy tried to contain his smirk. "While you're going to see him, you think it would make sense to take Lucy Stanton's laptop? It's in the same condition and I've made zero progress on it."

"Pack it up, also."

He snatched the phone off her desk and headed back to his work area.

She smiled at the thought of surprising Hunter, reached over and dialed the phone.

"Jackson here."

"Hey Sean, Stacy Morgan. You going to be around later this morning?"

*　　*　　*　　*

As Stacy pulled into the back parking lot of the FWPD's Central Division, she actually felt a hint of butterflies at the thought of surprising Hunter with a visit.

She hadn't been able to stop smiling all morning as she slogged through her paperwork on the two cases. Things had been going particularly well between her and Hunter over the past few months. Jake's visit this morning was just the icing on the cake.

Knowing that she needed to visit for a few minutes with the computer tech before going upstairs, she put on her game face as she pushed through the back doors.

After walking down a flight of stairs, winding through a maze of hallways and stepping around stacks of boxes, she found Sean Jackson sitting at his desk clicking away on his keyboard.

"Are all IT departments located in the basement?" She smiled.

"Kind of cliché', isn't it?" He leaned back, bumping the back of his chair on the cramped cubicle's wall. "What have you got for me?"

Stacy handed him the box containing the laptop and two phones sealed in evidence bags. "Strange situation. Two different cases between all these devices. But my guy Roy noted that the way each was disabled was very similar. To a point that defies coincidence. He was hoping you could dig deep into them to see if you can find out what disabled them."

Jackson's eyes lit up. "Really? Cool. I'll jump right on it. I can start with a—"

Stacy cut him off with a wave of her hand. "Stop. No need to rattle off a bunch of stuff I won't understand. All I need is for you to figure it out."

He smiled. "Got it."

Since Jackson was part of the core IT team, and not used to handling evidence, Stacy spent the next several minutes going over the rules of evidence with him to make sure that he kept everything separate, tagged and sealed, and that he made sure all evidence was

66

secured any time he left his desk.

His excitement was visible as he eagerly signed the evidence log. "Call me when you have something."

*   *   *   *

The knock on the conference room door caused both Hunter and Sanders to look up.

"Surprise." Stacy strolled in.

Both men spontaneously smiled. Hunter stood, stepped around the table and deftly gave her a peck on the cheek. "To what do we owe the pleasure?"

She spent the next ten minutes going over the story that Roy had presented to her and that she had relayed to Sean Jackson. As she concluded, she shrugged. "What do you think?"

Both men were silent for a long moment.

"That's bizarre." Hunter started pacing.

Sanders grinned. "Oh, shit. He's up and walking." He looked at Stacy. "Now you've done it."

She laughed. "I didn't do anything except follow the evidence." She looked toward Hunter. "What are you thinking?"

"First, we need to get in touch with Reyes and Parker." He looked at Billy. "By the way, have you seen them today?"

"Not since early this morning."

Hunter waved it off. "Second, we need to start cross referencing both victims and shooters to see if there are any connections between them."

Sanders scrunched his forehead. "You really think these have something to do with each other? We have the shooters in both cases. From the little I got from Reyes earlier, there doesn't seem to be anything linking these cases."

"Until now." Hunter arched an eyebrow, picked up his phone and dialed.

"Reyes here."

"Jimmy? Cowboy. Where are you?"

"Parker and I are serving a search warrant. Why? Did my mother call in sick and designate you as her replacement?"

"Funny. The CSI team found something interesting that might impact both our cases. Will you guys be back this afternoon, maybe 2ish?"

"Yep."

"Let's circle up then and Stacy will bring you up to speed." Hunter clicked off without waiting for a response.

He looked at his watch and then at Stacy. "Would you look at that? It's lunch time and you just happen to be here. How convenient?" He tossed his pen on the table and started for the door. "Shall we?"

As they left the room, Sanders called after them. "Don't mind me. I'll just grab something from the machine. It's okay. I'm fine."

Chapter 14

"Gentlemen." Hunter paused and smiled at Stacy. "And lady. Now that we've all had enjoyable lunches…"

"Speak for yourself." Sanders growled.

Hunter grinned and continued. "It seems our crack CSI team may have found something that links our two seemingly separate cases."

Parker and Reyes both frowned, looked at each other and then at Hunter.

Reyes tilted his head. "What case are you talking about? The only active case we're working is a murder suicide."

"And, by definition…" Parker paused and arched an eyebrow. "We know who did it." He smiled at his own joke.

"Yeah, we know who shot our guy also, but there still may be a connection."

"You're gonna need to explain what you're talking about Cowboy." Parker leaned back in his chair. "Last time I checked, once you've nailed the bad guy, which, in both our cases we've done, all that's left is the paperwork."

Hunter nodded. "That may still be the case. Humor me for a few minutes. I think we can spare thirty minutes to play this out."

"Okay." Parker shrugged.

Reyes shrugged, and gestured for Hunter to continue.

Hunter turned to Stacy. "The floor is yours, CSI Morgan."

Stacy spent the next few minutes explaining the similarities in how both shooter's cell phones and the laptop had been disabled. "So, I dropped off both phones and Lucy Stanton's laptop to Sean Jackson this morning to see if he can make heads or tails out of them."

Reyes and Parker had been sitting with their arms folded throughout her explanation, but now looked at each other as if they weren't sure what they'd just heard.

Parker cleared his throat and shifted his feet. "Her laptop was also disabled the same way?"

Stacy nodded. "Yeah."

Parker leaned forward in his seat. "Hmm…"

Sanders, who'd been quiet to this point, huffed. "Good grief Parker, spit it out. What's the issue with the laptop?"

"We just executed a search warrant on Dean Fritz's house and confiscated his laptop."

"And?"

"When we took it, his wife made a comment about not being able to get it to boot up this morning."

Everyone went quiet.

Hunter stood, momentarily lost his balance but caught himself against the wall.

What the hell?

He straightened up quickly hoping no one had noticed.

Parker grinned, started to comment but noticed the concerned look on Stacy's face and refrained.

Stacy eyed Hunter, but he shrugged it off and slowly began to pace. After a couple of passes, he stopped when he realized everyone was watching him. "Looks like maybe we should compare notes on the cases. See what other coincidences we find."

"Sounds like a good idea." Parker was more subdued than usual. He paused, cleared his throat, shook his head. "I'm willing to work through this, but let's not forget that in both cases, we have the shooters. One's dead and one's in custody. We also have both crimes on video, so there isn't any question who committed either crime."

Hunter nodded.

Parker continued. "So, we've got cell phones and laptops that belong to the two shooters that have been…" He paused, screwed up his face and looked at Hunter. "Sabotaged?"

Hunter pursed his lips. "I don't use that word often, but yeah, that sounds right."

Billy stood and walked to the whiteboard, wrote the word *similarities* at the top with bullet points notating the laptops and cell phones. He looked at rest of the team. "What else?"

"Our shooter, Dean Fritz, was a complete choirboy until yesterday. Absolutely no interactions with law enforcement. Hell, his wife didn't even know he owned a gun. Turns out he bought it last week." Reyes looked at Hunter. "What about your shooter, Cowboy?"

"Ditto. Lucy Stanton's past is bright, shiny and clean. Same situation with her gun. Staunch anti-gun activist until last week."

Sanders made several notations, looked at Parker. "How about your victim?"

"Completely different story. Marcus Howell had a long criminal history. Had even been associated with a local organized crime outfit headed up by the Rosa family."

"Organized crime?" Hunter cocked his head. "Okay, this is getting more than a little weird. Weston Caldwell was a lieutenant in the Mazanti family."

Reyes mumbled a few words in Spanish, looked at Hunter and amped up his accent. "Coincidences? We don't believe in no stinkin' coincidences."

After a round of chuckles, Hunter looked around the room.

"Alright, where does that leave us on the action items?"

Parker raised a finger. "I'm going to dig deeper into the backgrounds of Weston Caldwell and Marcus Howell to see if they've crossed paths somewhere."

"I'm going to do the same with our shooters, Lucy Stanton and Dean Fritz." Reyes shrugged. "There's got be some kind of connection."

Still standing at the whiteboard, Sanders twirled the marker in his fingers. "I'll document what we've got so far, follow up with Sean Jackson and work with Stacy to cross reference all the evidence between the two cases." He looked at Hunter. "How about you, Cowboy?"

Hunter exhaled. "I guess I got to go convince Sprabary that the storm doors on these two closed cases have just been blown off their hinges."

Chapter 15

Lieutenant Jeff Sprabary took the terms 'spit and polished' and 'straight laced' to a whole new level. In his early forties and known as a hard ass to most of the team, he wore a suit and tie every day and rarely took off either.

With the exception of Hunter, almost everyone on his team was openly intimidated by him. For some unknown reason, Sprabary was always pretty calm when dealing with Hunter. Of course, Hunter wasn't usually coming to tell him that he needed to take two wins off the board.

"Hi, Cowboy." Paige McLaren, Sprabary's admin, had a vocal tone that was like fingernails on a chalkboard. "I don't see you on his calendar. What do you need?"

Hunter tried to hide a scowl. "I only need about five minutes of his time."

"What's it regarding?"

He paused, irritated that she loved being overzealous in her role as gatekeeper for his boss, but knowing she could also make his afternoon far more painful than necessary if he rubbed her the wrong way. "Two recent unrelated cases that may be connected."

It was her turn to pause as she seemed to mull over his response. She made a show of pushing back her chair and sauntering over to the lieutenant's door.

Hunter couldn't quite make out what she said, but whatever it was, worked. She nodded for him to enter.

Now came the fun part. He took a deep breath and walked in.

Sprabary gestured for Hunter to sit and flashed his version of a smile, which always looked pained. "I've only got a few minutes. What's on your mind, Cowboy?"

"I may have some bad news." The chair creaked as he sat.

Spraybary's pained smile slid into a frown. He didn't speak, but paused waiting for Hunter to continue.

"The two new cases we caught this week…" Hunter swallowed hard. "There's some strange evidentiary coincidences. Too big to ignore."

"Stop." Sprabary held up his hand. "Cowboy, I'm used to others talking in circles, but when you start throwing out terms like 'evidentiary coincidences'…" He tilted his head. "Makes me nervous. Spit it out."

"We think there's a connection between the two cases."

"You mean the two cases that had essentially solved themselves before we got to the scenes?"

Hunter nodded. "Yeah."

"Great." He stretched the word out and exhaled loudly as he rubbed his forehead. "Please explain to me how that's even possible."

Hunter spent the next twenty minutes going over in detail how the team came to that conclusion. By the time he had finished laying out all the similarities, Spraybary's face turned a blotchy red.

After he completed his list, Hunter let the silence stand. He knew it was best to let the facts sink in before moving on to his request.

"We've just taken two high profile cases and moved them from the solved to the unsolved columns." Sprabary rubbed his temples. "Worse than that, these were cases where the victims aren't exactly local philanthropists and the shooters have spotless records."

Hunter nodded.

"All based on phones and laptops that don't work."

"Phones and laptops that appear sabotaged in the same ways."

Sprabary leaned his elbows on the desk and folded his hands together. "Now that you've ruined my afternoon, do you have a suggestion on how to fix this mess?"

"We've already put that in motion. We just need your official approval."

Sprabary motioned for him to continue.

"I think Reyes, Parker, Billy and I should combine forces and investigate the cases together. We met this afternoon, compared our notes, determined action steps and are now each working separate angles to see if we can find more connections. From there, we can hopefully either rule it out, or get some leads as to what or who is behind them."

Sprabary nodded. "Okay. Proceed. But you need to move fast. These have already been posted as solved. I've got my weekly briefing with the chief on Monday morning. I don't want to have to tell him that our numbers are wrong. He'll pop a vein, and I'll be the one that gets sprayed."

"Yes, sir."

"Give me daily updates including over the weekend."

"Yes, sir." Hunter stood and moved toward the door.

Before his hand turned the knob, Spraybary stopped him. "Cowboy, if you're right about this..." The tone of his voice turned ominous. "If you're right, the only explanation is a level of conspiracy well beyond a few people turning their grudges into rage vendettas."

"Yes, sir. The ramifications are scary."

Chapter 16

The phone buzzed on the breakfast nook table.

Hunter sighed. He'd just sat down on the couch with the remote in one hand, Panther head butting the other.

"Don't they know it's after hours." He rubbed Panther's head.

Panther let out a short meow, shot him a glance that clearly expressed his displeasure, hopped off the couch and disappeared down the hall.

"It's not my fault." Hunter yelled after him as he dragged himself across the room to the phone dancing across the table.

"Hunter." He used his professional voice since he didn't recognize the number.

"Cowboy. It's Colt. Where are you?"

"At the house. Everything okay?"

"Just wanted to make sure you weren't still on duty. Can you talk?"

"Panther's already pissed off so I've got nothing to lose."

"Tell him I'm sorry and I'll bring him a new package of catnip next time I stop by."

"Don't go making promises unless you intend to come through."

"Scout's honor." Barkley chuckled.

Hunter changed the tone of the conversation. "Where are you calling from?"

"It's a burner." Colt chuckled. "Wait until you see it. It's hot pink. Jot down the number for future reference. I'm not carrying anything that can tie back to my world. The asshats I'm tracking aren't exactly choir boys."

"Tell me what you've got."

"Our boy, Harley Lundsford, is a real piece of work. Just in the short time I've been tracking him, I could have already taken him down on drug charges, gun charges and if being ugly was against the law, I'd have him on that, too."

"What about the girl?"

"No sign of Kenzi yet, but he's been hovering around two different fleabag hotels, going in and out of the same rooms. Some of his boys are posted at both places."

"Sounds like it's time to call in the cavalry, kick down the door and throw their asses in jail. You got enough to drop the dime?"

"Not yet."

"Even if we got...creative?"

Barkley laughed. "If this was official business, they'd already be rotting in a cell. I have to be careful on this one. No sign of Kenzi, yet." He paused. "For that matter, I haven't seen any girls at all. I know they're there, but I need to get closer."

"What you need to do is be careful, call it in to the FWPD and let us take these jerks down. The girls in those rooms need to be rescued."

The line was silent for a moment. "Yeah, I know." Barkley's voice turned heavy. "Just give me another day or two. I'll get close enough to confirm and then we can call that SWAT guy of yours. The one that looks like an accountant."

Hunter laughed. "Yeah, Zeke's looks are a bit deceiving."

Barkley continued. "In the meantime, I'm going to send you some pics. They're pretty good shots of Lundsford's crew. You think you can call in a favor from that hottie CSI?"

"Hey now, just because you're a six-foot-five Texas Ranger, don't think I won't kick your ass."

"Duly noted." Barkley snickered. "My most humble apologies. Ask Stacy if she can get one of her techies to run facial recognition. Get names on these guys."

"Will do." Hunter grabbed a note pad from the counter. "Which hotels are they hanging out in?"

"Two of the finer establishments that Cowtown has to offer. Both just south of I-30 near Las Vegas Trail. The Express Inn and the Relax Inn. He and his crew bounce between the two of them. I need to figure out if he's got Kenzi stashed at either one. That's my mission over the next forty-eight hours."

"How can I help?"

"Just get me those ID's and I'll call you if I need you."

"You got it. I'll call you when I have something."

"Don't bother. I don't have my cell with me. Just this burner and I only use it for outbound calls and delete the history as I go."

Hunter paused. It wasn't Barkley's nature to be overly cautious. "You're being awfully cloak and dagger. Are these guys that good?"

Barkley laughed. "These guys are imbeciles. I'm not worried about them. But you never know who's hanging out in these places. I just can't have anything on me that ties me to Kenzi. I can't put her in any danger. Even these idiots would figure out the connection if a Texas Ranger is seen snooping around their nest."

"Okay." Hunter answered slowly, not sure if he was buying Colt's bravado. "When should I expect to hear back?"

"I'll check back in tomorrow or Saturday. Don't worry. I'll send up a flare if I need you."

Chapter 17

"It's time to go fishing on Instagram." He grinned as he pulled out his tablet and tapped on the icon. An account with the user name youreapwhatyousow popped up. After searching through the accounts he'd already infiltrated, he found the one he wanted.

Perfect. You've been a bad boy.

A few more taps and he found a file filled with video clips. He watched a short but vivid clip of two people fully engaged in the act, unaware their sexual exploits were being filmed. He found the account, attached the clip and typed out a short message.

Does your wife know?

He hit send.

"That ought to make him sweat. Mike Systrom, dear friend, before our time is through, you will beg for mercy. I guess you should have thought about that before all the gambling and whoring around."

He smiled.

"Of course, you'll direct your rage not at me, but at Nicholas Briggs. By the time I let that slip, you'll be more than ready to kill to keep him from telling your wife."

He clapped his hands.

"Places, my little puppets. Get ready for your fifteen minutes of infamy."

*　*　*　*

"Mike?" LeAnne tapped on the window to get his attention. "Honey, are you coming in for dinner?"

He waved an acknowledgement. "Just a second, babe. My phone just buzzed."

The October night was unseasonably warm, and Mike sat on his extended back porch in the Bear Creek neighborhood of Keller. He flipped channels on the HD flat screen trying to find the Cowboys score.

Over the summer, he'd sunk a ton of money into building an outdoor kitchen and covered cabana, and he took every opportunity to spend time outside enjoying it. After all, with all the other stressors in his life, he needed an escape.

He reached over and picked up his phone, noticed the Instagram icon highlighted. A smile came across his face. He wasn't big into social media, but he had to admit, getting a message always perked him up.

His fingers double tapped on the icon and saw the strange message. He scrunched his forehead as a video started playing. The jolt that went through his frame was like touching an exposed electrical outlet. Two forms moved in passionate high-definition, the bedroom unmistakable. A moment after the video ended, he gulped in air like a diver coming up from deep water. His vision blurred. The pulse pounding in his ears sounded like a kettle drum. An instant sheen of sweat formed on his forehead.

What the fuck?

He looked at the phone like it was a snake.

youreapwhatyousow

He didn't recognize the sender. His mind raced through the possibilities. Maybe this was a mistake; a doctored clip. Maybe it was someone else.

His hands shook as his finger hovered over the icon. The contents of his stomach churned and threatened to spew out.

When LeAnne rapped on the glass again, he jerked so violently, he dropped his phone.

"I'll be there in a minute. I've got to take care of something." His voice was so strained, he barely recognized it.

For several long moments, he just sat, stared at the phone on the ground and tried unsuccessfully to control his breathing.

*   *   *   *

He swiveled in his chair to click a few keys on his main

keyboard. Then pulled up a live camera feed of a well-dressed man sitting behind an executive mahogany desk. The camera angle from across the room showed a large office adorned with pictures of the man shaking hands with local politicians and dignitaries. A plaque on the wall commemorated an event and heaped praise on Nicholas Briggs.

Briggs read through some papers and made notes in the margins, completely unaware he was being watched.

The man glared at Briggs on the screen so intently, his forehead hurt. He could feel the hate bubble up in his chest.

"You clueless bastard. You have no idea what's coming. You think you're invincible with the family muscle protecting you. But when the threat comes from someplace you don't expect, we'll see just how good your protection really is."

* * * *

Mike's hands still shook, but he'd managed to gather himself enough to pick up his phone and watch the video two more times. It wasn't someone else. It was him, and Regina, at her house.

How could this be happening? Did she have something to do with it? She wouldn't do that. She's got as much to lose as me.

His thoughts and emotions lurched from one extreme to another.

Oh my God, what's going on?

Who's doing this?

How did they get that video?

They won't get away with this.

Fuck them!

His panic and fear morphed into anger, surging through his entire being. He wasn't going to take this bullshit from anyone. His fingers flew over the tiny keyboard, stumbling through a response that he had to rekey multiple times.

It was a short, simple message. His finger hesitated briefly, but then plunged down, sending his reply.

* * * *

A ding from his tablet interrupted the hacker's thoughts. "That didn't take long, Mike. So nice of you to respond so quickly." Now his smile returned. "Oh, but you really shouldn't use that kind of language on social media. I have no intention of doing that to myself. But since you're now engaged, why don't I tweak your rage just a little more?"

He went back to his file of video clips. Found one that portrayed Mike Systrom again. This time, he sat at a blackjack table in a private gambling room. He had a drink in front of him, a trashy looking blonde hanging off one arm and a cigar smoldering in an ashtray.

The man at the keyboard hit the reply button, attached the new file and typed another message.

The whore is just the start; does she know you're gambling your retirement away?

He hit send and once again, a self-satisfied smile filled his face. "That ought to keep him twitching for a while."

He leaned back in his chair, held out his arms as if to embrace the various computers and displays arranged around him. "I hate to pat myself on the back, but this is all coming together nicely. All you shameful people doing shameful things thinking no one is watching. Like you can get away with it. You're all cockroaches. It's amazing how you squirm as soon as I shine a light on you."

An amused look washed across his face as he shook his head. "How far you'll go to hide your sins. You make it so easy, my puppets. I've got a long list of wise guy scumbags to exterminate, and the second act is about to start."

*   *   *   *

For a moment after Systrom hit send, the world calmed. His heart rate slowed. He realized the TV was still on and the evening breeze started to normalize his body temperature.

Whoever's playing this game got my message. They know I'm not some wimpy pushover. Fuck them.

When his phone dinged again, his stomach tightened. He tapped the icon, saw the message as a new video began to play. Another one of him, this time of him at the blackjack table. The stack of chips as short as the whiskey glass in front of him. His eyes blinked uncontrollably. His body seemed to move without conscious thought. The next thing he knew, he was on all fours puking in the grass.

Chapter 18

The alarm clock jolted Hunter awake like a cattle prod. His hand fumbled in the dark to shut it off while Panther, who, in Stacy's absence, had staked his claim to the other side of the bed, let out a muffled mew and stretched.

It had been a rough night. Hunter had tossed and turned for hours just trying to find a comfortable position. His mattress felt like sleeping on a bed of nails. He'd even resorted to getting up around midnight and reading a few chapters of a John Sandford novel. Real sleep hadn't come until well after midnight.

He let his eyes adjust to being awake while mentally taking stock of the various aches and pains that had become normal over the past year.

If I feel like this at forty-five, what the hell will it be like at sixty?

Slowly sitting up, he placed his feet on the carpet, pulled himself up using his nightstand for leverage and shuffled toward the bathroom to start his morning routine.

His morning routine had stretched from thirty minutes, to forty-five, and recently almost sixty minutes. He had pondered this a few times, but hadn't been able to pinpoint why. It just seemed like everything was taking him longer.

As the steaming water from the shower splashed against his scalp, his mind drifted to the two cases. The strangeness of the murders and the odd connection between them. The sadness of the missing girl and the frustration of not being able to just kick the door down to get her.

He squirted some shampoo on his head as he continued to mentally review crime scenes and evidence. When he realized he was struggling to get the soap to spread evenly, he refocused on the task at hand. His hands seemed to need more mental direction than usual.

Since when do I need to consciously think about rubbing in shampoo?

After drying off and slipping into a pair of slacks, Panther fought for his attention by headbutting his shins.

"I know, I know. I'll get you some food in a minute."

When he finished shaving, he wiped off his face, leaned around the corner to check the time.

"Crap Panther, it's already seven. I need to get moving."

He grabbed a white T-shirt, slipped it over his head and took a dress shirt off its hanger. He slipped it on, but momentarily got tangled. His fingers fumbled with the buttons more than usual. By the time he'd gotten it straightened out and tucked in, another ten minutes had gone by.

What the hell? I'm so late.

The adrenaline from being late pumped through his system and he hurried through the rest of his morning routine. That same adrenaline caused him to dump too much cat food in Panther's bowl and to dribble coffee all over the countertop. Both transgressions were left uncorrected as he rushed out to his SUV, hurried down Western Center and joined the masses slowly creeping south on I35.

Hunter looked at his dashboard clock: already 7:35am. It had taken him over an hour to get out of the house this morning. As he stared at the glowing sea of red tail lights in front of him, he tried to replay his morning to determine why. His conclusion was no conclusion. There wasn't one thing that had slowed him down. It was everything. Death by a thousand cuts.

Maneuvering through traffic, his mind drifted back six months to his last doctor's visit. His annual physical. He felt fine. His bloodwork was great and his vitals were decent for even a twenty-year-old.

His doctor had been concerned about his posture and the way he moved around the exam room. Although he hadn't been specific about his concerns, he'd insisted Hunter see a neurologist. Which he'd delayed for longer than he should've. That appointment was scheduled for next week.

Could all this stumbling and fumbling around have something to do with that?

Chapter 19

Hunter cruised through the conference room door at 8:25am on Thursday, frowned and dropped his bag on the table.

"Has anyone heard from Jackson?" His question was the only acknowledgement that Billy was in the room.

"Not yet. I'm happy to call him, but…" Sanders looked at his watch and cocked his head. "You do know that this is an IT guy we're talking about. Chances of him being here before nine in the morning are slim."

"Call him." Hunter looked at his watch. "Hell, half the day's gone and I've already wasted enough time this morning." He started pacing the room, stretching his arms and loosening up his neck.

As Sanders listened to the phone ring, he arched an eyebrow at Hunter. "You okay?"

"Yeah, yeah. I'm fine. I just woke up thinking about this case. There's something wrong here, like a big piece we're missing. It doesn't make sense."

Billy held up a finger to hold Hunter's thought and left a quick message for Sean Jackson. When he hung up the phone, he leaned back in his chair. "Completely agree. I've been in here for an hour going over the two different files trying to find anything that connects them."

"And?"

"The only thing is the organized crime connection between the two shooting victims, and that's pretty weak."

Hunter slowed his pacing, slipped his hands into his pockets, and stared out the window.

What if it's right in front of my face, and I'm just getting too old to see it?

*   *   *   *

Sean Jackson didn't call back until ten in the morning. By then, all four detectives spun their speculations in circles in the stuffy conference room.

"Tell him to get his ass up here." Hunter barked as he glared at Billy.

"He's on his way."

When the man finally strolled in, four sets of angry eyes stared at him. He paused self-consciously. "Sorry guys. Didn't realize you were waiting on me."

"What did you find?" Hunter's tone hadn't lightened.

"To start with, whoever sabotaged these devices knew what he was doing. They were all completely inoperable."

"You said sabotage? Is that for certain?"

"Based on what little I could recover, I don't see how this level of destruction could happen by accident. Especially when you consider we have four different devices, all showing the same patterns and all associated with crimes that happened within days of each other." Jackson shook his head. "The statistical chances of that as coincidence are nearly zero."

Sanders leaned forward. "What could have caused it?"

"It had to be on purpose. An electromagnetic pulse or a very destructive virus. Either way, someone had to specifically target these devices."

Billy rubbed his temples. "Were you able to recover any data?"

"Nothing useful."

"Shit."

Jackson held up a finger. "But, keep in mind that any data that is transmitted through the internet most likely resides on a server somewhere."

Hunter perked up. "Okay, act like I have no idea how this shit works and explain that."

"Here's what I mean." He stood and walked to the whiteboard and drew some boxes with lines connecting them. "When you send data, say an email from one computer to another, it doesn't just go straight from your computer to the other person's computer. It makes at least two stops. First, it's stored on the server operated by your email service. You know, Gmail, Hotmail, etc." He looked up to see a few heads nod.

"Second, it's transmitted to the server operated by the receiver's email service. And then finally, it's sent to the receiver's computer." Jackson drew arrows following the path through the boxes. "So, if nobody deletes the records, or they're not overwritten, the data sits in four different places."

"Is it the same for things other than emails? Like texts?"

"It depends on what it is. Obviously, telephone companies keep detailed call records made and received, time and length." He rocked back on his feet. "Of course, they can't tell you what was said on the calls unless the line was tapped in advance. Text messages work similarly to emails. They are stored, unless specifically deleted."

"So, in theory, we should be able to get the emails and texts from these servers, right?"

"You'll have to find out their email and phone service providers, not to mention you'll need a warrant." He tilted his head. "You'll also need some luck and patience."

"Why is that?"

"Because whoever wiped out these devices may have deleted the records first. Service providers don't exactly view data requests as their top priority. It could take a while."

Hunter drummed his fingers on the table. His phone rang. Caller ID displayed Andre Kipton, again. He punched decline and motioned Jackson to continue. "Did you find anything else?"

"Forensically speaking, I think there are enough patterns and trails to prove the same person is behind the destruction of all of these devices."

Hunter's head popped up. "The cases are connected then."

"Yes. The odds of two different people sabotaging devices in the same way at the same time are astronomical." He paused. "I also think there was communication beyond email and text messages."

A look of confusion washed across Hunter's face. "What does that mean?"

"Well, this is where the similarities end and it gets a little fuzzy."

Jackson seemed to be finding his footing now. "I found traces of files and data on each device indicating the users had a number of different social media apps."

Hunter's expression hadn't changed and he met this statement with a shrug.

"Everything from FaceBook to Twitter to Instagram to SnapChat. There could have been messages, pictures and video's sent to and from any of these devices via those applications, but I couldn't recover them enough to confirm that."

"If you couldn't recover the data and you don't know what apps they had, how does that help us?"

"Most of the social media apps work much like email and text. If a picture or message or video was sent via the application, a copy of it exists on a server somewhere."

Hunter nodded. "But we don't have any way of knowing what app or what server."

Sanders leaned forward. "All we need to do there is ask their families. They'll know what social media platforms they were using. They'll probably know their user ID's as well. From there, we'll have to get a warrant for each platform."

Reyes shook his head. "We are going to be drowning in paperwork before this is over."

In spite of Reyes' comment, Hunter seemed to have perked up a bit. "Jackson, this was helpful. Thanks."

He turned to the rest of the team. "Parker, you and Reyes start working on warrants for the email, text and phone records. Billy, you and I will follow up with all four families and see if we can get a listing of their social media apps and user ID's."

Billy nodded. "I've also got some calls into the Organized Crime guys to see if they can shed some light on the connection between the victims."

"Good move." Hunter stood and stared at the whiteboard. "Whoever's behind all this, if destroying laptops and phones was that important, then there's an electronic trail somewhere. All we've got to do is find it. And follow it to the end."

MURDER BY PROXY

Chapter 20

"On behalf of the entire FW OCD, I'd like for you to pass on our most humble thanks to your shooters for closing the books on two scumbags." Detective Cosner Thompson of the FWPD Organized Crime Division made an overly dramatic gesture directing Hunter and Sanders to sit.

Hunter smirked. "OCD? Really?"

"It's a bit of a pun, but we enjoy it."

After lunch, Hunter and Sanders had made the short drive south across downtown to the FWPD Central Sub Station on Hemphill Street to visit with Detective Thompson about the tenuous connection between their shooting victims.

Thompson was tall, blond and held a constant expression that implied he knew something you didn't.

"How can we help our friends in Homicide today?"

Sanders leaned forward. "As I mentioned on the phone, our two cases appear unrelated on the surface, but as we dug a little deeper, they have some strange connections." He handed the files across to Thompson. "Including both shooting victims share a history with organized crime."

Thompson nodded. "More than just a little history. They were both top shelf assholes." He opened the top file. "Weston Caldwell has been a major player in the Mazanti family for years. Ran several of their strip joints and most of their prostitution rings."

"What about Marcus Howell?"

"Similar story, only with the Rosa family. He was a little classier than Caldwell, mostly white collar crimes and extortion." Thompson shook his head. "Couldn't have happened to two more upstanding gentlemen."

Hunter arched an eyebrow. "So, what's their connection?"

"Caldwell and Howell?" Thompson furrowed his brow. "None. I'd be surprised if they've ever been anywhere near each other. They certainly don't run in the same crowd."

Hunter frowned. "No connection at all?"

"Detective, these guys worked for rival families. They might have known the other guy's name, but that's about it. They didn't only work in different organizations, they operated in different criminal activities. Their paths would likely have never crossed." He stacked the two files together and handed them back to Sanders. "Other than them both winding up dead around the same time, why do you think they're connected?"

Sanders spent the next ten minutes summarizing the cases and outlining the similarities, especially the laptop and phones. When he was finished, he shrugged. "I know it's not bullet proof, but it's more than just coincidence."

Thompson rubbed his forehead like all of this gave him a headache.

"Here's the deal, guys. There's no connection between Caldwell and Howell other than they're both criminals. They're both mid-level managers who climbed their respective ladders, but were never destined to make it to the top because they weren't blood."

He reached toward his desk, grabbed a tissue and blew his nose.

"Sorry. Allergies." He wadded up the tissue and threw it away. "Guys, I think this is just a fluke of timing."

Hunter didn't respond. He just pursed his lips.

"I'll tell you something else. We'd better hope there isn't a connection."

"Why is that?"

"Fort Worth may not be a real hotbed of organized crime activity, at least not in the way you'd think about a New York, Chicago or Boston. But the Mazanti's and the Rosa's have plenty of muscle." He shook his head. "They have uncomfortably coexisted in this city for decades with very little direct confrontation. But if those two organizations were to ever declare war on each other... What is it that the terrorists like to say? The streets will flow with blood."

Hunter nodded. "At this point, it's just a little coincidental."

"Let's hope that's all it is. In the meantime, I'd be very careful about floating the idea of a connection. If that possibility got out into the media, we could have a full-fledged war on our hands. That's something none of us want."

Sanders tilted his head. "These clearly weren't mob hits. Not unless using a house wife as an assassin is a new method for them."

"It may seem obvious to you, but these guys aren't looking at your murder file, and they have no idea who did what. All they'll see is one of their guys got whacked about the same time as the other guy. They'll see tit-for-tat and might jump to a conclusion. I'm just saying, be very careful with that information."

Hunter stood, stuck out his hand. "Detective, thanks for your time. We'll keep you posted."

Thompson stood and shook his hand.

"I'm going to go pop a cork on a bottle of champagne to celebrate the demise of our two friends, but keep me on speed dial. If things go beyond these two, or if you find a stronger connection, I need to be your first call."

Chapter 21

"Hey, you still at the office?"

Hunter had just dropped Billy back at the station and now maneuvered through rush hour traffic heading south again. The sun dipped below the horizon to his right and he relished the crisp outside air coming through the vent as he progressed slowly down South Main. This time he headed for the FWPD Forensics Lab.

"I am, but I was just wrapping up my official business for the day." Stacy's smile in her voice made Hunter smile.

"Can I interpret that to mean you're available for unofficial business?"

Stacy let out a slow laugh. "Why do I think what you're wanting isn't going to be as fun as it sounds?"

"The first part might not be, but it is Friday night. Will it make it better if I promise to take you out to dinner afterward?"

"I guess every girl has her price." She giggled. "Damn, I'm a cheap date."

"Value isn't always measured in dollars and cents."

"Listen to you sounding all philosophical."

"Yeah, enough of that. I sent you an email with some photos attached. There are four guys in these shots I need ID's on. Can you run them through facial recognition for me?"

There was a pause on the other end of the line with clicking of a keypad in the background and then a moment of silence.

"From the looks of these guys, I'm guessing this is for our friend from Austin?"

"Yep."

"You better bring me a snack. Our dinner may be a little late. These pictures are good, but I'll need to do some cropping and adjusting, then process them through the system individually. Could take a while."

"Your wish is my command."

*   *   *   *

Hunter and Stacy sipped on their Starbucks, his straight black, hers a mocha Frappuccino, and munched on trail mix while the computer processed through the various facial recognition databases.

As she had speculated, the procedure was slow. The sun had already receded and rush hour traffic was long since a memory. They didn't seem to mind the time as they casually chatted about life and work, and enjoyed the quiet of a mostly empty office. It wasn't often they worked together when they weren't standing over a dead body or in a crowded conference room.

Three of the four searches had awarded them with hits, and they waited for the last one. Stacy tinkered with her computer while Hunter looked up information on the three ID's the system produced.

Every so often, Hunter looked up from his laptop to absorb Stacy's presence, and smiled. The pair of them were in a good place and he liked the feeling.

"Stop that." Stacy swatted her hand toward him without looking up.

"Stop what?"

"Staring at me."

Hunter chuckled and tried to act like he hadn't gotten caught. "What are you talking about, Ms. Morgan? We're in a FWPD facility. Staring longingly at a coworker would be frowned upon."

She stopped, gave him a mischievous grin, leaned over and kissed him. "If staring is frowned upon, what would they think about that?"

Hunter's smile broadened. He leaned forward only to be interrupted by a ding from Stacy's computer. "Damn."

Stacy arched an eyebrow. "Perfect timing. Let's save that thought for later, Cowboy."

Without giving him a chance to respond, she spun in her seat and clacked on the keyboard.

"Our elusive number four. Let's see who we have...Evan Monaco." She hit the keyboard. The printer on her desk came to life and spit out a sheet of paper. She handed it to Hunter. "That completes your set. Four little thugs all in a row."

"Thugs is right. These are some grade A assholes."

"What have you found so far?"

"Let's see." Hunter checked his laptop. "Thug number one is Ryan Williams, 25. Juvenile record is sealed, but I'm sure it's lengthy. Since he turned 18, he has been very productive in the criminal world. Several minor encounters with law enforcement including drunk in public, DUI, possession of a controlled substance and three assault charges. The final one earned him two years in the state pen. Out on parole for only three months."

"Considering that associating with convicted felons is a parole violation, shouldn't you guys just lock him up?"

"I've already made that suggestion. Seems our lanky friend with the big hat needs subtlety in his approach."

"Hmm." Stacy frowned.

Hunter grinned and put on his best game show host voice.

"But wait, there's more. Thug number two, David Gardner, 28, makes Ryan look like a slacker. He's been arrested for both rape and assault multiple times." He shook his head. "Take a guess as to why he hasn't been convicted."

"Witnesses and victims all got amnesia."

"Exactly."

"Bastard." Stacy's whisper was bitter.

"I'd tell you about thug number three...Joshua Floyd, but I'm afraid I'd start sounding like a broken record."

"Some real winners."

"Yeah, and I haven't even run thug number four, our boy Evan Monaco. My guess is he's going to be much the same."

Stacy's brow furrowed and she bit down on her lip.

"You okay?" Hunter arched his eyebrows.

"I'm just thinking about the poor girl, Kenzi. If she's mixed up with these scumbags, she's in real trouble."

Hunter nodded, not liking the dark turn in her voice. She really was getting concerned about the girl.

"Yeah." He paused for a moment. "The good news is that Colt is getting close, and once he confirms where she's at, he'll figure out a way to get her out."

"Speaking of Colt, when did you hear from him last?"

"Last night." Hunter reflexively looked at his watch. "He's working off a burner and said he'd call me back over the weekend. He didn't want me to call him in case he was somewhere he needed to be quiet."

Stacy folded her arms across her chest. "Are you sure he's safe, Cowboy?"

Hunter grinned. "I'm more worried about our four little thugs than I am about Colt. You know the old saying, don't you?"

She smiled. "One riot, one Ranger."

Hunter nodded. "Damn straight. Let's go eat."

Chapter 22

"Mike, you need to go to the doctor. This has to be the flu." His wife touched his forehead with the back of her hand to check his temperature. "You've been sweating like this for two days, and you've barely eaten."

"I'm fine." He gave her an annoyed look. He knew better. His symptoms had nothing to do with a virus.

She has no idea that our world is on the verge of imploding.

"It's just a little bug. I'll be inside in a minute."

As he sat on his back patio, even the cool October evening air wasn't enough to stem the flow of sweat. Speaking of flowing, it wasn't just sweat gushing out of him. Ever since he'd gotten the first messages, he'd spent more time on the toilet than he had anywhere else.

LeAnne sighed. "Make it quick. It's cold out here."

He could barely concentrate on her words. All he could think about was this bastard tormenting him on every social media platform. Deleting his Instagram account was a waste of time. The bastard just switched to FaceBook and Twitter direct messages and text messages.

How the hell did he get my cell number?

He'd tried to use a reverse directory for the cell number from where the texts had been sent. No luck.

She walked over, put her hand on his shoulder and furrowed her brow. "I'm worried about you."

He waved her off. "I'm fine. It's nothing." He patted her hand. "Get to bed. I'll be in soon."

She rubbed his shoulder and reluctantly went inside.

As soon as she'd gone, he let out a huge sigh and gulped in air. He'd had to hold his breath to keep it together. He leaned over and put both hands on his knees. After a moment of deep breathing, he realized his hands were shaking.

The phone dinged. His heartrate spiked.

Oh God.

He tried to ignore it, but couldn't. Jabbing his hand into his pocket, he pulled out his phone and opened the text messages.

There it was. Another text from that same number.

His eyes blinked rapidly and his hand shook so badly, he could barely get the message open.

Mike, don't ignore me. I have all the details. Dates, names, places. Your ass is mine and I'm bored with toying around. Does this phone number look familiar? 817-236-5502

Systrom gulped for air as he stared at his wife's cell number.

How on earth?

He caught himself against one of the outdoor lounge chairs as his knees buckled. Sitting down in the chair, he didn't know if he could take it anymore.

Whoever this guy was, he knew everything: the women, the gambling, the depletion of the investment accounts. How was that possible? Not only was his marriage in jeopardy, but as an officer in a public company, so was his career. He could lose everything.

Who is this guy and what does he want?

There'd been no demand for blackmail. No demand for anything really. Just a relentless barrage of torment.

Why? What did I do to this guy?

He shook his head to clear his thoughts. He had to keep it together. There had to be an answer. If his years in business had taught him anything, it was that there was always a solution. Sometimes that answer was expensive and sometimes you had to get your hands dirty, but there was always an answer.

Meanwhile, he was starting to feel his mood change ever so slightly. The scared, helpless feeling shifted to rage.

Whoever this guy is has never seen me pissed off before. When I find out who this son of a bitch is — and I will find out — he'll wish he was never born.

The bile in his gut roiled again, but this time it fueled his defiance.

The phone buzzed again. His blood pressure escalated. His face burned.

He grabbed the phone. Without even reading the new message, he ground his teeth as he stabbed in his reply.

Fuck you!

*   *   *   *

A smile slid across the face of the man behind the keyboard.

"Oh, Mike. Such language." He leaned back in his chair and studied the two word response. "I do believe the pump is just about primed. Give you another sleepless night and you should be ready."

He turned to another keyboard and looked at a different set of monitors. A few quick taps and several live feeds from various cameras filled the screens. On one, a man appeared to be having a late evening snack while sitting at a table in a breakfast nook.

"Enjoy your snack, Nicholas. Could very well be your last meal. Looks like Mike's just about ready to come calling. Shame on you for torturing him like you have. It's so rude." He smiled. "Beware Nicholas. Karma's a bitch."

Chapter 23

Hunter felt something, but at the moment he couldn't be bothered. His mind floated through time and space in that blissful realm somewhere between deep sleep and swimming to the surface. A hint of Stacy's perfume touched his senses. He smiled inside, adjusted the pillow and let his mind dive back into the depths.

He felt it again. A soft poke on his cheek.

No, no. Leave me alone.

Again, a poke.

He had no choice now. He cracked an eyelid just to be focused on the bottom side of a paw.

"Jesus, Panther, it's Saturday."

Stacy rolled over and squinted. "So, this is how it is? We had a great night only to wake up and find that you've invited someone else to the party." She reached over and petted Panther's head. "I'm not even going to comment on the fact that it's a 'he' and he's big, black and furry."

Hunter rolled his eyes, pushed the covers away, and stretched. "It's way too early for that." He nodded his head toward the door. "Come on Panther, let's get you some breakfast."

As Hunter headed for the door with Panther in tow, Stacy smiled. "What about me?"

"Oh, I'll be back for you."

*   *   *   *

Hunter slipped on a pair of jeans and headed to the utility room to feed Panther. As he moved through the living room, he felt something slapping against his left hand. Thinking that Panther was getting overly annoying, he started to say something but then realized that Panther was several steps ahead of him.

What the hell?

He stopped, looked down and around but saw nothing that could have hit his hand. As Panther meowed loudly from the kitchen, Hunter turned completely around and looked behind him. Nothing. He shook his head.

I'm losing my mind.

He turned to walk. It happened again and he realized that nothing was actually hitting his hand. It was his own hand, more specifically, his pinkie, that had caused the sensation. It was twitching. All on its own. Without him asking it to or wanting it to.

He stood still in the middle of the room and lifted his hand up from his side and stared at it. To his amazement, as the rest of his hand was completely motionless, his left pinkie was twitching spastically. It looked like a large caterpillar being electrocuted.

With his eyes watching this phenomena intently, he tried to stop the twitching, but his thoughts had absolutely no effect. It was as if his pinkie was completely divorced from his brain. He made a fist and splayed his fingers. His hand, including his pinkie, responded. But the moment he stopped the action, the twitching reignited.

Completely oblivious to Hunter's plight, Panther continued to protest loudly that his bowl was still empty.

"Yeah, yeah. On my way."

He slowly moved towards the kitchen, staring at, and shaking his hand vigorously as he walked. When he reached the utility room, he tested it again, holding out his hand and keeping it still.

Same results—rock solid hand connected to a spastic sausage.

A less than subtle headbutt from Panther reminded him of his mission. He grabbed a can of Fancy Feast and emptied it into the dish. "There you go. Thanks for your patience."

Panther paid no attention, just devoured the glob of meat byproducts in front of him while Hunter resumed his hand observation. He squeezed his hand.

Something's wrong.

* * * *

Stacy snuggled up behind Hunter in the kitchen as he worked the coffee machine. "How about a little almond mocha?"

He pressed his hand against the countertop to conceal the twitching from Stacy. Until he figured out what was going on, there was no need to freak her out.

"As you wish."

She smiled at his response, kissed him on the back of the neck and padded over to the table in the breakfast nook. The fresh almond coffee scent permeated the air.

Hunter shoved his left hand into his pocket and rattled open the fridge with his right trying his best to act casual. "Any special requests?"

"Something simple."

"Simple it is." Hunter grabbed a container of yogurt, and pulled out a bowl of grapes, strawberries and precut pineapple. He moved to the pantry and found a box of granola. After arranging everything on a tray, he carried it to the table and made a show of presenting it to Stacy.

"Mmm. Look at you, Mr. Healthy."

He sat, dropped his left hand down by his leg and smiled. "Got to look after this god-like body."

"God-like is right." She flashed him a wicked grin.

"Better be careful or that fruit might have to wait until lunch."

She slowly bit into a strawberry. "Promises, promises."

He grinned, fixed himself a bowl and unfolded the Star Telegram he'd brought in earlier.

She shook her head. "When are you going to get into this century? You know you can read the whole paper on your tablet."

He flipped a page. "I like the feel of the paper, the smell of the ink."

"And the residue all over your fingers?"

He nodded. "That, too." He raised his good hand and wiggled his smudged fingers in the air.

Stacy fixed herself some granola and smiled. "What's your day look like?"

He set the paper aside, noticed his finger still twitching in his lap but refocused on Stacy.

"Going to spend the morning in the yard before the weather gets wet and cold. After that, a little college football on TV while I finish up paperwork. Tonight..." He paused. "I'm hoping to hear from Colt. Maybe meet up with him."

"Sounds like an awfully busy Saturday."

Hunter flashed a sly grin. "Of course, all that could change if a better offer came along."

Stacy arched her eyebrow and smiled. Just as quickly, her face turned serious. "Any idea what's going on with Colt?"

"Absolutely none. I'd hoped to hear from him last night. I really need to give him that intel on the scumbags you ID'd last night. Once he knows who he's dealing with, I'm confident in his talents. As it is, he's dealing with unknowns, and that's always a disadvantage."

She reached over, took his right hand and gave him a concerned look. "You both need to be careful."

He pressed his left hand against his leg and smirked. "As you wish."

Chapter 24

Hunter sighed at the mass of crowds on the sidewalks as he strolled up N. Main towards Exchange early Saturday evening. He'd picked 7:00pm to meet up with Barkley so they'd miss the party crowds in Fort Worth's historic Northside area. He'd forgotten about it being college football season.

Even without being an ardent fan, he knew enough that when hordes of people roamed the Stockyard streets wearing various forms of burnt orange, it meant the UT Longhorns were in town to play TCU. Based on the plastered grins from the burnt orange fans and the conspicuous absence of purple clothing, he surmised the early game didn't fare so well for the hometown Horned Frogs.

Thankfully, his destination wasn't known for catering to the Saturday football crowd. The White Elephant Saloon on East Exchange was as traditional as a bar in Texas can get. The current incarnation had existed in the Stockyards since the 1970's.

When Hunter stepped in from the sidewalk, the sea of Stetson's made it difficult to find Barkley. In spite of the early hour, the bar already conducted a brisk business. Fortunately, Colt's hat poked up slightly higher than the rest of the crowd's.

The Texas Ranger had already secured a corner table. He nursed a beer and seemed lost in thought. When he looked up and spotted Hunter, he flashed his trademark lopsided grin and waved him over.

"Twice in one week? I must be living right." Hunter shook Barkley's hand.

"There is no doubt you're one seriously lucky man."

"Stacy routinely reminds me."

They both laughed and Hunter signaled to the waitress to bring him a beer. He laid a folder on the table and sat across from Colt. "I got the backgrounds for the four knuckleheads you've been watching. They look like grade A assholes. Any movement?"

Barkley shook his head. "Nothing significant. Just the same pattern between the hotels. Still no sign of Kenzi or other victims." He frowned. "I'm going to have to get closer."

"Or maybe just let the FWPD bust these guys for any number of parole violations." Hunter arched his eyebrows to stress his point as the waitress delivered his beer.

Raising his bottle, Barkley smiled. "We're close. I just need another day or two."

Hunter met his raised bottle with his own and frowned. "Before you discount using the FWPD, you need to read these backgrounds."

He opened the folder with the four profiles stacked in a pile on the table. Each contained a summary sheet with an attached mugshot. Hunter sorted through them one at a time, jabbing his index finger at each picture as he went. "Evan Monaco, Joshua Floyd, David Gardner and Ryan Williams."

He paused to make sure he had Barkley's full attention. "Every one of these guys has multiple prior arrests. All with violent offenses. Every one of them has served time." He stopped, looked directly at Colt. "Now, I know you're a badass Ranger, but these aren't choirboys you're dealing with."

Barkley nodded. "I hear you."

Hunter continued. "From everything I can gather, Ryan Williams is the group's alpha male. A real piece of work. Been in and out of the joint his entire adult life. My guess is he started much earlier than that, but I don't have access to his juvie records."

"Wouldn't want to tread on his civil rights." Barkley smirked.

"No shit."

"They all roll up to a serious asshole named Harley Lundsford. Based on what I've seen, Ryan Williams is definitely the boss's right hand man. The other three are his goons."

Both men went quiet. Hunter sipped on his beer and Barkley studied the four files.

The bar was beginning to fill up with the early party crowd. Hunter looked around the room and thought back to his younger days when hanging out in a bar on a Saturday night was the cool thing to do. Now as he studied the faces, all he saw were lonely people desperate to connect with another human being… Any human being.

He thought about Stacy. She filled his life. She'd made him happier than he'd ever been. He smiled inwardly.

Barkley's voice snapped him back to the business at hand. "This is good stuff. Thanks for your help."

"All this is just paperwork. How can I really help? We need to get these jerks off the street and get your friend's daughter back home."

"As soon as I can confirm she's actually there."

"How do you plan to do that? Based on the pictures you provided, you're already on top of these guys. You can't get much closer without being in the room."

Barkley nodded as if contemplating that very possibility. "Trust me, if I thought I could get in the room, I would. Not sure what I'm going to do, but I'll figure out something."

"I hear you." Hunter frowned. "Just so I can keep an eye on you, where are you staying?"

"I'm around the corner at the Courtyard on 26th and Main Street. I'm not there much, just crashing a few hours each night."

"Do me a favor and make sure you stay in contact with me at least once a day."

"Yes, mother." Barkley smirked.

"Don't give me that shit." He leaned back and frowned at Barkley. "I see you're still dressed like a civilian."

Barkley nodded.

"Let me get this straight." Hunter ticked off the points on his fingers. "You're stalking four really bad ex-cons, five if you count Lundsford. You're not carrying your badge. You're probably not even carrying ID at all, right?"

He nodded again.

"You're hanging out in a sketchy part of town and I'm guessing that whatever weapon you're carrying can't be traced back to you."

"That about sums it up."

Hunter squirmed in his seat. His exhale was louder than the chatter around them. "Hell, it's a tossup on which'll happen first. Either the thugs will beat you to death or you'll get arrested by FWPD."

Barkley shrugged.

Hunter picked at the label on his beer bottle. "No wonder I don't sleep at night."

Chapter 25

Diffused light broke through Kenzi's unconsciousness once again. The room swirled. Her tongue was dry and the bitter taste in her mouth made her gag. As she swam up through the haze in her mind, her surroundings became clearer.

Dread took over. Her heart raced and she couldn't get a deep breath, like a rabbit staring at a coyote.

Oh God, I'm still here.

She was in the same terrible room, sitting on the same disgusting bed.

Her eyes caught a glimpse of herself in the cracked mirror attached to the cheap dresser. She was unrecognizable. A sob broke the silence and she couldn't control her body convulsing.

Why? Why is he doing this?

Kenzi took a deep breath, tried to calm herself and slow her heartbeat. Sweat and dust permeated the stale air. She moved to wipe her face, and the chain of the handcuffs clanged against the headboard. That sound, and the bite of the metal cuff, ratcheted her heartrate again in a familiar panic.

The room blurred as her skin turned clammy with a cold fear.

Please, will this nightmare ever end?

* * * *

For an October Sunday night, the weather cooperated for Barkley's surveillance. A rare warm and clear evening. Stars spotted the darker patches of the sky. A beautiful night, if he weren't stuck staring at the ugly steel door of a seedy hotel room.

He'd managed to access the hotel's roof and tucked himself

between an air conditioning unit and the elevator shaft structure. His perch allowed him to watch the movements in and out of two rooms the four scumbags operated. Any decent human would've assumed Sunday meant slower business. That wasn't the case.

For three damn days, he still hadn't determined if Kenzi was in one of those rooms. Every evening that passed escalated Barkley's frustration. His patience wasn't paying off. The longer he waited, the worse things likely grew for Kenzi. No female had entered or left any of the rooms, but dozens of men had gone in, a revolving door of clients that made his blood boil. Deep in his gut, he knew they were there but had no concrete proof. At some point, he'd have to move even without confirmation. Kenzi's life depended on it.

*   *   *   *

"It's about God damned time you woke up," the man snarled from the doorway.

She recoiled at his voice, too scared to look at the source. Her heart jackhammered and she let out a squeak.

"You can't make me any money passed out." He paused, then laughed. "Well, you can, but that requires the right kind of kinky customer."

She reflexively tried to crawl away from the sound, and the cuffs stopped her again. The ratty mattress itched against her bare skin. Except for a pair of panties, she was completely naked.

Even without looking at him, she could feel the man's eyes feasting on her nudity. She twisted away from him in a vain attempt to cover herself.

"A little late for the shy act, don't you think?"

She cowered on the bed.

He shook his head in disgust and tossed a McDonalds bag on the bed. "Eat something, whore." He smiled. "You'll thank me later."

The smell of the greasy food made her stomach growl. She tore into the bag, barely removing the paper before biting into it.

"Hurry up. I've got customers on their way."

The words made her want to puke, but she couldn't afford to

waste the precious calories.

She sobbed in between bites.

Are you there God?

*   *   *   *

"Shit."

Barkley watched as two men knocked at the door. He took a quick picture with his burner phone despite knowing the final image would be too dark and too far away.

After the door opened and the two men entered, he squeezed his hand into a fist and pounded it on the rail in front of him. This was driving him crazy. Doing nothing but watching, and knowing... He couldn't do that much longer.

He processed what he knew from his surveillance.

The guys used two rooms and he figured out which one manned which. Since Harley Lundsford spent most of his time in the corner room and his four minions visited frequently, he surmised that room was their version of a headquarters. He'd also deduced that at this moment Harley only had one of his thugs in the room with him. Based on Stacy's research, it had to be Ryan Williams.

That guy had just brought in dinner from McDonalds. By the number of bags in his hand, maybe at least one of the girls was in there with them. His gut said it was Kenzi.

As for the other three thugs, one was in the room next to the headquarters and the other two had gone offsite about twenty minutes earlier.

If there was ever a good time to kick in the door, now was the chance.

*   *   *   *

The minimal food was cold and unhealthy but it was the first thing she'd eaten in a while. Between the drugs they'd pumped into her and the fact that she hadn't left the room in days, she had no idea what day or time it was. Since he'd just given her a small hamburger instead of a biscuit, it probably wasn't breakfast time.

In spite of only eating takeout food since she'd been here, the hamburger tasted divine. Amazing what hunger did to her taste buds. In a rare moment of calm and clarity, she thought about that documentary about the guy who only ate from McDonalds for an entire month. He'd hated it, even gotten sick toward the end.

I bet his attitude would've been different if he'd been caged up like an animal.

For just a flash, she smiled inwardly at the thought.

"What the fuck do you think this is, a spa?"

The voice jolted her out of her moment and sent her pulse thumping. She reflexively bowed her head and averted his glare.

"Give me that trash, bitch. It's time you pay me back for that dinner."

Her stomach churned as her mind began to disengage from her situation. She robotically handed over the trash.

He reached over, uncuffed her hand and growled into her ear. "Play nice. Take care of my two friends and I'll let your parents live for another day."

She felt her head nodding.

Two disgusting men stood at the foot of the bed, both already disrobing. Their eyes raping her.

Her skin crawled.

I'm not here. This isn't me. Pretend this isn't me.

*   *   *   *

Barkley ran various scenarios in his head. If he struck now, he'd have Lundsford and the sidekick subdued before the third guy reacted to the noise. At that point, if he was smart, he'd just run. Of course, if he wasn't smart…

Barkley smiled at the thought.

What if Kenzi isn't there? What if I'm wrong?

Worst case, maybe he'd rescue some other poor girl from this hell.

His brain spun through other possibilities, each one had some level of positive ending.

It's time.

While he didn't need backup to take down the three sleaze balls in the rooms, he would need Hunter to help him with the aftermath. He looked at his watch.

Sorry, Hunter, I'm going to interrupt your evening news.

Barkley reached into his jacket pocket, extracted the burner phone and started to dial.

When his finger tapped the fourth number, he heard the click of the trigger hammer cocked back.

He froze. The phone slipped from his fingers and crashed to the floor.

The barrel's cold steel touched the base of his skull.

Chapter 26

By the time someone reached the age of forty-five, they'd probably seen their fair share of doctor's offices. Hunter was no exception. In spite of the fancier than normal artwork in the waiting room, this one was just as sterile feeling as the rest.

It was 9:00am on Monday morning and there were a thousand places he would've rather been than at a neurologist's office. Filling out fifty pages of new patient information for the equally sterile looking lady at the front desk. Based on his very limited knowledge of neurological disorders, there were four levels of diagnosis – shitty, shittier, shittiest and Oh My God shitty. He wasn't thrilled about any of those options. Maybe that's why butterflies swirled in his gut.

He looked around the waiting room at his fellow patients. He was shocked to see they weren't just old, they were ancient. Two had walkers, one was hunched over his cane and a fourth sat staring at the floor, twitching and shaking.

What am I doing here? I'm not old.

The song from Sesame Street about how one thing isn't like the others and doesn't belong, popped into his head. In that moment, the happy little tune had a cruel tone.

The butterflies now started to completely spaz out in his stomach. The thought of leaving crossed his mind. He shook his head, refocused and began plotting out every detail of his medical life. With the exception of the issues he'd been having over the last several months, that medical history was incredibly boring. He was a healthy guy.

If I'm so healthy, why am I here?

After he'd answered the same questions a dozen times each, he turned in his clipboard, retrieved his cards and waited. He passed the time mulling over the two cases. He'd never had a murder that was clearly solved, but yet, didn't feel solved. Now, he had two.

The similarities—seemingly normal people woke up one day and murdered local organized crime players, to which they had no apparent connection. It was like these people had lost their minds and became robots on a mission. He shook his head at how crazy it seemed.

His mind then shifted to Barkley. He hadn't heard from him since Saturday evening. There was no doubt Barkley could take care of himself, but Lundsford and his thugs weren't lightweights. Without his badge and his team, Colt was exposed.

I should call him.

As he reached for his phone, a voice jolted him back to the moment. "Mr. Hunter?"

He nodded, pulled himself up and stood.

"This way, please." She led him through the door and began her routine cheerful banter.

Barely registering the questions, Hunter mumbled through his answers as he followed her to an examination room. They reviewed his responses on the paperwork and she made notes without ever letting her upbeat tone waver.

"Dr. Jorgenson will be in momentarily." She smiled and slipped out the door leaving him with his thoughts.

Those thoughts had him twitching and nervous. He looked around the room but found no worthy distractions, just posters providing way too much information about diseases he'd only heard of in passing. They all sounded terrible and the more he read the posters, the more he started to convince himself that he had every one of them.

His distress was interrupted with a short knock on the door before it swung open revealing a stocky man in his fifties wearing a white coat and a warm smile.

"Mr. Hunter, I'm Doctor Jorgenson. Nice to meet you." He gripped Hunter's hand and shook it in a firm, confident fashion. "I understand you and your Primary Care have some concerns." He commandeered the rolling stool and sat down. "Let's talk about what you've been experiencing."

For the next thirty minutes, through an intensive question and answer process, Hunter admitted to regularly feeling fatigued, struggling with balance occasionally, walking with a sporadic limp or shuffle and with slouching more than usual. He also told the doctor about his episode with the crazy twitching pinkie and with his overall sense that he was just moving slower in everything he did.

Throughout the conversation, Dr. Jorgenson took lots of notes, nodded regularly and displayed a calm but concerned façade. Eventually, with an almost imperceptible sigh, he put down his notepad, and asked Hunter to take off his shirt and shoes. Then to stand.

Hunter complied.

"Stand on one leg."

Hunter did.

"Look up... Now, close your eyes."

When Hunter obeyed, his inner gyroscope somehow was kicked across the room. He felt himself flailing to stay upright. Dr. Jorgenson caught him mere inches before he crashed into the wall.

Hunter's eyes flew open.

"What the hell?" He looked at the doctor, whose expression hadn't changed.

"Not to worry. Happens all the time."

Bullshit.

Hunter wasn't sold.

For the next fifteen minutes, the doctor put Hunter through an intense roadside sobriety test. Walking a straight line, touching his nose, and several hand coordination exercises. Some were easy, and others that should've been simple seemed almost impossible.

A sheen of sweat formed on Hunter's brow. He wasn't sure if it was from exertion or from concern.

If I had been pulled over, I'd have the cuffs on by now. What the hell is wrong with me?

Before Hunter had a chance to comment on his less-than-stellar performance, the doctor grabbed his notepad and stood. He blinked twice and looked Hunter in his eyes.

"Get dressed and come see me in my office, so we can talk about what's going on with you."

Hunter didn't need his observational skills to detect concern in the doctor's eyes.

Chapter 27

Mike Systrom sat behind his desk at work Monday morning and distractedly tapped his fingers on the wood. His mood swung wildly from fury to fear and back to fury. He had to stop this nut from ruining his life.

Over the weekend, he'd borrowed a hand gun from a buddy. He'd told his friend that he'd been invited to go to the range by his boss and he didn't want to show up empty handed. His buddy not only provided him with nice Mossberg M2c 9mm semi-automatic, he walked him through the basics of how to use it, loaded him up with eye and ear protection as well as two boxes of ammo.

He was all set to go to the range. He smiled at the thought.

Now, all I need to do is find this bastard. There has to be a way.

As he sat and stewed, he pondered how he could find him. He quickly realized he had no idea. He wasn't a techie. But...

But I know several.

He thought for a moment, trying to remember the IT guy who had helped him in the past. After a quick search in the company directory, he punched an extension into his desk phone.

"IT, this is Dustin."

"Hey, this is Mike Systrom up on the 10th floor." He put as much smile into his voice as he could muster. "Do you have a few minutes? I've got a rather urgent systems issue I need some help with."

"Sure, what app's giving you problems?"

"Well." He hesitated. "It might be best if you come up and take a look yourself."

There was a momentary pause on the other end of the line before Dustin responded with a conspiratorial tone. "Gotcha. No problem. I'll be right up. Don't worry, Mr. Systrom. We'll get it all cleaned up for you."

Confused by Dustin's tone, but happy he was on his way up, Mike walked across the room and stared out of the floor-to-ceiling windows. His role as partner in a mid-sized audit firm gave him an office facing south toward the Wells Fargo Tower in downtown Fort Worth overlooking Sundance Square. He normally enjoyed watching people scurry from place to place ten floors below. Today, he soaked in the landscape and let his mind process all the threatening messages.

I'm going to find you, bastard. When I do...

A knock on the door pulled him back to the moment. He turned and waived Dustin into his office.

Dustin went straight to Mike's desk and sat down. He pulled out a couple of disks and cables and started to hook them up to Mike's laptop.

"Don't worry, Mr. Systrom. This happens all the time. We'll get it cleaned up for you ASAP."

"Huh?" Systrom scrunched his face. "What are you talking about?"

A smile broke across Dustin's face. "Don't worry. I'll keep it confidential. It happens all the time." He gestured toward the laptop and shrugged. "You know, you go to a website you probably shouldn't have been on and your laptop gets infected with malware." He nodded knowingly. "It's happened to half the guys in the building."

"Website? What are you...?" The realization washed across him like a wave. "What? No. You got it all wrong. I didn't call you down here because I went to some porn site. That's not it at all."

Dustin's smile vanished. "Oh. Sorry. Then what did you need?"

Mike gestured for Dustin to move out from behind his desk. He pointed to the guest chair and they both sat, momentarily restoring a sense of order.

"Look, umm..." Mike struggled with phrasing. "I need some help tracing some messages."

Dustin cocked his head but didn't say anything.

"I've been receiving threatening messages through a number of different avenues. Some by email, texts, other times on FaceBook or Instagram." He paused, looked intently at Dustin. "I need to find out who's sending them so I can get him to stop, or at the very least, understand what he wants from me."

Dustin leaned back in his chair, exhaled deeply. "You have no idea who's doing it?"

"None."

"And they've sent you these threats through multiple channels?"

Systrom nodded. "Yeah, whoever it is knows how to contact me on just about every platform I use."

"Have you kept copies?"

"Some, yes." Mike shrugged. "In the beginning, I just wanted it all to go away, so I deleted anything that came in. Over the past few days, I've kept everything."

"Can I see them?"

Mike squirmed for a moment, leaned forward and rubbed his forehead. "This has to be kept completely confidential."

"Absolutely. Not a problem, Mr. Systrom."

He sighed. Then went to his laptop and pulled up a couple of direct messages he'd received on Twitter. They were from a user named @youreapwhatyousow.

Dustin read the messages over Mike's shoulder.

"Geez. This guy's creepy." He pointed to the user name. "Click on that."

Mike followed his instructions and the screen went to the profile for the user, but there was no information, no picture and no description.

Dustin frowned. "Unfortunately, unless you work for Twitter, getting to the real user information or to an IP address is almost impossible. That's going to be the same for just about any of the social media sites."

He stroked his chin. "You've gotten these messages on multiple social media platforms?"

Systrom nodded.

"But you've also gotten text messages and voicemails, right?"

Another nod.

"That may be our best hope. Do you have the numbers those came from?"

"I do, but I've already tried using a reverse directory to try to see who they belong to. That didn't work."

"Not surprising, but a buddy of mine works in IT in law enforcement. I bet he's got some resources we don't."

Systrom heartrate jumped, and he held up his hands. "Hold on. I don't want to get cops involved."

"Not to worry. This guy isn't a cop. He just works for them."

Mike chewed his lip for a moment. "Can you do it without showing him the messages?"

"If you've got the phone numbers from where the text messages and voicemails came, I can just have him trace those." Dustin shrugged. "Chances are they came from a burner phone, but if the guy's an idiot and sending you messages from his own phone, we might get something. It's worth a try."

Mike nodded, and scrolled through his texts and voicemails, jotting down two different phone numbers. His hand shook as he stared at the notepad. With a deep sigh, he tore the page off and handed it to Dustin.

Dustin took the paper. "I should have an answer for you by tomorrow." He paused, gave Mike an empathetic smile. "I'll do some other research to see how else we can find this guy. Don't worry. We'll get him."

Chapter 28

A blinding ray of sunlight lasered through a broken window and seemed to burn a hole in his retina. It didn't help that the eye was already swollen from sucker punches for much of the night before.

Colt squinted, then winced. With his good eye, he glanced around and took stock of the room.

Tied to a chair. Beaten up. Head pounding. In some sort of warehouse that looks like a set from The Zombie Apocalypse.

But he was alive. And alone, at least for now.

As rough as he felt, he'd taken worse beatings. Uncle Sam had trained him to endure physical pain. Lundsford's thugs were rank amateurs in comparison.

He replayed the events of the night. His spine tingled as he recalled the feel of the barrel touching the back of his neck.

How did they get the drop on me? I must be slipping. Old age sucks.

With a gun to the back of his head and realizing he was outnumbered, resisting seemed like a bad idea. The thugs were efficient in securing his wrists, disarming him and putting a bag over his head.

This obviously isn't their first rodeo.

They'd had a van waiting. With bolted down metal rings, it was clearly configured to transport restrained people. He'd let his senses absorb every twist, turn, bump and sound. It was mostly futile. They'd said nothing from the time they bagged him. His best guess was that he was a few miles east of the hotel. That detail was useless at the moment.

Arriving at the warehouse, they'd driven inside, pulled him down and secured him to the chair before removing the bag. Then he'd finally gotten a good look at his two assailants. Evan Monaco and Joshua Floyd. He recognized them from the files Hunter had given him. Up close, they were dirtier and scragglier than in the mugshots. However, this was his one advantage. He knew them, but they didn't know him.

They'd tried to question him with a fruitless result. His silence was complete, as was their frustration. They took turns trying to 'convince' him to talk, but he'd mentally disassociated from the moment and remained silent.

Somewhere in the night, they'd either given up, gotten bored or needed to sleep. Whatever the case, they'd left him with threats about bringing their boss. It sounded an awful lot like his mother threatening, "Wait until your father gets home." The memory made him smile, which made him wince.

He tested his restraints to no avail. They were solid. He looked around for tools, weapons or avenues of escape. Nothing.

The garage door squealed open, and interrupted his analysis. Before the door had completed its upward trajectory, a black Ford van pulled into the warehouse, kicking up a cloud of dust as it braked. The particles hung in the tracks of light streaming in from the open door.

In the few seconds the door was open, Barkley squinted against the light to snap a mental picture of the immediate surroundings. There was a familiarity to the scene, but the moment was so brief, bright and dusty, his mind couldn't process it.

"Well, what do we have here?" Harley Lundsford's voice was loud, gravelly and arrogant. "Seems my boys caught themselves a spy." His eyes were wide and he gestured with his hands when he stressed the word 'spy'.

Barkley watched as Lundsford put on a show for Evan Monaco and Ryan Williams.

Floyd must have gone back to the hotel.

Lundsford turned to Barkley. "Kind of tall for a spy though." He stood directly in front of Colt, reached out, put his index finger in the middle of Barkley's forehead and pressed hard enough to make Colt look up. "Who the fuck are you?"

Colt's brown eyes darkened and focused as he stared directly into Lundford's. His silence answered the question.

After a momentary staring contest, Lundsford smiled sadistically, snorted a short laugh. "Oh, that's right. My boys said your ability to speak was impaired." He smiled. "We'll have to work on that."

Lundsford pulled his hand away, leaned back and looked around as if perusing a luxury apartment. He turned to Monaco and Williams. "Let me see if I've got this right." He started to pace around, checking to make sure that Barkley was following his dramatics. "We found this guy last night spying on our operation. He has no identification on him. No car keys or money or credit cards. The only thing he's carrying is this really cute, hot pink, burner cell phone. The cheap piece of shit shattered into a dozen pieces when he dropped it, so I have no way to see his call history or stored numbers."

He turned to Barkley and sneered. "Quick thinking."

He paused for a moment, walked over to Evan and held out his hand. Monaco handed him Colt's gun. "But..." He turned back toward Barkley. "You're packing kinda heavy, aren't ya?" Lundsford held up his finger to emphasize the next point. "A .45 caliber, solid steel Kimber. Holding the gun up near his face, he looked at it admiringly. Now, this is a nice gun. The kind a real pro would carry." He lowered the barrel of the gun and pointed at the spot where his finger had been. "Who are you, 'Mr. Cat's Got My Tongue'? A Cop? A Fed? My competition?"

Barkley didn't say a word. The two stared at each other, unflinching. As if waiting for the other to blink.

Only the sounds of traffic filtering in through the broken windows filled the silence.

Lundsford's eyes narrowed as he slowly nodded. "Okay... Your choice. We can play this however you want."

He stood, tucked Colt's pistol into the small of his back, looked at Evan.

"Take me back to the room." Then he turned toward Ryan. "Have some fun with him, but save some for me..." His grin turned gruesome. "I'll be back."

Chapter 29

Neurological disorder…
Progressive…
Degenerative…

Hunter's brain twitched in fifteen directions as he drove south on I35 toward the downtown station. What the doctor had said couldn't possibly be right. He was a healthy man.

Early onset…
Incurable…

He shook his head, regained focus to get his mind back in the game. He'd get a second opinion. Right now, he needed to work. People were counting on him.

Remembering Colt, he tapped the button on his Bluetooth car connection and barked out a command.

"Call Colt Burner."

The phone connected, but after one ring, bounced to a phone company recording.

"The cellular phone you are trying to reach is either turned off or no longer in service."

Hunter frowned. Not good. Barkley had been out of communication since Saturday night.

He glanced at the dashboard clock. It was now over thirty-six hours.

Something's wrong.

"Call Billy."

His mind drifted as the system connected, the phone rang twice. Billy answered without preamble.

"Hey, Cowboy. You on your way in?"

"I am, but I've got to make a little detour and I need your help."

"Fire away."

"I need you to quietly trace a phone number. Triangulate its last known location." He read off the number.

"Okay. How should I note this in the case file?"

Hunter paused. "You shouldn't."

The long silence on the other end of the line made him nervous. Finally, Billy responded hesitantly.

"Okay, Cowboy, when do you need it?"

"Yesterday."

"I'll call you back."

Hunter clicked off and replayed his conversation with Colt at Risky's.

He's staying at the Courtyard at 26th and Main.

He mentally rerouted, then looked up just in time to see the 28th Street exit about to pass. With a quick glance in the mirror, he steered right, slid across two lanes of traffic, ignored the symphony of car horns and barreled off the freeway down the exit ramp.

Hunter headed west on 28th, turned left on Main Street and navigated the two blocks to the Courtyard.

As he walked across the parking lot towards the entrance, he pondered his approach. He had no search warrant or legal reason for getting into Barkley's room. If the manager decided to be uncooperative, there wouldn't be much recourse.

When all else fails...bluff.

Bursting through the doors like he owned the place, Hunter ignored the customers waiting in line and flashed his badge at the young man at the kiosk. "I need to speak to your manager immediately, please."

"Sure. Just a minu—"

"What part of immediate did you not understand?" He glared at the man, then quickly acknowledged the woman the clerk had been helping. "Sorry, ma'am. It's an emergency."

Her eyes widened as she mumbled something unintelligible.

The manager emerged from his office. "I'm Elliott Meyers, the Manager. How can I help you?"

Hunter motioned him to step away from the crowded check-in

area to the empty bar. "Detective Jake Hunter with the FWPD. I need to gain access to a guest's room. Colt Barkley."

Meyers squirmed. "Unless you have a warrant, I'm not auth—"

"Colt Barkley is a detective with the Texas Rangers. He and I are working a joint investigation and I have reason to believe his life may be in danger." He looked directly into the man's eyes trying to impart the sense of urgency. "You can help me make sure his daughter grows up with a dad."

Meyers nodded, walked over to an open computer, tapped in a few keystrokes and motioned for Hunter to follow him. Both men fidgeted as the elevator slowly reached the third floor.

As the door opened, they hurried down the corridor and stopped at Barkley's room. Meyers started to knock, but Hunter's fist was already pounding on the door.

"Colt? Open the door." Hunter's bark was urgent.

No response.

Hunter nodded to the manager. "Open it up."

He used his master key and unlocked it.

Hunter burst into the room. Hand resting on his Glock, his gaze swept the space, checking the bathroom and closet as he passed.

The room was empty, silent and orderly. Hunter stared at the bed. It was made up with a pair of jeans laid neatly across the foot.

"Has the maid service been in today?"

The manager had gone pale. "No. They're still on floor two."

Hunter absorbed the scene. "Maids haven't been here. Beds made. He never came back here last night. Shit."

Hunter's head spun as he processed the situation. He was stuck.

Colt wasn't here on official business.

Technically, he was just another citizen.

But he's not.

He grabbed his phone and hit speed dial.

"Hey, handsome."

Stacy's voice caused him to pause. He pictured her in his mind. His stomach turned as his mood swung wildly. He was all business when he'd dialed the phone. Her voice had made him smile. Thinking of her threw him back to the doctor's words. His diagnosis...their relationship…the future they now won't have. The myriad of thoughts tore through his chest. Remembering Colt, and why he had called, brought back his urgency.

"Cowboy?" Her voice concerned.

"Colt's in trouble. I need your help."

"Absolutely. What do you need?"

"Can you package up all that information you put together on Lundsford and his crew? Pictures, backgrounds, the whole enchilada. Email electronic copies of all of it to both Billy and me."

"Billy? I thought this was all under the radar?"

"Not anymore. Colt is missing. This just turned into a huge blip on the radar. I've gotta go. I'll catch you up soon. Thanks."

Hunter's eyes surveyed the room. The manager still stood there, listening.

"Mr. Meyers, I'm going to need a few minutes. Can you please make sure this room remains off limits to all personnel until further notice?" He gestured toward the door.

"Uh, sure. Absolutely. Just let me know if you need anything." He turned and left.

Alone in the room, Hunter tried to settle his mind. His synapses fired in too many directions at once and he felt a little dizzy. He closed his eyes and took a deep breath.

Barkley was his priority.

His pulse slowed and he centered himself back on the task.

Where did he go?

He slowly perused the room. Colt's organized personality was evident. The few items in sight were neat and orderly.

A stack of photos printed on copy paper sat on the side table. He flipped through them. The photo and print quality were poor, but it was clear they were surveillance photos of the hotel rooms used by Lundsford and his crew.

He didn't recognize the hotel or even the area of town from the pictures.

From their phone conversation a few days before, Colt had said something about two hotels on the west side of town, near Las Vegas Trail.

What were the names? Something really cheesy…

After several moments, he snapped his finger. The Express Inn and Relax Inn. He grabbed a pen and notepad off the desk and wrote them down. The addresses were easy to find on Google.

He continued his search of Barkley's hotel room, but the Ranger was experienced in keeping a low profile. Nothing identifying of his I.D. or his purpose.

Frustrated, Hunter folded the printouts and slipped them into his jacket pocket before punching in Billy's number on his phone.

"Hey, Cowboy. I'm still waiting on a call back for the trace on that number. Shouldn't be much longer."

"Thanks, Billy. In the meantime, I need you to do something else. I'll explain all of this when I get to the station, but just trust me."

"Yeah, sure. What is it?"

"Stacy is emailing you several background files on some suspects."

"Suspects?"

"Stay with me." Hunter headed for the door with the phone cradled on his shoulder. "When you get them, print them all out and get them ready for a debrief with Sprabary."

Billy's voice turned wary, bordering on annoyed. "Sure, Cowboy. What's this all ab—"

"I'll explain when I get there." He punched the button on the elevator. "I've got one more stop to make. Call me if you get that trace."

I hope I'm in time.

Chapter 30

Hunter flew down I-35, weaving in and out of midday traffic, toward I-30 West. Both of the potential hotel locations were near the Las Vegas Trail exit off the freeway on the west side of town. Both cheap, roadside hotels catered to hookers, druggies and other lowlifes.

All he had were the pictures from Colt's room, but once he was on site, those photos should not only narrow down which hotel he was surveilling, but should also be able to provide insight to where Colt was hiding when he took the photos.

His mind was racing in time with the roar of the V8 in his Explorer. He took the ramp to I-30 so hard, he almost scraped the concrete guiderail.

I-30 West unfolded in front of him as he whipped below downtown. Once he crossed the Trinity River, the landscape changed from high rises to an mix of commercial, industrial and residential buildings. Older neighborhoods sandwiched between new developments, and the freeway expanded to six lanes.

As he blew past Alta Mesa, south of the Fort Worth Naval Air Station, his mind drifted to memories of when the military base was called Carswell Airforce Base. As part of the Strategic Air Command during the cold war, B-52's constantly rattled the local area with their takeoffs and landings. Charlie had taken him to air shows there as a kid where he got to see the Navy Blue Angels acrobatic flight demonstration squadron and the Army Golden Knights parachute team.

The sign for Las Vegas Trail passed over his head. His mind snapped back to the moment and he took the off ramp, braking hard. He managed to maneuver through the two left turns under the bridge without incident. Merging onto the access road and sliding across two lanes of traffic elicited multiple horns from the cars he cutoff. The middle fingers some of them threw at him were the least of his concerns as he took a right into the parking lot of the Express Inn.

People actually stay in places like that? Damn.

The car rocked to a stop in front of a haggard, sleazy hotel that appeared more rundown and abused than old. His eyes surveyed the surroundings. It was the middle of the day and the area was quiet.

Prime sleeping time for nocturnal degenerates.

Barkley could be in one of these rooms. Reaching for the photos he'd found in his friend's room, Hunter's mind processed the scene in front of him. The building didn't feel right. He compared the photos to the architectural features of the view before him.

While all cheap concrete box hotels look similar, they all had their own uniquely disgusting features. The shit box out his window and the photos didn't match. This wasn't the place.

Without wasting more time, he slammed the SUV into gear and smoked the tires as he screeched out of the parking lot and back onto the access road. One possibility left.

He turned right onto Laredo Drive, then another onto Calmont Avenue, and a third onto Las Vegas Trail. That positioned him across an empty lot from the Relax Inn. The trip only took a matter of minutes, but this time he approached with more caution. He headed west on an unmarked asphalt road which curved north. The front of the Relax Inn filled his windshield.

A rush of adrenaline ran through him instantly.

This was the place. It had to be.

He slowed. The printouts matched the building features as he rolled past.

He scanned the area. Not much activity. He continued driving the length of the building until he got to the back parking lot near the swimming pool. The wrought iron fence around the pool was rusted and leaning. The asphalt parking lot was faded and crumbling.

He pulled in and parked. Without knowing Barkley's status or location, nor the men he'd been surveilling, he knew he needed to move cautiously.

Maybe busting into the manager's office with a show of force would give him intel if any of the identified suspects were around. But most likely in a place like this, the manager was involved with whatever activities that took place. At the very least, the man was being paid to look the other way. Word would get back to the bad guys quickly.

If Colt was in trouble, he couldn't afford for Hunter to broadcast that law enforcement was on their trail.

His alternative was to quietly reconnoiter the area to see if he could determine Colt's observation point. And possibly identify any of the perps. He checked his Glock in the holster and stepped out onto the parking lot.

The sun was bright and almost directly overhead so he kept his aviators on. His dress shirt and jacket over nice jeans made him feel conspicuous. Practically screaming *outsider*. He might as well have worn a tuxedo.

Scanning the parking lot, he tried to remember what kind of rental car Barkley had been driving. His brain seemed to lurch in multiple directions at once, but not retrieving the information he needed. He flashed back to earlier that morning.

Brain fog.

He shook his head and refocused. With his head on a swivel, he maneuvered through the parking lot, skirted around the swimming pool and reached the back of the building quickly.

With his back against the wall, he looked at the surveillance photos once again. The shots were angled downward, indicating Colt took them from a higher perch. The building was only two stories tall and there were no other taller buildings around.

Must have been on the roof.

He looked around to see if he could find an easy access to the roof. Nothing was obvious from the outside. Eventually, he found the stairs that got him to the second floor. Like most roadside motels, the design was simple. A long exterior walkway with guest room doors facing out.

On the second floor, he walked as casually as possible around to the east side of the building. He found a stairwell that gave him some cover and ducked into it. Now, with a better view of the length of the building, he studied the photos again.

The building had an offshoot that sat at a ninety degree angle to the east. Colt had clearly been on the roof of that offshoot looking back and downward on the rooms just ahead and below where Hunter was standing.

How did he get up there?

Hunter stopped for a moment when he realized that going any further would make him visible to the rooms that Barkley had been watching. He backtracked, and was able to take another hallway to the south side of the building. This provided him cover until he could make it to the end of the building.

As he turned the corner, he grinned at the sight of a built in ladder that provided roof access.

Even a blind squirrel…

The security screen designed to block access to the ladder showed no sign of having seen a lock in ages. Hunter moved quickly, opened the screen and was up the ladder in a matter of seconds.

Once on the roof, he crouched down to be less obvious. The chances of anyone noticing him or caring enough to call someone about him were slim, but he needed to be careful.

The rooftop was tar and gravel and on a slight grade with air conditioning units spaced out in rows. He worked his way down a row of units, getting closer to the edge that overlooked the doors to the rooms.

When he got to the third row of units, he stopped and ducked down behind one. He pulled out the photocopies, looked closely at the one that showed the doors to the rooms.

Bingo.

He had found the perch Barkley had used for his surveillance. For a moment, he absorbed the scene, paying close attention to the two rooms on the bottom floor where Barkley's photos had shown the activity.

Hunter tried to put himself in Colt's frame of mind. What could've happened to him? Did the whole operation move to a different location? Was he found? Is he in one of these rooms? Or worse?

He had no answers.

He ducked back down behind the unit and let his eyes drift for a moment.

A splash of color crossed his line of sight. He looked down and saw a small piece of hot pink plastic. It took a moment for it to register, but his mind flashed back to his lunch with Barkley.

The hot pink burner phone.

Hunter picked up the plastic and stared at it. His stomach clenched as his mind confirmed his fear. It was clear.

Colt had dropped his phone. He was in trouble.

Shit.

He quickly searched the gravel for anything else. His heart raced as his gaze darted around. He searched around the bottom edge of the A/C unit, found nothing. He moved to the unit behind him, ran his hand along the edges. Something scraped his right index finger. Crouching lower gave him a different angle.

He reached in and pulled out a single car key. Attached to a plastic key ring was the Avis logo.

Barkley's rental.

Both the phone and his car keys.

He's *really* in trouble.

He slid the key and the hot pink plastic piece in his pocket, and pulled out his phone to call his partner.

"Sanders here."

"Billy, I'm on my way. I'll be there in fifteen minutes. Colt's in trouble. We've got to go see Sprabary."

Chapter 31

Hunter burst through the back door of the station moving past people in a blur. His mind frantically bounced from topic to topic. He raised his foot to take the first step up the stairs. Without warning, his hand slipped from the rail, and the ground fell out from under him.

His shoulder crashed into the wall and he crumpled to the floor. His body lay awkwardly on the bottom steps.

Heads turned, conversations stopped and for a moment the bustling went quiet.

Did I just fall? What the fuck?

A uniformed officer stepped toward him to help. "You okay, Detective?"

Hunter waived off his hand and grumbled. "I'm fine." His face flushed, and he mockingly announced to the gathering crowd, "Nothing to see here. Move along."

That brought a few laughs as he stood up and dusted himself off. He nodded his appreciation to the officer and headed up the stairs.

When he reached the top and out of sight of anyone who'd witnessed his spill, he stopped and took a deep breath.

What the hell just happened?

While he wasn't a teenage athlete any more, he was normally very coordinated and fit. How did he miss the rail and the step and end up on his ass?

For a moment, his heartrate jacked up and his breathing went shallow. Was this related to what the doctor had told him? A new realization and concern that this thing could impact his work washed over him. He hadn't thought about that. If he couldn't walk upstairs without falling down, how was he supposed to deal with the physical requirements of arresting people?

He pushed those concerns from his mind, put on his game face and headed for Sprabary's office. When he rounded the corner, Billy made uncomfortable small talk with Paige. Neither seemed like they enjoyed it.

"You got the files?"

Billy nodded, held them up and frowned. "Might be nice for my partner to clue me in to what's going on."

"Sorry. This was all kind of unexpected." He looked through the office window and caught Sprabary's stare. Their boss waived them in. "We'll talk more after this meeting."

Sprabary gestured for them to sit, his expression all business. "Why do I sense you're not going to improve my day?"

"Well, um..."

"Shit, Cowboy, spit it out. The taste won't get better the longer you chew on it."

Hunter cleared his throat. "I have reason to believe Detective Colt Barkley is in serious danger. He needs our help."

"Barkley? The tall Texas Ranger? I didn't know the Rangers and the FWPD were working a case together."

Hunter shifted in the chair. "We aren't."

"Shit." Sprabary looked down and rubbed his forehead with his hand and let the silence hang for a moment. He looked up at Sanders. "Billy, could you close that door? I think we're going to need some privacy."

Billy obliged, muting the outside chatter.

Sprabary rocked back in his chair and clasped his hands together at his belt buckle. "Let's hear it." He frowned. "Don't leave out anything."

Hunter ran his hand through his hair. "This wasn't supposed to involve the FWPD. In fact, it doesn't technically involve the Texas Rangers. Colt isn't working in an official capacity."

"You're not helping my indigestion." Sprabary rolled his hands to prod Hunter forward. "Enough preamble. What the hell is going on?"

Let the shit storm commence.

"Colt reached out to me last Tuesday..." He spent the next thirty minutes walking Sprabary and Billy through all that had happened up through Saturday evening when they'd connected for beers and he'd last seen Barkley. The runaway girl, her family, the suspects he'd tracked and the hotels he'd scoped out...all of it. More importantly, why he'd had to keep it all a secret.

He handed the folders across the desk to Sprabary. "These are the guys Colt has been surveilling. Up until this morning, he had everything under control, checked in with me daily. Colt was going to call us in when he'd confirmed Kenzi was in one of those rooms." He paused, swallowing back the bitter taste accumulating in his throat.

"The problem is I haven't heard from Colt since Saturday night, and I haven't been able to contact him. I went to his hotel this morning and convinced the manager to let me into his room. He didn't sleep there last night."

Both Sanders and Sprabary listened intently.

"I remembered the information on the locations of his surveillance, so I went to those two hotels for a quick look around." Hunter rubbed his chin. "No luck finding him, but..."

He pulled out the car keys and bag with the broken piece of plastic from Colt's phone, plopped them on the desk. "I did find these."

Both men looked confused.

Sprabary tilted his head, waiting.

"The car keys to Colt's rental, and a broken plastic piece from his cell phone."

Sanders face scrunched. "He has a pink phone?"

Hunter shrugged. "It was the only burner the store had in stock. He was in a hurry. I gave him shit about it, too."

"You're sure about this?" Sprabary took the bag and examined the piece closely.

"Positive. I found it on his perch at the hotel where he'd been watching them. Billy ran a trace on the burner. It's not online."

"Shit." Sprabary rubbed his forehead. "What's your theory?"

Hunter set his jaw. "My guess is somehow he got caught surveilling them. Without his credentials, there's no telling who they think he is. And he sure as hell won't tell them."

Sprabary nodded. "So, if he's not already dead, he's probably wishing he was."

"Exactly."

"Do we have any idea where they might have taken him?"

Hunter shook his head. "No, but we do know the players and we also know the location of their operations."

His boss tossed the bag on the desk, and scraped his hands across his forehead. "This going is to be a mess. But if your theory is right, the clock is ticking. We need to find him now." He looked at Hunter. "Any thoughts on how we do that?"

"I do." He paused. "But we'll have to break a few rules."

Chapter 32

The cold, black steel felt foreign in Mike Systrom's hand. He was *not* a gun guy. Sure, he'd gone to the range a few times with buddies, but he was always the novice, using someone else's gun and needing constant coaching on how to reload. Now, here he was, holding a deadly weapon in his hand, the weight and power unnatural.

As much as he wanted to wipe this stalker off the face of the earth, he now found himself thinking more of using the weapon on himself.

It's my fault I'm in this mess. All those nights, gambling, drinking, cheating on LeAnne. All this guy did was call me out on my behavior.

A wave of depression washed over him as his mind kept processing the damage done if the stalker revealed his secrets. He'd lose his wife, his kids, most likely his job. His life would be over, and his family destroyed.

I'd rather be dead and leave them with happy memories.

He shifted the gun in his trembling hand, rubbed the metal ridges on the handle. His stomach turned and sweat formed on his forehead. He set the gun down on his desk and wiped his face with the back of his hand.

I'm shaking so bad, I'd probably miss.

He smiled weakly at his gallows humor.

Standing up from behind his desk in his home office, he paced around the room. The house was quiet and empty in the mid-afternoon. He should've been at the office, but he'd told his assistant he wasn't feeling well. Took the day off.

The silence of the house felt like hopelessness. He couldn't stand it. It seemed to amplify the stress of the situation. All he wanted was for it to stop. He'd do anything to make it stop.

A gurgle twisted his stomach, which had been upset for days. He ran for the bathroom, getting to the toilet just in time, his bowels emptied like a firehose.

He sat there, spent, desperate, lost.

Please God, help me. I promise to straighten up and fly right.

As he gathered his strength, stood and buttoned his pants, he shook his head at the thought of praying. He wasn't a religious man. He'd never seen the point before.

What's that old saying? No one is an atheist in a foxhole.

Weekly church service sounded like a pretty good bargain in exchange for making all of this disappear.

He slumped back in his desk chair. No god would make this go away. Only he could do that. But how? He had no way of knowing who this lunatic was.

As the hopelessness of the situation swelled in his chest, his eyes drifted to the gun on the desk. He touched it. His hand recoiled as if it were a snake that had bitten him. He reached out again. This time his hand didn't flinch.

Without realizing it, the gun was in his hand. The grip's rough pattern pressed against his palm. He had to remember the steps, ingrain them in his mind.

Check the magazine…

Snap it in…

Rack the slide…

The gun was ready. At this point, the slightest tug on the trigger would send a 9mm bullet hurtling into space at over 1,000 feet per second. That bullet would crush through his brain in a fraction of that second.

Mike stared at his hand holding the weapon. How strange it looked. How wrong his fingers felt on this thing. His heart pounded. A tear ran down his cheek and his chest heaved with a sob.

I'm so sorry, LeAnne. This is all my fault. You don't deserve this.

He leaned back in his chair and slowly lifted the gun. It felt like an anchor dragging him down. His hand shook so badly, he had to stabilize it with his other. The barrel pressed under his chin.

His mind raced with images of his life. His wife, his children, his work…his childhood. All of that was gone.

It's better this way.

He closed his eyes. He inhaled, desperate to find the courage to pull the trigger. To end everything. He exhaled, ignoring the tears streaming down his cheeks.

Do it. Do it. Make this all end.

The phone buzzed across the desk.

He jumped. The jolt nearly made him pull the trigger.

He slapped the gun down on his desk and shoved it away.

He gasped for air and wiped the tears from his cheeks.

The phone continued to buzz. Finally, he shook his head and picked up his phone.

A FaceBook message. He tapped a few times and read it.

I'm done fooling around. Calling LeAnne tomorrow. I'm taking you down. You're going to lose everything. Sleep well tonight.

Rage boiled up from the depths of his soul. Any thought of hurting himself flew out the window. This bastard would not get away with this.

He picked up the gun. This time it felt warm and natural in his hand. He absorbed its power. No more fear.

I'll find you, you son of a bitch. If it's the last thing I do, I'm going to kill you.

Chapter 33

Evan Monaco guided the 1998 Ford E150 Van into a parking spot at the Relax Inn. He liked October. Summer faded into shorter days and cool, crisp air. Football weather.

He switched off the lights and key, but the engine fought back and coughed a couple of times before it gave up. He leaned over and cracked off a ferocious fart. The sound reverberated in the empty van. Almost immediately, the smell hit his nostrils and he waived in front of his face to dissipate the odor.

"Damn. That MacDonalds' stuff is lethal." He smiled at the present he left for the next one of Lundsford's guys who'd use the van.

As he ambled through the external hallway connecting the Relax Inn's parking lot to the inner courtyard and rooms, he thought about the girl that Harley brought up from Austin.

What's her name? Oh yeah, Kenzi. Damn, she's fine. I gotta tap that next time the boss is away.

A sly smile had just started to wash across his face when a muscular arm swept over his shoulder and nestled quickly across the front of his throat. A second arm locked in place on the back of his neck. Before he could squeak, the two squeezed together like a clamp cutting off his air supply. His brain grew heavy, then his body. He was out within seconds with no sound or struggle.

*   *   *   *

Choke holds violated every FWPD regulation. Billy Sanders would've never used one on duty. Tonight, he wasn't on duty. He was conducting a personal mission helping Hunter find Colt.

"Package one acquired." He spoke quietly into the two-way

radio that connected to the team.

"Roger that. Get his keys. Jimmy will help you get him into his van."

Sanders rifled through his pockets and found the keys. After securing the perp's revolver tucked into the back waistline of his pants, along with the knife in his back pocket, he lifted up Monaco and tossed him over his shoulder like a roll of carpet and moved quickly toward the parking lot. Thank God the guy was a skinny thug.

He kept to the dark shadows around the building. At the edge of the parking lot, an old, fading light post lit up the van. Jimmy Reyes stood behind it.

Sanders double checked for onlookers, then bolted for the vehicle. Jimmy signaled for him to toss the keys, caught them, popped the back doors open and followed Billy inside.

Once they had Monaco's hands zip tied, Jimmy leaned back against the side and took a deep breath. He coughed and waived his hand in front of his face. "Damn Billy, what did you do to this guy? I think he shit his pants."

Billy scrunched up his face. "That's the van, not the dude."

Reyes shook his head. "Great."

Sanders ignored him, dug in Monaco's front pocket and retrieved his cell phone. He tapped on the screen and smiled. No PIN needed.

He tossed a canvas bag to Jimmy. "Get the blindfold on him and duct tape his mouth before he wakes up. Make sure he doesn't see you."

"Ten–four, good buddy." Reyes gave him a mock salute.

Sanders headed for the back doors. "I'm off to get number two."

*   *   *   *

Cowboy watched from the surveillance perch Barkley had used. Billy's stealth and precision against that perp was impressive.

Remind me never to piss him off.

As he waited for an update from the van, he kept an eye on the rooms where he assumed some of the other scumbags loitered. There was no way to know for certain. Without any real intelligence, they were flying blind tonight. Up until Monaco had shown up, there'd been no movement.

With a quiet burst of static, his radio crackled to life.

Package one wrapped up. Positioning for package two.

Hunter smiled and settled in. Without knowing where all the players were positioned, the timing on this vigilante mission was a crap shoot.

*   *   *   *

Sanders slipped back into the dark void behind the broken soda machine. He pulled out Monaco's phone and tapped into the contacts. The short list was made up mostly of nicknames. He tried to find any names that matched up to their suspects.

There you are.

He tapped on the entry for J-Flo and wrote out a short text message.

Need help at the van.

Billy leaned back against the wall and watched the rooms. It was a calculated risk. If Joshua Floyd was in one of them, there was a good chance in a few seconds he'd come out to the parking lot. If he wasn't here, the whole operation might be blown.

*   *   *   *

Hunter perked up when the hotel door opened and a man slowly ambled his way toward the parking lot.

Holy shit. It's our lucky day.

He keyed the mic. "Heads up. Package two heading your way."

"Roger that. In position." Sanders snuggled in behind the soda machine and waited.

Hunter watched the man move down the sidewalk. Just before he disappeared into the vending machine hallway, he whispered into the mic, "Twenty feet."

*   *   *   *

Sanders listened intently, following Floyd's approaching footsteps. His timing was perfect. His foot flew with the force of a sledgehammer. A direct hit to Floyd's crotch.

Floyd's exhale sounded like a car's airbag deploying. He dropped to the ground with a moan, completely disabled.

Billy once again hoisted a limp, motionless body over his shoulder and moved quietly toward the parking lot.

Jimmy had been monitoring the radio and popped the van's back door just as Billy arrived. Without saying a word to each other, they repeated the process of searching, disarming and securing Joshua Floyd. As they had done with Evan Monaco, Floyd was zip tied, blindfolded and gagged.

Using hand signals only, Sanders directed Jimmy to drive. As they pulled out of the parking lot, they headed toward a predetermined meeting spot, Billy keyed the radio mic with a four burst sequence letting Hunter know they were on the move. Hunter replied with a two burst confirmation sequence.

*   *   *   *

Hunter remained crouched behind the air conditioner on the roof of the Relax Inn after responding to Billy's signal. The night was crisp and quiet with just the ambient sounds of traffic on I-30.

He stared at the doors where Floyd had emerged. His mind twisted and his chest felt heavy as he thought about the girls who were likely left in those rooms.

What kind of hell are they living through?

Scratch that. He didn't want to know. He just had to save them.

For a moment, he considered kicking in the doors and going in gun blazing. He gritted his teeth and shook his head. Finding Colt was their priority. They had no idea what or who lived behind those doors and they had no warrant justifying a forced entry. As soon as they found Colt, they'd be back to finish the job.

Chapter 34

Without asking for details, Lieutenant Sprabary had provided the keys to a nearly empty warehouse the FWPD used for storing office furniture.

Reyes drove down the dark street, and pulled the van into the warehouse driveway a few blocks east of the Jones Street Central Division Station. Billy jumped out of the van and opened the garage door. A moment later, the van was inside, hidden from sight. Hunter arrived a few minutes later, parked on the street, and entered the building.

The team had set up their interrogation area. Perfectly situated to scare one or both their captives into spilling their guts on where Colt was being held.

Both of their involuntary guests had regained consciousness on the drive over. Evan Monaco had merely fidgeted around and tugged on the restraints. Joshua Floyd, on the other hand, had doubled over in pain, holding his balls and moaning during the whole ride.

Billy and Hunter yanked the two men out of the van, and dragged them across the uneven concrete floor, careful not to dislodge their blindfolds. The wooden chairs creaked in protest when they slammed the pair into them. Legs and arms zip tied to the chairs, they both breathed heavily through their duct tape. Fear filled the stale and musty air.

That was the point. They wanted these men terrified. Prime them for questioning.

Hunter let them sit for a moment, the uncertainty amping up the tension. He purposely created sounds to play on their fears. He clanked a hammer against the metal table, revved a power drill and sparked jumper cable leads together.

Monaco flinched. Floyd moaned.

When he noticed Floyd's pants darken with urine, Hunter signaled to Reyes. He nodded and pulled off their blindfolds.

*   *   *   *

Evan Monaco looked around wildly as his eyes adjusted. What he saw was a scene staged for maximum terror inducement.

A single overhead light illuminated their chairs and a small circle around them. Beyond that was nothing, just pitch black. Yet the earlier sounds had echoed off walls in what felt like a bigger room.

Three men stood directly in front of them. Each wore all black military-style fatigues with full black hoods, black gloves and smoky ski goggles. Monaco couldn't even identify their race, much less what they looked like. One of them, the most muscular of the three, held a black AR-15 with a large capacity magazine. The other two, one tall and lean, the other short and pudgy, fingered 9mm semiautomatic pistols in thigh holsters.

Monaco's heart raced. He struggled to breathe with his mouth taped.

Who are these guys?

To Monaco's right, a low table with a number of instruments laid out made him swallow hard. A claw hammer, a drill, pruning shears, a meat cleaver, a propane blow torch and a car battery with attached jumper cables.

Monaco jerked around wildly, straining against the zip ties cutting into his skin. Anything to break free from the chair. He screamed against the duct tape.

The muscular guy stepped forward and ripped the tape off both captive's faces.

Monaco screamed as his flesh ripped. "What the fuck do you want? You got the wrong guys! Who are you?" Fear escalated his voice to a piercing cry.

Joshua Floyd merely moaned, leaned over and puked in his own lap.

The tallest of the three men in black stepped over and stood in front of Monaco.

"I didn't do anything!" Monaco screamed. "Who the fuck are you?"

Without warning, the man backhanded each of them hard across the face.

The sting exploded across Monaco's cheek. He blinked through the pain. Somehow, he expected the tallest one to have a harder punch.

The man pointed to a white board behind the tools table. In serial killer handwriting, four bullet pointed statements stared at them in black marker.

- *You work for Lundsford*
- *He's holding a man captive*
- *Tell us where that man is*
- *Or you'll wish you were dead*

As Monaco read each bullet point, panic gripped his chest and he couldn't breathe.

Floyd moaned and puked some more.

Monaco stammered, "Oh God. Oh God. Oh shit. Oh God."

The man backhanded him again and signaled for him to be quiet. He immediately stopped talking, but replaced it with a high pitched keening sound.

Floyd continued to moan, but it now sounded more like crying.

They aren't talking. Why aren't they talking? Who the fuck are they?

The man took the marker, circled the third bullet point and off to the side wrote a single word: where.

Anguish washed across Monaco's face. "I don't... I mean... Oh God. I can't..."

The big guy struck like a snake with another backhand, searing Monaco's cheek again. He pointed to the smaller guy and gestured toward the jumper cables. He grabbed them, turned toward Monaco and tapped the two metal clamps together, causing an electric buzzing sound. Sparks flew in all directions some landing on Monaco's pants.

"Wait!" He screamed. "Oh fuck. Please. I don't know, I swear."

The tall guy made a gesture. The small guy took a step toward him.

Monaco's entire body contorted, spasming out of control. "No!

Please. Stop! I mean, I know where he's at, but I don't know the address." He shook his head and tried to kick his feet loose, but the restraints were too tight. He couldn't get out. He couldn't even back up. "Fuck Lundsford. I didn't sign up for this shit."

"Dude…" Joshua Floyd's voice was cross between a groan and a whisper. "He'll kill you."

The short guy tapped the clamps again, holding them together for a long moment as the electric buzzing growled and the sparks flew in all directions.

Monaco's eyes widened as the short one moved toward him.

"Fuck Lundsford. Fuck him. I'll tell you where he's at."

Without saying a word, The tall guy grabbed the pruning shears. Then stepped toward Monaco.

"No!" He began twitching and squirming wildly in his chair. His voice pitched up an octave. "Wait! Stop! I'll tell you. I'll tell you what you want to know."

Without slowing down, the tall guy grabbed his right forearm.

Monaco jumped as if he'd been electrocuted and braced for the pain. Screaming wildly.

Snip. The zip tie came loose and dropped to the floor. His right hand was free.

The tall guy held out a small white board and marker, dropped them in lap.

Monaco's chest heaved. His whole body shook. There was no holding back the tears streaming down his face.

He scribbled an address on the white board.

*   *   *   *

Hunter's mind raced as he powered through light traffic. The GPS wound him around into an industrial area south of downtown. The specific building was a long thin warehouse at the corner of South Houston and West Daggett.

He replayed what had just happened in the warehouse, what he'd just done. Had he crossed the line? Everything the three of them had put those suspects through was completely against any and all

146

regulations as a detective. Against his oath as a civil servant. But Barkley's life was on the line. They didn't have time to run it by the book. He'd chosen a good man's life over the rules.

He could lose his job, his career. Hell, even go to prison for it.

Right now, all he could do was push those thoughts away and focus on Colt's safety.

Hunter parked in a shadowy spot a block away. There was no other way to verify Colt was in the building than peeking through a window. Which could give away their element of surprise.

Time slipped away too quickly. He took a deep breath and started moving toward the building. He stayed close to other structures in the shadows, keeping his head on a swivel and his ears tuned for voices or footsteps.

He darted across West Daggett and tucked in behind the warehouse. A huge open construction pit sat to the west. Tall oak trees gave him cover from any cars on the street. The ambient traffic sounds from I30 hummed.

The building was in bad shape, but interior lights were on and rooftop exhaust fans clattered. Fortunately, there were no exterior lights on the back side of the building. He strained to see what kind of openings existed. He noted a couple of doors and a series of windows.

Strands of light emanated from various cracks and holes along the back of the building. Someone was inside.

As he crept along the wall, he noticed a rusted air vent halfway up. Several vent flaps had fallen off over the years. A faint light shined through.

He needed to see in there. But that was a good three feet higher than his head.

Surveying the area, he found a discarded wooden cable spool. He quickly dragged it over against the wall and climbed on top. He grabbed ahold of the vent's bottom edge and pulled himself up. Muscles strained in ways they hadn't in years. He'd certainly feel all that in the morning.

He only caught a glimpse, but it was enough. The scene was just as Evan Monaco had described. A man stood in front of someone slumped in a chair. The faces were too obscured in the distant dim lighting to identify Colt.

Whoever was sitting in that chair was in bad shape. There was no time to waste.

*   *   *   *

Hunter burst through the warehouse door, which made both Monaco and Floyd jump. Blindfolds and duct tape back in place, they were still secured to their chairs.

Without a word, Hunter gave a thumbs up to Reyes and Sanders.

On the drive back from Colt's location, he'd used a burner phone to call another burner he'd given to Lieutenant Sprabary. He'd let him know the address and that there'd be a 911 dispatch to that location shortly. Sprabary left his office to get in position.

Sanders and Reyes had packed up all the toys into boxes. They were ready to move. The next step was the tricky part. Up until this point, everything was off the books. Now, they had to transition back to a legitimate FWPD operation so SWAT could help rescue Colt.

Hunter walked straight to the whiteboard and began writing. Once he finished, he reread it to make sure it was exactly what was needed. Sanders and Reyes nodded their approval.

He put on the hood and ski goggles one last time, to make sure they weren't identified.

Evan Monaco yelped when Hunter ripped off the blindfold and tape. He blinked several times until his gaze landed on the board.

Hunter pointed to the first bullet.

I'm dialing 911 on your phone. You will read the following script exactly as written. Understand?

Monaco nodded.

Hunter pointed to the second bullet.

If you break from script in any way, we'll use the toys on you all night.

Monaco shook his head. "I understand. No problem."

Hunter pulled out Monaco's cell phone, put it in speaker mode and dialed.

"911, what's your emergency?"

Monaco stammered. "Uh…"

Hunter drew his Glock and shoved the barrel into Monaco's crotch.

The guy yelped.

"Sir, what's your emergency?"

He read the script from the board. "My name is Evan Monaco and I need to report a kidnapping and torture. There's a man being beaten in a warehouse at the corner of South Houston and West Daggett. The people holding him are armed and dangerous. Please hurry."

"Sir, do you…"

Hunter hung up and turned off the device. He signaled to Reyes and Sanders. They re-secured duct tape over both Monaco and Floyd's mouths, and pulled hoods over their heads.

The game was set in motion.

* * * *

Once Reyes had left with the two thugs wrapped up tightly in the van, the silence in the warehouse weighed down on his shoulders. Hunter removed his goggles and hood, sat down in the now empty chair, and rubbed his forehead.

Sanders followed suit and sat in the other chair. For a long moment, both stared at their hands. A long time passed before he finally spoke, more gravelly than usual.

"Cowboy, I'm not sure I'm okay with what we did tonight."

Hunter stared blankly out into space. Billy's statement hung in the air. He was just as torn up about the whole thing.

Finally, he shook his head. "I understand." His voice sounded like he'd been smoking all day. He cleared his throat. "I'm not either." He paused. "But, you know what I'm even less okay with?"

Billy looked over to Hunter, the creases in his forehead deep.

"I'm not okay with driving to Austin, knocking on Chelsey Barkley's door, and telling her that her husband isn't coming home because I wouldn't bend the rules a bit."

Slowly, Billy nodded. "Roger that."

"Let's go get Colt."

Chapter 35

All units in the area, report of a man held captive and tortured in a warehouse at the corner South Houston and West Daggett. Please respond and advise.

The police radio in Lieutenant Sprabary's car crackled to life.

He waited a beat, feeling the adrenaline amp up his heartrate. Breathing through it helped, and he relied on his years of training to stay calm for the shit storm Hunter said would come.

He picked up his microphone and responded. "This is Lieutenant Jeff Sprabary. I'm in the area and will manage the scene. All responding units, Code Blue, approach without lights or sirens."

Sprabary pulled to the curb at the intersection near the warehouse, positioned his car to see approaching vehicles in all directions. He picked up his cell phone and dialed.

"Dickson here." The SWAT commander sounded alert.

"Zeke, this is Jeff Sprabary. I'm at a scene and we need your assistance."

"We're ready to roll. What's the situation, Lieutenant?"

Sprabary laid out the details as best he could.

"We'll roll quiet. Our ETA is less than ten minutes."

Sprabary slid his phone back in his pocket just as a patrol unit arrived from the west on West Daggett. He exited his car, waved the unit down and spoke through the driver's window. "Secure this intersection. We've got a potential hostage situation. SWAT's en route. ETA ten minutes."

"Yes, sir." The officers parked their patrol unit, got out and ducked behind the corner to wait for backup.

More units arrived. Sprabary stationed them at the various corners to keep things cleared and secured.

When Hunter pulled up two minutes later, he and Billy wore jeans, tennis shoes and sweatshirts. He nodded to Sprabary.

"Rumor has it you might have a situation we can help with."

Sprabary nodded, his voice tight. "You might say that. How has your evening been?"

"Just another quiet night as planned."

"Good." Sprabary reached into his pocket, pulled out a cheap phone. He pulled a handkerchief from his other pocket, wiped down the device, then handed it to Hunter. "Dispose of this."

Before either was tempted to say any more about the evening's events, the FWPD SWAT armored vehicle wheeled around the corner. It stopped behind the lieutenant's parked car, out of sight of the targeted warehouse.

Sprabary set his jaw, ready for the assault.

*　*　*　*

Reyes drove in silence, Monaco and Floyd wrapped up tight in the back of the van. Unlike their first ride, they were quiet. Before leaving the warehouse, he'd changed back into street clothes and had stuffed the black fatigues into a backpack. He kept the hood and goggles on in case a traffic camera caught an angle of him driving the van.

The streets of downtown Fort Worth were essentially empty at midnight, as they should be. He'd found a place in the downtown area with minimal CCTV camera coverage, but also where there was enough traffic around that the van parked oddly would be noticed.

The timeline was tight to make this work. He had to get back to the station ASAP.

Seventh Street and Grove Street was the prized location, mostly industrial, some residential, and no retail or office space. And only a short four-block walk to the station.

He surveyed the intersection thoroughly until he was sure no pedestrians or occupied vehicles watched him. Then he quickly pulled into the middle of the intersection, cut the engine, and taped a note to the windshield: "Look in the back."

Leaving the van in the middle of the stoplights, he grabbed the backpack and darted away. A small, dark alley gave him the perfect cover to whip off the hood and goggles and stuff them into the backpack.

He continued moving north on Jones Street. As he walked, he took out the burner phone and dialed.

"911, what's your emergency?"

"Well, I'm not sure it's an emergency, but someone parked a van in the middle of the intersection of Grove and Seventh. It's locked and the engine is off."

He didn't wait for a response. He turned off the cell phone and slid it into the backpack. The backpack and its contents would be burned in the fireplace before the night was over.

*   *   *   *

The SWAT armored vehicle was essentially a bullet proof military troop transport with room in the back for eight officers and a steel front grill capable of ripping through the walls of most buildings. Zeke Dickson dismounted from the passenger side door, walked around the truck and nodded. "Lieutenant, Cowboy, what's our situation?

Sprabary was all business. "I'll let Cowboy fill you in on the details, but we believe a Texas Ranger Detective is being held captive and tortured by local scumbags."

Zeke's head cocked around toward Hunter. "Texas Ranger? That tall one? Barkley?"

"Yep." Hunter nodded. "He's been surveilling these guys for a few days. We weren't officially working with him, but providing support. He went off grid sometime late Saturday or early Sunday. We've, uh...worked the local grapevine for information. Apparently, we managed to motivate one of his guys, who called in a 911 tip."

Zeke squinted. "He just spontaneously called in a tip?"

Hunter cleared his throat. "Something like that."

A smirk slid across Dickson's face. "What an upstanding citizen. You need to make sure he gets some acknowledgement."

"If it's up to me, he'll get exactly what he deserves."

"Alright then." Zeke waved over one of his guys. "First things first. Let's get some eyes on the inside of that building. Baker, run a snake camera under that garage door. I want to know exactly what we're walking into."

Baker nodded, grabbed the equipment and trotted toward the building.

"If he can confirm our hostage is in a safe spot, we'll breach the garage door with our truck and engage the suspects with overwhelming force. Assuming all goes well, we'll be out of here and having a few beers within the hour."

*　　*　　*　　*

Blaine Parker gave Reyes a conspiratorial look. "Hey, amigo, how was your evening?"

"You tell me. I've been here the whole time." Reyes plopped down into one of the conference room chairs. He'd kept a low profile on his trek through the station's back hallways and stairs.

Parker nodded. "That's what I've told everyone I've seen tonight." He smiled. "And I've made sure to see a lot of people." He tossed Reyes his cell phone. "I've been all over the station tonight and everyone I've bumped into, I made sure to tell them that you, me, Cowboy and Billy were working in the conference room. I've also kept all four of our cell phones on and active. I've made and received calls on each one. Trust me. There'll be twenty people swearing the four of us were here all night, with phone records to prove it."

"Excellent." Reyes smiled. Then lowered his voice. "Everything else went off without a hitch. Cowboy, Billy and the Lieutenant are positioned as we speak at a warehouse where we think they're holding Barkley." He looked at his watch. "In fact, we should head there now to get these phones back to the guys and help with the cleanup."

Blaine smiled. "I thought you'd never ask. Let's roll."

*　　*　　*　　*

"Answer the phone, goddammit." Harley Lundsford slammed his cell phone down on the passenger seat. Two of his guys had gone dark on him. Over ten phone calls unanswered, and he hadn't heard from them in the last few hours. Maybe his operations were compromised.

He'd left David Gardner back at the hotel with the girls and had spent the last couple hours trying to find or contact his guys. It was now well past midnight and his sixth sense was tingling to the point that he was about to vibrate out of the car.

After our tall, lanky guest, this is just too much coincidence.

His mind raced as he headed toward the warehouse where Ryan guarded the guy. It had been over 24 hours. He needed some answers. Fast.

One way or another, this bullshit ends tonight.

He pulled onto West Daggett. Ahead of him two blocks up, several parked cars including one police cruiser blocking the intersection of St. Louis Avenue.

He crept through the green light and slowed his approach.

What the hell?

His hand felt around for his cell phone, only to realize it had bounced to the passenger side floorboard. He pulled to the curb.

A military style truck pulled away from the parked vehicles, the tires nearly squealing on the pavement. It made a hard turn north on South Houston Street.

Fuck.

It was too late to reach his phone and warn Ryan. All he could do was just watch.

It was time to cut his losses and bail.

*   *   *   *

The garage door exploded into the warehouse, shaking the whole building. Metal shards careened past the front battering ram on the SWAT tactical vehicle as it barreled inside.

The wheels crunched over debris at full speed until it hit the back wall. A hail of twisted beams and shredded metal flew in all directions.

Ryan Williams landed hard on his rump from the explosion. He'd been dozing in that chair for God knew how long when the sonic blast knocked him to the floor. Several seconds passed before he realized it wasn't a bomb, but a truck. Full of cops.

Somehow, his instincts kicked in. He grabbed his Beretta M9 and rapid fired at the vehicle. Using the tiny, flimsy chair as his cover.

The magazine was empty before he realized the only person in the bulletproof truck was the driver.

The SWAT team surged through the gaping hole on foot. They all held much bigger guns than him.

Ryan reached for a second clip in his back pocket, fumbling with the casing.

How the hell did they find us?

He looked up just in time to see the leading officers point their guns at him.

Ryan Williams was dead before his body crumpled to the cold concrete floor.

*   *   *   *

With military precision, the SWAT team fanned out through the warehouse searching every storage row, container and office in the building. The random, staccato sound of their voices echoed as they declared each area "clear."

Hunter and Sanders trailed the SWAT team through the hole. By the time they entered, the shooting was over, Williams' body was secure and the SWAT team had cleared the building.

Hunter ran straight to Colt.

The man was slumped in a chair and hadn't moved during all the chaos.

"Aw, shit." He winced as he surveyed the damage to his friend. He dropped to his knees in front of Colt, reached up and gently lifted up his chin.

The sight of his face shook Hunter. He looked like he'd been stomped by a pissed off bull.

Colt moaned.

"We need an ambulance, now!" Hunter yelled at anyone listening.

Sanders nodded, grabbed his phone and dialed as he ran back toward the door.

"Hey, buddy. Are you with me?" Hunter grabbed his handkerchief and gently wiped away some of the blood and grime.

Barkley's mouth moved, but nothing came out. His good eye opened ever so slightly. The left one was swollen shut.

One of the SWAT officers handed Hunter a bottled water. He fed a few sips to Colt and used more to keep wiping away some of the crusted blood. "The ambulance is on its way. We're going to get you to the hospital ASAP. You'll be okay."

What might have been a smirk broke through the carnage on Colt's face. One of his front teeth was chipped. His voice was barely audible. "What took you so long?"

Hunter broke into a strained smile. "Glad to see you too, buddy."

By the time they freed him of his constraints, the EMT's unfolded a gurney in front of him. His wrists were sliced to hell and back from the zip ties. They situated Colt on the stretcher, started an IV and strapped him down.

As they started to roll him away, he signaled for Hunter to come over with a raise of his bloodied hand.

Hunter bent down to hear.

"He took my Kimber."

"Well, shit."

* * * *

As Lundsford raced through the empty early morning roads, he called the only man left on his team, David Gardner. He took a hard right on Galveston Avenue, desperate to put distance between him and the warehouse.

"Hey, boss," David answered.

"Pack everything up. Get the girls ready to move. I'll be there in ten minutes. Everything better be ready to go by the time I get there."

"Okay." Gardner sounded surprised. "What about the guys?"

"The guys are gone. Don't sweat it. Just you, me and the girls now." He tried to sound authoritative, but he felt like puking. "Get going. I'll see you in a minute."

For all he knew, Ryan Williams was either dead or spilling his guts to the cops at this very minute. It didn't matter. They'd be back up and running as soon as they found another safe place.

His earnings might suffer until he regroups, but it was still better than prison.

Chapter 36

Early morning light bounced off the laptop screen. Mike Systrom rubbed his raw, dry eyes.

Is it morning already?

His all nighter had been a crash course in researching how to find his tormentor's identity. Email domains. Internet protocol addresses. Network routing. Internet service providers. Application security.

After everything he'd been through, including the near suicide, it was a wonder he ever saw daylight again.

The sleepless, feverish night proved worthless. Unfortunately, while he felt like he could teach a master seminar on the internet, he wasn't any closer to finding this guy.

Exhaustion permeated every fiber of his being. It felt like he was wearing a weighted suit. Strung out on adrenaline, no sleep, no food, barely any water… He was useless like this. He took a whiff of himself and realized he smelled like the ass end of a horse on a hot day.

He rubbed his eyelids and felt the ache in his shoulders. He needed a shower to wake up and get focused. He had to find this son of a bitch. He had to get his life back, even if it meant ending someone else's.

* * * *

An evil grin washed across the hacker's face. "Oh Mike, did you enjoy your crash course on the internet last night?" He laughed. "Good God man. All those pricks in Silicon Valley with decades of experience aren't nearly as smart as you to have learned it all in twelve hours." He scoffed. "Guess that's why you're not driving a Ferrari and living in a million dollar home."

He reviewed the multiple screens arrayed around his work station. Nicholas Briggs' office prominently displayed on one of them, the hidden camera giving a decent definition. As usual, Briggs worked hard at his desk, unaware he had a spectator watching his every move.

"Nick, Nick, Nick, all work and no play makes you a bad boy." He frowned. "Particularly since you've built your fortune as the mob's head bean counter. What a waste of that high dollar education. Your parents must be so proud."

He leaned back, played with a rubber band in his hand. "That's okay. You're about to get yours." He pulled back on the rubber band wrapped tight around his thumb to form a gun. "One of my little puppets is ready to pop, and when he does, he's going to pop all over you." He let the rubber band go and it struck the image of Nicholas Briggs.

*　*　*　*

Systrom soaked in the shower for ten minutes, letting the hot water and steam unknot his shoulders and clear his mind. By the time he got out, his crashing level of adrenaline weighed on his eyes. Going to the office wasn't in the cards. He needed some sleep so that he could think straight.

After sending a quick text to his assistant explaining he didn't feel well, he slid into sweatpants and a T-shirt, and pulled back the covers. He could almost taste the sweetness of sleep.

The phone buzzed. He shook his head and ignored it assuming it was just his assistant responding. He leaned toward the pillow.

The phone buzzed again.

Shit.

He wouldn't be able to sleep without knowing who called. As dread washed over him, he let out a heavy sigh and reached for his phone to read the text.

I'm done playing, Mike. Today's the day.

Rage boiled slowly. Mixed with his exhaustion, they overwhelmed his circuits. He stared at the message so hard, his vision blurred. He felt faint. Maybe he was experiencing a stroke.

As the emotions shot through his system, he noticed the text came from a different phone number than before. All of the other numbers came back empty on a phone identification website. If he was lucky, he'd get a hit. But the way things were going lately, he'd come up with zilch on this one, too.

He wearily trudged over to his laptop, opened his browser and punched in the number on the website.

In less than a second, a name popped up.

Nicholas Briggs.

* * * *

"Congratulations, Mike. You win the prize!" The hacker clapped his hands and spun around in his chair. He was getting so good at this, and the best part was just coming up. "Now, what are you going to do, Mike. The ball is squarely in your court.

"What about all that big talk? Do you really have what it takes to take a life? Have I primed the pump enough?"

His hands flew over the keyboard as he staged just the right amount of Nicholas Briggs' personal information into the hacked version of Google he'd loaded onto Systrom's laptop.

Full name.

Home address.

Employer.

Work address.

Several pictures.

Fake news articles.

"There you go, Mike. Follow those breadcrumbs. Let's see if you've got the balls to pull the trigger." He leaned back and flexed his hands together. "Happy hunting."

* * * *

Nicholas Briggs.

Systrom stared at the screen, at the name. He didn't recognize it, but that didn't matter. This was the bastard who'd been tormenting him. This was the bastard who had made his life a living hell for the last two weeks.

Now, he had him.

You son of a bitch! You fucked with the wrong guy.

Mike reached for the keyboard. His hands shook and his heart pounded. The relaxation from the shower vanished and the adrenaline returned, amping up his system. He panted as if he'd just finished sprinting a mile.

He pushed back from his desk, interlocked his hands on top of his head and forced several deep breaths. Slowly, he regained his composure. The lack of sleep and rollercoaster of adrenalin overload had his head swimming.

Eventually, his hands were at least functional enough to work the keyboard. He pulled up Google, typed in the name, began clicking on the links and absorbing the available information.

Works at Othello Industries…

Chief Financial Officer…

Othello Industries under investigation for organized criminal activities… Lives in Hulen…

Home address…

Office address…

As he clicked and read, a plan formed in his head.

This was going to be easy. Quick in. Quick hit. Quick out.

He pulled up Google Maps to find the location of Othello Industries, made mental notes about how to approach, where to ambush and how to escape.

He leaned back in his chair and stared at the screen.

"I have no idea why you chose to fuck with me, but it was a bad decision."

In the last text, this guy planned to tell LeAnne today. To destroy his family.

"Like hell you will."

This was escalating fast, but there was no other option. He picked up the 9mm pistol, held the weapon in his hand for a moment to let the power fuel his courage. Then he headed for the door.

Chapter 37

Sunrises may be beautiful when on vacation and sharing them with a loved one, but not so after a full night of hell.

Nine o'clock on this Tuesday morning felt way too early to Hunter. By the time Colt was transported to the hospital and they'd secured the crime scene and turned it over to the CSI team, the eastern horizon had lightened up the sky as Hunter pulled in his driveway.

He'd stumbled in, fed Panther, set his alarm for 9AM and fell into bed. Five minutes later, his alarm shrilled through the room, the sun was bright in the windows and he hadn't moved a muscle.

His head was foggy, his mouth was dry and every joint in his body ached. His hand was bruised from smacking around the thugs.

He crawled out of bed and slowly processed through his morning routine. In his mind, he replayed all that happened the night before, checking off each step to ensure they'd covered their tracks flawlessly. The final step had been to dispose of all identifying clothing, duct tape and zip ties. He'd done that step personally.

No way anyone can tie us to Monaco or Floyd.

The cold water on his face didn't revive him the way it used to. The reflection in the mirror made him scowl. His face looked older today. The night before weighed on his mind.

We did what we had to do. We rescued Colt and nobody got hurt.

His memories flashed back on Floyd. The sight of him pissing himself. He winced.

Well, almost nobody.

His mind moved like it was stuck in wet concrete, drying too fast to escape.

Why is it so difficult to focus?

He was certainly exhausted, but was there more to it than just being tired? His internal dialogue seemed to work overtime this morning.

Looking at his text messages, he saw one from his pharmacy. He'd forgotten to pick up the prescription from his neurologist.

Do I really need it?

After all, he'd performed well last night. He'd manhandled two scumbags, climbed up a wall and was in the thick of things when they'd busted into the warehouse. Maybe the doctor was wrong. Maybe there was some other explanation.

All this medical shit was messing with his head. He needed to figure it out. He needed to talk it through with someone he trusted. But as he mentally ticked off names, he wasn't comfortable with any of them, even Stacy. Especially Stacy. He couldn't risk telling her. Not yet.

He sighed, realizing there was only one person left to whom he might be comfortable enough talking.

* * * *

In the harsh light of the hospital room, the bruising on Colt's face seemed to glow. It looked like a purple, green and yellow piece of modern art.

Hunter looked at Colt from the doorway and assumed he was asleep. It was hard to tell if his eyes were closed due to slumber or if they were just swollen shut.

Geez, he looks bad.

He had gone by the Courtyard, checked Colt out of his room and retrieved his suitcase. He'd brought it with him and now stood at the door a moment longer before quietly stepping away and flagging down a nurse. He flashed his badge.

"Is there someone I can speak with to get an update on Detective Barkley's condition?"

"I'll page Dr. Johnson for you."

Hunter paced outside Colt's room for the next fifteen minutes until a tall, lean, blond man in a white coat barreled around the corner stopping just short of running into him. He towered over Hunter. "I'm Dr. Conway Johnson. How can I help?"

"Detective Jake Hunter. I was part of the team that freed Detective Barkley." He gestured toward Colt's room. "Any update on his condition?"

The doctor nodded and twitched with energy. His eyes were intense, but just below the surface there was an unmistakable kindness. "Your colleague is a very lucky guy. He took one hell of a beating, but other than severe bruising over much of his body, a few stitches and a mild concussion, there doesn't appear to be serious damage." He glanced at a folder he'd had tucked under his arm, his eyes darted quickly over the documents. "We performed a full body MRI once we got him stable. No breaks or tears or internal bleeding. He's just beat up."

"So, what's next?"

"We cleaned him up, pumped him full of anti-inflammatories, pain meds and sleep aids. If he's smart, he'll stay in bed for the next few days while we monitor his concussion." He closed the file and smiled. "My guess is he'll sleep most of today."

He took a deep breath, relief easing some of the worry after that report. "Thank you."

They shook hands, and the doctor hurried down the hallway as Hunter stepped back to Colt's room. He didn't want to disturb him, but without more information from him or Lundsford's guys, they wouldn't be able to justify a warrant to search the hotel rooms. Officially, the FWPD had no knowledge of the activity at the hotel. Their only involvement began when Evan Monaco, out of his sincere sense of civic duty, called 911 about Colt being held captive.

He quietly placed Colt's suitcase by the closet and turned away to leave when Colt groaned softly behind him.

"Hey."

Hunter stopped, and smiled at Colt.

"Hey, yourself. How are you feeling?"

Barkley blinked a few times, tried to sit up but aborted the attempt quickly. "Fuzzy."

"Considering the alternative, that's pretty good." Hunter approached the side of Colt's bed, shoving his hands in his pockets. "You tangled with some serious assholes. Two are in custody. One's in the morgue. Not sure on the rest. You feel up to talking? I need to get your information so we can raid the hotel rooms."

Colt's responding nod was barely perceptible and his voice was strained. "I wish I had more for you, but the truth is, I was never able to confirm that Kenzi, or any women at all for that matter, were in either of the rooms." He frowned, winced with pain. "I've got nothing that would justify a search warrant." He paused. "Did you say you had two of Lundsford's guys in custody?"

Hunter pursed his lips. "Yeah. Pretty interesting turn of events last night. Evan Monaco was the one that called 911 to tell us where to find you, and then amazingly, he and Joshua Floyd were both found bound and gagged in the back of a van parked in the middle of an intersection just around the corner from the station." He smirked. "No idea how that happened. They apparently told some wild story about being kidnapped and tortured."

"Really?" Colt smiled. "I'm sorry to hear that."

"The good news is that, even though they were bound and gagged, they were both carrying weapons." Hunter shrugged. "Since they are both convicted felons, they're being held on possession of illegal firearms and my lieutenant has arranged for me to interrogate them." He looked at his watch. "In fact, I'm already late. Gotta go."

"Good luck."

Hunter headed for the door. "Don't go anywhere. Don't torment the nurses, either. I'll be back."

Colt scoffed. "Yes, Mother."

Chapter 38

Systrom's heart hammered He could barely catch his breath and sweat poured from his forehead. The gun sat on the passenger seat. His gaze vacillated between watching the office building and the area in front of him and glancing at the gun.

Deciding to kill Nicholas Briggs was one thing. Actually doing it was something else entirely. He'd never been a violent man. Not even a confrontational guy. He'd always had more of a 'live and let live' view on life.

But this was different. He hadn't done anything to this guy. Hell, he didn't even know this piece of shit.

Nicholas Briggs, you picked this fight. I don't know why you chose to destroy my life, but I won't let you.

He glanced over to the gun lying on the passenger seat. It was small for a 9mm, but it was black and cold and hard. All business.

I'm going to finish it.

As part of his research, he'd found that Othello Industries was headquartered just west of South Hulen Street at the corner of Overton Plaza and International Plaza.

The six-story, white tile building curved on the south end with upper floors that fanned out further than the lower floors, supported by standalone columns. Uniquely designed and a modern look for the Hulen area. On the north end of the building was a circular silo structure that accessed all floors. For some reason, the whole thing reminded him of the famous Opera House in Sydney, Australia.

He'd been amazed at how much information he found on Nicholas Briggs on the internet, in just a few keystrokes.

I guess the internet really is more than just free porn and advertising.

The thing that surprised him most was that he was able to find the make, model and plate number for Briggs' car. With a little cruising the parking lot, he spotted the vehicle in a few minutes.

He was now backed into the spot directly across from the car, with a direct view of the windshield. He sat, contemplating exactly how this would happen. The plan was simple. He'd read about a professional hit by a drug cartel in Southlake a few years back. The shooters just simply waited for their victim to pull into a parking spot in broad daylight in the middle of Southlake's Town Square. As soon as he stopped, they walked to the front of the car and shot him a dozen times through the front windshield. Then they casually got in their car and drove away. It took less than a minute. By the time anyone had realized what happened, the shooters were on the highway and gone, never to be seen again.

If they can do it in the middle of an upscale Town Square with hundreds of shoppers as witnesses, doing the same thing in this sleepy parking lot should be a breeze.

Systrom surveyed the area. Though he didn't see any security cameras, he was sure he was on video somewhere. He'd worn a plain black baseball cap and sunglasses just in case. He'd also obscured his license plates with mud.

Now, all he had to do was wait. And not lose his nerve.

*   *   *   *

"Well done. Well done." The hacker lightly clapped as he watched the dot on the map. He knew exactly where Mike Systrom was parked. He'd engineered it so that Mike would have all the information he needed to find Briggs.

The internet is a wonderful thing…if you know how to use it.

He looked at the clock on his screen. Close to lunch time. He needed to nudge this process forward to avoid the lunchtime crowd. The more people around, the better chance Mike would panic and not follow through.

He thought for a moment, then smiled. He pulled up a program he'd created that allowed him to send a text message to a cell phone, but let him define the number of origin. He typed out a text to Nicholas

Briggs.

Need you at the house. Water pipe burst. Kitchen is flooded. Plumber on his way.

He punched in Briggs' wife's cell as the sender's number.

That ought to do it.

A moment later, the system indicated a return text.

On my way.

He smiled. Hook, line…and now the sinker.

Time for some fishing, Mike.

*   *   *   *

Out of the corner of his eye, Mike saw movement.

Someone walked toward the parking lot from the building.

He glanced at the photo of Nicholas Briggs one more time to cement it in his mind, then turned his attention to the man hurrying in his direction.

It's him. That son of a bitch.

His system surged to overload. His heart rate soared. Rage coursed through his whole body as his vision tunneled and focused on the man now a few feet from his car.

As Briggs turned between his car and the next, Systrom slid his hand down to the door handle, his other gripping the 9mm so tight, the grip's ridges cut into his palm.

In an almost subconscious movement, Systrom stepped out of his car as Briggs stepped in his.

Systrom barreled straight to the front of Briggs' car. He stopped just at the bumper.

Briggs looked up, and frowned, confused.

In one swift motion, Systrom raised the gun. His finger squeezed the trigger. Briggs had no chance to react. The gun exploded. Glass shattered, and bullets ripped through, leaving a staggering wave of destruction.

After all fourteen shell casings littered the ground around him, a silence filled his ears, except for the tinkle of glass pieces dropping from what was left of the windshield and the faint echo of the gunshots. The smell of burnt gun powder hung in the air.

Nicholas Briggs slumped behind the wheel. His face, chest and shoulders were obliterated, almost unrecognizable.

Mike Systrom stared at what looked like a scene from a war zone. He blinked several times, focusing on the sound of his heartbeat pounding in his ear. Then he slid the gun in his jacket pocket, returned to his car and casually pulled out of the parking lot.

Chapter 39

"Okay, okay. I see you moving, but did you do the deed?"

The hacker straightened in his chair, intently tracking Mike Systrom's cell phone on a hacked version of Life360. The dot turned south on South Hulen Street.

"Time to go old school."

He flipped the switch on an old fashioned police scanner on a separate desk, then sat back and listened.

After thirty seconds of random calls, the radio crackled with a dispatcher's voice cutting through the static. "Shots fired at 4055 International Plaza. Units in the area, please respond. Paramedics dispatched."

Two different units responded and headed to the scene.

The man switched his radio from the general dispatch channel to the tactical channel where on-scene officers communicated with each other. It took a few minutes to scan through several channels to find the responding units.

"Unit 537 on scene at 4055 International Plaza. We're located in the reserved parking area just northwest of the building. One deceased. No sign of the shooter."

"Roger that, 537. I'm two minutes out. What's it look like?"

"Like a mafia execution. Man, this guy is shot up bad. I'm calling in for Homicide and the ME. Taping off the area now. Will need some help with crowd control. There's a flood of people coming out of the building."

"Roger that. Almost there."

The hacker smiled and thought for a moment. Things were going as planned. Third target on his list now dead.

So far so good.

He turned his focus back on the map with the moving blue dot.

"Well done, Mike, but where are you going now?"

He pulled up a hacked version of OnStar, found Mike's car on his list of tracked vehicles, brought up a homemade dashboard and clicked on the microphone button.

The hacker jumped for the volume knob and turned it down as Pharrell Williams' song Happy blared through the speakers with Mike Systrom singing along in full voice.

"Oh, damn, Mike, you're a terrible singer. I'll never be able to listen to that song again." He paused.

What the hell is going on?

The hacker drummed his fingers on the desk as he listened to Systrom's out of tune singing and watched the blue dot move only a few miles per hour over the posted speed limit.

Mike Systrom was so calm and relaxed. After having gunned down another man in cold blood.

Oh my god, I've created a monster. Shit.

Other puppets he'd used were frantic and panicky after pulling the trigger. But not this one.

He swung into action to clean up his tracks. As he'd done before, he pulled up Systrom's laptop, accessed his online backup and pressed 'delete.' Step two was to let his worm loose on the laptop.

Boom. That'll take care of any traces of me meddling with him.

Finally, he pulled up Systrom's cell phone and sent the command to fry the operating system. Now, it was nothing more than a fancy paperweight.

He leaned back, and took in a deep, cleansing breath.

"Okay, Mike, now let's take out the monster I've created." He raised an eyebrow. "Thanks for the fun, but I don't keep loose ends."

With a flurry of keystrokes, he brought up a series of traffic cameras along I-20 East. His array of wall mounted monitors allowed him to watch as Mike left one camera's view and entered another.

He didn't know where Mike was headed, so he just watched and thought. His eyes glazed over as he watched Mike's car move steadily along I-20. The vehicle passed over Granbury Road, then McCart Avenue.

171

As the car approached Hemphill Street, the hacker sat up and leaned toward the screen.

"Interesting."

His eyes widened as Mike piloted the car toward the ramp to I-35 North through the I-20 / I-35 mix-master.

Now his puppet moved north on I-35, and the hacker jumped into action. A new set of traffic cameras gave him visibility all the way to the I-30 / I-35 mix-master with its highly elevated connecting ramps.

His grin widened across his face. He zoomed in on the ramp connecting northbound I-35 with westbound I-30 and smiled. "That's brilliant."

From where Mike was, there was only about four minutes to pull this off. Digging quickly into a desk drawer, he pulled out a device that looked like a game controller for a racing video game. A miniature steering wheel connected to a hand operated gas pedal.

Cables twirled around in a frenzy as he connected them to the gaming console, and he pulled up a control screen on an adjacent display.

"Well, Mike, this is what we call the 'nuclear option.' It's been nice knowing you."

*   *   *   *

Mike Systrom turned east onto the I-20 access road from South Hulen Street. His hands tapped on the steering wheel as he sang along with the blaring radio.

He smiled at the tune selection, "Happy." It was not only a catchy song, but it seemed so appropriate for the moment. He was 'happy' and he did 'feel like a room without a roof'.

For the first time in over two weeks, he could breathe. His chest didn't feel like there was an elephant sitting on it. It was a beautiful morning now that his immediate problem was obliterated. Now, maybe life could get back to normal.

He pulled onto I-20 East, accelerated to merge into traffic and moved on, leaving Nicholas Briggs in his rear view mirror.

Systrom was lost in his moment of bliss as he turned north and cruised up I-35. Finally, he felt free and he was going to enjoy the relief.

He looked over at the gun that he'd tossed onto the passenger seat. His mood shifted as he thought about his buddy who'd let him borrow the thing. He didn't want his friend to get into trouble. He had no choice but to throw it in the river.

I'll just have to apologize to John and pay to replace it.

As he came up on the Hattie Street exit, a slower car moved into his lane. He lifted his foot off the accelerator to slow.

Not only did his car not slow down, it felt like it was speeding up slightly.

That's odd.

He tapped the brakes. No effect. He hooked his foot under the accelerator and lifted up in case it was stuck. Nothing.

Oh shit.

He was coming up fast on the car in his lane. Before he could react, the steering wheel turned right on its own. His car shifted, smoothly changed lanes and accelerated past the car.

What the fuck?

The car gained speed as he flew under the Hattie Street bridge. Systrom looked up as the I-35 / I-30 mix master loomed in his view. There were no options that he could take at a high speed.

He gripped the steering wheel, tried to veer to the left, but it wouldn't budge. He stomped hard on the brake pedal. Panic ripped through him as the car drifted to the right and moved toward the I-30 West exit ramp. It was one of the highest elevated ramps in the intersection. At its peak, it was almost one hundred feet off the road below it.

He grabbed the emergency brake and yanked. Nothing. The car accelerated through the exit ramp at ninety-three miles an hour.

His heart pounded. A scream filled the car, and he realized it was him. He reached for the door handle.

The car raced up the ramp, hugging the inside of the curve, continuing to accelerate. The engine roared. The tires squealed. He yanked at the steering wheel and stomped the pedals.

In a flash, the steering wheel jerked hard to the right, turning the car sideways.

The vehicle crashed through the concrete barrier and railing. For a split second, a weightless silence replaced the panic as the car vaulted off the side of the bridge.

Gravity caught up. Systrom screamed and clawed as the view in the windshield changed from sky to concrete. The car fell nose first down a hundred feet. The surface of I-35 raced up toward him.

He never saw the car impact the pavement below. An eighteen wheeler cruising southbound on I-35 T-boned Systrom's car in mid-air. Both vehicles exploded into a thousand pieces of metal, glass, rubber and plastic, the bodies of the two drivers disintegrated on impact.

Chapter 40

"Well, it's about goddamn time."

Hunter let the door to the interrogation room close behind him and looked over at Evan Monaco sitting, handcuffed to the table in the middle of the room.

"I apologize for the delay, Mr. Monaco. I hope we haven't inconvenienced you."

"Inconvenienced? I was locked up overnight and now I've been sitting here for almost two hours. It's more than inconvenient. It's a pain in the ass. I'm a victim here and I'm being treated like a criminal." He shook his hands and rattled the chains on the handcuffs. "You can start by getting me out of these."

Hunter casually nodded, sat down in the chair across from Monaco, opened the folder he'd carried in with him and perused the contents. All for show. He knew the whole file by heart. After a moment, he cleared his throat. "Victim. Hm… According to what I'm reading here, you are a two-time convicted felon found in the possession of an illegal firearm."

"Oh, come on. That was planted on me. I was kidnapped, tortured, and tied up in that van."

"Interesting. Doesn't explain how your fingerprints weren't only all over the weapon, but on the shells loaded in the weapon, too."

"That's bullshit. What part of kidnapped and tortured don't you people get?"

"Tortured… Yeah, again, according to my notes, the intake officers performed a thorough examination of your…" Hunter gestured at Monaco. "…body, and found no signs of torture. Not so much as a scuff, scratch or bruise."

"It was psychological. It doesn't matter. Clearly, I was

kidnapped. I can't tie up, blindfold and gag myself in the back of that van."

"Well now, you've finally hit on something we can agree on. That was rather odd, especially since you'd called 911 an hour or so earlier, from your own cell phone, gave us your name and explicit information on where another man, coincidentally, was being held captive and tortured. Now, how do you explain that?"

"Like I said, I was kidnapped and forced to do it."

Hunter nodded. "Okay, I'll go with that. Can you describe your kidnappers?"

Monaco shook his head in disgust. "No. They wore hoods."

Hunter tilted his head. "Can you at least tell their race?"

Monaco's agitation grew. His voice was emphatic. "No. They were covered from head to toe. Gloves, hoods, dark goggles. Totally concealed."

Hunter frowned, clasped his fingers on the table. So far so good. "Can you at least tell me what their voices sounded like?"

Monaco's head shook violently before Hunter finished his question. "No, no, no. Like I told the cop that found us, they never said a word. They wrote everything on whiteboards."

Hunter sighed, tossed the folder on the table and leaned back. "Let me get this straight. These people kidnapped you, tortured you without leaving a mark, concealed themselves so well you couldn't identify them. On top of that, they never said a word so you wouldn't recognize their voices. Even if they were right here in this room." He leaned forward. "Did I summarize that about right?"

Monaco nodded.

Hunter smiled. "Hell, maybe they were aliens."

Monaco glared at him.

"Can you tell me anything to identify these people?"

He sat for a moment, apparently lost in thought. "There were three of them. One was tall and lean." He looked at Hunter. "About your size. One was short and kind of soft looking. The third was built like the Hulk."

"Okay. I'll make a note of that." Hunter jotted something down on his notepad. "Evan, let's just cut to the chase. I have no idea how much of your bullshit story is true. Quite honestly, I really don't care how you ended up bound and gagged in a van owned by Harley Lundsford. What I do care about is that, for whatever reason, you called 911 and gave all the details of where another man was truly being held captive and tortured." He stood and leaned his hands on the table. "So, you clearly knew of a crime in progress."

"Man, they made me say that stuff."

Ignoring him, Hunter continued. "What you may not know is the guy you and your buddies kidnapped and beat to a pulp was a Detective in the Texas Rangers."

The man's face drained of all color. "Ah, shit. I didn—"

Hunter slammed his palm down on the table. "I don't give a shit what you did or didn't know. You're going down for the kidnapping and assault of a law enforcement agent, and by the time we get through with everything, my guess is we'll throw at least a dozen more charges at you including possession of an illegal firearm and human trafficking."

Monaco's eyes widened. "What?"

"That's right. We know all about your operation, so if you don't want to spend the rest of your life being some dude's bitch down in Huntsville, you're going to tell me everything you know about Harley Lundsford, the kidnapping, the girls, and anything else you or anyone you know has done wrong since you hit puberty."

"Shit." Monaco buried his face in his hands. "Shit. Shit. Shit."

"Here's the good news." Hunter smiled like a game show host. "Since your buddy, Joshua is in the hospital with a ruptured testicle." He swallowed the acrid taste in his mouth, and continued. "And your buddy Ryan is in the morgue, you get the first shot at 'let's make a deal.'"

His head shot up. "What? Ryan is dead?"

"What did you expect when you torture a Texas Ranger?" He cocked his head. Then pulled out a recording device, slipping it onto the table. "So, what's it gonna be?"

Chapter 41

"This had better be important," Hunter barked into his phone as he stepped out of the interrogation room. His notepad was full of all Evan Monaco's confessions of everything he'd done since the second grade.

"We've got a homicide we need to work. I'm already en route." Sanders voice was muffled.

"Shit." Hunter fumed. "Why us? Are we the only Homicide Detectives in this damn city?"

"Came down from Sprabary. Looks like it might be another one of our..." Sanders paused. "What the hell do we call our murders where a normally inconspicuous office worker takes out a bad guy?"

"Really? Huh..." Hunter backed off a little. "Text me the details. I'll wrap up with Monaco and head over."

"See you there, Cowboy."

*   *   *   *

A large chunk of the parking lot where the murder took place was taped off with patrolmen securing the scene and providing crowd control. Sanders coordinated everything under the bright sun.

Hunter traipsed over to the scene, badged the patrolman, and headed toward the center of the action.

Stacy and the CSI team were already marking evidence and documenting the scene with photographs. The ME team stood by off to the side to transport the body once released.

Hell, this one might take a while. He bit the inside of his cheek. With all the information Monaco had provided in interrogation, he really wanted to get to those hotel rooms fast. He didn't have time for this.

Even through the shattered windshield, their victim looked more like a busted piñata with all the bullet wounds in his torso.

"Crap." Hunter lowered his sunglasses. "How many holes does that guy have in him?" Even for Hunter, the scene was fairly gruesome.

Sanders cocked an eyebrow. "Far more than needed to get the job done."

"No kidding." Clearly, a crime of passion. Hunter stepped back and surveyed the surrounding area. Low rise office buildings to the east and west, a large Methodist church to the north, and a lot of open space between buildings. "Any witnesses?"

"Of the shooting itself, no." Billy pointed to the nearest office building. "Several people in those offices heard all the noise, looked out the windows to see a guy getting in his car and driving away."

"Did they get plate numbers?"

Sanders shook his head. "Only a partial. A guy claims the plate was covered in mud. We got a pretty consistent description of the vehicle." He looked at his notes. "Late model Toyota mid-sized SUV. Another guy said he was pretty sure it was a Highlander. Dark blue, first two letters on the plate MN."

Hunter jeered. "That should narrow it down to a couple of million possibilities."

"Got a BOLO out on it anyway." Billy pointed toward the corner of the building. "One of Stacy's guys is tracking down the video from that camera. Should be able to confirm what we've been told."

Hunter nodded. "Yeah, but from that distance, we're not going to get much of an ID."

"Nope."

Stepping gingerly through the crime scene and avoiding anything marked as evidence, Hunter looked in the driver's side window.

This guy never had a chance. Didn't see it coming until it was too late.

Shell casings littered the ground in front of the car. Lots of them. Hunter pointed to them. "Doesn't look like a pro. Way too many shots. Didn't pick up his brass."

Sanders nodded. "I bet we'll get some prints from a few of them. This is looking oddly similar to our other two cases."

"Yeah... Let's not get ahead of ourselves. So far, the only thing they have in common is they're sloppy. Hell, do we even know the victim's name?"

Sanders held up an clear plastic evidence bag containing a man's wallet. "Sitting in the console. Nicholas Allan Briggs, fifty-five years old. Lives two miles up the road. Haven't run any other background on him yet."

Hunter's shoulders slumped. "Guess you and I are on deck for notification duty."

"Yeah. Guess so." Billy looked deflated.

"I always hate this part the most." Hunter nodded to multiple news trucks setting up for live broadcasts. "But we should get that done before these guys go on the air."

*   *   *   *

Hunter pulled away from the curb in the high end residential neighborhood just off South Hulen Street. They had just delivered the news to the newly-minted widow and left her in the care of a neighbor as she waited to tell her now-fatherless, teenage children.

"That sucked." Billy exhaled and stared out the windshield of the passenger seat.

"Never gets any easier." Hunter frowned, looked at his watch, and shifted back into crime scene mode. He read the notes on his pad, and stopped. "I know she was too distraught to tell us much, but she did say he worked for Othello Industries, right?"

"Yep."

"Isn't that the same company where Weston Caldwell worked?"

"Yep."

"Didn't our OCD detective...what was his name?" Hunter scrunched his face trying to remember.

"Cosner Thompson."

"Yeah." Hunter snapped his finger. "Didn't he say that company was a front for the Mazanti crime family?"

"Yep."

The SUV went silent except for the hum of the tires on the road.

This just went from zero to fucked up in a flash.
After a long pause, Hunter pursed his lips. "Shit."
"Yep."

* * * *

When they pulled back into the scene, the media presence had grown and multiple outlets cranked out live updates.

Hunter pulled around to the back of the parking lot as far away from the cameras and microphones as possible. "I am not ready to deal with that."

"At this point, all we have is a great big bag of nothing." Sanders grinned. "They won't like that."

Hunter reached for the door handle. "Let's go see if we can rectify that situation."

They badged the patrolman controlling access to the scene. Hunter caught Stacy's eye, smiled and gestured for her to come over.

"Hey, Cowboy, were you two hiding from the media hordes?"

"Something like that." He smirked. He really couldn't help himself when he was around her. He just felt like smiling. "Didn't you have one of your guys looking for CCTV footage?"

"Yeah. Roy just got back." She held up a small USB memory stick. "It's hard to see them, but four cameras caught at least something. He downloaded footage from each."

"Yeah?"

"Don't get too excited. He watched the critical parts. All he saw was a dark colored Toyota Highlander coming into the parking area and parking. Then he saw the driver, dressed in black with a black baseball cap and sunglasses get out, walk over to the front of our victim's car, and unload his magazine. Then casually walk back to his vehicle and leave." She shrugged. "It's grainy and from a distance. There's no way to ID the shooter."

Hunter frowned. "Was there anything useful?"

"We saw a few more digits on the plate. We've already updated the BOLO."

Hunter ran his hand through his hair, took a moment and

surveyed the scene again. "Hopefully that'll narrow it down a bit." He paced around for a few minutes contemplating what other actions they could take.

"Hey, Billy." Hunter waved him over.

"What's up?"

"You have this scene humming pretty well. I got enough out of Monaco to get a search warrant for the hotel rooms. Hopefully, Reyes will have it signed by a judge by now." He glanced at his watch. "I really want to get to that hotel. Mind if we divide and conquer?"

Sanders frowned.

"By the time I get back to the station, get the warrant, and update Barkley at the hospital, you'll be wrapped up here and you can meet me at the hotel." He smiled. "Hell, I'll even let you kick the door if necessary."

Billy smiled. "You always know my weak spot."

Chapter 42

"You look worse than this morning. Must be the jello they're feeding you." Hunter strolled into Colt Barkley's hospital room and chuckled.

"Unless you're here to break me out, you can walk out the same way you walked in." Barkley fidgeted, squirmed and looked around. "I don't see how Chelsey deals with working in a hospital. These places are nothing but depressing if you ask me."

"Are you kidding? Chelsey's married to you. Any woman who can deal with that is a saint." Hunter grinned. "Dealing with a hospital is easy in comparison." He shook his head. "You may not look any better, but clearly, you're feeling better." He stopped at the foot of the bed, his tone turning serious. "Glad to see it. I was worried."

"It'll take more than a couple of low rent dipshits to take me out of the game." Colt arched an eyebrow. "Speaking of which, how'd your interrogation go? Did Monaco squeal?"

"Based on his performance, he might land a spot on The Voice. He sang like a bird."

Barkley had sat up straighter in his bed and listened intently.

"He confirmed they're running prostitution out of the two rooms you were surveilling. And that Kenzi Cheek is one of the girls."

Hunter reached into the breast pocket of his jacket and pulled out a folded piece of paper. "Here's the search warrant." He looked at his watch. "I'm meeting Billy at the hotel in thirty minutes. We're going to round up what's left of Lundsford's crew and shut them down."

Barkley didn't say anything, he just pulled back the covers on his bed.

"What are you doing?"

Barkley pulled the pulse monitor off his finger, gingerly slid the

IV needle out of the back of his hand and planted his feet on the floor. "I'm going with you."

"Like hell you are. You're in no condition to walk to the bathroom much less raid a prostitution ring."

Colt grimaced as he limped and shuffled across the room to the closet. "Cowboy, unless you want to see my manhood in all its glory, turn away." He grabbed some clothes, set them on the bed and started to pull the hospital gown off.

"Geez. You're serious." He turned around. "You're absolutely nuts."

"I started this thing. I'm finishing it." It took a few minutes for Colt to struggle into his clothes. He sat on the edge of the bed and caught his breath. Sweat covered his forehead and his body shook from the effort. "We may need to stop and get me a hamburger. I'm a little weak."

Hunter ground his teeth. "They'll never let me back in this hospital again. You're staying out of the fray when the shit goes down. Sanders and SWAT are both meeting us there."

Barkley nodded. "We'd better get going. Check to make sure the coast is clear."

*   *   *   *

Hunter distracted the floor nurses as Barkley shuffled to the elevator. They somehow managed to avoid security and other staff on their escape into the parking garage. Like two teenagers successfully skipping class at school. They couldn't stop laughing. Only every time Barkley laughed, the pain made him moan and buckled his knees.

Hunter helped him up into the SUV. "Why do I think I'm going to regret this decision?"

Barkley smirked. "The decision you're regretting was meeting me last Tuesday for lunch."

"Good point."

Hunter maneuvered the truck out of the garage as his phone rang. He looked at the caller ID.

"Geez, that guy is persistent." He punched decline and shoved his phone back in his pocket.

Barkley attempted to arch an eyebrow. It looked more like a grimace.

Hunter laughed. "It's a reporter from the Star Telegram. Guy named Kipton." He shook his head. "He's like a dog with a bone. He's gotten wind that the cases I'm working right now are possibly linked. He's drooling for a story."

"You gonna help him out?"

"I wish I had enough information to help him out. As it stands, none of it makes sense. We've got normal, everyday people executing mob guys in broad daylight for no apparent reason."

Barkley smiled. "You'll figure it out."

"Wish I shared your confidence."

*   *   *   *

"I need to see the manager now!" Hunter burst through the front door of the Relax Inn holding his badge high. Sanders stepped in right behind. "Don't touch the phone."

The clerk froze, her eyes wide.

"Open the door. Now!" Hunter roared.

She pushed a buzzer. The door lock clicked.

Sanders yanked it open, and pushed through down the hall to the manager's office. "Fort Worth Police Department. Let me see your hands!"

The manager pushed back from his desk and raised his hands. "Don't shoot! Don't shoot! My hands are up."

Sanders filled the doorframe with his broad shoulders, his badge in his left hand, his right hand resting on his holstered Glock. "Is there anyone else in the office?"

The manager shook his head furiously. "Just me and Betty." He nodded to the front desk.

Sanders stepped into the small office as Hunter escorted Betty in behind him.

Hunter stepped back to the door, glanced in both directions in the short hallway to confirm the manager's statement. He turned to the manager, pulled out the search warrant, slapped it on the desk. "The

185

Fort Worth Police Department appreciates your cooperation as we execute this search warrant for rooms 105 and 106."

The guy started shaking. "W-why?"

"My partner here enjoys kicking in doors, so unless you want to spend money on replacing shattered doorframes, you'd better give us a key card to unlock the doors. I'd also appreciate if you could provide information on the guests in those rooms as well."

The manager stammered. "There's no one in those rooms."

Hunter arched an eyebrow. "There was yesterday."

"They cleared out in the middle of the night. Left the key cards in the night drop. They'd paid in cash in advance for the rest of the week."

Fuck.

Hunter clinched his jaw. "Who were the rooms registered to?"

The manager gave a sheepish shrug. "I think the name was John Smith."

Hunter glared at him. "Let me guess. You've already cleaned the rooms."

His head dropped. "Sorry."

"Damn it!" Hunter slammed his fist on the top of a metal filing cabinet. He pointed at the manager. "Get up. You're going to open the rooms for us. Then, we're going to have a chat."

*   *   *   *

The rooms were empty and cleaned.

Hunter dispatched the SWAT team, called and requested Stacy and her team to dust for prints. He stood in the doorway and stared into the empty room. His stomach twisted.

Barkley paced outside the rooms in the courtyard, his face tense, his eyes distraught.

Hunter stepped outside and absorbed Barkley's anguish. Every fiber of his being ached. It had been barely over a week since Lucy Stanton had gunned down Weston Caldwell. Now, there were three killings and no real progress despite having identified the killers for two victims.

Colt had requested his help exactly a week ago with an off-the-books investigation. Now, there was one dead bad guy, two more in jail and two on the run.

But no sign of Kenzi Cheek.

Too much was piling up in his mind, with little to no answers.

In the midst of all this chaos, he was still trying to wrap his brain around the doctor's appointment...the diagnosis.

Where do we go from here?

He looked down. His hand shook again.

Chapter 43

"Cowboy! It's been so long." An effeminate male voice cut through the noise of the busy Starbucks. "How have you been?"

Hunter smiled. "Sorry for my absence, Bernard. Bad guys have been keeping me busy."

Bernard smile a mischievous smile. "Where's your prettier half?"

"Stacy's been even busier than me." Hunter grinned. "After all, she does all the real work."

"Some traditions live on. Your usual? Drinking in or taking out?"

"I need a couple of jugs of coffee and some pastries to keep the team happy."

*   *   *   *

"Alright boys, I brought fuel to jumpstart our brains. We need to make progress on these killings before we end up with a full blown mob war." Hunter set down the jugs of coffee and bags of pastries on the conference table.

Sanders already made notes at the white board. Parker and Reyes clicked away on their laptops and jotted down notes.

Hunter poured a cup of coffee, stood against the wall and nodded to Sanders. "Billy, looks like you've been busy. Why don't you catch us up?"

"Let's start with the victim." He pointed toward the board and started ticking off data points. "Nicholas Allan Briggs, fifty-five. Married with two teenage children. Listed as CFO for Othello Industries. As you guys know, Othello is a front for the Mazanti organized crime family."

"So, he's the mob's accountant," Hunter filled in.

"Yep." Billy checked off each bullet point he'd written on the whiteboard. "The connection to Othello is important. Our first victim, Weston Caldwell, was also a key employee of Othello. The second victim, Marcus Howell, was a known organized crime figure from the Rosa crime family." He looked at the other detectives. "The fact that all three victims are organized crime figures is a clear indication these three crimes are connected. At the moment, it's the only factor that links yesterday's shooting to the other two. I expect that to change as we dig deeper."

Hunter stared at the notes on the whiteboard. "I'll reach out to Detective Thompson with OCD and see if we can get on his calendar for today. He's going to want to get ahead of this thing with the Mazanti folks." He pointed to the board. "What else?"

Sanders frowned. "It becomes more gray area from there. We did get a hit on the prints found on the bullet casings in the Briggs murder. Came back to a guy named Benjamin Serrie. Not surprisingly, much like our last two shooters, he has no criminal record. Not even a traffic stop in the last ten years. The only reason we have his prints on file was because he's a regular volunteer at Cooks Children's Hospital, and they require background checks."

"Great. Another saint shooting a sinner." Reyes laughed. "Lucky us."

"He does have a concealed carry permit and a 9mm pistol registered to him. I've already got the process moving for a search warrant. Should be ready later this morning. But..." Sanders held up his hand. "Serrie doesn't drive a Toyota Highlander. Based on his physical description, he's smaller than the guy on the CCTV footage."

"Speaking of which," Hunter jumped in. "Have we gleaned anything from that?"

Sanders looked through his notes. "Other than the vehicle information and a ballpark height and weight of the shooter, it's pretty useless. Yet..." He frowned. "Good news and bad news." He tossed the pad on the table. "With the additional digits for the plate, we got a solid hit on the BOLO. The vehicle spotted driving away belongs to a Michael Systrom."

"What's the bad news?" Hunter asked. That was a solid lead.

"Shortly after the time of the shooting, Michael Systrom was involved in a fatal automobile accident."

"How convenient." Parker smirked.

"Where?" Hunter asked.

"The High-Five interchange. Speeding on the top bridge, lost control, crashed through the barrier and fell onto southbound I-35. An eighteen wheeler smashed through the car in midair."

"That'll leave a mark." Reyes grimaced.

"From the report, it sounded like both vehicles exploded into a few thousand pieces. Both drivers were killed on impact."

"Coincidence?" Reyes cocked his head.

"I think not." Parker finished his thought.

Hunter ignored the two detectives, looked at Sanders. "Do we have anything that ties Systrom to the scene, to Othello or to Briggs?"

"Other than the CCTV footage, no. But I've got the process rolling for a search warrant for him as well."

Hunter crossed his arms. "That ought to be a joyous notification meeting. Dear Mrs. Systrom, we're awfully sorry for your loss, but we need to search your house because your husband may have shot someone."

"Yeah." Billy frowned. "That's gonna suck."

They spent the next thirty minutes going over the detailed backgrounds of Benjamin Serrie and Michael Systrom. Neither one of them fit the pattern. No criminal background. No ties to the victim. Both had to be processed as the potential shooter. Serrie had to be considered armed and dangerous. They planned accordingly.

After reviewing their plan for serving the warrants, Hunter checked his watch. "Great work, guys. Let's roll mid-afternoon. I want to talk to the OCD guy right after lunch. Call me with any issues in getting the paper. I've got something I need to take care of before then."

An equally unpleasant something.

Chapter 44

"I'm intrigued." Dr. Chapman Murray directed Hunter to sit on the couch. He had worked with Hunter before, after Hunter had shot a suspect. As usual, he wore faded blue jeans, white running shoes and an untucked golf shirt. "I don't usually get calls from the illustrious Cowboy Hunter wanting a visit." His smile held a hint of a warm smirk.

Hunter's smile was more uncomfortable than warm. "Yeah, I can see how that might have been a surprise." He sat on the front edge of the couch, leaning forward with his elbows on his knees and his hands clasped in front of him. Eye contact was too difficult.

"Can I get you some coffee?" Murray probed. "You seem a little tense."

The uncomfortable smile flashed again. "I'm good, doc." He nodded. "You're right, I guess I am a little tense."

"You know everything we share is confidential. Anything you say is just between us."

"That's not the issue." Hunter paused, took a deep breath. His stomach started to churn. "It's... Something happened... Well, I mean... I learned something, and I don't know what to do with it." Hunter stood and started to pace. He stopped. "Is it okay if I walk?"

"Whatever makes you comfortable."

"It's not even a psychological issue really, it's more, well, neurological."

Dr. Murry tilted his head, but let Hunter continue.

"Maybe I should start from the beginning." Hunter fidgeted as he paced.

"That's always a good choice."

"Over the last year or so, things have been happening to me... With me. Little things. Subtle things." Now that Hunter was going, he sat on the couch and looked at the doctor, his eyes radiating concern. "Nothing dramatic. A stumble here, a trip there, fumbling with buttons. It was sporadic."

Dr. Murray matched Hunter's seriousness and listened intently.

"Also, it's been like my whole world has been stuck in molasses. Everything has just slowed down. My walk. My talk. My brain." He shook his head. "My normal thirty-minute wake-and-out-the-door routine stretched to forty-five minutes and then an hour. I didn't change anything, it was just everything took longer."

Hunter stared at his hands, his stomach on the verge of somersaults. "I've known something was wrong for a while. I didn't know what, but I knew it was getting worse." He looked up. "I could go on for the whole hour about all the little shit that just wasn't working right, but that's not the point."

Dr. Murray stayed silent, content to let Hunter work through this conversation.

"The point is…" His voice strained. "I finally went to my doctor. He checked me out and sent me to a neurologist." He inhaled. "I finally saw him on Monday." He cleared his throat. "He diagnosed me with Parkinson's Disease. Technically, based on my age, he referred to it as Early Onset Parkinson's."

Hunter stopped and let the comment hang in the air. The room went silent.

Damn, I said the words. They're out in the open now.

Hunter's face flushed with heat. Just the effort exhausted him, but for the first time in three days, he felt relieved. He'd told someone. It was no longer bottled up inside.

Dr. Murray set down his notepad, his face calm but clearly a shade paler than before. "I'm so sorry to hear that, Cowboy. I imagine you're feeling a little overwhelmed at the moment."

Hunter nodded. A nervous laugh mixed with an exhale as he stared at his hands.

"That's probably a good word for it." He spoke as if he were reading a text book. "Parkinson's is a neurological disorder where the brain doesn't create enough dopamine. It affects how your brain sends messages to your muscles causing everything from uncontrolled movements to no movement at all. It's degenerative and incurable." He looked up. His voice cracked. "I'm forty-five, doc. Not eighty-five. It's only going to get worse. I'll likely get tremors. It may affect how I think. The list of symptoms is a mile long." He stopped, blinked rapidly. "I don't know how I'll be able to work."

Dr. Murray nodded. "Cowboy, I know this sounds devastating right now. And I'm not going to bullshit you. It's serious. I know. My dad suffered from Parkinson's for almost two decades"

A weight pressed down on him, making his whole body heavier.

"You're right." Murray continued. "There's no cure. Over time, some symptoms are going to get worse. But...the medicines and technology available today to manage them are light years ahead of where they were when my dad was diagnosed. People can live normal, productive lives for decades with the proper medications and care."

"Maybe for someone at a desk, but...I'm a cop. People's lives depend on me. My reactions, processing and coordination. How can I..." He let the statement fade off into his fears.

"Jake, let's take a breath and process through this. Nothing has to happen today. We don't know how it will affect your job. Did the neurologist prescribe medication for you?"

Hunter nodded.

"Have you started taking it?"

"I, uh, haven't picked it up from the pharmacy yet."

Dr. Murray arched an eyebrow. "Well, there's step one. Go get it. Start taking it. It will help. Trust me." He smiled. "My dad referred to his meds as his Superman pills."

Hunter smiled.

"Why don't we talk for a bit about what the neurologist told you and what he recommended. I might be able to supplement that a little based on my experience with my Dad."

Hunter relaxed back into the couch for the first time during the discussion. He explained what he'd learned, and Dr. Murray expanded on several topics.

As with many patients who hear bad news from a doctor, much of what the neurologist said had gone in one ear and out the other. He'd been so taken aback by the diagnosis that he'd asked very few questions.

Dr. Murray recommended he research the disease, the symptoms, the progression and treatments. The best place to start was the website for the Michael J Fox Foundation. The famous actor had been diagnosed at age 29, and over the past two decades, his foundation had funded over $800M in research. He also highly recommended Michael J Fox's memoir called Lucky Man.

"Jake, I know this sucks, but you're not alone. There are over a million Americans living with Parkinson's. Almost sixty thousand more get diagnosed every year. Beyond Michael J Fox, there are lots of other celebrities... Linda Ronstadt, Alan Alda, Muhammad Ali. Hell, I think I heard Ozzy Osbourne was recently diagnosed." He paused. "My point is most of these people live productive lives. Do they have challenges and hurdles that others don't? Sure. But this isn't 1950. There are a ton of resources out there."

As their appointment neared its end, Hunter set down his notebook and gave Dr. Murray a relaxed smile. "This was helpful." He tilted his head slowly. "When you hear the words neurological disorder, degenerative and incurable tumble out of a doctor's mouth, it's kind of a kick in the crotch. It's hard to figure out where to go from there."

Dr. Murray nodded. "I know. It's not much easier on the family." He paused. "Speaking of which, have you told Stacy?"

Hunter's body stiffened for a flash before he looked down and cleared his throat. "Not exactly sure how to do that. This isn't exactly something that just pops up in conversation." He paused. "Besides…I'm not ready to lose her."

Dr. Murray frowned. "Jake, you're not giving her enough credit. From everything I can gather, as unfathomable as it might be, she seems to be head over heels in love with you."

Hunter swallowed hard. "I can't do that to her. I don't want to be a burden on her. She deserves better."

"Look, Cowboy, you're about to step in the ring for the fight of your life. It's a fight that's going to last years. You're going to need people in your corner. Especially someone like Stacy." He looked at his watch. "Can I recommend we continue this conversation next week?"

Hunter nodded. "Yeah, that might be good."

"In the meantime, take your Superman pills. You'll feel better."

Chapter 45

"Maybe we should have gotten take out and eaten at the station." Hunter looked around the courtyard at Joe T Garcia's. Countless patrons stared at Barkley and his completely battered face. "They must think you're the elephant man."

The beautiful October day gave them the perfect ambiance to eat outside in the string-lit patio with the fountain trickling in the distance. As always, the restaurant was packed with a mixture of locals and tourists.

"Are you kidding?" Barkley straightened in his chair making his six-foot-five-inch frame even taller. "There's no way I visit Fort Worth and not eat at Joe T's." He smiled. "Even if my raw hamburger face intimidates them. At least they know not to mess with me."

After coming up empty at the Relax Inn on Tuesday, Hunter had insisted that Barkley check into a hotel, get a good night's sleep so they could regroup Wednesday.

While Barkley's face looked like roadkill and he was still moving gingerly, the rest had done him well. But the man was obviously itching to get going.

They ordered their food and waited, lost in thought, enjoying the beauty of the day, the smell of spices and the hum of the crowd.

Hunter broke the silence. "Now that you've had some time to think, any idea where you go from here?"

"Historically, Lundsford is an Austin-based guy. My guess is he high tailed it back there when his Fort Worth operation was compromised. He'll regroup and get some reinforcements, maybe lay low for a while. I've got good intel on his Austin based network. I should be able to pick up his trail quickly." He paused, the creases on his bruised forehead deepening. "The real question is, in his haste to go underground, what will he do with the girls, specifically Kenzi?"

"Have you spoken to her parents?"

"I called them last night. As you can imagine, they're distraught."

Hunter sipped his iced tea. "Are they ready to make your investigation official by filing a missing person's report?"

Barkley chewed on the inside of his cheek. "They may not have a choice. I was summoned to my boss's office first thing in the morning. As your lieutenant predicted, once the FWPD rescued me, red flags shot up throughout the system."

"Shit." Hunter rubbed his face. "If there'd been a way to get you out on my own, I would've. We had to find you and time was running out. I'm sorry."

Barkley held up a hand. "Cowboy, this is not your fault. You did exactly what you had to do." He leaned back. "Hell, you saved my life. I wouldn't have made it through the night. I got into this mess on my own. The consequences are on me."

"Any idea what your boss will do?"

If it was possible for Barkley's face to look worse, it did. "This'll be bad." His voice was barely audible over the din of the restaurant. "Going off book is a mortal sin in the Rangers." He played with a tortilla chip. "It may cost me my badge. I'm not sure what I'd do without it. Being a Ranger is all I ever wanted to do."

Hunter inhaled deeply, thought about his diagnosis. "I understand how you feel."

Concern washed across Barkley's face. "You're not getting busted for helping me, are you?"

Hunter waved off his concern. "No. Sprabary's pissed, but his concern for your safety sucked him into the vortex, so he had to cover for me."

"Then what do you mean?"

Hunter waved him off again and was saved by the waitress arriving with Fort Worth's best Tex-Mex. "Nothing. Let's eat and talk about how you're going to find Lundsford and how I can help."

Barkley eyed him for a moment, then attacked his enchiladas like a man rescued from the pits of hell.

Between crunching on tacos, savoring enchiladas and gulping fork loads of rice and beans, the two of them worked through the details of how Barkley would chase down and find Lundsford. Assuming he still had a badge.

For good measure, they strategized on how to accomplish all that without the badge. At the end of the day, the approaches weren't all that different. One was easier and legal. The other required significant help from Hunter.

"Was it worth it?"

Barkley tilted his head as if he was trying to understand the question. "Who knows? I guess that'll all depend on the ultimate outcome. If we get Kenzi back alive and reasonably intact, then there's no doubt." He shrugged. "In the end, it doesn't really matter. A friend asked for my help. Saying no wasn't an option. Regardless of what happens tomorrow, if I had to do it all over again, I wouldn't change a thing."

Hunter arched an eyebrow.

"Well, maybe I'd have called in the cavalry a little sooner." Barkley smiled.

"You know what they say about hindsight."

Hunter flagged the waitress down for the check and they made their way to Hunter's SUV.

The ride back to Colt's hotel was quiet, both men lost in their own thoughts. When they pulled up to the hotel entrance, Hunter extended his hand.

"Regardless of what happens in the morning, I want a phone call and an update. I also expect whatever your next step is, I'm right beside you."

"I wouldn't have it any other way."

Chapter 46

"No offense guys, but I was really hoping I wouldn't see you again." Detective Cosner Thompson with the Fort Worth Police Department's Organized Crime Division flashed his I-know-something-you-don't smile and shook their hands.

Hunter and Sanders took their seats and handed him a file. "I feel the same way, but unfortunately, it seems the strongest connection between our three murders lands right in the middle of your world."

"Yeah, I saw the note on Briggs. That's now two from the Mazanti family and one from Rosa." He shook his head. "I gotta tell you boys, this isn't good. I've already left a message for the attorney for the Mazanti's. I stressed to him that the Rosa's aren't behind this and asked him for a meeting with Alfred Mazanti." He looked at Hunter. "I need you at that meeting."

Hunter nodded. "Just let me know when and where."

Thompson leaned back. "So, are we sure it's not the Rosa's?"

"Ever known them to enlist accountants and businessmen to do their executions? Besides, keep in mind they've had one of their own guys picked off as well." Hunter shook his head. "It makes no sense. You said yourself these two organizations have coexisted in this city for years with minimal conflict. What would make them break that pattern now? If they did, why would they do it like this? Broad daylight?"

Thompson shrugged. "Beats the hell out of me, but if we don't get to the bottom of this soon, none of that's going to matter because these guys will go to war." He frowned. "If that happens, every single morgue in the Metroplex will be overrun."

"That's the issue, and if you ask me, that's what's motivating our player." Hunter got animated. "It's exactly what he wants. Somehow, someone is conspiring with...or using...everyday people to stoke the fires of a mob war by killing players on both sides."

Thompson nodded. "Whoever he is, he wants them to go to war. He's counting on these organizations not to react rationally. They'll get violent in order to save face." He paused for a moment, looked at Hunter, then Sanders. "This is bad. While I can get us a meeting, I can't guarantee they'll listen. I mean, come on, we're the police."

The three sat in silence for a moment before Thompson continued. "Is there anything at all connecting these crimes other than the criminal backgrounds of the victims?"

"Well, the laptops." Sanders shrugged.

"Laptops?"

Sanders spent the next ten minutes going over in detail how the laptops and cell phones of the first two killers were completely fried. "We've got search warrants for two different suspects in the third killing, and analyzing their electronic devices will be a priority."

"You think someone is sabotaging their electronic gear as part of this process?"

Sanders nodded. "Looks that way. Covering their tracks."

"That takes some real skill." He shook his head. "Unfortunately, that won't help convince them the other family isn't behind all this."

Hunter cocked his head. "What do you mean?"

Thompson shrugged. "It's the modern world gentlemen. These families have a dozen topshelf cyber criminals working for them. These days they make more money off internet fraud than they do running drugs or prostitution."

"Really?" He paused as he mentally chased that thread, but he couldn't work out a clear connection. There was something there, though, and he made a mental note to talk through it with Billy later.

Sanders looked at Thompson. "Any thoughts on how we block a potential war?"

The OCD Detective smiled. "Other than the obvious…find the guy behind this. We need to sit down with both families and convince them to remain calm, maybe share some of our information. Get them to take some precautions."

Hunter nodded. "The sooner you can get those meetings set up, the better. We've already got a high enough body count."

Chapter 47

"How do we want to do this?" Hunter asked both Sanders and Zeke Dickson, the SWAT Team Leader. The three of them huddled in the back corner of a Starbucks on Davis Blvd. on the border between North Richland Hills and Keller. The SWAT team was staged around the corner in a Target parking lot.

"This guy has no idea we're coming, right?" Zeke blinked through his wire-framed glasses.

"Right." Hunter downed a bottled water.

"Are we sure he's there and do we know if he's alone?"

"We've had a unit parked down the street from his house since dawn. The wife and kids all left as expected this morning and haven't been back." Sanders gave a quick shrug. "No sighting of Benjamin Serrie, but based on our research, he works from home. So, we believe he's there and alone."

"How sure are we that he's our guy?" Zeke looked at Hunter.

"It's fifty-fifty. We found his prints on some shell casings, but we've got nothing else and the guy's background is spotless. In fact, we only got his prints because of his volunteer work." Hunter held up his finger to make another point. "It's also interesting that both of our potential suspects live in the Bear Creek area of Keller. A stretch to think that's merely a coincidence."

Zeke nodded, paused for a moment as he absorbed the information. "Man, I'd hate to crash his door only to find out he's completely innocent. That's an expensive civil lawsuit waiting to happen." He looked at Hunter. "I have a suggestion."

He laid out his plan and they collectively poked holes in it. Then filled the holes until they were foolproof.

Zeke swigged the last remnants of his coffee. "Saddle up boys.

Meet you there in ten."

* * * *

Hunter stood in front of the front door of a large, red brick two-story home on Lakeway Drive in Keller. The manicured lawn matched the meticulous landscaping. The upscale neighborhood boasted a top-notch golf course community built along the winding Big Bear Creek. The Serrie house backed up to the sixth hole with a par-four water trap.

They had decided to make the approach as soft as possible. The SWAT truck was staged several houses down the street. Hunter had pulled up and parked in front of the house next door. He had Sanders, Zeke and one of the SWAT team members in his SUV.

Hunter rang the doorbell and tried to look as nonchalant as possible. He stepped back off the porch leaving several feet between him and the door. The other three men positioned themselves out of view, on each side just a few steps away.

The door cracked open a few inches and the curious face of a fifty-something male appeared in the opening. "Can I help you?"

Hunter flashed his badge. "Mr. Serrie, I'm Detective Jake Hunter with the Fort Worth Police Department. Would you mind if we spoke for a moment?" As he said the words, he stepped back more and made a subtle gesture for Mr. Serrie to come out of the house.

Serrie scrunched up his face, opened the door a little wider, but stayed inside the house. "Is everything okay? Did something happen?"

"No, sir." Hunter motioned again for him to step out of the house. "Nothing's happened. I just need some information from you."

With that, Serrie tentatively opened the door further and stepped out.

Hunter nodded.

In an instant, Zeke and his SWAT officer emerged from their corners onto the porch, each grabbing an arm. They pulled Serrie off the porch, shoved him face first against the wall, and cuffed his hands behind his back.

"What the fuck? What are you..." Serrie's words were muffled as he was slammed into the wall.

"Is there anyone else in the house?" Hunter's voice commanded.

"What? No. What's—"

Zeke led him into the house. The rest followed. As Zeke guided Serrie to the couch in a small living room off to the left, Sanders and the SWAT officer fanned out through the house clearing each room.

"What the hell are you doing? This is my home." Serrie regained his bearings, and his face contorted with fury. He struggled against the cuffs.

"I'm sorry, Mr. Serrie. Under the circumstances, we couldn't take any chances. We have a search warrant for the premises. Your cooperation will make this go smoother."

"You're treating me like a criminal. What's going on?"

A moment later, Sanders and the SWAT officer completed the sweep of the house and returned to the living room. Hunter and Zeke sat across from the now perturbed, sweaty man.

Hunter gave a nod to Billy. Sanders stepped over, pulled Serrie up, frisked him thoroughly and took the handcuffs off.

He calmed a bit. "Thank you."

"Mr. Serrie, do you own any weapons?"

Serrie went quiet for a moment. "Why?"

"Mr. Serrie, please. The more you cooperate, the faster we get done here."

After another long pause, Serrie nodded. "Yes. They are all legal and registered and I have a Conceal Carry Permit. I own two 9mm pistols and one AR15 rifle."

"Please tell Detective Sanders where he can find those."

Serrie looked a little uncomfortable, fidgeting under their stares. "My Springfield 9mm and AR15 are in my gun safe in the garage. The Mossberg M2C is going to be a problem."

Hunter arched an eyebrow. "Why is that?"

"I loaned it to a friend last week."

"Can we call your friend and go get it?"

"Well, you see, that's the problem. The friend I loaned it to was killed in a car wreck yesterday." He shrugged. "I really didn't think getting my gun back was a high priority. I figured I'd wait until after the funeral before I asked his wife about it."

Hunter and Sanders looked at each other, registering his words. Hunter cleared his throat. "That friend wouldn't happen to be Mike Systrom, would it?"

Shock slapped across his face. "How the hell did you know that?"

"Did you load the magazines for him?"

Serrie tilted his head. "Yeah. He's not that experienced with guns, so I thought I'd make it easy for him. He said he was going to the range with his boss, I think."

Hunter leaned back in his chair, looked at Zeke. "I think you and your guys can bail. Billy and I will finish up here. Thanks for your help."

Zeke nodded and the two SWAT guys moved out swiftly.

"Mr. Serrie, we're going to make the search quick today. Can you take us to your gun safe to verify those two weapons? After that, we'll get out of your hair. I apologize for this inconvenience."

Serrie looked confused, but relieved. "Follow me."

*   *   *   *

"He'll have a story to tell." Hunter smirked.

He and Billy pulled away from the curb.

"Let's just hope he tells his friends and not his attorney."

"Not to worry." Hunter smiled. "By the time we left, we were old buddies talking guns and ammo. Hell, he's going to invite us to his next barbeque."

Hunter's face sobered. "This next stop is going to suck."

Their drive wasn't far. Not nearly enough time to harden the resolve they'd need to serve a search warrant on a widow. They went west on Bear Creek Parkway and turned south onto Promontory Drive. A couple of quick turns got them to Tealcrest Court.

As with Benjamin Serrie's neighborhood, the homes were beautiful and large, with immaculate landscaping. The home of the late Michael Systrom sat at the end of the cul-de-sac facing east. The two-story, tan brick home flaunted a large, four column front porch supporting a faux balcony. The expansive front yard was bright green even this late in October, accented with two oak trees.

Hunter eyed the houses as they pulled to the curb. "Keller has come a long way since I was a kid. Back then, all of this was trees and bushes. Keller was considered country."

"Not anymore." Sanders smiled. "Looks like money found the country."

"Yeah, well. Money may have found the country, but it isn't making this situation any better." He nodded to the cars parked at the curb. "She's got company."

Sanders inhaled deeply. "It just keeps getting better."

"Follow my lead."

Billy stepped out of the truck.

The sun sank behind the Systrom's house, the later afternoon shadows making it look even bigger than it really was.

Hunter rang the doorbell and stepped back. A teenage boy with sullen, bloodshot eyes opened the door. "Yeah?"

"We're detectives with the Fort Worth Police Department. May we please speak with LeAnne Systrom?"

The teenager stared for a moment and looked confused as he processed the request. Without acknowledging them further, he stepped back, let the door open wide and wandered down the hall.

"Mom, there are a couple cops at the door for you."

A fifty-something woman walked through the entry hall toward them. Had it not been for the intense grief and exhaustion that emanated from every part of her, she would've been stunning with her curly, blonde hair and bright blue eyes. "I'm LeAnne Systrom." She extended her hand. "Please, come in. I wasn't expecting a follow-up from the police."

Hunter introduced both he and Billy. "Ma'am, is there a place we can speak privately?"

The grief and exhaustion seemed to turn to curiosity and concern. "Certainly." She directed them to an office just off the main hall. "This is…was Mike's office. Have a seat."

She hesitated over the leather chair behind the desk for a moment, then sat. "I'm confused. You introduced yourselves as detectives. Why would there be detectives involved with a traffic accident?"

"Ma'am, we're very sorry for your loss. If we had the option of delaying this visit until somewhere down the road, we would. Unfortunately, this is time sensitive and not directly related to your husband's wreck."

Her face somehow appeared to become a shade paler. "That sounds scary. What's going on?"

"My partner and I are homicide detectives. We're investigating the death of a man named Nicholas Briggs. To your knowledge, did your husband know anyone by that name?"

She shook her head slowly, staring at Hunter. "I've never heard of him before. As for Mike..." She cleared her throat. "He was a senior partner in an audit firm and worked in that industry for over twenty-five years. He has hundreds of business contacts I wouldn't know." She stood abruptly. "Look, I have no idea what this is about and I'm not comfortable being interrogated by the police without an attorney. If you want to continue this conversation, we'll need to schedule it so I can make arrangements."

Hunter made no move to stand. "You're certainly entitled to have an attorney present, but I assure you, you're not a suspect in any crime." He reached into his jacket pocket and pulled out the search warrant. "Unfortunately, with or without an attorney, we have a search warrant for the premises. My intent with the questions was just to gather some baseline information."

"A search warrant?" She almost shrieked. "What are you talking about? Why on earth would you have a search warrant for my home?"

"Ma'am, with your cooperation, we can do this as quickly and quietly as possible. We'll limit the intrusion as much as we can. The warrant is for specific items. If you help us collect them, we can speed up the rest of the search."

The resolve solidified on her face. "Detective, you didn't answer my question. Why do you have a search warrant for my home?"

Hunter had hoped to avoid this conversation stream, but now he had no choice.

"Mrs. Systrom, your husband is a person of interest in our investigation." He softened his tone. He gestured back to her chair. "I know this is a terrible intrusion, but the list of items is very limited and with your help, we can be out of here in a very short time."

Her glare faded. She folded her arms in front of her. She was clearly not happy, but seemed resigned to the inevitable. "What are you looking for?"

Hunter nodded. "Just three types of items. First, any computers or computer equipment your husband used. Second, any and all firearms. Third, any communication devices such as cell phones or tablets your husband had."

"I can only help you with the first item. We don't have any firearms in the house. I won't allow them around my children. He didn't own a tablet and his cell phone was with him." Her mind seemed to shift back to her husband's crash. "My assumption is it was destroyed in the wreck. The police told me it wasn't recovered."

"Thank you, ma'am. We'll note your comments about the firearms and the cell phone." He paused. "As for the computers?"

She looked to her left at the credenza. A laptop and a few pieces of computer paraphernalia sat on the smooth mahogany. "That's the only computer he used." She unplugged it and handed it over.

"Thank you, ma'am." Hunter stood as if about to leave.

Sanders spoke up. "Ma'am?" He pointed to where the laptop had been. "Was that external hard drive used by your husband?"

She looked at the device like she'd never seen it before. "I'm sure it was. I don't use it."

"We'll need that as well."

*　　*　　*　　*

Hunter read the text message from his pharmacy reminding him that his prescription was ready for pickup. He stared at the message and felt the world weighing heavy on his shoulders.

"You okay, Cowboy?" Sanders gave him a concerned look from the passenger seat.

"Huh? Uh...I'm fine." Hunter shoved his phone back into his jacket and plastered on a smile. "What about you in there, Bill Gates." Hunter laughed as he started the SUV. "External hard drive? Good catch." He exhaled. "I was just trying to get the hell out of there as fast as

I could."

"No kidding. That was an uncomfortable conversation."

"If you thought it sucked from your point of view, try being the one doing the talking." Hunter shook his head.

"How much you wanna bet this laptop is as deep fried as an onion ring?"

"I think that's a given. If so, it'll at least confirm this is another rerun in the same series." Hunter shrugged. "Who knows? Maybe we'll get lucky."

Chapter 48

"I'm not so sure about this, Panther. What do you think?" Hunter sat at the table in the breakfast nook, Panther in his lap. He rubbed the enormous black cat's head, eliciting a purr loud enough to echo in the empty house.

After he and Billy had left the Systrom's home, he'd dropped Billy back to the station with the collected laptop and external hard drive. Sanders had volunteered to log the evidence and get it ready for the tech team to review.

On the way home, Hunter had stopped by the pharmacy and picked up the medicine the neurologist had prescribed him. Now, he found himself staring at the bottle hesitantly.

He read the label out loud. "Carbidopa Levodopa 25-100." A mild anxiety fluttered through his system. "According to the doctor, this is supposed to replace the dopamine my brain no longer produces. He says many of my symptoms will improve. Do you believe him?"

Panther mewed, staring up at him.

He sighed heavily. "I know. But I don't want to take it."

The cat mewed in protest when Hunter picked him up and set him in the chair beside him. His arm strained due to the cat's weight, the result of years of being spoiled. But Hunter needed to pace. To think.

Panther bristled before he settled into his new resting spot.

Hunter's feet scraped against the linoleum floor in the kitchen, back and forth for countless turns. He fiddled with the bottle of pills, twirling and shaking it as he walked. "He said the best way to confirm a Parkinson's diagnosis was to take the PD meds. If the symptoms went away or improved, then I definitely have Parkinson's."

Several more turns around the kitchen.

"What if the symptoms don't improve? Does that mean I don't

have Parkinson's? What the hell do we do then? "

He picked at the plastic bottle cap. "If the symptoms go away, that means…"

He stopped and stared again at the label. Why was his heart beating so fast? "The problem with that is…" His voice was so strained. "I don't want to have Parkinson's."

I don't want to have to quit my job.

I don't want to lose Stacy.

I don't want to be a burden.

Panther head-butted his leg. He realized he stood in the middle of the kitchen, frozen in space.

"I know, buddy. This isn't like taking aspirin for a headache or some sort of antibiotic for an infection, Panther. This isn't a cure. All this does is help manage the symptoms."

He squatted down to pet Panther prompting the cat to roll over and stretch.

"Well, that's easy for you to say. Life is a lazy, relaxing one for you. Once I start taking these, I resign myself to the fact I'm going to be taking this every day, or some other medication, for the rest of mine."

He shook his head and looked at the bottle again.

"Superman pills, huh?"

Panther mewed.

Hunter stood, opened the bottle and doled out two tablets in his palm. He grabbed his water bottle.

"Let's see what you've got. Just hope you're not my kryptonite."

Chapter 49

Much like someone with a newly repaired vehicle, Hunter paid extra close attention to every aspect of his body on Thursday morning. Was he moving faster or slower? Did his joints hurt? Could he button his sleeves?

All he'd managed to accomplish was to drive himself mildly crazy and distract himself from work. As far as he could tell, he felt exactly the same as before.

Superman pills my ass.

Hunter walked into the conference room a few minutes after eight, and Sanders was already updating his notes on the whiteboard.

Hunter looked at his watch and smiled. "You got an early start."

Without taking his eyes off the board, Billy smirked. "I thought you were on vacation today."

"Touché." Hunter settled in at one of the tables. "Do we have anything new since yesterday? We need to think about what we will or won't say at the press conference this morning."

"That's at ten, right?"

"Yep."

"Not much new. Systrom's laptop and hard drive are with Jackson in IT. I expect to get some preliminary info from him later today." He looked back at the board. "If the laptop turns out to be sabotaged in a similar way, that will fit the pattern." He ticked off the bullet points. "Shooter with no criminal history. No known connection between the shooter and the victim. No known connections between the three shooters. All three suspects have sabotaged laptops, along with their cell phones. All three shooters are either dead or incapacitated. Finally, all three victims have connections with organized crime."

Hunter looked at the whiteboard. "Seems like a lot of

connections, but whatever, or whoever is driving this bus isn't in the mix of stuff we've found so far."

"Doesn't appear to be." Sanders shrugged. "Certainly nothing we've deciphered yet."

Hunter rubbed his face, stood and began to pace. Yet again, his subconscious continued to distract him by focusing on his movements. Normal or slow? Clumsy or smooth?

On the verge of the right answer, or nowhere close?

*   *   *   *

The hum of the servers and keyboard clicking filled the quiet room. Once again, he perused his monitors and files for his next opportunity.

"Three down, and… How many more to go?" He smiled. "Oh, so many options." His smile slipped. "They won't discount me again. Treat me like a two-bit computer geek. They have no idea who they fucked with."

He looked up at the bank of monitors. As before, each one displayed live video of someone who appeared to be going about their daily life, oblivious that someone was watching them.

"Let's select our victim." He played with a large rubber band and spoke like a game show host. "Bob, who do we have as our next contestant in the game of 'Mob Thug Gets Shot'?"

In a lower voice, he answered. "From the Rosa Family, we have Carlton Nunzio." With a few taps, he brought up a file. "Carlton is your typical mafia sleaze bag who's been in and out of prison most of his life. It's suspected that he's killed at least three people, assaulted countless more and has climbed his way into middle management of the Rosa Family. All with the IQ of a dipstick."

The hacker smiled. "This is going to be so much fun." He checked his watch. "Oops. Sorry, Carlton, the selection of your executioner is going to have to wait. The news conference is about to start. Apparently, law enforcement needs help from John Q Public to find someone who's whacked three guys just like you. We'll continue the reaping after a brief commercial break."

He brought up one of the local networks on his screen, increased the volume, and settled back in his chair for the show.

*   *   *   *

The large multipurpose room looked more like a rugby scrum than a news conference. A whoosh of sound filled the space when Hunter entered with his team. Cameras clicked and flashed, video cameras froze him in place with their little evil red lights recording live, and reporters, technicians and spectators turned toward the open door.

Holy shit.

A horde of psycho butterflies rushed through Hunter's nervous system. He'd expected a handful of reporters from the local stations and newspapers. Beyond the blinding glare of the lights, the logos of the heavy hitter news organizations made him chew on his tongue. Including CNN, Fox, MSNBC, ABC and CBS. The entire alphabet soup of the news world.

The Public Relations Officer stood at the podium, gesturing for Hunter to step over.

He took a deep breath and willed his feet to move.

The crowd quieted, the Public Relations Officer gave a brief intro and then stepped away from the podium.

Hunter felt his feet move forward. His first truly out of body experience because he sure as shit didn't know how he made it up to the stand. He retrieved a sheet of paper from his jacket pocket, flattened it onto the podium and cleared his throat. "As mentioned by…" He looked at the Public Relations Officer and realized he had forgotten the guy's name. "Um… My name is Jake Hunter, Homicide Detective with the Fort Worth PD." He gestured toward Sanders, Reyes and Parker as he introduced each in order.

"I have a short prepared statement."

*   *   *   *

The hacker watched the team of detectives enter the room. The lead guy stepped up to the microphones looking more like a lost puppy than a seasoned investigator.

He grabbed a pen and notepad to take notes. See if they announced anything that could indicate they were on his tracks. Or more importantly, see if he could use anything against them. As they were introduced, he jotted down each detective's name.

He put an asterisk beside Hunter's name.

"Welcome to my party, Detective Jake Hunter." He smiled at the aging man with wide eyes on the monitor. "You seem a little surprised by the level of attention I've generated. To be honest, I'm a little surprised myself." He pursed his lips. "Not part of my original plan, but I'm sure I can use it to my advantage."

The detective started with a statement.

"Over the last two weeks, there have been three fatal shootings in the Fort Worth area that are potentially connected. The root cause for these shootings is being investigated by the team of detectives behind me. The department has assigned this task force out of an abundance of caution to ensure there will not be similar crimes moving forward. At this time, while we have identified the actual shooters in each of the cases, we have not determined if there is a direct connection and if so, what or who that connection is. Even though we are treating this as a priority case, we do not believe there is any immediate danger for the general public."

The hacker sat motionless throughout Hunter's statement. When the man finished talking, he tapped a few keys to print off screenshots of all four detectives. He picked up the picture as it printed out and grinned. "Let the games begin, Detective Hunter."

*   *   *   *

Hunter finished his statement. "I'll take a few questions now."

A roar of noise and questions unleashed from the crowd with everyone in the room speaking at once.

He reflexively stepped back and held up his hands to quiet the room. Which had the opposite effect.

The Public Relations Officer came to his rescue, leaned over to the microphone. "Quiet please." He pointed a reporter holding a CNN microphone. "Bill, why don't you go first?"

The reporter straightened himself, put on his best anchor voice and introduced himself. "Detective Hunter, you mentioned you've identified the shooters in all three incidents. Are those suspects in custody?"

"One is in custody and the other two are deceased."

Another reporter jumped in. "Doesn't that mean that you've solved the crimes, and if so, what is the purpose of the task force?"

"While it's true we've identified the perpetrators in each individual crime, we also believe there's a bigger picture connection that if not stopped, may result in future attacks."

A third reporter shouted. "What specifically makes you believe these crimes are connected?"

Hunter held up three fingers. "Three things." He ticked them off as he spoke. "The shooter profiles are similar. The victim profiles are almost identical. Lastly, some specific evidentiary components share unique patterns."

The reporter asked louder through another barrage of questions. "What are those evidentiary components?"

"Due to the ongoing investigation, we can't disclose those specifics at this time."

Andre Kipton spoke up, his tone lazy and annoyed. Like he wasn't pleased with being just part of the scrum. "Is it true all three victims have criminal pasts, and are all associated with organized crime families?"

Hunter paused, and gave him a distinct stare. The man was smart. "We aren't in a position to disclose that information at this time."

The grilling went on for another twenty minutes with no real information divulged. Finally, the Public Relations Officer stepped in between Hunter and the podium, thanked everyone for coming and briskly escorted him and the team out the door.

In the quiet of the hall, relief washed through Hunter's entire body as he felt the adrenalin subside. "Thank God that's over."

The Public Relations Officer smiled. "Evidentiary components? Nice one. By the way, my name's Clark. Lieutenant Rodney Clark." He winked, turned and headed down the hall.

Chapter 50

"Hey Cowboy, I think I need to loan you some of my self-tanning cream." Reyes laughed. "You looked a little pale in there."

The team had meandered back into the conference room after escaping the media circus in the press conference.

"Next time, I'll let you do the talking."

Reyes dramatically shook his head. "Oh, no. *No comprendo. No hablo ingles.*"

"Yeah, I hear you." Hunter dismissed him with a hand wave and plopped down into a chair. How could he feel so drained this early in the day? He shook it off with a scraping of his face, and tried to refocus. "Now that the vultures have flown off, let's figure out where we're at."

Sanders held up his phone and arched an eyebrow to Hunter. "Got a voicemail during the press conference. From a Dustin Harris. He's the IT support guy for the company where Mike Systrom worked. He thinks he has some relevant information for us."

"The IT guy, huh?" Hunter tilted his head. "That would fit with our whole electronic device connection."

Sanders nodded. "We can call him back shortly. In the meantime, Jackson's on his way up to brief us on Systrom's devices."

On cue, there was a knock on the door frame and Sean Jackson was there with an excited expression.

"Don't just stand there." Hunter gestured. "Come on in and tell us why you look like you're about to wet yourself."

Jackson talked as fast as his feet moved into the room. "We've found something. You're not going to believe it. It blew my mind."

Hunter smiled. "Don't leave us in suspense, man. Spit it out."

Jackson turned so he could address all four detectives at the same time, his eyes wide with excitement. "First, just like with the other two cases, the laptop was completely fried. It was clearly done in the same fashion as the other two laptops. I think we can safely say that the same person sabotaged all three."

All four detectives jotted notes. So far, none shared his level of excitement. Hunter gestured for him to continue.

"Second, we didn't have a cellphone to compare." He paused and looked at Sanders. "As I understand it, Systrom likely had his cell phone with him in the car crash. My guess is it's in a few hundred pieces across I-35. But my assumption is we would've found it in the same condition."

Hunter nodded. "Probably, but we really can't do much with assumptions."

Jackson smiled. "Got it. Right. But here's the homerun. I was able to crack Systrom's external hard drive." He looked at Sanders. "Good catch to whoever spotted that. It was a goldmine." For the first time, he referenced the notepad in his hand. "That hard drive contained a complete backup of his laptop. His IT guy must have set it up because it didn't just backup the basic documents and photos like most people do, it backed up all of the underlying system tables and registries. I backtracked for the last month almost every communication transaction that came into or went out of his laptop."

All four detectives sat up in their chairs, fully interested.

Hunter gestured again. "And?"

"Oh, it gets better. Systrom took screen shots of things he wanted to save. Posts and messages from Twitter, InstaGram, FaceBook. Some of these are incredible." He opened the laptop he'd carried in with him and looked at Sanders. "Turn on the projector. You need to see these."

He plugged in the cable as Billy hit the power button. Jackson didn't wait for the projector to warm up. He started clicking away on his keyboard.

"Check this out."

An image of a FaceBook message came to life on the monitor. "This is just one of several messages on different platforms, but they're all similar."

The personal message read, *I know everything. I know about the gambling and the whoring around. I have LeAnne's email address. I'm going to send her the videos. There's nothing you can do to stop me.*

Reyes whistled. "Holy shit. This guy was getting blackmailed."

Jackson slowly shook his head. "Not exactly. Certainly threatened, but I read through dozens of messages and there's no kind of ransom or action request. In fact, when Systrom asked what the guy wanted, all he got in response was more threats. At no time, does the guy taunting him identify himself, so there was no way for Systrom to make any kind of payoff even if he wanted to."

Reyes frowned. "Then what was the point?"

Jackson shrugged. "Seems like he was just trying to harass Systrom, drive him crazy to send him over the edge."

"Well, mission accomplished." Hunter leaned forward. "So, there was never a point where his tormentor promised, 'If you kill Nicholas Briggs, I'll leave you alone?'"

Jackson shook his head. "Not that I could find."

"Then why the hell did he execute Briggs? Is there something in the screenshots that indicates the tormentor was Briggs?"

Jackson shook his head again. "Nothing I saw. In fact, even with the information I pulled from the registries and logs, the initiating IP location was too well hidden, I couldn't figure it out." He shrugged. "I'm sure a true expert in internet security could, but my guess is it would take some serious time and effort."

Hunter frowned. "The initiating IP location? Pretend I'm a normal human being and have no clue what that is."

"IP stands for Internet Protocol. It's the address of the computer that initiated the communication. The problem is whoever sent these messages bounced them through multiple servers in various countries. Reverse tracing back through all of that would take far more powerful tools than I've got. And even then, there's no guarantee we'd identify him."

Hunter nodded. "Okay, we know someone was tormenting this guy with the apparent intent to push him over the edge." He stood and paced again. "But we don't know why. It doesn't appear like your average blackmail scheme because they never ask for money or anything else."

Sanders rubbed his smooth scalp. "This is all interesting, and while my gut tells me this is tied to Systrom killing Briggs, there's nothing in any of these messages that specifically ties to the action." He shrugged. "No message telling him to kill Briggs. No indication that the tormentor is Briggs. The only link is the timing and the buildup of the threats."

Blaine Parker, who'd quietly listened and took notes raised a finger to get Hunter's attention. "You know, Cowboy, it should be relatively easy to figure out if Briggs was the tormentor. If he was sending all these messages to Systrom, wouldn't the outbound messages be on his laptop?"

Hunter stopped pacing, pointed at Parker. "Bingo." He turned to Jackson. "He's right, isn't he?"

Jackson nodded. "Theoretically, yes. But unless this Briggs guy was technically savvy, he's not the one who sent the notes. Whoever sent these messages is a serious geek." He shrugged. "I've been in IT my whole career and how he routed the messages is way beyond my capabilities."

"Still worth checking out." Hunter looked at Reyes. "Get a search warrant for Briggs' home and office. Can you and Parker get out there today?"

"Roger that, Cowboy." Reyes gave a thumbs up.

Sanders looked at Hunter. "That's a thread we need to pull, but what if Jackson is right and Briggs didn't send the messages?"

Hunter pulled out a chair and collapsed into it. "No idea. We got lucky Systrom kept an offline backup of his laptop. It seems logical to assume whoever sent the messages to Systrom did the same to Dean Fritz and Lucy Stanton. But because he was able to sabotage their laptops and cell phones, we have no way to see what he was doing."

"Cell phones…" Sanders snapped his fingers. "We forgot about the cell phones. Those were sabotaged as well. That means he must've used texts and maybe voicemails to communicate. Would it be easier to track this guy that way?"

All eyes in the room turned to Sean Jackson.

He tilted his head. "Possibly. But surely the sender would use a burner phone, wouldn't he?"

"It's worth checking out. Billy, can you get the phone records for all three shooters. Focus on the two days before each shooting and see if we can identify the owners for all incoming text messages."

"On it."

Hunter drummed his fingers on the table. "That still leaves us with figuring out who sent the messages via social media. Sean, do we have anyone technical enough to do that?"

Jackson shook his head. "Not on staff. I've got connections into the local hacker scene and the FWPD has some contractors on retainer. We can find someone, but they won't do it for free."

"You find someone. I'll get Sprabary to approve the budget."

"Will do."

Hunter looked at Sanders. "Why don't you call Systrom's IT guy and see if he's available for a chat this afternoon. I need to return Cosner Thompson's message from earlier. He's arranged a meeting with the Mazanti family." He nodded, surveying the whiteboard and the team clicking away on their computers with more confidence than in the press conference. "Feels like we're finally riding some momentum."

As he glanced over the taunting text message still displayed on the projector, a disturbing thought crossed his mind.

"Is it really possible to intentionally threaten, coerce, torment and manipulate someone enough to get them to kill someone?"

Sanders chewed on his lip. "The better question might be, if they did, exactly what law did they break?"

Chapter 51

"Colt's Bar and Grill, would you like the margarita special to go?"

Hunter snickered into the phone. He had grabbed an empty office to return several phone calls, including checking in on Barkley. "You sound awfully damn chipper for a guy who was wondering if he was gonna lose his badge."

"Well, Cowboy, the status of my badge is still up in the air. In the meantime, they've sent me on an unpaid week long vacation. So, if I'm on a forced vacation, why not act like it?"

"Unpaid for a week, huh?" Hunter's voice lowered, taking on a somber tone. "That's pretty heavy as a starting point."

"Yeah." Barkley matched his tone. "I really stepped in it this time. Internal investigation, conduct assessments, and a disciplinary review next Monday."

"Ouch." Hunter paused for a moment. "What's happened to the case?"

Several beats of silence passed. "Officially...I turned all my information over to another detective in my squad." Barkley let the statement hang in the air.

"Unofficially?"

"Kenzi still hasn't been found, and Congressman Cheek and his wife are more distraught than ever. They're worried since we only caught a couple of Lundsford's gang, he may decide to cut his losses. If that happens, Kenzi will be collateral damage." Barkley's voice turned strained. "I can't let that happen. I promised them I'd bring her home. Badge or not, I have every intention of doing just that."

Hunter smirked. "So, you're still working it, aren't you?"

"I've made a few calls."

"And?" Hunter stretched out the word.

"It's possible I might know where Lundsford's going to be tonight."

He sat up straight. "Son of a bitch. You're going after him, even without your badge, aren't you?"

Barkley didn't respond.

"Why can't you be reasonable and turn the intel over to the detective working the case?"

"It's not his fight. I'm the one who made the promise and I'm the one who messed up." He paused. "I'm also the one that Lundsford nearly beat to death. So, now it's personal."

"Damn it, Colt. You're either going to get fired or killed, maybe both."

"It is what it is... Besides, Lundsford still has my Kimber .45, and no Texas Ranger can let that stand."

Hunter choked back a laugh. "When you put it that way, I understand. But I'm not letting you go alone. What time do you expect the festivities to start?"

It was Barkley's turn to laugh. "What? You're going to drive down from Fort Worth?"

"It's a three hour drive, two and a quarter with lights and siren. If I leave here at five, I'm there in time for a late dinner and strategy session."

After a long silence, Barkley responded. "You're serious, aren't you?"

"Damn straight. Going alone is foolish. Hell, look what happened to you the last time I let you out of my sight. I know all about that Texas Ranger legendary stuff — one riot, one Ranger. We all know that's bullshit. Besides, you won't be carrying that badge tonight, and Lundsford has already proven he's ruthless."

"Cowboy, that's crazy. I can't ask you to do that."

Hunter cut him off. "I didn't ask. I'm telling. My only conditions are, I have to be back here by 8am tomorrow and you're buying dinner."

"Getting back by 8am is going to mean driving back in the middle of the night."

"I'm aware of that."

"As for dinner, I can do that."

"Okay. So, where are you taking me?"

*   *   *   *

Detective Thompson's voice sounded strained and tired on the phone with Hunter. Like he'd been filibustering a mob family for hours. "One of my colleagues in OCD has a relationship with a top associate in the Rosa family and he was able to calm the waters on that side. Thank God."

"Good."

"Mazanti is the bigger concern. He's known to be a little less rational, but… I got a face-to-face scheduled with Alfred Mazanti this afternoon at four."

"Sounds great. Where?"

"Whoa, slow down. I know you're not an organized crime guy, so let me dial you in. Alfred is way, *way* up the food chain, and as you can tell by his name, he's not just another employee. For him to accept a meeting with lower life forms like you and me, that means this is a top priority for him."

"Good, maybe we can get some cooperation from him."

Thompson snickered. "I appreciate your exuberance, but let me tamp down your expectations a touch. The chances of him uttering more than a few words are slim. Our objective here is to keep him from unleashing his goons on the streets of Fort Worth."

Hunter sighed. "Got it. But we have to at least ask the basic questions, right?"

"Of course. Just follow my lead and try not to piss off this guy."

Hunter laughed. "You're making this sound like a scene out of The Godfather. Who is this guy? Marlon Brando?"

The enduring silence made him stop chuckling.

"Like I said, this guy is no one you want to mess with. I'll text you the address. Meet me there at a quarter to four. Oh, and unless you want your weapon confiscated for good, leave your gun in the car."

*   *   *   *

"Hey, handsome, how can I make your day?" The smile in Stacy's voice lifted his spirits. Even eased the tension in his shoulders a bit.

"All you gotta do is be you."

"Now, that's what I'm talking about." Stacy giggled. "Are you taking me to dinner tonight?"

Hunter groaned. "Um. Not exactly. I'm sorry. I won't be around this evening and I was hoping you'd swing by my place and feed Panther."

"Of course, I will. But don't think you're getting away with that explanation. Spill. Where are you going?"

Hunter cringed. The woman was smart and she'd read right through him, he was certain of it. "Austin. I need to pop down there to catch up with Barkley."

"Catch up?" Her tone turned south. "You mean help him do something off the books." Her sigh sounded like a scoff. "Are you crazy? You and Colt both barely escaped last time with your badges. You know if you get caught this time, you won't be that lucky."

"Don't worry. It's not like that. We're just going to tie up some loose ends." The lie tasted bitter on his tongue. He could feel the sweat forming on his brow. "We'll be careful."

She didn't respond.

"Are you there?"

"Yelling at you won't change your mind. Just please be careful… Text me when you're on your way back."

He hated the hint of an edge in her tone, like he was letting her down.

"Yes, dear…"

Chapter 52

The doors opened directly into a plush lobby area on the eleventh floor of the Wells Fargo Tower in downtown Fort Worth. A large mahogany receptionist's desk kept anyone from walking beyond it without unlocking the glass doors on either side. The air was frigid, with the A/C clearly set on high.

They walked across, discretely presented their badges. "I'm Detective Jake Hunter. My partner and I have an appointment with Dustin Harris in IT."

She nodded and said the wait would be a few minutes.

The lobby was immaculate. Expensive furniture. Windows with an amazing view. Sparse, yet impeccable decorations to flaunt the appearance of prodigious success.

"How does this happen?" Hunter asked the question almost to himself.

"What?"

"Mike Systrom. Look around this place. He was a partner in an outwardly successful firm. He owned a beautiful home to match what appeared to be a beautiful family. He had it all. He was living the American Dream." Hunter shook his head slowly. "How do you go from that to executing a stranger in broad daylight and driving your car off a bridge? All because someone sent you threatening notes on your computer?"

"The unknown is always scarier than the known."

Hunter arched an eyebrow.

Sanders leaned forward and lowered his voice. "Think about it. If this had been a typical blackmail scheme, Systrom would've paid the money or called the cops or hired a private investigator. But it wasn't. It was just two weeks of relentless torture. Every day. More threats. He never knew if, or when, he would come home to a pissed off wife and a wrecked home life. There was no remedy. No demand. No way to make it stop." He shrugged. "Would drive anyone crazy."

"Good point. But he did kind of bring it on himself. He was doing shit he shouldn't have been doing. The gambling, sleeping around."

"What's that saying? Who among us is without sin?" Sanders smiled broadly. "I bet even the legendary Jake 'Cowboy' Hunter has secrets he doesn't want the world to know."

Hunter squirmed. He opened his mouth to reply, but a very non-corporate looking man interrupted them. His arms were covered with tattoos, and he sported multiple facial piercings.

"I'm Dustin Harris. Follow me, we'll grab a conference room."

They followed him through a side door into a bustling office area with a combination of cubicles in the middle of the space encircled by private offices and conference rooms lining the windows. Harris ushered them into the first conference room.

He closed the door and sat across from them at the table. "Thanks for coming. I hope this is worth your time."

Hunter nodded. "Thanks for calling us. Our condolences regarding Mr. Systrom."

Harris waved it off. "I didn't know him that well. He seemed like a nice enough guy, but I only interacted with him once. Just before… Well, you know."

"So, what information did you want to provide?

He fidgeted, his white knuckles clasped together on the table. "I guess that depends. Rumor has it Mr. Systrom is a suspect in a murder from just before his car crash." Harris stopped and let the statement become a question.

Hunter cleared his throat. "We're really not in a position to disclose that kind of information. Why did you call us, Mr. Harris?"

"Well, if he really did kill someone, I may know why." He gestured with his hands and spoke rapidly. "I had no idea he was going to do something like that. I would've never… I mean, he just asked me for some help with his computer. He's a partner, for God's sake. What was I going to say, no?"

225

"Slow down." Hunter laid both hands on the table to help calm him. "Just tell us what happened."

Harris took a few deep breaths. "He called me to his office on Monday, said he was having some issues with his laptop. Based on how he said it, I just assumed he'd gone to a porn site and infected the device with malware."

Hunter and Sanders exchanged glances.

Harris noticed. "Happens all the time. I clean it off and everyone acts like it never happened."

Hunter gestured for him to continue. "But it wasn't?"

"Not at all. Someone was sending him all these terrible messages threatening to tell his wife about things he'd done. Whoever was behind it was very good with technology. There was no way for me to trace the origin of the threats. At least not the ones coming through the laptop."

Sanders leaned forward. "But..."

The guy paused and rubbed his palm with his thumb. "Well, he'd also gotten threats on his cell phone. Those, I was able to show him how to find the sender. Some of them had been from a generic burner phone, but based on a message he left me on Tuesday morning, I think he may have been able to trace one." Harris stopped rubbing his hand, and glanced between Hunter and Sanders. "He seemed satisfied, said thanks and hung up."

An energizing excitement welled in Hunter's chest. This explained how Systrom could've known Briggs sent the threats.

The three spent another thirty minutes going over in detail everything that Systrom had shown or said to Harris. The data all corroborated what they'd found on the external hard drive.

After thanking Harris for his information, he escorted them back through the reception area to the elevators.

When the doors closed, Hunter smiled. "It's starting to make some sense now."

Sanders's face scrunched. "Explains how Systrom found Briggs and why he shot him, but there's still a piece missing."

"What?"

"We still have nothing that shows a connection between Systrom and Briggs. If they didn't know each other, then why would Briggs torment him. Hell, for that matter, how would Briggs even know who Systrom was?"

"We gotta keep digging." Hunter held up a finger to issue the next step.

Sanders interrupted. "I'll get Briggs' phone records to confirm he sent the texts."

Hunter frowned. "You take all the fun out of being the boss."

Chapter 53

Holy crap. What a view.

Outside on the balcony on the top floor of The River Tower luxury condominium, the sun glimmered off the Trinity River streaming lazily under the Seventh Street Bridge and through Forest Park. The cloudless sky provided just enough radiant heat to offset the cooler late October temperature. With no breeze, it felt almost perfect. From this vantage point, Fort Worth looked pretty incredible.

Amazing how well mob-life paid off. If one lived long enough to enjoy it.

The River Tower, sometimes referred to as Trinity Terrace, towered twenty-three stories over the city since 2017. It sat on the western edge of downtown just south of West Seventh Street east of the Trinity River, and offered lavish accommodations for its residents.

Still didn't make Hunter feel any safer, having to leave his Glock 9mm in his truck in the underground parking garage. Despite all this wealth and extravagance around him, it was still a meeting with a crime boss. His safety net was now locked in the console, completely useless if things went south.

Thompson better know what he's doing.

A staff member had met them at the elevators, frisked them for weapons and escorted them to the balcony to wait for their audience with Alfred Mazanti.

Hunter leaned on the chrome railing and nodded toward the view. "Who says crime doesn't pay?"

"Oh, it pays alright. At least for the handful who can survive long enough to make it to the top." Thompson smiled. "Problem is most of them get pushed off somewhere along the way."

Hunter took a step back from the edge. "Yeah, let's not talk about getting pushed off when we're twenty-three stories up and about to meet with a guy who's probably responsible for the downfalls of a few people along the way."

Thompson laughed.

The glass door slid open. Alfred Mazanti stepped through.

A short, round, fifty-something Italian guy wore multiple gaudy rings along with his seventies-style jogging suit. A walking cliché if Hunter had ever seen one.

He stifled a smile.

As he waddled out and sat down, he gestured beyond the balcony. "How do you like my view?" A thick New York accent filled his gravelly voice.

Hunter smiled. "Not bad."

Mazanti nodded. "Ain't exactly Central Park, but what the fuck, it's warmer." He pointed to the empty chairs. "Take a load off."

The detectives sat.

"How can I help local law enforcement today?"

Hunter had agreed to let Thompson take the lead in the conversation. His main objective was to listen, observe and take notes.

Thompson leaned forward. "First, our condolences for the loss of your two associates, Weston Caldwell and Nicholas Briggs. We—"

"Acquaintances," Mazanti interrupted.

"I'm sorry?"

"They're more acquaintances, than associates. Although I am certainly saddened by their passing."

Hunter once again stifled a smile as he watched Mazanti play the word game and distance himself from his two lieutenants.

Mazanti took advantage of the pause while Thompson composed himself and waved a hand for one of his minions. "Would you gentlemen like some coffee, or what is it you guys like down here, ice tea?"

Both detectives declined and waited while Mazanti arranged for one himself. "You were saying?"

Thompson jumped back in. "We wanted to let you know we're making significant progress in both investigations, as well as a third related incident. We want to assure you that, based on everything we've determined, we don't believe the Rosa family had anything to do with these shootings."

Mazanti nodded his head slowly, absorbing the view instead of looking at them. He let his shoulders settle with a deep exhale. "I really appreciate that information, but I'm not sure I understand your need to assure me of anything."

"We thought it might be important for you to know in case any of your associates...I mean acquaintances decided to take justice into their own hands. With this information, you might be in a position to convince them to let our investigation run its course."

"Certainly." His casual tone hardened slightly. "What in your investigation gives you reason to believe this isn't related to the Rosas?"

Thompson cleared his throat. He and Hunter had expected this question. "It really boils down to two facts. First, we know all three shooters had no connection with the Rosa family. They have no criminal histories at all. Second, without revealing too many details we're not permitted to, there is significant evidence that all three shooters were coerced and manipulated via technology by someone highly skilled with computers and networks."

Mazanti's whole body shifted. Despite trying to hide his reaction, Hunter caught the mob boss' widened eyes when Thompson mentioned the last detail.

"Gentlemen, I appreciate your visit. Your information and position is noted." Mazanti stood abruptly. "Unfortunately, I have some pressing business." He waved to his minion. "Tony will see you out."

With that, he walked through the glass door and disappeared inside.

Hunter and Thompson exchanged glances, but said nothing. Tony escorted them back to the private elevator without a word.

When the doors closed, Hunter couldn't wait.

"Did you see that?"

"Yes." Thompson adjusted his suit coat like the temperature just escalated in a few seconds.

"Look likes we just kicked up a big hornet's nest."

They exited the elevator into the lobby, Thompson talked as they walked. "Looks like there might be some kind of connection between our hacker and Mazanti. You remember our first conversation. As I said then, both the Mazanti's and the Rosa's have full staffs of cyber criminals generating enormous revenue for them."

Hunter rubbed his temples as they walked. "I need to process this." He looked at his watch. He wanted to get on the road to Austin, but this revelation couldn't turn cold. "I'll ping Billy on my drive out. Does your team have any way of identifying the Mazanti cyber staff, past and present?"

Thompson puffed out his cheeks on an exhale. "That's not easy. Hackers are notoriously protective of their identities. *Mob* hackers even more so… Shit."

"I need you to try."

"We'll do our best."

As Hunter fired up his SUV, he could feel the momentum building.

*   *   *   *

Alfred barreled through the living room, his face growing redder with every step. When he reached his office, his jaw was clenched so tight he may have cracked a tooth. He slammed the door behind him.

"Fuck." He muttered under his breath.

By the time he'd made it around his desk, his fingers were already jabbing at the phone.

"Carlos here."

"It's me. We've got a problem. We can't discuss it over the phone. Meet me at the cyber center at eight sharp tomorrow morning. I want every one of our tech guys there."

"Uh, sure boss, but you know those guys aren't exactly early risers."

"I don't give a flying fuck." His voice roared through the room, rattling the window. "They'd better be ready to work. Because none of them are going home until this is fixed."

Chapter 54

"When you said the place was funky, you weren't kidding." Hunter looked around the restaurant at the eclectic artwork, décor and wait staff. He'd never seen so many people with purple hair.

Barkley smiled, his face only showing minor remnants from the previous week. "Everything in Austin is funky. Trudy's is an Austin original. Some of the best Tex-Mex you'll ever eat and an atmosphere that makes even curmudgeons like you smile." He pointed to the walls. "All the artwork you see is made by local artists and it's all for sale. We're just a few blocks north of the University of Texas campus, so you shouldn't be surprised. All their locations are great, but this is the original, and my favorite."

Hunter had left Fort Worth a little after five and had made the drive in less than three hours despite all the construction and traffic on I-35 South. Looking through the menu made him famished.

"Any suggestions?"

"Of course, *mi amigo*. If you want to give your taste buds a treat, I'd recommend either the migas enchiladas or the stuffed fried avocado." Barkley never opened his menu. "I'm going with the carne guisada." He waved to the waitress as she buzzed from table to table.

With the food ordered, Barkley laid out the intelligence he'd gathered.

"I've got a reliable source that tells me Lundsford and his lone remaining minion, David Gardner, are hanging with a friend on the east side." He paused for a beat. "How familiar are you with Austin?"

"Not very. I can usually find a blues bar on Sixth Street without much help. Beyond that, I'm dependent on you."

Barkley nodded. "Okay, just for reference. First of all, nothing truly runs north, south, east or west because everything is built in relation to the river which runs northwest to southeast. And, of course, the river isn't called a river, it's called Lake Austin."

Hunter smirked. "Only in Texas."

"Yep." Barkley sipped his tea. "I-35 runs roughly north and south on the eastern edge of downtown. The capitol, UT, all the restaurants, bars and hotels people associate with downtown Austin are on the west side of I-35. Everything else you want to avoid is on the east side of I-35."

"Then they are clearly in their element."

"Exactly. As I understand it, Lundsford and Gardner are essentially living in their buddy's trailer parked in his backyard."

Hunter frowned. "That could be dicey. How do we get into the trailer without a riot breaking out?"

"The good news is, according to my source, they're using the trailer for the girls. To keep a revenue stream flowing while they regroup. Lundsford and Gardner are essentially camping out in the yard." He smiled. "Complete with a campfire and lawn chairs. The whole bit."

"What's the plan?"

"We keep it simple. You take one side of the house. I'll take the other. We meet in the middle, get the drop on them in a crossfire and take them down nice and easy."

"Okay." Hunter's voice signaled a question. "Since you're suspended and I'm out of my jurisdiction, exactly how are we going to get them from that backyard to jail without making more trouble?"

"I liked what you guys did up north. We secure them, rescue the girls, and then drop a dime to the Austin Police Department. Let them find the boys locked up in the trailer. We'll conveniently leave enough contraband so the APD will have to take them in. Then we'll make sure the girls file complaints within twenty-four hours."

"Slam, bam, thank you ma'am."

"It'll be like taking candy from a baby." Barkley smiled.

"Yeah, well, the last time I did that, all hell broke loose."

"Okay, maybe not my best analogy, but you got the plan." Barkley finished as the waitress set down their plates. "Now, enjoy the meal. Your taste buds are about to orgasm."

*   *   *   *

The food was better than advertised. So was the conversation as Colt and Hunter talked about life, work and family for the next few hours to kill time.

Several times Hunter tried to bring up his diagnosis, but never quite got the words out. That wasn't something that just flowed naturally in a conversation. Not to mention it would completely derail the conversation and the focus. They couldn't afford to lose their focus as the night's plan unfolded.

Darkness settled over the city as they finished up shortly before ten.

Hunter absorbed Austin's night vibe as he followed Colt across town in his own truck. They traversed down Guadalupe through the UT campus and over to I-35. Once they reached 12th Street, they cut east for a while. At Walnut Avenue, they turned left and Colt pulled to the curb. Hunter parked behind him and jumped into Colt's truck.

They cruised slowly through the rundown neighborhood. Older cars and beat up pickups lined the street. The target house sat at the end of the block among overgrown bushes and a dilapidated fence. As they slowly drove past, they caught a glimpse of a flicker of a campfire beyond the trees. With shadows dancing around it.

Colt smiled at Hunter. "Piece of cake."

He U-turned at the end of the block and parked in front of the neighbor's house. Although they'd seen signs of life in the backyard, the house was dark and quiet.

"Let's roll." Colt checked the clip in his pistol, and climbed down from the truck.

As planned, Hunter took the west side of the house and Barkley the east. They moved slowly along the brick walls to the back, ducking under the windows just in case people were inside. The plan called for Hunter to wait until Barkley made his move, and they'd step out together.

When Hunter reached the end, he peeked around the corner. Someone stood less than a foot away, his back turned.

He pulled back quickly.

A wave of adrenaline washed over him.

What the fuck?

The unmistakable sound of a guy taking a piss in the bushes made him shake his head.

He'd seen just enough to recognize the pisser was David Gardner. The man stood only a few paces away. Gardner finished his business and zipped up his pants.

As he finished, Gardner stepped back and almost bumped into Hunter.

Silent as a snake, Hunter stepped forward, looped his left arm over Gardner's shoulder and under his chin. He clamped down on his throat and pressed the barrel of his Glock to Gardner's temple.

"Don't make a sound," Hunter whispered. "I'm a cop. Drop to your knees."

Gardner's body tensed like he was going to resist, try and wriggle out and toss him off. Hunter clamped down harder on his throat. The man's body relented and he dropped to his knees.

As Hunter clicked the cuffs on the guy's wrist, he spotted Lundsford sitting in a lawn chair, holding a beer and staring at the small campfire.

He'd stumbled onto Gardner so quickly, Hunter wasn't sure if Colt was even in position yet. He remained quiet as he and Gardner stood in complete darkness.

Lundsford glanced toward their shadowy corner. "Hey, what's taking so long? You playing with that thing?"

"Freeze! Police!" Colt's voice ripped through the night air.

As if tasered, Lundsford dived for the ground. He twisted onto his back, and from out of nowhere pulled a gun.

The Kimber .45 exploded into the quiet, like a cannon on a battlefield. Two cracks from Colt's 9mm followed instantly.

Hunter watched Lundsford fall limp to the ground.

Well, fuck. So much for the plan.

Hunter holstered his Glock, wrestled Gardner to his feet and pushed him forward into the backyard, towards Lundsford and the campfire. "Colt, I've got Gardner secured."

Lundsford's blank eyes stared up to the night sky. Blood trickled from two small holes in the center of his forehead.

"Lundsford's gone."

Barkley didn't respond.

Hunter kicked the pistol away from Lundsford's body. Then he yanked Gardner to the ground.

"Face down in the dirt, asshole."

Barkley still hadn't emerged. "Colt?"

No response.

Darkness encased the corner of the house where Colt was supposed to be.

Hunter shifted, and the flames moved the shadows against the wall to reveal a large mass on the ground.

"Shit." He stomped down on the middle of Gardner's back to get his attention. "Move one muscle, I'll shoot you." He spun around where he had line of sight on Colt, the backdoor of the house, the trailer and Gardner.

"Colt, hang on, man."

Hunter pulled out his phone and hit 9-1-1. Then pulled out his Glock, keeping it trained on the backdoor of the house. He had no way to know who was in the house or trailer. Someone could easily get the drop on them in this position.

"Austin 9-1-1, what's your emergency?"

"Officer involved shooting at 1211 Walnut Avenue in East Austin." He spoke rapidly, clearly and controlled. "One Texas Ranger wounded, status unknown. One suspect dead on scene. Another suspect in custody. Roll Austin PD and paramedics immediately. Law enforcement on site but scene is not secure. I repeat, law enforcement on site but scene is not secure. We're in the backyard."

The operator started to ask a question, but Hunter kicked at Garner to get his attention. "Who's in the trailer?"

Gardner didn't respond.

He jabbed him harder, right in the kidney area. Hard enough to get his attention, but not to injure him. "Hey, asshole, I'm talking to you. Who's in the trailer?"

"Just the two girls."

"What about in the house?"

"Nobody. They went out tonight."

Hunter stared at him. "If you're lying to me, I'll aim through you to shoot them."

Hunter spoke back into the phone. "We have at least two human trafficking victims on site. Will need to transport to the hospital and arrange for social services."

"Help is on its way, sir. To whom am I speaking?"

"This is Fort Worth Detective Jake Hunter." Sirens already wailed in the distance, echoing off the skyline. "I need to put the phone down to get to the wounded officer." He dropped the phone, her voice still coming through the speaker.

Grabbing Gardner by the collar, he yanked him up and headed toward Barkley.

"Colt, you with me man?"

As he slid down beside Barkley, he shoved Gardner against the wall sitting in the dirt.

Colt moaned, his right hand gripped his left shoulder. Blood flowed freely through his fingers. He looked up, his eyes glassy, and spoke in a labored voice. "It's a mere flesh wound."

Hunter holstered his gun again and smiled. "At least they didn't hit your sense of humor." He pulled off his jacket and pressed it into the wound. His friend grimaced.

"That's a Brooks Brothers. You owe me."

"Put it on my tab." His eyes closed, his breathing shallow.

The sirens blared louder, drawing closer with each second. Tires screeched to a stop. Doors opened, voices called out and footsteps clambered close from all directions.

Hunter yelled as loud as he could. "We're in the backyard. I'm a cop. Don't shoot."

From all the jostled bushes, it sounded like an army headed his way. Light beams from a dozen flashlights danced around, eventually landing on Hunter and Barkley.

Hunter raised his hands high in the air. "I'm a cop. Don't shoot." He nodded toward Barkley. "We have a wounded Texas Ranger here. He needs immediate medical attention."

There was a voice from behind the light beams. "Austin Police. Keep your hands in the air and take a step back."

Hunter complied. "I'm a cop. My ID is in my jacket pocket." He nodded again toward Colt. The jacket had fallen down to his lap. Blood resumed flowing down his arm.

Two officers stepped forward with guns drawn. One frisked, disarmed and cuffed Hunter. Then he reached for the jacket and retrieved Hunter's ID. "Fort Worth PD? A little off the reservation, aren't you?"

"Can you please plug his wound? I was working in conjunction with the Texas Rangers on a case that started up north."

Paramedics surged forward and began to work on Barkley.

"Hang on, Colt." He called over their shoulders.

Two other cops secured Gardner.

Hunter nodded toward the perp. "Be careful with that asshole. He's a human trafficker." He nodded toward Lundsford by the still flaming firepit. "The other one's dead over there. Their victims are in the trailer. It's not secured." He turned back toward the cop standing beside him. "Can you uncuff me now?"

A sergeant emerged from behind the trio. He nodded his approval and the officer took the cuffs off Hunter. He gave the ID and gun to the sergeant.

*   *   *   *

The explosion of gunshots had jarred Kenzi out of her brief moment of peace. They were loud, just outside the trailer. Her heart jackhammered. She bolted upright, and panted for air. The room went fuzzy as she almost passed out, but she fought to stay awake.

What happened?

Who did they shoot?

Am I next?

She heard muffled voices. No intelligible words.

She fought against her restraints and frantically searched the room for a weapon, anything to protect herself. Nothing but filth and disgust.

Her whole body trembled as her vision locked on the closed door. Time stopped. One minute? Ten minutes? An hour? She didn't know. All she knew was that her life depended on who walked through that door next.

She jumped when she heard the outer door open. Footsteps approached. Her chest tightened with each footfall. She stared at the doorknob and shook.

The knob turned and the door opened. The silhouette of a man filled the space. She reflexively crawfished backward on the bed. The flesh on her wrist ripped as she reached the limit of the handcuffs. She violently shook her head and covered up with her arms.

"No. Please. No."

Terror tore through her as she fought to get away.

The man stopped, and held up his hands. "It's okay. I'm a cop." His voice soft.

She was beyond consoling. Panic drove her as she thrashed around.

"This is unit 271. We need an additional ambulance on scene." He spoke quickly into his shoulder microphone, then refocused on her. "You're safe. I'm here to help."

He took off his jacket, made two quick steps and draped it over her shoulders covering her nakedness.

When the soft, smooth inner lining touched her bare skin, she froze. Her sight cleared and her heartrate dropped. She blinked quickly when she saw the badge on his chest. Sobs racked her entire being as she tugged the jacket close and curled into a ball on the bed.

* * * *

"I'm Sergeant Calhoun Michaels." He was a big guy, likely eyeball-to-eyeball with Barkley, but outweighed him by at least fifty pounds. His thin eyes gave off an Asian ancestry, but his mannerisms were all Texan.

He compared Hunter to the ID. "Looks like you and I need to chat, Detective Jake Hunter."

"Happy to fill you in on everything. Do you mind if I tend to my partner first?"

The paramedics had already discarded the jacket, cut away Barkley's shirt and covered the wound. They were shifting him onto a gurney and strapping him down.

"No problem." The sergeant held up his Glock and his ID. "I'll hold on to these while you get him loaded up. See you out front. Don't dawdle now, you hear?"

The gurney rolled over uneven dirt and grass toward the ambulance at the street, the thing jostling with every bump. Hunter followed the paramedics and watched as they loaded Colt into the back and started an IV.

Countless red and blue lights danced off the houses along the street, the road blocked with a dozen law enforcement vehicles. Dozens of people stood beyond the perimeter watching them, or spying through the front windows.

"Can you guys give us a minute?"

The paramedics nodded and Hunter crawled up into the back of the ambulance. "How are you doing, bud?"

"I've had better weeks." He smiled weakly. "They gave me something for the pain. Not too bad."

Hunter laughed. "Oh, don't kid yourself, it's bad alright. That son of a bitch shot you with your own gun."

Barkley shook his head, and looked like he was about to vomit. "I wish that was the worst part."

"What the hell's worse than that?"

"They're taking me to the only Level One Trauma Center in Austin, Dell Seton Medical at The University of Texas."

The statement hung between them for a minute while Hunter processed it.

Then it clicked.

"Oh, shit. Is Chelsea working tonight?"

"Yep. She's gonna kick my ass."

*   *   *   *

As the ambulance pulled away, Hunter patted around feeling his pockets and realized his phone was still on the ground in the backyard. He quickly made his way down the side of the house to retrieve. On his way, Sergeant Michaels caught his eye and gave him an 'I don't expect to wait all night' look.

Hunter held up a finger. "Just one more thing and you'll have my undivided attention."

The look he got in return was not a happy one, but he kept moving and found his phone right where he'd dropped it during all the chaos.

He punched in the number and heard it start to ring.

"Chelsea Barkley, how may I help you?" She sounded like she was moving fast.

"Chelsea? This is Jake Hunter."

There was a pause on the line. He could tell she had stopped.

"What's wrong? You wouldn't be calling if something wasn't wrong."

"He's okay. Everything's going to be fine…"

"What the hell happened, Jake?"

"He's on his way to Dell Seton with a gunshot wound to his shoulder." Hunter sped up as he explained. "But he's okay. He's awake, alert and cracking jokes. He should be there in about ten minutes."

"Oh, Jesus." She sounded like she was about to cry, then it morphed into anger. "Damnit, I'm going to kick his ass." Then back to concern. "Are you sure he's okay?"

"Trust me. Your guys will be able to patch him up in no time. As soon as I get through talking to a rather pissed off Austin Police sergeant, I'm heading your direction."

Chapter 55

Sargeant Calhoun Michaels glared down at Hunter. He'd clearly waited long enough for an explanation.

Hunter took an involuntary step back to create some space, but even with that extra room, his neck angled back awkwardly.

"Any chance we could sit down for this conversation? I'm getting a crick in my neck." Hunter thought about Barkley's height. "Is everyone from Austin tall?"

A smile cracked across Michaels' face. "I'm actually from Kansas. And I'm the short one in the family." He gestured to the lawn chairs. "Why don't you catch me up on what led to this...kerfuffle? Exactly how does a Fort Worth detective end up in an Austin shootout?"

"Long story, and technically, I never fired my weapon."

Michaels scoffed. "Why do I think I'm going to have a headache by the time this conversation is over?"

Hunter walked him through from the very beginning. He explained how Barkley had tracked these guys to retrieve Congressman Cheek's daughter, following their trail to Fort Worth and back, including getting kidnapped and tortured by Lundsford.

Hunter left out the few details of how Evan Monaco and Joshua Floyd ended up in custody, but was clear about how Barkley was rescued, including the SWAT team shooting of Ryan Williams.

That all lead to this house, and the expectation that, if they could get the drop on Lundsford, it'd be a quick and easy arrest.

"And you never thought of calling us to let us know y'all were here? A little professional courtesy maybe?"

"Yeah, sorry about that. We really thought we could do this quietly."

"So, what went wrong with that plan?" Michaels wrote quickly in his notepad as Hunter spoke.

"Lundsford must have had a death wish. He obviously didn't want to go quietly. Gardner was already in cuffs when Detective Barkley identified himself and told Lundsford to freeze. The guy did just the opposite. He turned and shot at Barkley. Colt immediately returned fire, fatally wounding Lundsford."

At this point, Michaels leaned back with an incredulous look. His eyebrow raised nearly as high as his hairline. "Let me get this straight. Our friendly Texas Ranger, while in the process of taking a .45 caliber slug to the shoulder, returned fire placing two bullets in the suspect's forehead? That's pretty impressive, even for a Ranger."

Hunter smirked. "Had he not been shot as he fired, those two bullets would've entered through the same hole." He smiled. "He's a damn good shot."

*   *   *   *

Like all big cities' emergency rooms, Dell Seton Medical Center bustled with activity like prime time television. Even for two o'clock in the morning. Nurses and doctors moved from room to room like choreographed spinning tops, sometimes whirling past each other and sometimes bouncing off each other.

Hunter politely tried to gain the attention of a few as they sped by, but he seemed to be invisible. He finally resorted to spotting the nurse who looked like she was in charge, and flashing his badge directly in her path.

With a dismissive frown, she stopped. "How can I help you, officer?"

"I'm looking for one of your nurses, Chelsea Barkley "

Her frown turned defiant. "I'm afraid she's not available at the moment. She's with a…patient."

"Yes, I know, ma'am. I'm that patient's partner. I need to see them both."

"Oh." The frown softened. "Are you a Ranger as well?"

"No, ma'am. I'm a homicide detective from Fort Worth."

Her face went blank as she processed his words.

"Again, long story, but Chelsea knows me and I need to see Colt as soon as I can."

She nodded. "Follow me."

*　　*　　*　　*

Colt looked close to death. Between the remaining bruises on his face, the wrapping holding his shoulder stable, all the needles and tubes pumping medicines into him and the beeping and whirring of the machinery around him, no wonder he hated hospitals.

Hunter glanced at Barkley, but quickly shifted his attention to Chelsea. He wanted to gauge her disposition not only to see Colt's medical condition, but also to gauge her level of pissed-off.

I should've brought flowers and a white flag.

Even with her eyes red-rimmed from crying, she still looked gorgeous. She was tall and lean, like her husband, but golden hair and with bright blue eyes. When she saw Hunter enter, she smiled and pulled him over for a hug.

"Oh, Cowboy, thanks for coming."

"How's he doing?"

"It was a close call, but nothing we can't repair."

"Thank God. What did the doctor say?"

Colt fidgeted and cleared his throat. "I may have been shot, but that doesn't mean you can talk about me like I'm not in the room."

"There's that charming personality." Hunter smiled. "Okay, tough guy, what did the white coats say? Can they do anything about your face while you're in here?"

He flashed a lopsided grin, his eyes a little distant. "You're such an ass." He looked at Chelsea. "Honey, what did the doctor say?"

"You had half the staff working on you. They did a quick surgery to remove the bullet fragments and to stabilize his shoulder. They didn't want those metal pieces causing more internal bleeding. You're lucky that thing didn't shatter the bone. The orthopedic surgeon will be here at seven for another surgery to actually repair the shoulder. Apparently, a .45 caliber bullet does a lot of damage."

"No doubt." Hunter smiled. "Especially one fired from your

own gun."

Barkley rolled his eyes. "You're never going to let me live that one down, are you?"

"Not a chance, big guy."

Chelsea gave her husband a stunned look. "Your own gun?"

He grimaced. "At least I got it back. I'll explain later, sweetheart."

She sighed and kissed his forehead. "I need to check in with my team. I'll let you boys chat." She gave Hunter a quick hug and left.

Almost instantly after she cleared the door, Barkley's expression darkened. "Cowboy, I think I really fucked up tonight. It might cost me my badge."

Hunter didn't sugar coat his response. "You may be right, but you accomplished what you set out to do. Kenzi Cheek is safe and will likely be home long before you get released from the hospital. You kept your promise to her parents." Hunter shrugged. "There may be consequences, but you saved a life and in the process, took several bad guys out of the game."

"Yeah." Barkley nodded unconvincingly. "I'm just not sure what I'd do if I wasn't a Ranger."

Hunter nodded, thought about his own situation. "I understand."

For the next twenty minutes, Hunter caught him up on how the crime scene wrapped. He gave him a heads up that Sargent Calhoun Michaels would be in soon for a follow up.

Finally, Hunter stood from the chair. "Hang in there, buddy. I have five hours to drive home and be in that conference room, so I need to hit the road."

"You sure you're okay to drive?"

Hunter paused before he answered and realized that, for the first time in months, despite the lack of sleep, he actually felt great. He wasn't struggling to focus. He wasn't fatigued. He didn't hurt all over. He felt...normal.

"Yeah, I'm good. I'll text you when I get there."

Superman pills indeed.

Chapter 56

"I have one simple question for you gentlemen." Mazanti paused and glared around the room, sure to make eye contact with each of them. "Where's my nephew Frankie?"

Carlos del Gado had pushed open the door leading to a large workroom filled with tables, chairs and a wide assortment of computers, peripherals and accessories. His custom suit was tailored to fit his muscular frame and to provide some concealment of the multiple firearms strategically carried on his person. His black leather briefcase was top of the line.

He set the briefcase down on the conference table and then held the door open while Alfred Mazanti stalked into the room, his face scrunched up as if he'd smelled something bad.

Unlike when Thompson and Hunter visited him at his condo, Mazanti was all business. His dark, pinstriped suit was razor sharp and somehow managed to make his portly frame look fit.

Carlos had assembled the unkempt group of cyber criminals around the conference table where they now sat as Alfred Mazanti spoke.

His question was met with confused looks and dead silence. He let the silence hang for a long moment.

"Let's try this again. Francis Conte... I call him Frankie. I think he prefers Frank. Where is he?" He looked around the room. "What? Cat's got your tongue?"

Still silence.

"I don't have all day." He slammed his fist on the table and bellowed. "Where the fuck is Frankie?"

Finally, a brave soul shrugged and opened his arms, palms up. "How would we know? He's been gone almost a year. It's not like we were buddies."

His statement was followed by nods from around the table.

"Bullshit. You computer geeks all live in your online playground and he was supposed to be a hotshot in your world."

Another guy chimed in. "Exactly, he was a hotshot, or at least he considered himself a hotshot. He treated the rest of us like dirt." He shook his head. "Hell, we were happy he left."

Mazanti squinted and surveyed the faces around the table. He noticed one of the hackers who hadn't commented or reacted sitting quietly, staring at his hands.

Mazanti pointed at him. "You. What's your name?"

The small man with stooped shoulders, stringy hair and sunken eyes looked up startled. "Who, me?"

"Yeah, you."

"D-Darrel."

Mazanti cocked his head. "You know where he's at, don't you?"

"No. No, I don't." He stammered. "I barely knew the guy."

"Bullshit." Mazanti nodded to Carlos.

Carlos moved around the table before anyone could react. He grabbed the hacker by his collar, dragged him to the head of the table and shoved him into an open chair.

Panic swept across the guy's face. "I told you. I don't know where he is. I swear."

Mazanti nodded toward the briefcase. "Maybe some extra motivation will jog your memory."

Carlos opened the briefcase and pulled out a hammer.

Darrel tried to jump up, but Carlos slammed him face first onto the table.

Every man in the room jumped back.

Carlos handed the hammer to Mazanti, and then splayed Darrel's hand out on the table.

He squirmed and moaned. The rest of the group looked on in horror. Mazanti wasn't fazed.

"One more time. Where the fuck is Frankie?"

Darrel thrashed about, squealing and pleading. "I don't know! I swear to God, I don't know!"

Mazanti made the sound of a buzzer. "Wrong answer."

He raised the hammer high above his head.

"Wait!" A voice called from the other side of the table.

Mazanti stopped. The pinned down hacker whimpered.

A man on the other side of the table stood and pointed at his friend. "Mr. Mazanti. Darrel's telling you the truth." Unlike the rest of the team, the man was clean cut and wore a buttoned down dress shirt. "Once Frank left, we never heard from him again, but…" He held up a hand as if trying to calm the situation. "Frank *is* one of the best hackers I've ever met. I guarantee he's out there cracking systems and causing havoc. It's what he does." He motioned around the table. "It's what we all do."

Mazanti glared at the man. "I don't care what he's doing. I want *him*."

"We can find him. Give us some time. We know his signature and his style. Let us focus on finding him and we will."

It was as if all the air was sucked from the room. No one breathed.

Mazanti twirled the hammer.

After a long moment, he handed it back to Carlos, who released Darrel and replaced the hammer into the briefcase.

Darrel squirmed away, stumbling back to his chair. He heaved over his lap, twitching and staring at his hand.

Mazanti studied the man who'd spoken up, the only one with the balls to give a straight answer. "What's your name, Bigshot?"

"Cliff Wangler." The man fidgeted.

Mazanti nodded. "Alright, Cliff Wangler. You, your buddy Darrel, and the rest of you computer freaks have until Monday to find that little son of a bitch. If you don't, your broken hands will be the least of your worries."

Wangler paled, but nodded. "We'll find him."

Chapter 57

Being alone with his thoughts for the three-hour drive back in the middle of the night was almost worse than the shootout. Hunter worried about Barkley and fallout from last night's shooting.

Only one thing overshadowed those concerns.

His own future with the FWPD once he revealed his diagnosis to Lieutenant Sprabary.

Even if his symptoms were under control, the department's policy probably would relegate him to a desk. He'd rather turn in his badge.

Before the day was out, both he and Barkley could end up off the streets at the same time.

The mental bloodletting didn't diminish the fact that apparently the meds were working. He really did feel great. He'd focused better than he had in months, and given how long he'd been awake, it was a damn miracle he hadn't passed out by now.

The sunrise climbed over the horizon just as he pulled into town. The pinks, yellows and blues chased away the dark in a beautiful message welcoming him home.

Driving all the way to his house just to turn around and drive back to the station didn't make much sense. He'd have to beg Panther for forgiveness later. Fortunately, he'd thrown an extra set of clothes in the backseat the night before. He used the station's locker room to clean up and change and sat in the conference room with a less-than-gourmet cup of coffee when Sanders arrived shortly before eight.

"You're here early." Sanders freshly shaved head glistened. "Did you have some sort of epiphany?"

"No such luck. Just a long night and it was easier for me to get here early than it was to go home."

"Sounds like there's a story there. Care to share?"

Hunter sighed, and tossed a dry erase marker to Billy. Sanders settled in, and he gave him the complete blow by blow.

"Holy shit." Sanders shook his head. "Colt's going to be okay, right?"

Hunter looked at his watch. "My guess is he's in surgery with the orthopedist right now. Assuming that goes well, physically, he'll be fine." He paused, shook his head. "Not so sure about his career. Hell, once Sprabary gets wind of what happened, I'm not so sure about my career."

"If you hadn't been there, it might've gone really bad. Probably a good thing you didn't fire your weapon."

"Hope you're right."

*   *   *   *

"Good morning, gentleman." Reyes looked at the table and frowned. "What? No Starbucks?"

The team had planned a regroup session for nine. With several minutes to spare, Reyes and Parker had wandered into the conference room.

"Gotta fend for yourself today, Jimmy." Hunter shrugged. "If I'd have brought it with me this morning, it'd be stone cold by now."

Parker arched an eyebrow. "Sounds like a personal problem to me." He sat down. "What's on the agenda this morning?"

"Recap where we are and brainstorm where we need to go." Hunter looked at his watch. "Let's wait until Jackson gets here. He's apparently found a top shelf hired gun to help us find our mystery hacker."

"Did I hear my name?" Sean Jackson stepped into the conference room trailed by another man carrying a laptop bag in one hand and another slung over his shoulder.

Jackson pointed to his guest. "Detectives, this is Richard Malone. Cyber security expert highly recommended by multiple sources. He's going to reverse engineer the information on Systrom's external hard drive to see if he can identify the sender."

Hunter shook Malone's hand. "Welcome aboard. Do you go by Richard or Rick?"

"Richard. Thanks."

Malone wasn't a big guy, but at the same time didn't look like the stereotype of a nerdy hacker. At about five ten, 165 pounds with brown hair and brown eyes, he would have blended in with almost any crowd.

Hunter smiled. "I've never met a hacker before. Not sure what I was expecting, but you look pretty normal."

Malone smiled. "Thanks...I think. For the record, we don't really use the term hacker. I'm a cyber sercurity specialist. In the cyber security world, there are white hats and black hats. I'm a white hat. The guy you're after is definitely a black hat."

"We're just glad to have you. We've been at a loss on how to identify this guy. Hopefully, you can help."

"Hope so."

Hunter turned his attention to the team. "Alright, guys. Let's start the party." He nodded to Sanders. "Billy, catch us up."

For the next hour, Sanders painstakingly walked back through everything the team knew about the three cases. He spent a lot of time outlining the technology connections between the cases including the shooters' sabotaged cell phones and laptops, as well as the external hard drive the black hat missed.

Sanders, Malone and Jackson had a detailed back and forth discussion about the hard drive and what the data meant. Malone seemed to jump right into the discussion. Hunter was impressed with his questions and engagement.

This guy may get us where we need to go.

Sanders continued with the technology overview. "While Systrom's hard drive tells the story that Briggs was tormenting him through technology mediums, when we examined Briggs' laptop and cell phone, they show no evidence that Briggs ever contacted Systrom, or for that matter, even knew he existed."

He put a checkmark by a couple of bullet points on the whiteboard. "Since the laptops and cell phones for Lucy Stanton and Dean Fritz were trashed beyond salvage, we don't know if they were getting messages. But it seems safe to assume they were. However, when we checked the victims' devices, Weston Caldwell and Marcus Howell, we find nothing that shows they'd ever contacted their shooters. So, in all three cases, it appears a third party sent the messages. To make it look like the victims were sending them."

Parker leaned back in his chair. "That's a really roundabout way of getting from point A to point B. If he or she wanted Caldwell dead, why not just kill him directly? Why involve Lucy Stanton?"

Hunter shrugged. "Maybe he or she doesn't have the means to kill someone directly."

"Or the balls." Reyes got a round of laughter from the team.

Sanders cocked his head. "Maybe he's trying to kill two birds with one stone."

Hunter leaned forward. "How's that?"

"All the messages to Systrom threatened to reveal his sexual escapades and gambling. I mean, this guy was torturing Systrom, but it wasn't blackmail. It seemed more like punishment."

Hunter nodded. "So, torturing him for bad behavior is the first bird, and having Briggs killed because he's a mob guy is the second bird."

"Right. Maybe this black hat sees himself as some sort of avenger, like a super hero." Reyes grinned.

"That's it. Maybe we should be looking for a guy wearing tights." Parker laughed. "But seriously, using a third party to do the actual killing insulates him from the crime."

Hunter looked at Sanders. "Do we know if Lucy Stanton or Dean Fritz were doing anything in their world worthy of this kind of torture?"

"Since we have none of the messages, we don't know."

Hunter turned to Parker and Reyes. "Then let's dig deeper on our first two shooters. See if you can find anything nefarious they were doing to attract this guy's attention. Anything that deserved punishment."

The team carried on with their assigned tasks. Hunter turned to Malone.

"Well, Richard, now you've gotten to see how the sausage is made. Investigations are hot and messy under the covers, but something will eventually finish cooking."

Malone smiled. "This was enlightening."

"Based on what you've seen on the hard drive, do you think you can find this guy?"

He nodded. "Definitely possible, but it'll take some time and work. If your theories are accurate, he's experienced in high level intrusion and manipulation. This guy's good. But we can get there."

Hunters phone buzzed. He looked at the display and his shoulders sank. "Hunter here... Uh huh... Okay... I'll be up in a minute."

He looked at the team. "I've been invited to chat with our lieutenant."

The detectives all groaned.

Hunter arched an eyebrow. "If you haven't heard from me by mid-afternoon, send up a rescue team."

Chapter 58

"Exactly what the hell were you thinking?"

Lieutenant Sprabary didn't waste time with pleasantries when Hunter came to his office. He pointed Hunter to sit and jabbed at the air as he yelled.

Ass chewing time.

Sprabary was up on his feet behind his desk, his suit jacket not only off, but crumpled on the credenza. His tie was skewed to the side under his unbuttoned shirt collar. Signs of a seriously unhappy lieutenant.

"Well, um…"

He cut Hunter off with a wave of his hand. "I've got an Austin police captain so far up my ass, he can count my fillings. He's rattling on about interdepartmental cooperation. Threatening to arrest you. Demanding to know why one of my detectives and a suspended Texas Ranger were involved in a shootout in his city without so much as a courtesy call."

"Well, um…"

"This is the second time in a week I've had to cover your ass, because you and your buddy, Barkley were out playing superhero." Sprabary took a breath, ran his hands through his hair and rested his hands on his belt. His tone quieted. "Seriously, Cowboy. What the fuck?"

Hunter paused to make sure Sprabary was finished. Sweat trickled down the back of his neck.

"Lieutenant, I shouldn't have done it, but I didn't want Barkley to go in alone. We really thought our plan would avoid fireworks." He frowned. "If Lundsford hadn't been certifiably insane, our plan would've worked. No casualties, no injuries, green lights all around."

"Regardless of your plan, you ended up in a shootout outside your jurisdiction."

Hunter held up a finger. "Technically, I was more a witness than an actual participant. I never fired my weapon."

"You're kidding." Sprabary's eyes narrowed. "That's your best defense?"

Hunter shrugged. There wasn't much more to say.

Sprabary continued to finger through his hair. "Okay, walk me through what happened in detail. I want to know everything you did from the minute you entered the Austin city limits."

Hunter walked his boss through the night in detail. Including a positive review and recommendation for Trudy's. That was the only part of his story that coaxed a slight smile from Sprabary.

"Let me guess." He arched an eyebrow. "Even after being shot in the shoulder, Barkley still hit exactly where he aimed."

Hunter smiled. "The two entry wounds in Lundsford's forehead were an inch apart, so he wasn't quite up to his normal level of accuracy. But it worked."

"How is he doing?" Sprabary's voice calmed significantly.

"I haven't checked since I left Austin at three, but they'd already removed all the bullet fragments." Hunter looked at his watch. "He should be in recovery from the orthopedic surgery to repair the damage."

Sprabary nodded. "If you talk to him, tell him we're all thinking about him."

"I will."

Sprabary face looked strained. "You know he's in deeper trouble than you."

Hunter lowered his gaze to the desk, and nodded.

"His lieutenant was one of the many phone calls I received this morning after your Austin escapade." Sprabary shook his head. "He was distraught. He thinks very highly of Barkley, but doesn't see how he's going to save his badge."

The coffee turned rancid in Hunter's gut and threatened to come back up. The words were hard to get out, but he pushed them through. "I was afraid that might be the case. The congressman begged him for help. He saved the girl. He reunited that family. That was all he was trying to do."

"I know. Excuse the pun, but he had no business riding into the fray like a Lone Ranger. He had other options, and so did you."

Hunter nodded, but didn't speak.

"Look, Cowboy, what Colt did... What you did... It was commendable, but you colored way outside the lines. You're really on thin ice here. I'll give you as much cover as I can. I've got some favors left I can call in, but you need to be on your best behavior for a while."

"Absolutely, Lieutenant." Hunter nodded.

Sprabary leaned back in his chair and sighed. "It's Friday. You guys have had a brutal couple of weeks. With all the press, my guess is that our computer puppet master won't push his luck for a few days. I want you and the team to chill over the weekend, unless something big pops."

"Yes, sir."

"I want you guys back in here Monday morning ready to take this guy down. We've got to close this. We need a win." He paused, waiting for Hunter to look him in the eyes. "*You* need a win."

Chapter 59

Singing to himself, Francis 'Frank' Conte entered his command center, and admired the array of monitors on the three walls surrounding his work station.

So many opportunities. But they'll need to wait.

He smiled as he dropped his keys in the top drawer of his desk and pulled his wallet out of his pocket. He extracted a Texas driver's license and a Department of Defense ID and clearance card. A slight giggle rose up as he dropped them on the work surface. The two cards landed face up. Both pictures showed a smiling Conte.

He tapped the driver's license with his finger. "Great job today, Richard Malone. Over an hour in the lion's den and they didn't have a fucking clue. Like a fox in a henhouse."

Conte plopped in his chair letting it spin a few rotations. He interlaced his fingers across his stomach. "What a rush! What a rush!"

He rolled his chair forward and tapped away on the keyboard. The main monitor in front of him flickered as a new image appeared. He smiled and stared at the live video feed. He increased the volume.

Detective Billy Sanders' voice resonated through the speakers as he compared notes with Detective Blaine Parker.

"Well, boys, smile nice for the camera. The little surveillance kit I planted appears to be working quite nicely. Definitely worth the cost. All your security protocols are shit when up against me."

He stared until his noticed Reyes. He jabbed at the screen with one hand, and grabbed his crotch with the other. "Suck on these, Detective Reyes. They're bigger than yours, jackass."

He clicked a few keys to bring up a dictation application. He grabbed the microphone beside his keyboard, set it in its stand and began to dictate notes. The system converted his spoken words into text on the white page.

"What did we learn today? Let's see… First, at some point in the near future, I'm going to take great pleasure in shoving something long and hard right up Detective Reyes' happy ass. Second, I need to pay close attention to Detective Billy Sanders. He gets it, and that's dangerous."

He ran his hand through his hair and absently stared at the images on the various monitors. "They really lucked out when they found that external hard drive. They're now clued into my game and between that press conference and Hunter's visit to Uncle Al, I've clearly got to change courses. But how?"

He stood and moved and stretched a bit. His little space wasn't conducive to pacing. "What are my alternatives? I really can't just continue on my original path." He looked again at the monitors with video images of other potential victims. "Looks like you folks are going to have to wait a bit. I have higher priorities at the moment."

"I wonder…" He rocked back and forth and continued to speak out loud so the system would capture his thoughts. "I need to know how much information Hunter provided to Uncle Al? If good old Uncle Al knows it was me who was responsible for the demise of Weston Caldwell and Nicholas Briggs, he'll pop a cork. He'll have his whole army looking for me."

He sat down, leaned back and interlaced his fingers behind his head. "Of course, even if Uncle Al thinks it's me, he and his goons couldn't find me if I was living in his condo. Bumbling fools."

"The real question with Uncle Al and the family is… Since my method of having minions do my dirty work is clearly off the table for a little while, do I need to take more direct action? Technology as a weapon offers so many creative ways to inflict pain. The possibilities are endless…"

He scowled at the thought of the detectives. How to prove to these assholes that his balls were plenty big enough? Prove that he was better and quicker than anything they could throw at him.

An eyebrow arched up when came to a decision. "Uncle Al and his hoodlums will have to wait a bit. The boys in blue are screaming for retribution."

He tapped a few more keys and a second monitor brought up a map.

"Let's see if we can find your fearless leader. The tall one with the pacing addiction."

A dot appeared on the map near the Summerfields area of North Fort Worth. "Look at that, boys. While you're still toiling away on a Friday afternoon, Detective Hunter ran home for a nap."

He smiled and steepled his fingers together. "You better rest up, Detective Cowboy Hunter. I'm going to keep you two-stepping this weekend."

Chapter 60

Hunter stared at his reflection in the mirror in his bathroom. He wore a pair of nice, comfortable, faded jeans, leather sandals and a cream colored linen shirt with the sleeves rolled up. The ensemble presented a very islands feel.

He studied every crack and crevice on his face. Judging his posture, any shake or flickers of his hands and fingers. Testing the weight on his feet.

He searched for any sign of Parkinson's.

Does she know? Can she tell?

After his conversation with Sprabary and informing his team to stand down over the weekend, he'd cut out early and came home for a power nap before getting cleaned up for his evening with Stacy. It was a little before six on Friday night. She was set to arrive any minute.

The thought of revealing his diagnosis cluttered his mind all week. How could he tell her? How could he not? The thoughts in his head were swirling around like a tornado.

She deserves to know.

God, I don't want to lose her.

But I can't be a burden on her.

She doesn't deserve this.

She didn't sign up for this.

The queasiness he felt in Sprabary's office was nothing compared to the nausea facing this life-altering moment. It wasn't about keeping his job or his badge. It was about his life. Her life. Their life together.

While he loved his work, this was ultimately more important. He realized that now. Based on how more acute his fears were standing here contemplating what she'd say.

How do I tell her?

The sound of the front door opening interrupted his mental yoga. Stacy's voice danced from down the hall.

"Hey, Cowboy, I brought some wine." She closed the door. "We've got an entire weekend free."

He emerged from the hall and met her in the front room.

She smiled and folded into his arms. He didn't let go. Just held her and breathed her in.

Amazing how she could settle him so easily, despite his fears clawing at his insides.

She pulled back, gave him a quick kiss and a wary look.

"I like this. Maybe you should drive to Austin more often." She smiled and handed him the wine. "Why don't you get this opened. I'm going to grab some clothes from the car and freshen up." She turned toward the door, but stopped and looked back at him. "I like that look."

He smiled and pretended to tip his hat. "Just for you."

As Stacy cleaned up, Hunter prepared one of the few meals he excelled at. Filet mignon grilled to perfection on the back patio along with a wonderful medley of yellow squash, zucchini, onions and baby potatoes baked with extra virgin olive oil and lots of garlic and pepper.

Stacy made her entrance just as Hunter plated the meal. He stopped, stared at her and smiled. She was what Hunter called 'casual gorgeous.' With her damp hair pulled back, wearing black tights, a baggy lime green blouse and white Vans, she managed to look both relaxed and smoking hot at the same time.

She noticed his stare. "What are you looking at?"

"A work of art."

She snuggled into him for a kiss. "Mm, that smells delicious. I'm starving. Let's eat."

Hunter finished filling their plates while Stacy poured the wine. Panther strutted into the room and claimed his spot in the chair at the head of the table.

"I guess we know who's boss around here." Hunter arched an eyebrow as he moved the place settings to the other end of the table and they sat.

"Have you heard from Colt?" Stacy dug into the steak first and smiled.

"Spoke with Chelsea. Surgery went well this morning, but he'll be in the hospital until at least Sunday."

"Didn't you say Sprabary told you guys to take the weekend off?"

"Yep."

"Sounds like an opportunity for a road trip." Stacy sipped her wine. "What do you think? You and me in Austin for a Saturday night?"

A broad smile burst across his face. "As you wish. We can drive down in the morning and back on Sunday."

They clinked their glasses as a toast to the plan.

Hunter picked at his food. "I like that idea. Colt may need some cheering up."

"You mean beyond his messed up shoulder?"

"Yeah. Based on what the lieutenant said, there's a good chance he'll lose his badge."

"No? Really?" Stacy frowned and pressed her lips together. "I know he broke the rules, but at the end of the day, he saved those girls. And put a half dozen traffickers out of business. Sounds to me like he ought to get a medal."

"No argument here."

They settled into their meal and talked over the plans for the weekend. Hunter found himself lost in Stacy's presence. Over the past few weeks, and especially the past few days, the realization of how important she was to him had become overwhelming. The thought of possibly losing her was devastating.

After having to pull Hunter out of his fog and back into the conversation for the fourth or fifth time, Stacy got irritated. "Okay, Cowboy, what's going on?"

"How do you mean?"

"You're a thousand miles away. Something's going on in that brain of yours."

Hunter started to smile and opened his mouth to say something smart, but nothing came out. The smile died and fell away. He felt his throat constrict to the point that he had to clear it just to make sure he could breathe. He tried to look at her, but all he could do was blink.

Stacy's eyes widened. She put down her fork, and shifted her legs to face him full on. "You're scaring me, babe. What's going on?"

He nodded and took a long sip of wine.

No backing out now.

"Well, uh... It seems Barkley may not be the only one in jeopardy of losing his job."

Stacy looked confused. "But this afternoon, you said Sprabary was okay with what you did and was going to take care of it."

"Yeah, he is. My issue has nothing to do with the Colt thing."

She stared intently at Hunter, waiting for him to continue.

Hunter struggled for the words. His voice sounded like sand paper. "You remember..." He paused, loosened his jaw.

She took one of his hands in hers. Her skin was so warm, so soft.

"Over the last few months, you've commented several times on my..." He searched for the right words. "Physical condition. My limping, my fatigue, even me stumbling sometimes."

"I didn't mean anything—"

He cut her off. "No. It's okay. You were right. There were many more things you didn't notice." He took a deep breath. "Those didn't just happen. There was a reason."

The color faded from her cheeks slightly, but she remained quiet.

"On Monday, on the advice of my doctor, I went to see a neurologist. After a battery of tests, he diagnosed me...with Parkinson's Disease."

Confusion swept across Stacy's face. "Parkinson's? There has to be some kind of mistake. You're forty-five. People your age don't get Parkinson's."

"Yeah, sometimes they do."

She shook her head defiantly. "But look at you. You're in great shape. You're lean and fit. That can't be. There's clearly some kind of mistake."

"Physical fitness has nothing to do with it. It's a brain disease. No matter how in shape or strong you are, it's about the signals getting from your brain, through your nervous system and to your muscles."

Hunter watched as Stacy nodded. Her analytical and deciphering mind clearly worked hard to come up with a plan. He loved that about her, always dedicated to solving problems.

"So, what do you have to do to fix it?"

Hunter gave her a sad smile. "You can't fix it. It's incurable and degenerative." He shrugged, and squeezed her hand. "It's just going to get worse."

Her face contorted into something of pain and anger. Then just as quickly, she launched herself into his arms. She kissed him deeply and then slid her head over his shoulder and hugged him tightly.

Her hug felt right. It felt natural. But what did it mean?

She doesn't understand.

"It's going to be alright. We'll figure something out. It's going to be fine."

Hunter held her, but didn't respond. This was just her way of digesting the news. He'd already experienced those same thoughts, that first initial stage of grief. Denial.

Chapter 61

"How long?"

"How long what?" Hunter changed lanes driving south. They'd just passed downtown Fort Worth, heading for Austin. Just a few puffy white clouds floated in a sea of blue October sky. He adjusted the heater to offset the morning chill.

"How long have you known about your diagnosis?"

After dinner the night before, they hadn't discussed it further. His instinct was to spend the evening in each other's arms, focused on being in the moment and trying to forget what the diagnosis meant for his future, for their future.

Hunter scrunched his face. "I was just diagnosed on Monday."

Stacy rolled her eyes and gave him a sideways glance. "Don't be dense. I know that. I mean, how long have you...known? That something was off."

He stared out the windshield, happy to have something to concentrate on as this conversation interrupted their beautiful morning. He blinked a few times as he thought about his answer. "It's hard to say. Hindsight is always clearer, and thinking back it's more obvious. At the time though, most of it didn't register as something to worry about." He shook his head. "They were little things, starting probably two years ago. I kind of ignored them, shrugged them off as being tired from a bad night's sleep or not hydrated well enough. Deep down though, I knew something was wrong. I just didn't know what."

"What's it like?"

Hunter squirmed against his seatbelt, his eyes locked on the road. This was the first time he had been asked this question by someone other than a doctor. He knew it wouldn't be the last. It was hard to answer, even in his own head.

"I don't know, it's...different every day. Some days everything's normal." Hunter swallowed, stretched his neck hoping to release the tension growing on his shoulders. "Truth is, those days are fewer and fewer."

He went quiet for a moment as he continued to process the question.

Stacy didn't speak. She just reached over and squeezed his arm.

Hunter didn't look at her. Afraid that if he did, he'd completely lose it and not be able to drive. Admitting to the woman he loved he was no longer as physically and mentally capable as he used to be was a real gut punch. Even worse, that it would never get better. The thought that she didn't deserve this played on a loop in his mind.

"That's the interesting thing about Parkinson's. Because it's a brain and nervous system issue, it can manifest itself in a thousand different ways. And it's different for every patient."

He ran his hand through his hair and kept his eyes fixed on the road. "Some mornings, putting on a shirt and buttoning it up takes so much effort and concentration I literally break a sweat. Some days, walking in a straight line down the hall without bouncing off the walls is a challenge. Other days, I feel like I'm walking in sludge."

"Oh, Cowboy, why didn't you say something?"

Hunter just shook his head.

"That's just the basic, get-through-the-morning and out-the-door issues. Staying focused during the day, making sure no one notices my hand shaking or my foot dragging..." His knuckles whitened against the steering wheel. "The mental side is made worse by the fact that sleeping at times is just impossible. Every nerve in my body feels like it's bruised, my entire core vibrates and my mind is racing. I spend most of the night wandering the house, hoping exhaustion will eventually win."

"I've never noticed any of that when I've stayed over."

Hunter smiled. "When you stay over, my mind is focused on much happier things."

"Maybe I should stay over more often."

He started to respond, but his throat constricted and suffocated the words. He just nodded, blinked and accelerated around a slower driver.

The silence hung in the air for a few miles.

"Stacy, this thing… I'm in the early stages, so things may look normal, but they're not. They're never going to be *normal* again. It's just going to get worse."

"I know."

"No, you don't." The words came out much harsher than he'd intended. "Sorry. I didn't mean to snap."

She rubbed his shoulder. "It's okay."

"Do me a favor."

"Okay."

"Get on your phone. Go to YouTube. Search Michael J Fox."

She did as he requested. "What am I looking for?"

"Find a recent interview with him, something in the last few years. I think there's an Oprah thing."

She scrolled through the options. "Okay."

"Watch a few minutes of that interview. Watch how his movements are out of control. His head bobs and weaves. His hands twitch constantly."

She watched. "Yeah, but—"

He cut her off. "Honey, that's him when he's on his meds. Not to mention with the best doctors, medicine and therapy that money can buy. Imagine what he's like when he crawls out of bed in the morning? When the meds haven't kicked in?"

"I get that, but—"

He kept going with his point, his eyes almost burning. "Can you imagine the burden his wife and family endure?" He shook his head because even he didn't want to imagine it. His voice cracked into a mere a whisper. "I can't do that to you."

Her head snapped around and she looked at him, her green eyes glowed. "That's not your decision."

"Yeah, it—"

"I'm a grown ass woman and you don't get to decide what I can or can't deal with. Especially when it comes to someone I love. That's my call, and I have no intention of going anywhere."

"But—"

"Don't even think about pulling any of that macho, Lone Ranger,

I'll-suffer-alone crap."

"You have no obligation. It's not like we're married."

"What?" She recoiled. "What kind of... I happen to be in love with you. That doesn't change just because there's a pothole in the road. And if making it official is that much of a difference, then as the song says, maybe you should 'put a ring on it.'"

The conversation silenced. The whining tires against the road roared in his ears as they passed through Hillsboro. That thought hung in the air all the way to Waco.

Chapter 62

"Oh my God, this room is beautiful." Stacy dropped her bag on the bed and absorbed the ambience.

Built in 1886, the historic Driskill Hotel on Sixth Street and Brazos Street in downtown Austin was the oldest hotel in Austin halfway between the Texas State Capital and the Brazos River.

The external architecture is breathtaking and the old world charm of the lobby, event area and guest rooms will transport you to another time. Hunter had stayed there once in his early thirties and was so mesmerized by the place, it had become his regular spot when he traveled to Austin.

While Stacy spun in amazement, Hunter spun for a much different reason.

"I can't believe it. None of my credit cards would work. Not one! What the hell is going on?"

"Calm down, honey. Just call the card company and get it straightened out."

"I'll call them alright." He stomped around the room and jabbed his finger at his phone punching in the number.

As he fumed and fussed at the unlucky customer service representative, Stacy unpacked and took advantage of the luxurious shower to get freshened up after the drive down. The hot water rushing through the oversized shower head drowned out the ranting coming from Hunter.

"You're not going to believe this." Hunter barged into the bathroom and interrupted her moment of bliss. "According to Mastercard, I cancelled my account this morning." He paced back and forth. "I'd know if I cancelled my account, and I sure as hell wouldn't do it right before a trip."

"So, what are they going to do?" Stacy poked her head out of the shower.

"They're sending me a new one." Hunter frowned. "But I won't get it until Monday."

"That's alright." Stacy gave up on the shower, stepped out and dried off. "I'll cover it. Relax."

"I've got to check on the other two cards that didn't work." He stormed out of the bathroom.

*   *   *   *

"How the hell can three different credit card companies make the same mistake on the same day? Each one told me the same thing…I cancelled my card." Hunter shook his head and stormed through the parking garage as they headed to his truck.

Stacy had to jog to keep up with him. She finally caught him, grabbed his arm and pulled him to a stop.

"Cool your jets, Cowboy. Clearly, there was some kind of glitch. You fixed it and you'll have new cards on Monday. In the meantime, I'll take care of this weekend. I want to have a good time with you in this awesome city." She pulled him down to her mouth and gave him a quick kiss. "Now, let's go see Colt and Chelsea, visit a while and then have a nice dinner."

Hunter gave a frustrated nod and took a deep breath. "I'm sorry. You're right. Let's go."

Since they had some time, they decided to drive up Congress to the Capital and take a right on Fifteenth Street. Just as they did, Hunter noticed an Austin PD patrol car pull away from the curb and slip in directly behind them. Before he had a chance to comment to Stacy, the lights came on and the officer hit a short whoop on the siren.

"Seriously?" Hunter shook his head as he pulled to the curb. "Could this day get any worse?"

Stacy glanced over her shoulder to see the patrol car. "That's really odd. There's no way you were speeding. You were barely moving."

The officer sat in his car and talked on the radio for a moment leaving Hunter to boil. "What the hell's he doing back there?"

After a moment, a second patrol car arrived and rolled past Hunter's parked SUV pulling to a stop in front of them.

Hunter looked behind them and then in front as both officers remained in their cars. "What the hell?"

A voice crackled over the loud speaker on the patrol car behind them. "Please step out of your vehicle and keep your hands where we can see them."

Hunter put his hands palms up in the universal 'what' fashion.

"I repeat. Please step out of your vehicle and keep your hands where we can see them."

Stacy raised her hands above the dashboard and stared ahead at the patrol car in front of them. "Cowboy, just do what he says. It'll all work out."

Hunter nodded, opened the door. In very slow, deliberate movements, making sure to keep his hands visible, he stepped out of the truck and raised his hands above his head.

Stacy started to do the same, but stopped when the officer in front of them joined in the fun. "Ma'am, stay in the vehicle with your hands on the dashboard."

She nodded and complied.

By now, both officers had exited their cars with weapons drawn. They approached Hunter as he stood motionless without saying anything until they got within a few feet.

"I'm a Fort Worth cop. My ID's in my jacket pocket. I'm unarmed."

They continued as if he hadn't said a word. "Step to the back of the vehicle. Put your hands on the truck and spread your legs."

Hunter complied.

While one officer kept his gun trained on Hunter and his eyes tracking both Hunter and Stacy, the other officer frisked and cuffed Hunter.

Once Hunter was secured, they turned their focus on Stacy and kept her under close surveillance while she exited the SUV. By the time they had gotten her to the back of the vehicle, a third patrol car had pulled up. This third officer was female and took the lead on frisking and securing Stacy.

"Now that we have the formalities taken care of, would someone please explain why we're standing here in cuffs? As I mentioned, I'm a Fort Worth Police Detective and she is a Fort Worth Crime Scene Investigator. We're in Austin visiting a friend in the hospital, who happens to be a Texas Ranger."

"Sir, we've detained you because this car has been reported stolen and the bulletin listed you as 'armed and dangerous'. Are there weapons in the vehicle?"

"My service Glock is secured in the console." Hunter glared at the officer. "Once again, if you'd take two seconds to reach into my jacket pocket, you will find my ID."

While one officer took the car keys and retrieved Hunter's Glock, the other reached in his pocket and extracted his ID. As he looked at him, he arched an eyebrow. "Hm…"

"Well, Detective Hunter, any idea why you're driving a vehicle that's been reported stolen?"

"I own it. I've driven it every day for the past two years. I have no idea why it would've been reported stolen." His attitude was beginning to sour. "Look, can you call Sargent Calhoun Michaels? He can vouch for me."

The officer continued to eye Hunter suspiciously, but reached up to his shoulder and engaged his radio. "Dispatch, this is Unit 534, can you have Sargent Michaels roll to our location? We have a situation here that needs his attention."

"Roger 534."

"While we're waiting, make yourself comfortable. My partner's going to search your vehicle."

"What…" Hunter started to say something, but was immediately cut off by Stacy.

"Not a word, Cowboy." She glared at him. "Not until the sergeant gets here."

Hunter huffed and leaned against his truck.

The officer finished his search just as a fourth patrol car pulled up. A mountain of a man stepped out and sauntered over to the scene. He looked at Hunter and shook his head. "I've met you only twice in my life, and both times you've caused me heartburn."

Hunter started to respond, but Michaels waived him off and turned to the officer. "Can you explain why we have a fellow law enforcement officer in handcuffs on the side of the road?"

The officer explained the situation. When he finished, Michaels nodded.

"Take off the handcuffs from our guests." He looked at Hunter. "Any idea why your car was reported stolen and you two were flagged as if you were Bonnie and Clyde?"

Holy shit. First my credit cards. Now, a fake stolen car report. This is no coincidence.

"I've got a sneaking suspicion this has to do with a case I'm working. Our suspect is a cyber criminal. Earlier today, all of my credit cards were cancelled."

Michaels winced. "Sounds like you pissed off the wrong guy."

"He's pissed me off right back." Hunter frowned.

They went back and forth about the case, why the pair of them were in Austin, and how to resolve the truck issue.

Michaels finally turned to the officer. "Have dispatch take the flag off the vehicle record and to put on another to disregard the stolen vehicle complaint." He turned to Hunter. "That should get you through the weekend and out of my city. When you're back home, you'll have to figure out how to clear it up permanently."

Hunter nodded. "Sergeant, looks like I owe you again. Thanks for your help."

Michaels just stared at him for a moment. When he turned and walked away, he shook his head. "Get out of my city, and please don't come back."

Chapter 63

"I've got a really bad feeling about the next few days." Hunter pulled into a parking spot at the hospital, turned off his truck and exhaled. His head was pounding and his left hand was twitching. "If our suspect is behind today's events, we've got a real problem."

They sat for a moment in silence.

Stacy reached over and rubbed his shoulder. "We don't know. It could just be a really freaky coincidence."

"I don't believe in coincidences, especially not freaky ones. The worst part is he knows who we are, but we still have no idea who he is. That's one hell of a disadvantage."

He stared out the windshield for a moment. "We need to warn the guys and take some defensive measures." His mind was spinning in a dozen directions. "If he's able to hack my credit cards and the police systems, we've got to assume he either has, or will, crack into my phone. I bet he's already going after Billy, Reyes and Parker as well."

As he spoke he occupied his left hand by tapping his fingers on the steering wheel. "The press conference made it really easy for him to find us. The good news is he shouldn't know about you. I need you to text Billy. Tell him to call you back from a land line immediately."

Stacy whipped out her phone and sent the text in seconds.

Hunter continued to process as they waited for the call back.

A moment later, Stacy's phone rang. "Billy? Hang on." She handed the phone to Hunter.

"Billy, I think we've got a problem."

He recounted everything that happened that morning.

Billy exhaled. "Shit."

"Exactly. Here's what we need to do. Call Reyes and Parker. Don't use your cell or theirs. Use only landlines. Tell them what's going on and to meet me at three o'clock tomorrow afternoon at the Starbucks on Rufe Snow north of 820. Tell them to contact all their credit card companies and explain they've been compromised and to take whatever precautions they need. Make sure you all have plenty of cash."

"Gotcha."

"Also, I need you to buy four prepaid cell phones. Use cash." He paused.

What else? What other areas can he track?

"Call the station motor pool. We need to reserve four department vehicles so that we don't have to drive our own. If he's going to hack our worlds, I want to make it as difficult as possible."

* * * *

"You look like you've had a shittier day than me." Barkley winced when the nurse changed his bandage just as Hunter and Stacy entered his room. "And I'm the one in a shoulder sling."

"Let's just say it's been a tough morning." Cowboy waved it off. "How's our patient doing?"

"He'd heal faster if he kept his arm still." The nurse finished rewrapping the wound and left.

"I'll survive the gunshot." Barkley eyed the door as if to make sure they were alone. "Whether I ever get back on Chelsea's good side is the important question. And significantly more dicey."

"What do you expect?" Stacy smiled. "It's not every day a wife sees her own husband wheeled in on a gurney with a bullet in his shoulder. You'll be lucky if you're not grounded for a year."

"A year?" Chelsea's voice sang from the doorway as she strolled in. "More like grounded for life." She gave hugs to Hunter and Stacy.

"What if I agree to rub your feet every night that whole year?"

Her smile beamed, and she leaned down to kiss Colt "Who am I kidding? I can't stay pissed at this guy."

Barkley grinned. "She says that now. Gimme a couple weeks and she might be singing a different tune. Tired of her man sitting on his ass all day."

"Yeah, she will." Hunter looked around the room. "Looks like a florist truck exploded in here. When are you getting out of this place?"

"First thing in the morning, and it can't come soon enough." Barkley arched an eyebrow. "This place may have the best nursing staff in the country, but the food sucks and this bed is terrible."

"You'll survive." Hunter fidgeted at the foot of the bed.

Stacy eyed him and then looked over at Chelsea. "How about you and I grab some coffee and let these two catch up. I think they both wanna talk shop. Might be easier without a crowd." She gave Hunter that 'you need to tell him' look before turning back to Chelsea. "Besides, I haven't seen any recent photos of Cassie. I bet she's already a heartbreaker."

Chelsea nodded. "She knows it, too. She thinks the planet revolves around her." The two of them headed for the coffee shop.

Hunter grabbed one of the guest chairs, pulled it around to the side of the bed. Using that time to let his mind wrap around how to broach the topic. The longer he delayed, the better. "Looks like your shoulder's healing up nicely. Can we say the same about your career?"

Barkley didn't even attempt to dodge the question with humor. "My guess is it's dead on arrival. Disciplinary hearing got pushed back a day, to Tuesday, but only because they wanted time to expand the charges against me." He shook his head. "By this time next week, you'll be referring to me as 'former' Texas Ranger."

Hunter frowned. "There's nothing that Congressman Cheek can do to influence the process?"

"Cowboy, you should know better. This is the Texas Rangers. Even if there was a possibility of influencing their decision, a mere congressman wouldn't carry nearly enough clout."

"What are you going to do?"

"No idea." He shrugged. "I'll spend the next couple months rehabbing. After that, I guess I'll explore the commercial security market." He smiled and gestured like he read a sign. "Colt Barkley, Private Investigator."

The jocularity died down, and Colt looked questioningly at Hunter. "Don't think I didn't catch that stink eye Stacy gave you. What's going on?"

Hunter fidgeted through a shrug. "Who knows? Although something crazy did happen on our drive over. You won't be…"

Before he could begin the stolen truck story, his phone started ringing, beeping and vibrating all at once. The thing just exploded with activity. Hunter tried to see what was happening, but the phone wouldn't respond to his touch.

He watched as the number of email notifications went from five, to fifty, to one hundred in a matter of seconds. Text messages exploded, too. All of this while every alarm and notification set off repeatedly.

Nothing responded to his commands. The noises grew louder and louder. He frantically pressed the power button, but it didn't respond.

"What the fuck?" Barkley plugged one ear with his good hand. "Turn it off!"

"I'm trying. I'm trying." Hunter pulled at the case. After a few excruciating moments, he managed to get the phone extracted.

A nurse burst into the room. "Sir, you need to turn that thing off. You're disturbing the whole floor."

"Shit. I'm trying." He tore at the back cover, trying to get his fingernails under the edge. It finally popped off and he ripped out the battery. Silence.

The wall of sound made his ears ring.

"Finally." He looked at the nurse. "Sorry. I have no idea what just happened."

She just glared at him, spun on her heels and left.

Barkley snickered. "Dude, I think you need a new phone."

"Unfortunately…" Hunter shook his head. "I don't think there's anything wrong with my phone."

"You're making me question your detective skills."

"It's not the phone that's the problem." He took a deep breath. "I've pissed off someone with the skills to make life a living hell."

Chapter 64

"What day is it?"

"What difference does it make?"

"Seriously. I've lost track." Darrel's face was pale, his eyes hollow, the bags under them looked more like bruises. He stared out the window into the darkness of the night.

Cliff Wangler stretched. "It's early Sunday morning. Again, what difference does it make?"

"We've only got one day left before that madman comes back, and we haven't found him yet."

Wangler rubbed his face. "We're getting there. We've made progress. We've just got to keep looking. He's out there somewhere."

"Progress? What progress? We haven't even caught a whiff of him yet." Hopelessness oozed from Darrel's voice.

Wangler frowned, then nodded. "You're right." He turned back to the room where the rest of the team clicked away, all looking like death warmed over. "Hey guys, gather round the table. We need to regroup."

Like prisoners in a death camp, they slowly trudged to the front of the room and slouched in chairs around the table. Cliff watched as they sat. "Does anyone have any good news?"

Silence.

"That's what I thought. Damn it."

"Cliff, we've looked in every hacker forum out there." A pudgy, curly-haired guy in his late twenty's shrugged. "No one's seen any activity for any of his known ID's. We've reached out to everyone who knows him and they all say he's vanished."

"I hear you, but unless he's dead or out of the country, we know he's out there in the ether. We just need to get creative." Wangler pinched the bridge of his nose. "Think about his quirks, his idiosyncrasies. What were unique things he liked or did?"

Darrel smirked. "He always drank Big Red and ate Pop-Tarts."

The room laughed halfheartedly.

Wangler smiled. "Unless he's ordering them by the pallet, I don't think that's going to help us find him."

The pudgy guy perked up. "Hey, remember how we used to give him shit because the only brand of laptop he'd use was Toshiba?"

Darrel sat up straighter. "Yeah, he's the only black hat I know that uses a Toshiba laptop. Of all the random things…"

"I wonder…" Wangler's mind was racing. "How hard would it be to build a worm to search for all the Toshiba laptops out there? I guarantee you they have unique identifiers. They've got product codes built into them. At the very least, their serialization structure is probably unique."

"We could build one." Darrel frowned. "But it would take days or weeks to search the entire internet for every Toshiba laptop out there. They may not be popular in the US, but I bet they're all over the place in Japan."

"Yeah, but…" Wangler held up a finger. "What if we built in a geo fence and coded it so it only searched in Northeast Texas. Essentially, DFW. I bet that would narrow the field enough to get results in a few hours."

"Okay, but even with Toshibas not being a big brand here, we're still talking about hundreds of machines out there."

"True, but think about it. He's a cyber geek. He's not using just any Toshiba laptop. He's using a high end, new one, so we could build the search patterns to take that into account. That probably gets us into the double digits, maybe even low double digits."

Darrel nodded, but didn't seem to share Wangler's enthusiasm.

Wangler slapped the table hard, jolting everyone. "I've got it." He looked around the table. "What's the first thing we disable on any piece of equipment we use?"

He looked around the table at blank stares.

"The GPS sensor." He stood straight, smiled and looked around the room. "Guys, come on. All we've got to do is find all the high end, new, Toshiba laptops in the DFW area with the GPS functionality turned off." He stood triumphantly.

"Then what?"

"What do you mean, then what? Then we do what we do best. We hack the shit out of him. We find a Zero Day vulnerability in the Toshiba laptops. We exploit it to gain access to his machine. We turn on the GPS tracker. And we send an alert back here with his coordinates."

For a moment, there was silence. No one moved. No one spoke. One at a time, smiles crept across faces. People squirmed in their chairs and sat up straight.

"That's fucking brilliant." Darrel had come to life. He looked at his watch. "We've got about twenty eight hours before that psycho with the hammer comes back. Let's divide and conquer. Tom, start searching for any known Zero Day vulnerabilities for Toshibas. Mike, start coding the search worm. Dave, you build the code to find and turn on the GPS function. I'll build the alert to triangulate his location. By the time that fucker knows what hit him, Carlos will be knocking on his door with that hammer."

Chapter 65

"That son of a bitch. I'm going to kill him when I find him." Reyes' eyes bulged as he fumed at the small table in Starbucks.

"Jimmy, you've got to calm down." Hunter patted Jimmy's shoulder, glancing around the busy coffee shop. "People are staring. If you're not careful, they're going to call the cops."

"We *are* the cops. That's the problem."

Hunter eyed Parker. "Do something with your partner."

Blaine Parker scoffed. "Do something? Hell, he's right. If he doesn't kill the mother fucker, I will. Do you know what kind of hell we've been living the last twenty four hours?" He jabbed his finger in the air to make his point. "My credit cards. My phone. Hell, he even cut off my home internet service and my damned cable TV. My wife is pissed."

After visiting with Colt and Chelsea, Hunter and Stacy had tried to make the best of their one-night vacation in Austin despite all that happened. They had dinner at an Austin classic, the Magnolia Café, serving a great mix of Tex Mex and American food since the late seventies. The funky side of the river on South Congress Avenue gave them ample people-watching entertainment.

Then they'd caught a drink in the hotel bar and made it an early evening for a good night's sleep. As the early morning sun danced across the downtown Austin skyline, they took a long, peaceful, walk on the trails around Town Lake near Zilker Park.

The drive back to Fort Worth had been quiet as they both were lost in their thoughts, Hunter racking his brain to figure out what to tell the team and how to fend off the cyber criminal's attack.

Now at the Starbucks, their animated conversation made several patrons eye them, grab their cups and rush out the door.

"I've got news for you both..." Hunter squeezed his cup,

stretching the cardboard sleeve to its limit. "If you think having your credit cards cancelled is tough, try having the Austin Police pull you over and handcuff you on the side of the street like a common criminal because your truck was reported as stolen."

Reyes and Parker's jaws dropped. "Are you serious?"

Billy walked up just in time to hear the last few words. "Your truck got stolen?"

"No. That shithead somehow reported my truck stolen and I nearly got arrested." Hunter gestured for them all to sit.

Sanders smirked. "Damn. That must've sucked."

Reyes looked at Sanders. "You're awfully chipper considering everything that's going on."

Billy shrugged. "What's going on?"

This set off another round of angst filled complaining by Reyes and Parker. They spent the next ten minutes spewing out a profanity laced dissertation about the events that had tormented them during the weekend.

"Man, that sounds awful." Sanders shook his head. "I haven't had any issues at all."

The rest of the team looked at him blankly.

He set a bag on the table. "As you requested, four prepaid burner phones. I've also got four FWPD cars reserved to pick up in the morning."

"Good. From this point forward, nobody uses their cell, home or office phones. Use only these burners or the FWPD radios. Same for the cars. If he can't find us, he can't hack us."

Hunter looked at Sanders. "Since you're the only one with a working credit card, you get to buy these guys coffee."

Sanders smiled. "Under the circumstances, I don't mind at all." He took everyone's orders and made his way to the counter as the team settled in with more complaining.

Once coffees were in hands and the level of rage had calmed a bit, the team fell into small talk. Hunter and Stacy filled everyone in on Barkley's recovery.

Hunter leaned forward and looked at the team. "Guys, there's not much we can do today. We'll regroup in the morning, with Sean

Jackson and that super hacker contractor of his." He tried to remember the guy's name. "Richard Malone."

Reyes smirked. "Yeah, don't call him Rick."

Hunter grinned. "Nice to see your sense of humor wasn't permanently impaired by recent events."

Reyes shrugged.

"Maybe Richard will have found something on this guy. Someone has to be able to find him." Hunter cocked his head. "Other than that, we just need to get back to good, old fashioned detective work."

From their dejected expressions and slumped shoulders, their weekends really had taken a toll. They all seemed to share the same sense of defeat. Unless something changed soon, what little trail existed to follow would grow cold and disappear.

Parker shook his head, his coffee untouched. "I'm not sure how good, old fashioned detective work finds someone who's invisible."

Chapter 66

"I've been studying this guy nonstop for the past three days. He's a real piece of work." Malone leaned against the conference room wall and addressed the team.

"No kidding. He took some preemptive action against the team." Hunter motioned to the group. "We all had a pretty rough weekend, dealing with cancelled credit cards and blown up phones." Hunter nodded to Malone. "Hell, I nearly ended up in jail for stealing my own truck."

"What the hell?" Jackson looked shocked.

Hunter spent the next ten minutes recounting to Jackson and Malone all that had happened to him, Reyes, and Parker.

Sanders smiled. "Reyes is still pouting."

"Easy for you. Just wait till that son of a bitch decides to wreck your life. You won't be laughing then."

The team returned their attention to Malone, and he continued. "First of all, he's really good. I've run every kind a reverse trace I know of, and all I've ended up with is a mountain of aliases. Secondly, he's a real sadist. The way he tortured Mike Systrom..." He let the sentence trail off as he shook his head.

"What do you think the chances are that you're going to be able to find him?" Hunter sat with his arms folded.

Malone shrugged. "I'm not completely out of tricks yet, and I've pulled in some favors from buddies, but...I'll be honest. It doesn't look promising."

Reyes pushed his chair back from the table. "Shit. You mean that son of a bitch is going to get away with what he did to us."

Malone smiled. "Detective Reyes, I can assure you, the little bit of misery he caused you over the weekend was child's play. Had he really wanted to fuck you over, you probably wouldn't be here this morning."

That comment seemed to send a cold chill through the room. Everyone went quiet and seemed to be lost in thought when the conference room phone rang.

Hunter punched the button. "Conference room. Detective Hunter speaking."

"Cowboy? Hey, this is Cosner Thompson in Organized Crime. Glad I caught you."

"You're on speaker. What gets us a call from the OCD studs this early on a Monday?"

"Needed to pass some information along. I don't have the full story yet, but I wanted to give you a heads up."

"We're all ears."

"Our visit to Alfred Mazanti may have done some good. I've got a confidential informant who's pretty close to the organization. He called me this morning and told me Alfred went ballistic after we left."

"Did he say why?" Hunter leaned over the phone while looking at his team gathered around the table.

"He couldn't give me a lot of details because we were on the phone. I'm going to meet with him in a couple hours to get the rest. What he did say was Alfred yelled at everyone, demanded they find his nephew. He apparently completely lit up his cyber team. Even threatened to break a guy's hand."

Hunter scratched his forehead. "Who's his nephew?"

"I'm not really sure. They have a big family and my C.I. was reluctant to say anymore over the phone. But whatever was going on, it was directly related to our visit."

"Great, let's talk again as soon as you know more. Maybe we'll get lucky. We could sure use some luck."

Thompson laughed. "Yeah, well, based on what I know about Alfred, it's his nephew who's going to need the most luck."

Richard Malone stood quietly against the wall of the conference room, absorbing the call.

Chapter 67

"I think I'm going blind." Darrel rubbed his eyes with the heels of his hands.

Rows and rows of numbers scrolled across one display while a second showed a map of the greater Dallas / Fort Worth area with blocks grayed out.

"Stop staring at the screen. Just let our beast do its magic." Cliff Wangler looked over his shoulder and seemed energized despite the fact he hadn't slept in two days. "We're good. I spoke to Carlos and explained the plan. He actually seemed to understand. He said he'd keep Mr. Mazanti occupied to give us more time."

"What if Frank's not out there?"

"He's out there." Wangler sounded confident at first. "With his ego, he's got to be." The confidence tapered as he spoke.

A loud buzz scared both men to the point that they jumped.

"Holy shit." Darrel almost hyperventilated.

The rest of the team dropped what they were doing and gathered around the monitors.

Wangler smiled.

A second loud buzz shocked them all again. This time, there was confusion.

"Two hits?" Darrel scrunched his face. "What the fuck?"

Two IP addresses emerged from the scrolling wall of numbers.

A slow smile washed back onto Wangler's face. "That's him. That's fucking him."

"Which one?"

"Both! Think about it. Frank would absolutely have two laptops rolling at the same time." Wangler slapped Darrel on the back. "Damn, we're good! Okay, before we do anything, we need to all be ready to move. Once we flip the switch on the GPS sensors on those laptops, we'll probably have less than a minute to get the coordinates before he realizes he's compromised. Once he does, there's no telling what he'll do."

* * * *

Hunter surveyed the city view outside the window in the conference room. Absorbing the late morning sun as his mind sifted through all the pieces to the puzzle. The real problem wasn't the pieces he knew and couldn't fit together, it was the pieces that were still missing.

"Gentlemen." Detective Thompson entered the room and grinned like he'd just finished off the cookie jar. "How are you all doing this fine morning?"

Reyes was still grumpy. "We'll be doing better if you've got some actionable intel for us."

"Prepare to drool." He held up a folder and slipped it onto the table in front of them. "I think we've got something. Christmas came early."

"Tell us about it." Hunter turned, but kept his arms crossed. Any good news he'd take with a big grain of salt.

"Happy to." Thompson dramatically opened the folder. "Francis, a.k.a. Frank, a.k.a. Frankie Lorenzo Conte is a former Mazanti family hacker. Apparently, one of the best. He also happens to be Alfred Mazanti's nephew." Thompson couldn't contain himself, stopping every few sentences to watch the awe on his audience's faces. When they all just stared back at him waiting for the punchline, he continued. "It seems Francis wasn't a very happy player in the family business. Thought his talents were wasted. About a year ago, after a nasty throw down with his father and uncle, he vowed revenge and disappeared. No one's seen or heard from him since."

Hunter straightened and gestured for the folder. "They have now."

"Heeeee'ssss baaaack." The glint returned in Reyes' eyes.

Thompson handed the folder to Hunter as Hunter rolled his eyes at Reyes. He skimmed through the documents in the folder, stopping at a set of photos. The top picture was a large headshot of Francis Lorenzo Conte.

Hunter's face dropped and he went pale for a brief moment before exploding.

Sneering back at him from the color photo was Richard Malone.

"That son of a bitch!"

*   *   *   *

"I'm back is right boys. How's that for spitting in your eye?"

Frank clapped his hands with delight as he watched the scene unfold from the conference room on one of his monitors.

All the time and effort to get into the team's war room was well worth it. The shock on Hunter's face was priceless.

"My show is so much better than reality TV. I should call it the Frank Conte Hour. A cross between True Detective and Toddlers & Tiaras."

He turned up the volume on the video feed to Hunter's stumbling over his words, angrily pacing, yelling and kicking chairs.

*   *   *   *

Hunter held up the photo, almost crushing it in his grip. He looked at Thompson. ""This is Francis Conte?

"Uh, yeah." Thompson was confused by Hunter's reaction.

"You'd better not be punking me. I will come across this table and whip your ass if you're fucking with me."

"Dude, I'm not fucking with you. Do you know him?"

"Do I know him?" He shot back.

He held up the photo so the team could see.

He might has well have dropped a lit match into a bucket of gasoline. The room just exploded. Each man spat out his own profanity laced rant and tossed over the rest of the chairs.

Thompson watched in wonder. "What the hell is wrong with you guys? Will someone please clue me in?"

"I'll clue you in." Reyes sputtered. "Francis Lorenzo Conte is

Richard Malone."

"Who?"

"We hired an outside cyber security expert to help us with the case. Richard Malone was here less than two hours ago. In this very room." Reyes shook his head. "Richard Malone and Francis Conte are the same fucking person."

"The guy we were looking for is the same guy we hired to find him!" Hunter threw a marker so hard, it exploded on impact with the wall.

Thompson blanched. "Oh, my God."

*   *   *   *

"I wanted to have you on the phone when we set everything in motion because you're going to have to move fast. As soon as we turn on the GPS sensors, he's going to know, and my guess is that he'll be out the door in minutes." Wangler struggled to catch his breath.

Carlos' smile could almost be felt through the phone. "Great. Where is he?"

"Oh, well, we don't have an address yet, but we're a couple of keystrokes away. We've found his computers, and wherever they are, he'll be close by."

Carlos was quiet for a moment. "Okay." His voice was overly calm. "Can you at least give me an area or part of town?"

Wangler nodded as if Carlos could see him. "Somewhere north of I-30."

"Hmm." Carlos groaned. "That leaves a hell of a lot of ground to cover."

"I think we can apply some logic and eliminate more." He started walking around the table as he spoke into the phone. "He was born and raised in Fort Worth. What are the odds of a Fort Worth native relocating to Dallas?"

"Okay."

"I think they're slim. So, he's probably west of DFW Airport. He's too city-fied to be on the northwest side of town. He's not a Lake Worth or Saginaw kind of guy. So that means he's probably east of I-35."

"Okay." Carlos slowed as if he wrote down the directions. "North of I-30, east of I-35 and west of DFW Airport?"

"Most likely."

"I'll call you when I'm ready."

Cliff Wangler's chest tightened. Giving this information to Carlos meant that Frank Conte would be kidnapped, torutured and likely killed. He fought to convince himself that wasn't his fault. He was just providing information, and making sure Darrel and the team survived. "I'll have my finger on the button."

* * * *

Hunter feverishly sorted through the pages in the folder, now determined to find this piece of dirt. He'd easily screwed with so many people's lives, destroyed dozens more, and then had the audacity to go after Hunter himself.

Not on my watch.

"So, where is he?"

Thompson shrugged. "We don't know. He's been off grid for a year."

Hunter turned to Sanders. "Get Sean Jackson's ass up here now. We need to see if he's got an address, phone number…something."

"Will do." Billy reached for the phone.

Thompson leaned against the wall. "Cowboy. If it's any consolation, it may not matter."

"Why's that?"

"Because according to my C.I., Mazanti's tech team think they're close to finding him. When that happens, he'll be nothing more than digital dust."

"Hell no. This guy's *mine.*

* * * *

"Aw, your tough talk is so cute. Fools." Frank spun in his chair and laughed as he watch Hunter throw his fit. "You really think you're going to find me. As if I'd give that dork IT guy my real contact info. C plus for effort boys, but you'll never make the big leagues."

He stopped spinning and smiled at the monitor. "As for Uncle Alfred's B team… Are you kidding me? Those dorks couldn't hack their way into a library, much less find me. I carried them on my backs the whole time I was there."

He stood and sashayed over to the kitchen. "I think this calls for a Big Red and a Pop Tart."

* * * *

"We're in position." Carlos breathed through the phone. "Punch your fancy button."

"The second we find him, he's going to see us." Wangler explained.

"Just do it!" The man barked back. "I don't have all day."

Wangler twisted in his chair, and took a deep breath over his keyboard. He tapped out a set of short commands.

The monitor started flashing. A set of coordinates popped up. Then another.He turned to the monitor with the map and transferred the coordinates onto the map.

"Both laptops are showing at the same address. 909 South Main Street in Grapevine. Go. Hurry!"

Silence filled the phone.

* * * *

"What the hell?" Frank's face paled. He dropped his drink and snack onto the tabletop. "Oh no. No, no!"

The main monitor flashed an ugly red warning message.

"That's impossible. How the hell did my GPS sensors turn on?"

He frantically pounded on the keyboard. Within seconds, he'd successfully turned off the sensors. For a moment, he just sat and stared at the settings screen.

How could that have happened?

Screens flashed across the monitor at a blinding pace as his hands flew over the keyboards. He checked firewalls, registers and logs.

Then everything stopped. It finally hit him.

"Oh, God. They found me. How the fuck did they find me?"

His stomach churned, and the Big Red infused pop tart threatened to come back up. He'd wasted almost ten minutes trying to figure it out. Those bastards were probably down the street at this point kicking in doors.

He had to move fast.

He yanked all the cords out of both laptops, grabbed their power cables and ran for the bedroom. In the back of the closet, he tore open a black duffle bag. Inside the go-bag were all his essentials. Including a stack of cash, a bundle of fake documents, and a loaded 9mm semi-automatic pistol with a box of ammo to go with it.

He tucked the gun in his waistband, tossed the laptops and cables into the bag, zipped it up and ran for the door.

"Not today, you bastards."

*   *   *   *

"Enough of this bullshit. I want everyone focused on this completely. We're going to find this asshole." Hunter was up and pacing. "Billy, pull in help from patrol if we need. I want multiple teams working. We need someone scouring the county property records, automobile titles, DMV, voter registration, credit cards and phone records."

Sanders nodded.

"He's got to have bought something, drove something or lived somewhere in his own name. Whatever that was, we're going to find it. And when we do, we'll find him."

*   *   *   *

Frank didn't bother to wait for the elevator. That thing was slow as hell and he didn't have the cycles. He took the stairs two at a time down to the apartment complex's parking garage. He tossed his bag into the front passenger seat and smoked the tires as he backed out. He had to get out of here, find a new base of operations, and then figure out how to get out of the country.

The exit for the garage poured out onto West Nash. He took a hard right and another onto South Main Street in Grapevine. At the intersection of South Main and East Dallas Road, three shiny black Suburbans blew through the red light. Then screeched to a stop in front of his apartment building.

He ducked his head.

An army of men all in street clothes piled out of the SUVs. Several of them had failed to properly conceal long shotguns at their sides, while others grabbed for their pistols. They raced into his building.

His light turned green. He accelerated slowly through the intersection, and drove north through downtown Grapevine.

In the rearview mirror, none of them followed.

His heart thundered out of control, and he swallowed back vomit.

Chapter 68

Hunter was back at the window again, staring at the sun, which had moved four hours further west since the morning session. His shadow now projected against the far wall. He felt like his head was going to explode. Every part of his being ached, but he suspected it had nothing to do with his diagnosis.

"Hey, boss." Reyes shuffled into the room.

Based on his friend's crestfallen tone of voice, Hunter didn't even bother turning around. "Let me guess. You got nothing."

"I think I checked every car title and car lease in the state for the past ten years. No version of Francis Conte. Apparently, that bastard must use a magic carpet, because he sure as hell doesn't drive."

"He's apparently never voted or had a driver's license either." Blaine Parker walked in and slapped his notebook down on the table. "We're chasing a fucking ghost."

"If he can make false records appear, he can certainly delete records that prove he exists." Hunter pursed his lips.

In the window's reflection, Sean Jackson sheepishly stood at the door, avoiding making eye contact with anyone.

"Don't just stand there." Hunter turned around. "You really can't make my day any worse."

"I'm so sorry, Detective Hunter." He stepped into the room, his hands in his pockets. "I still can't believe that Richard Malone is really Francis Conte. I had no idea. All the identification he provided looked so real." He lowered his head. "I feel so stupid for bringing him into the investigation."

"It's not your fault. The guy's a pro. He fooled us all." He shrugged and gripped the back of a chair. "Did you find anything on him?"

Jackson shook his head. "Every shred of information he provided was false. His ID, address, phone numbers, email. Everything."

Hunter frowned. "As expected."

Sanders burst into the room. "We got him!"

All heads turned his way as he almost levitated from the door to the whiteboard. "Ten months ago, a 'Frank Lorenzo' rented an apartment in Grapevine. It's got to be him."

Hunter moved toward the door, scooping his burner phone from the table. "Reyes, get to work on a warrant. I don't care who you have to piss off or run over to get it, but you've got about thirty minutes." When he reached the door, he snapped his fingers and pointed at Parker. "Get Zeke on the phone. Give him the address and tell him to meet Billy and me there ASAP."

Billy tossed Parker the folder with the information. "I'll call you from the truck. Everything's in there."

Sanders sprinted to catch up with Hunter as they flew down the stairs and out the back door of the station.

"This better be him. I'm tired of chasing my ass."

*   *   *   *

The team moved down the hall in formation, quietly and quickly, working off of hand signals from Zeke. Hunter and Sanders followed the heavily armed and armored SWAT teams from Grapevine and Fort Worth. Once they found the door to Frank Conte's apartment, they split with equal numbers on each side of the door.

Standing to the side of the door, Hunter reached his arm across and pounded his fist on the door. "Frank Conte, this is the police. We have a warrant. We're coming in."

Hunter nodded to the SWAT officer with the battering ram. In one swift move, he slammed the huge hunk of metal against the door. The wooden thing exploded into the apartment. Before the splinters hit the floor, SWAT members surged through the threshold and inside the apartment.

It sounded like a category five hurricane as the officers identified themselves and cleared rooms. In seconds, all the chaos was over.

Empty.

Hunter stepped over the door splinters inside the apartment. A massive typhoon of destruction lay before him, none of it caused by the SWAT team. Furniture was overturned, drawers and cabinets were open and papers littered everywhere like confetti. The twisted perp had converted his bedroom into a high-tech workstation. The destruction was even worse in here, with shattered monitors, severed cables and busted cameras.

He ground his teeth together.

"What the hell?" Sanders looked from behind Hunter's shoulder.

"Mazanti beat us here."

"How?"

Hunter thought for a moment, and then remembered what Thompson had said. "Mazanti's tech team. Frank was the leader of it for a while. They must have found him online somehow and then backtracked to a physical location. His thugs did the rest."

"I wonder if they got Frank."

Hunter shook his head. "Doubt it. They wouldn't have needed to trash the place."

"So, Frank's now on the run from both the Mazanti family and the police?" Sanders huffed. "Serves the bastard right."

Hunter nodded. "Get a BOLO out on him. Every airport, bus station, train station, and toll booth. I want them using everything at their disposal—facial recognition, patrols, helicopters, dogs, drones, whatever they've got."

Sanders nodded, took out his phone and headed for the hallway.

Hunter surveyed the apartment. Before the destruction, Frank had lived a sparse, but meticulous life. He took out his burner phone and punched in a number.

"Detective Cosner Thompson, how can I help you?"

"Thompson, this is Jake Hunter. We need another audience with Alfred Mazanti."

"Um, okay. I'll see what I can do."

"This is not a request. I'm going to be at his door first thing in the morning."

Thompson paused. "I'll meet you there."

Chapter 69

"What's our game plan?" Thompson looked concerned when he met Hunter in the lobby of Afred Mazanti's building. "You look very...focused."

Hunter had been up early on Tuesday morning. The reality was that he slept very little, so when the sun cracked the horizon, he decided to beat the traffic to get to the west side of downtown. He stopped at a Starbucks on University, just north of West Seventh. He sat, absorbed the vibe, and sipped his coffee. With each sip, he sorted through the case in his head until it was time to drive around the corner and meet Thompson.

"It's simple. For once in the history of man, Mazanti and I want the same thing, and neither of us are equipped to achieve it by ourselves."

Thompson tilted his head. "I see your logic, but I'm not sure I agree with your baseline assumption. While you may want to capture Frank Conte, Alfred wants to kill him."

"Well, there's that." Hunter arched an eyebrow. "Let's just hope I can convince him that my way is better for everyone."

"Good luck."

*   *   *   *

"Gentlemen, follow me." Carlos del Gado met the detectives at the door, repeated his security process the same as before, complete with frisking, and led them to the balcony once again. This morning was cooler, but the view was just an impressive.

"Apparently, you two must really like my balcony." Alfred, in his matching jogging suit, gestured for them to sit. "How can I exhibit my cooperation and help local law enforcement today?"

Hunter didn't sit this time. He looked Mazanti directly in the eyes. "We need you to help us find your nephew."

The slightest tick raised Alfred's brow before he smiled. "Detective, I'm Italian. We have big families. I have over a dozen nephews. You're gonna have to be a little more specific."

"The same nephew your...associates missed in Grapevine yesterday. Francis Lorenzo Conte. Better known as Frank or Frankie."

Mazanti waved him off. "I'm not sure what you're talking about with that Grapevine stuff, but I haven't seen Frankie in almost a year. He wasn't cut out for the family business, so he decided to go off on his own." He leaned back in his chair, stretching out his legs in front of him like a lounger. "Why are you looking for Frankie?"

"The same reason you are. He's responsible for the shooting deaths of two of your associates."

Mazanti laughed. "You must be thinking of the wrong Frankie. My nephew would barely know how to fire a gun, much less actually shoot someone."

"Mr. Mazanti, let's stop playing games." Hunter finally sat opposite the mob boss, leaning forward. "You and I both know Frank used his cyber skills to manipulate innocent people into committing those murders. We also both know that your tech team found him, but your retrieval timing was just a few minutes off yesterday."

Mazanti merely sat and stared at him, waiting for him to continue. Not even a flicker of an eyelash.

"Here's the deal. If you continue down the path you're currently on and you find him, and you take matters into your own hands, I assure you I will find enough evidence to lock you up for a few decades on conspiracy to commit murder charges."

Mazanti yawned and crossed his feet in front of him. He said nothing.

"However, if you cooperate with me and we work together to find him, you can continue to enjoy this lovely view for a little while longer."

Mazanti nodded slowly, breathed in the crisp air and observed the sights around him. "You've made a lot of assumptions." He nodded toward Thompson. "After all, your buddy there has spent half his career trying to put me behind bars, and yet, here I sit on my luxury patio furniture overlooking the skyline like a king."

"Mr. Mazanti…" Hunter's voice remained calm. "We both want the same thing. We want Frank to pay for what he did." He shrugged. "You have a small handful of associates, but my team is huge. My team includes every law enforcement agency in the country from the TSA to the FBI and everyone in between. We've got every transit point in North Texas covered."

"Then why do you need me?"

"Because your team of *hackers* proactively found him once, and my gut says they can find him again. When they do, instead of chasing around town with a couple of SUVs full of muscle, I can mobilize an army where he won't get away."

Mazanti seemed to contemplate the possibility, but didn't respond.

"Besides…" Hunter raised an eyebrow. "Once he's in the Texas Prison System, you'll know exactly where he is. In case you want to visit him." He paused. "It goes without saying that Frank being in prison beats the hell out of you being in prison."

Several beats passed and clouds shifted overhead, scattering the sunlight across the balcony. Mazanti finally lifted a hand and motioned for his second. "Carlos, can you please introduce these two fine detectives to our team of nerds. Tell that ballsy one to cooperate and help them find Frankie."

*　　*　　*　　*

The room smelled like the remnants of a week-old pizza party in a men's locker room. Hunter and Thompson nearly gagged when they walked in.

Carlos pointed to a ragged looking group of eight pale, sleep-deprived men scattered throughout a large conference room cluttered with laptops, desktops, servers and cables.

Like a refugee camp for nerds.

"This is the team." Disgust wrapped around the man's words.

He gestured for one of the men to come over and introduced him as Cliff Wangler. "These men are detectives with the Fort Worth Police Department. Mr. Mazanti wants you to help them find Frankie."

Wangler gave Carlos an incredulous look. "You're kidding, right?"

Carlos glared at him, his shoulders arching back slightly. "Do I look like I'm kidding?"

The smile slid off Wangler's face. "No. uh, exactly what do you mean by cooperate?"

Carlos fisted his hands as he turned toward Wangler like he might punch him.

Hunter stepped in between them. "Maybe I can explain."

Carlos took a half step back.

Hunter held out his hand. "I'm Detective Jake Hunter. This is Detective Cosner Thompson."

He shook Hunter's hand. "I guess you'd call me the team supervisor. This is a little...abnormal for us."

"I can imagine." Hunter nodded. "We just left a meeting with Mr. Mazanti. I convinced him that since we're both looking for his nephew, Frank, it would be in everyone's best interest if we worked together."

Wangler cocked his head. "Mr. Mazanti working with the cops? Impressive."

"I have my moments." Hunter kept a close sideways eye on Carlos, just in case he decided to move things in the wrong direction. "The reality is you found him before we did yesterday. My guess is you're probably our best shot at finding him again."

Wangler shot one last concerned glance at Carlos. "You're sure Mr. Mazanti wants us to work together? With the police?"

Carlos arched an eyebrow. "Are you really going to make me say it twice?"

After a deep, disbelieving breath, Wangler nodded. "Well, then, detective, how can I help you?"

"Why don't you start by telling us how you found him yesterday."

The man's face lit up. "That was a work of art..."

For the next thirty minutes, Wangler used the whiteboard to explain about worms, zero day software vulnerabilities, weaponized exploits, geo fencing, GPS sensors, IP addresses and back doors.

Through most of it, Hunter and Thompson listened intently, nodded occasionally and asked a few questions.

"As soon as he booted up, we engaged the GPS sensor and triangulated his coordinates. Of course, he also knew instantly we'd done it, and he was able to disappear from his location before our team arrived." Wangler shrugged like he'd lost a life in his video game.

Hunter nodded. "So, that's where I think we can add some value to this equation. You guys may be better at finding, but we've got law enforcement resources essentially everywhere, so we can deploy faster and with more force." Hunter paused. "That is, of course, if you think you can find him again."

Wangler smiled. "Assuming he hasn't ditched his laptops… I'd be stunned if he did because I'm sure he's got them tricked out in every possible way. But as long as he's still using them, we can find him again. The real question is, do you want him to know we found him, or do you want it to be a surprise?"

"We have a choice?"

"Maybe." Wangler drew on the whiteboard again. "When we cracked his systems the first time, we embedded a program we can activate anytime we want, which will give us essentially the same results as before. But he'll know it instantly, and since he'll be looking for it, my guess is he'll disappear even faster this time."

"What's the alternative?"

"It's a bit of a longshot. We assume he's on the move now, which means the next time he connects, he'll be somewhere public, like a hotel, restaurant, bar, train station or airport. We can plant a surveillance worm onto any public or semi-public wifi network within a geographic area. That worm is programmed to do only one thing, sit and wait until one of those two laptops signs onto that network. When it does, we get a notification. At that point, we'll know what network he's on, which will give us a location."

"And he wouldn't know he's been detected?"

"Nope, because nothing ever hits his system." Wangler smiled with pride.

Hunter almost matched it. Maybe...just maybe they could nail him this way.

"How long will it take to get this worm in place?"

"A couple hours to build it, and if we restrict it to the DFW area, another couple hours for it to be distributed." He shrugged. "Then it's just a waiting game."

Hunter nodded. "How accurate is the location? What radius are we talking about?" Just the possibility of nailing this guy while he was busy tinkering on his laptop jazzed up his adrenaline.

"Depends on the size of the network, but within a city block, give or take. Most of these networks are designed to service one set of customers. A Starbucks network covers the size of the store. It bleeds over into the parking lot a bit, but not much. Whereas the public wifi at DFW is designed to cover an entire terminal. Just depends on what they need."

"Let's hope he signs on at a Starbucks."

Chapter 70

"Detective Barkley, this is not a court of law. However, you should consider all decisions from this panel to be as binding, with no appeal."

The panel of three high-ranking Texas Rangers officials might as well have been a court, his judges and jury all wrapped into this one hearing. A Texas Ranger Inspector General played the prosecutor. He was the defendant. His life and career in their hands.

The Inspector General grilled him on the witness stand for the past hour. The lawyer stood ramrod straight, his chiseled features stern and severe. His suit, while not expensive, was crisp and clean. Each question more damning than the previous.

"Detective Barkley, upon your return to Austin after the injuries you sustained in Fort Worth, were you put on unpaid administrative leave and told not pursue this case further?"

"Yes, sir."

"Were you told to transition your case notes and all leads to a fellow detective?"

"Yes, sir."

"When you learned of Harley Lundsford's location, did you pass that on to your fellow detective?"

"No, sir."

"When you and the Fort Worth PD detective found Harley Lundsford in Austin, did you call for backup?"

"No, sir."

"Did you call for a warrant?"

"No, sir."

The Inspector General scowled and stalked in front of the

witness stand like a lion. "Let's summarize. You disobeyed direct orders to stand down. You hunted Harley Lundsford to an Austin backyard with no warrant, engaged in a shootout with him, during which he shot you with your own weapon, all of which ended in his fatality with two shots to the head. Is that correct?"

His stomach clenched. Every single statement he made was a nail in his coffin. But at the very beginning, he'd sworn on the Bible to tell the whole truth. "Yes, sir."

The inspector general faced the panelists. "I have nothing further."

What was left of Barkley's energy drained.

His union-provided attorney shuffled over and stood in front of him. The fifty-something man moved more like he was in his sixties, and his clothes seemed a size too large.

"Detective Barkley." His slow Texas drawl was almost as slow as he walked. "You've been a Texas Ranger for ten years, correct?"

"Yes."

"In that time you've received five special commendations, right?"

"Correct."

"Why did you proceed with Congressman Cheek's request to find his daughter without backup or an official case opened?"

Barkley kept his deep breath discreet. He knew better than anyone these answers would probably end his career. But he promised to tell the truth.

"Congressman Cheek was concerned the traffickers holding his daughter would injure her worse or even kill her if they suspected law enforcement was involved. I did this as a personal favor to him and his family."

"Did your investigation lead to any arrests?"

"Yes. Three human traffickers, Evan Monaco, Joshua Floyd, and David Gardner."

"Did your investigation end a human trafficking ring?"

"Yes."

"Did your investigation recover illegal firearms and money?"

"Yes."

"Did you rescue Congressman Cheek's daughter, Kaci?"

"Yes, sir."

"You risked your own life several times to ensure her recovery, correct?"

"Yes, sir."

He smiled. "That sounds more like an entire career, than a week."

The panel of judges didn't return the smile. The prosecutor scowled.

His lawyer continued. "Detective Barkley, were your instincts correct?"

"Yes, sir."

"Did you accomplish your mission?"

"Yes, sir."

His attorney nodded slowly. "I have nothing further."

The ranking member of the panel acknowledged the conclusion of questioning. "This court will take a short recess as we deliberate. Our decision will be rendered shortly."

His gavel slammed down, the sound ripped through Barkley. He stood until all panel members stepped out of the room, and then he followed his own attorney out into the lobby. His steps on the granite floor echoed off the wood paneled walls.

He gulped from the water fountain, hoping the cool water would ease some of his anxiety.

"How long do you think they'll take?" he asked.

"I don't think too long. Maybe an hour?"

"Is that good or bad?" He adjusted his suit coat, and tapped his foot.

Away from anyone else's earshot, his lawyer kept his voice low. "No telling at this point. We did our best. You told the whole truth up there, which is what they needed most. The letters from Congressman Cheek and your commanding officer requesting leniency should help. Let's hope your long and distinguished career can save this thing."

The main doors creaked open and an aide stepped out calling them back in.

"Less than five minutes?" Barkley muttered under his breath.

His breakfast threatened to come back up.

His lawyer sighed. "We're about to find out."

Once everyone filed back into the main room, Barkley stood before the panelists, his head high. The temperature in the room had skyrocketed in the last minute.

The Inspector General and all three panelists wore the same stoic expressions.

"We're ready to render our judgement." The lead panelist cleared his throat.

*   *   *   *

"Can I tell you something?" Wangler nervously tapped his fingers on the table as he and Darrel stared at the monitor. Fighting boredom was quickly becoming a losing battle.

It was late afternoon on Tuesday. After several days of working almost around the clock, the rest of the team had gone home.

"What's up?"

"Mr. Mazanti called me directly earlier today."

Darrel straightened and arched an eyebrow at Wangler. "No shit? What did he want?"

"He made it clear when our worm finds Frank, I'm to call him and not the cops."

"Okay? So what?"

"So what?" Wangler looked at Darrel incredulously. "Dude, Mazanti is going to kill Frank. I mean, like chop off his head and stuff it full of shit dead."

"Yeah, well, not our issue."

Wangler let his mouth drop. "You're okay with contributing to someone's murder?"

"Better him than us."

Wangler folded his arms across his chest. "You may be okay with it, but I'm not. I don't want his blood on my hands."

Darrel frowned. "It's your call, but you'd better be prepared. If Mazanti thinks you disobeyed his direct order, it'll be your blood spilled, not Frank's."

Wangler leaned back in his chair, his face a little pale and his voice raspy. "Yeah, I know."

*   *   *   *

"Have we gotten anything?" Hunter had stepped out on his own for lunch and had walked down to Sundance Square to clear his head. It may have helped his head, but his mood was the same erratic and anxious.

"Some false alarms on facial recognition at DFW. Wasn't close enough to bother calling you." Sanders shrugged.

Hunter frowned. He was back in the conference room, but didn't bother sitting down, he just started pacing and rubbing his forehead.

"You know what the song says?" Reyes grinned. "Waiting is the hardest part."

Hunter rolled his eyes and kept pacing.

Sanders followed Hunter with his eyes. "Have you heard anything from Mazanti's team?"

"They deployed the surveillance worm just before lunch. Takes a couple hours to spread through the metroplex." Hunter stared at the whiteboard full of case notes. "Now, we just wait and hope he isn't already out of the country."

*   *   *   *

Barkley stepped out of the building and into the early afternoon sunlight. He adjusted his white Stetson and tugged on the sling. It didn't help. Something just didn't feel right.

He patted his blazer's chest pocket.

The familiar weight wasn't there.

He closed his eyes and fought against biting his lip.

No badge.

Ten years with the Rangers, gone.

Without even an opportunity to walk around the office and shake hands.

His chest felt as empty as his pocket.

What am I supposed to do now?

"Colt." His lawyer stepped up beside him. "I'm sorry we couldn't do more to save your career with the Rangers." He sighed heavily. "Under the circumstances, keeping you out of jail was the best I could do."

Barkley nodded and stared at the Austin cityscape. The sky looked smaller somehow.

"I know. I appreciate all you did. It's just gonna take some adjusting."

"Didn't Congressman Cheek offer you a job? I'm sure someone with your reputation won't have trouble landing somewhere."

A sad smile crept across Barkley's face as he looked down at the ground. "I'm not too worried about finding a job. I wasn't looking for one when I joined the Rangers."

*　　*　　*　　*

Hunter stopped pacing when the burner phone in his pocket buzzed. He hadn't bothered to upload his contacts to the temporary phone so no caller ID appeared. But the familiar 512 area code indicated an Austin number. He headed for the conference room door as he punched the button to answer.

"Hunter."

"Hey, Cowboy, it's Colt."

For a long moment neither man spoke. The silence hung on the line.

Hunter finally broke that. "How'd it go today?"

"The good news is I won't be going to jail."

He leaned against the wall in the hall. "And?"

"Looks like I'm officially a free agent."

His heart fell.

"Damn." Hunter searched his mind for the right thing to say, but with something like this nothing would suffice. "I'm sorry. Is there anything I can do?"

"No. I just need some time to digest. I'll be fine."

"Have you told Chelsea?"

"No. I'm headed home now. She has the day off."

Hunter didn't respond.

Barkley filled in the silence. "If you ever need a free agent, give me a call."

Hunter thought about his own situation. Once he told Sprabary about his condition, he would likely also be a free agent.

"You never know what the future might hold. Give Chelsea a hug for me."

Chapter 71

"You have plans this evening?" Hunter rubbed his eyes and looked over at Billy. He leaned back in a chair with his feet up on the conference room table.

"Just hanging out at the house waiting for your call."

Hunter nodded. "Here's a thought. We've purposely kept Frank's face out of the media so he'd feel comfortable staying in the area. While we have no way to know where he's hiding out, we do know he's spent the last year living in Grapevine." He pulled his feet off the table and leaned forward. "Assuming he's even still in the country, he probably hasn't gone too far."

"Right. So?"

"So, my guess is that he's somewhere in Northeast Tarrant County. If that's the case, I want to have some of us in that region."

"Okay. Makes sense."

"So why don't you come hang out at the house with me? We can order a pizza, watch ESPN and chill until Wangler calls."

"Sounds like a plan." Sanders smiled. "As long as you keep that monster cat away from me."

* * * *

The Grayson Resort Hotel was one of the largest hotels in the country. With over 1,800 guest rooms on the shores of Lake Grapevine, the expansive destination boasted its own convention center and water park. The magnificent ground floor atrium included six restaurants, two bars and multiple shopping outlets. If someone was looking for a place to get lost in the crowd, he couldn't pick a better spot.

Frank Conte hid in plain sight enjoying the luxury provided by a four-star resort the size of a small city. For now, all he needed to do was relax, sip world class tequila and get his laptops back fully operational. Before his flight to Costa Rica on early Wednesday morning.

Once he'd calmed down and was certain he wasn't followed, he had to admit he was impressed with his former colleagues. They'd created a worm that found him easily with a fine piece of computer coding. Of course, he'd been able to disable it with just a few keystrokes, but he was still impressed.

"Can I get you another drink, sir?"

Frank sat at the Texan Station bar located in the resort's center atrium. The wall of televisions from floor to ceiling displayed various football and soccer games with the plush leather seats mostly full for game day drinking.

"I'm good for the moment, but can you tell me the wifi code?"

"It's just your last name and your room number."

"Thanks." Frank needed to make some final arrangements for his departure. He took another sip and popped open his laptop.

*   *   *   *

"Let's do something other than pizza tonight. After these last few days, I never want pizza again."

Cliff Wangler smiled. "I'm up for anything that'll deliver. I want to make sure we're both here when the alarm goes off."

"Don't you mean 'if' the alarm goes off?"

"Have a little faith."

Darrel frowned. "If I were in Frank's shoes, I would've been in Mexico months ago."

"That's the point. Frank always believed he was bulletproof. He was the smartest guy in the room. His arrogance kept him here for the past year, and before this is all over, that's what's going to get him killed."

"Better him than us."

Wangler swallowed, his mouth turning dry.

A loud buzz from his laptop jolted his nerves. Adrenaline coursed through his system. He began clicking away on the keyboard.

311

"Where is he?" Darrel looked over Wangler's shoulder.

"Shit," Wangler breathed, then laughed. "Well, that sure as hell isn't a Starbucks."

"Where, dammit?"

"He's at the Grayson Resort."

Wangler just sat there and stared at the monitor. The gall on this guy amazed him. He was no more than a few miles from the last time they'd found him. But he'd found him. The best black hat he'd ever met, and Cliff Wangler had found him, twice.

Take that, you prick.

Darrel shook his shoulder. "What are you waiting for? Call Carlos."

Any happiness or excitement drained from his face. "I don't know."

"What the fuck do you mean, you don't know? Do you want to die? Call Carlos and call him now."

Wangler picked up his phone, then set it back down. He stared at it. There was a lot to gain by picking up that phone...and even more to lose.

"Dude! Call him!"

"Okay." Wangler picked up the phone and punched in the number.

Carlos answered in his understated way. "Yes."

"Carlos, it's Cliff. We found Frank."

"Where?"

"At the Grayson Resort in Grapevine."

The slight delay before Carlos responded sent a shiver down Cliff's spine.

"You think you could narrow it down? That place is enormous."

"It's all on the same wifi network, so all I can see is that he's on the property."

"Shit. Okay. You haven't call the cops have you?"

"Not yet."

"Give me fifteen minutes before you do." He clicked off.

Cliff set down the phone on the table.

Darrel smiled. "No fucking pizza tonight. I'm going home. See ya." He was up and out the door in seconds.

Cliff Wangler sat in the silence. He looked at his watch. Two minutes had passed. He thought about Frank.

The guy really was a dick.

Everything he'd done was more of a family matter than anything. There was no need to intervene or get involved. He needed to just step away.

All I did was my job.

I'm not one of Mazanti's thugs.

I'm not pulling the trigger.

His stomach twisted. For a moment, he thought he was going to puke. He looked at his phone, tapped his fingers on the table. He felt dizzy and his hands turned clammy.

"Shit." He reached for the phone and punched in a number.

* * * *

"I hope you like pepperoni. It should be here any minute. I ordered it on the drive." Hunter walked in the front door with Sanders trailing him. "Grab some beers from the fridge. I'll meet you on the back patio in a minute. Panther needs dinner, too."

The rotund black cat eyed Hunter as if he wondered why the man was in his house.

"Don't give me that attitude. Remember, I'm the one that feeds you. Besides, we have company."

Hunter finished dishing out his food about the time the doorbell rang. He paid for the pizza and joined Sanders on the patio as the sun faded in the western sky. He dropped the pizza on the table, popped the top on a beer and nodded toward the horizon. "I can't believe I'm wasting that gorgeous sunset on a slug like you."

Billy smiled. "The feeling is mutual, my friend."

They clinked their bottle necks together and relaxed with their dinner.

Sanders choked down a couple of bites and wiped his mouth. "Did you hear from Barkley today?"

Hunter nodded and frowned. "Yeah. Not good. He lost his

badge."

"Shit." Sanders bowed his head. "That sucks."

Hunter didn't respond immediately. He just watched the sky and absorbed the colors as they swirled and flowed. He hadn't had a chance to talk with Billy about his situation. Maybe there was a better time and place to start that whole debacle, and he certainly didn't want to add any more stress on top of anyone else's shoulders.

But maybe there really isn't a better time.

He forced a deep breath. "Speaking of sucking...there's something I need to—"

His phone buzzed. He grabbed it and punched the button.

"Hunter here."

"Detective, this is Cliff Wangler. We found him."

Hunter jumped up, gestured for Sanders to follow, and headed toward the front door. Leaving the uneaten pizza and full beer bottle behind. "Where is he?"

"The Grayson Resort."

"Shit. That place is massive. Anyway to narrow it down?"

"Unfortunately, no." Wangler paused. "You should know Carlos and his men are already on the way. He forced me to tell him first. He told me to give him a fifteen minute head start. I only gave him three."

Hunter jumped into the driver's seat of the unmarked FWPD sedan. "Call Reyes, Parker and Zeke. Tell them to get their asses to the Grayson Resort immediately. Frank's there somewhere. Mazanti's goons have a head start."

Chapter 72

Oh shit.

Frank almost dropped his glass as he looked across the open expanse of the hotel ground floor and saw eight identically dressed men enter from the valet parking entrance. Each wore a tightly tailored, expensive suit stretched over their muscled torsos. He'd seen dozens like these before when he worked in his uncle's organization.

The men stopped in the open air space where the restaurants, bars and shopping outlets converged to serve hundreds of hotel guests. Their gazes scanned through the scenery and crowds. The leader of the group — so Frank surmised from all the hand signals — sent the men off in pairs in four different directions.

This is definitely not part of my plan.

Frank dropped a twenty dollar bill on the bar, nodded to the bartender, and headed for the elevator. He camouflaged himself as much as possible, staying behind the crowds of guests and his head down.

His mind raced as he moved quickly, discreetly trying to keep the eight men in his sight.

How the hell did they find me this time?

*   *   *   *

The tires smoked on the asphalt as Hunter turned north on Grayson Trail off Highway 26. Sanders gripped the handle and worked his phone in the passenger seat. Three Grapevine PD patrol cars followed closely, along with Reyes in his unmarked sedan. Lights and sirens bounced off the building and landscape when the caravan roared to the back of the resort. The vehicles screeched to a stop under the covered valet parking area, several lanes wide.

The officers poured out of the cars. Hunter yelled to Reyes to get Frank's room number from the front desk.

Reyes nodded. "On it, boss."

Just outside the main doors, a lean man in a blue blazer and nametag waited. Hunter assumed this was the Head of Security Sanders had called to text him a photo of Frank Conte.

They needed all the help they could get to corral this guy.

"Detective Hunter? I'm Matthew Peer, Head of Security." The guy spoke as the group jogged through the main entrance. "I've got men deployed on each floor. They all have the suspect's photo and radios to call it in. We'll know immediately if they spot him."

"Great. You need to let them know to be on the lookout for members of the Mazanti family. They're probably already here as well and they'll be armed and dangerous."

"Anyway of identifying them?"

"Nope. Other than they'll be moving as fast as us, and surveying the area looking for Conte."

As they jumbled into the ground floor atrium, Hunter stopped. A policeman's worst nightmare in looking for a suspect. The scene was straight from a movie. Hundreds of civilians milled about, people moving everywhere through the center section of the ground floor atrium. Kids dashed in and out of bends of a small river walk, families took photos next to picturesque corners specifically designed for interesting snapshots, and dozens more wandering the pathways to the bars, restaurants and stores. The area resembled a rural Spanish village they called Mission Plaza, complete with trees, a winding river with trickling falls, bridges, standalone buildings and a bell tower.

The place was enormous. And packed. With far too many potential casualties.

"Holy shit."

*　*　*　*

Hunter scanned the crowd, searching for one particular face. He paid extra attention to people in hats or sunglasses, anyone trying to conceal themselves.

"This is going to take too long." Sanders stood next to him. "How are we supposed to find him in this mess?"

Two explosions echoed through the cavernous building. Gunshots. For a split second, every person in the building froze in place. Complete silence except for the trickling water in the river.

Suddenly, hundreds of people panicked. They knocked over chairs and tables to escape in every possible direction at once. The exits flooded with people pushing each other, kids crying and women screaming for their lost children.

The team of police officers found themselves swimming upstream against a tsunami of human beings. Mass chaos erupted as hundreds of panicked people pushed, shoved and trampled each other to get outside.

Hunter, Sanders and Matthew Peer pressed against the wall to avoid the mass exodus.

"Where did that come from?" Hunter franticly swiveled his head and searched in every direction he could.

"No idea. The acoustics in this place are shit." Peer looked up and searched the walkways on each floor. "I think it came from upstairs." He pointed up toward the guest room balconies on the upper floors.

Hunter followed his direction, but the hallways weren't visible from their vantage point. "Billy, get Grapevine PD to accompany us. Deploy three on each floor and start looking for both Frank Conte and Mazanti's guys. Be careful."

Sanders yelled the instructions into his phone, barely heard over the roar of the crowd.

Hunter pulled out his phone and dialed. "Zeke? Where are you?"

"We're pulling up outside. What the hell is going on? There are people everywhere."

"Shots fired. Set up a perimeter. Don't let anyone out of the area. Mazanti's goons are searching the place and Frank Conte is here somewhere. My guess is he's going to try to crowd surf his way out of here."

"We'll try, Cowboy. But I've only got a team of eight, it's getting dark, and there are hundreds of people scattering in every direction."

"Do what you can. We have to find him."

*   *   *   *

Frank stuffed everything he could fit into his go-bag inside his room when two muffled pops stopped him short.

Were those gunshots?

What the hell?

He stuck his head out onto the balcony of his sixth floor room. Chaos boiled on the ground floor. People running for the exits and scattering like roaches. Running against the current were two of his uncle's men dashing through an elevator lobby on the fifth floor.

Shit.

He grabbed his bag, tucked the gun into his waistband and bolted out the door.

Can't use the elevator. Gotta take the stairs.

He ran down the long hallway toward the exit sign and hit the door at full speed. He barreled down the stairs two at a time, his chest heaving.

*   *   *   *

"We need to know where those shots came from," a Grapevine police officer called next to Hunter. "All my men are accounted for."

Hunter pointed at Matthew Peer, the security head. "Have all your guys checked in?"

The man spoke into his radio as calm as he could, but concern filled his eyes.

Reyes came swimming through the crowd. "Cowboy, I've got something."

"You got a room number?"

"Three possibilities."

"Read 'em off."

Reyes looked at his note pad. "There's a Frank Lawrence in

room 7110, a Frank Condit in room 6150 and a Fred Conte in room 5212."

Hunter turned back to Peer. "Do you have master keys to all the rooms?"

"We all do. It's an electronic keycard."

The radio in Peer's hand crackled to life. "Boss, Charlie's been shot. In the hallway on level five. He approached two guys and they shot him without warning."

"Oh my God." Peer's face turned ashen.

"Hang on." Hunter grabbed his phone and punched a number. "Billy, start your search on level five. One of the hotel security guys is down. Call for an ambulance. Be on the lookout for Mazanti's guys. It was likely them."

Hunter nodded and look at Reyes. "In addition to the Grayson guy, take a Grapevine uniform with you. Start on seven and work your way down. Call me if you find him."

One of Peer's team came from around a corner. He and Reyes bolted for the elevator.

Hunter scanned as much of the ground floor as he could see. By now, most of the guests had made their way outside. The huge open air atrium was eerily quiet.

"Any suggestions on how to make this search easier, Mr. Peer?"

"Actually, yes. Follow me."

*　　*　　*　　*

"Freeze! Police!"

The words echoed from somewhere above. Followed instantly by a volley of gun fire.

Hunter and Peer instinctively took cover. Hunter drew his Glock and tried to determine where the shots came from. He grabbed his phone and dialed.

"Jimmy? Was that you?"

"No, we're on seven. I think it was below us."

Another round of shots cracked the air.

From the volume and cadence, there were multiple shooters.

Three Grapevine patrolmen burst through the doors, running

past Hunter and Sanders toward the elevators.

"What's going on?" Hunter fell in behind them.

"Two of our guys on five are trading fire with at least two unsubs. A hotel security guard is down."

Hunter surveyed the area. "I've got one of my guys heading that way with an ambulance en route." He stopped and let them go on. He had to let them fight it out with Mazanti's guys.

His focus was finding Frank.

He signaled Peer. "I'm following you."

Peer led him to the now abandoned front desk. Through a door behind the desk, Hunter followed him into a command center that looked like NASA's mission control. There were ten command pods, each manned by a security guard with multiple monitors displaying closed circuit television feeds from all over the resort.

"Damn." Hunter could see the activity unfolding on every floor and in every nook and cranny of the entire complex.

Hunter's phone buzzed.

"Hunter here."

"Cowboy, it's Jimmy. The seventh floor Frank Lawrence wasn't him. The sixth floor room might've been him. Looked like someone left in a hurry, but he's gone."

"What section is that room in?"

"Northwest quadrant."

"Thanks. I'll see if I can find him." Hunter glanced over the shoulder of a guard. "Meanwhile, you've got a pair of Mazanti's guys a hundred feet up the hallway from you. Be careful, but take them down."

"You got it, Cowboy."

Hunter hung up, stuffed his phone in his pocket and continued to watch several screens. Searching…

"Detective." A guard waved him over to his command pod. "Here's someone moving fast down the stairs. Is this your guy?"

Hunter moved across the room and watched a man dashing down the stairs, a black canvas bag slung over his shoulder. He stopped at the bottom, then leaned against the wall. Out of breath.

A smile broke across Hunter's face. "I got you, you son of a bitch. Where are those stairs?"

MURDER BY PROXY

*   *   *   *

Frank was so out of breath, he had to lean against the wall in the stairwell. He was doubled over, sucking in gulps of air and working his brain to figure out his next move. On the outside of the door marked Lobby, it sounded like a war raged with more gunshots and screams.

The only other door available was marked Vineyard Tower on the other side. He had no clue where that led.

He poked his head out the Lobby door.

Even though the crowds had thinned, the number of cops roaming around was more than he wanted to risk. When he poked his head out the Vineyard Tower door, he smiled. Exterior lights led to a view of the small lake directly in front of the valet parking area.

An easy, clear exit and he could blend into the crowd, and be just another panicked patron of the Grayson Resort.

Freedom was just a few feet away.

*   *   *   *

Reyes moved fast down the hallway with one of Peer's guys and a Grapevine officer on his hip. They stayed close to the wall and strained to look around the curves to catch a glimpse of Mazanti's guys.

As they rounded a corner, Reyes pulled up his weapon fast and locked into a shooting stance.

"Freeze Police!" His voice boomed in the hallway.

Thirty feet in front of Jimmy, two men dived for the ground. In different directions, they spun and raised their weapons to fire.

Reyes pulled the trigger.

Gunshots rang out in a deafening roar. Bullets flew in all directions, blowing out light fixtures and ripping through walls.

One of Mazanti's guys dropped. Something hit Jimmy with a force he couldn't fathom. It was like being kicked by a mule. He was on the ground looking up at the ceiling before he realized he'd been hit.

The second Mazanti thug spun and took off down the hallway, leaving his partner lying on the floor.

The Grapevine patrolman fired three quick shots in the direction of the fleeing subject while the security guard knelt beside Jimmy. "Detective, where are you hit?"

"I don't know." Jimmy's voice turned raspy. Hot liquid poured over his hand clutching his side.

*   *   *   *

Hunter struggled for speed as he ran through the lobby toward the set of elevators on the northwest edge of the complex. His legs fought him as he neared an annex building called Vineyard Towers.

He rounded the corner connecting the Vineyard Towers to the main hotel, just as Frank stepped through the door to the elevators.

Their eyes locked. Both men froze.

Hunter reached for his Glock. "Stop right there, Frank."

Frank retreated back into the elevator lobby.

By the time Hunter made up the hundred feet to the door, Frank was nowhere to be found.

Hunter had to guess.

Did he get back on one of the elevators and go up?

Did he take the door to the lobby?

Or the hallway toward the Mission Plaza?

His brain processed the options like a super computer on speed.

He wouldn't have gone up.

The lobby's full of cops.

Hunter had a Grayson Resort Security radio clipped to his jacket, the earpiece shoved in his right ear, and his cell phone in his left hand. His right hand shook as he held his Glock, and headed for the Mission Plaza.

*   *   *   *

"Do you have eyes on the guy that was just in the elevator lobby near the Vineyard Towers?" Hunter struggled to whisper into the radio, hold his phone, hold his Glock and run at the same time.

"We caught a glimpse of him. You're headed the right way, but he slipped out of view."

Hunter stopped just inside the door leading out into the huge center atrium. Not only did he not want to just bolt through the door without knowing Frank's position, he also needed to reshuffle his resources.

"Zeke?" Hunter put the cell phone to his left ear.

"We're working it, Cowboy, but it's chaotic out here." Zeke yelled over the sounds of sirens, engines and panicked people.

"Don't worry about crowd control. Frank is still in the building. I need you to split up your men and deploy them to cover every hotel exit. He's in the center atrium and we have to keep him there."

"Roger that, Cowboy. Watch your six."

*   *   *   *

"Hang on, Detective. Help's on the way." The Grapevine patrolman knelt beside Reyes. He pressed a towel against Jimmy's side. The fabric was soaked bright red.

"Let...Hunter...know..." Reyes' chest heaved as he gasped for air between words.

The patrolman nodded. "We'll take care of it. You focus on breathing." He turned to the Grayson Security Guard. "Where the fuck are the EMT's?"

"They're on the elevator. Almost here." He reached for his radio. "Matt? You there?"

Mathew Peer's voice crackled over the radio. "What's your status?"

"We've got two down. One suspect is dead. Detective Reyes has been hit. EMT's arriving now. He's conscious, but losing a lot of blood. He wants to make sure Hunter knows."

Peer responded on the radio. "Take care of him. I'll pass on the news."

*   *   *   *

Hunter started to move through the door from the elevators to the ground floor atrium, but the radio squawked in his ear.

"Detective Hunter. This is Matthew Peer. Detective Reyes has been wounded."

"Shit. How is he?"

"Alive, but critical. Care Flight is en route. ETA five minutes. Once they load him up, they'll head to John Peter Smith Trauma Center. He'll be in great hands there."

Hunter paused, and took a deep breath. More gunshots rang out from somewhere in the complex. The sound jarred him back to the task at hand. "Thanks, Matthew. Keep me posted."

"Roger that."

Hunter punched a number into his phone and listened for the ring.

Parker answered. "Almost there, Cowboy. What's up?"

"Turn around and head to JPS. Jimmy's been shot. He'll be there via Care Flight in twenty."

"Oh, God. How bad is it?"

"No idea. Bad enough for Care Flight. Just get there. I don't want him to be alone."

"On my way."

Hunter pocketed his phone. He forced himself to breathe.

Focus.

He had to know which way Conte went. He got back on the radio.

"Any sightings of our guy?"

"Not yet. We're scanning every camera we've got. There are a lot of blind spots in Mission Plaza."

Hunter signed off. He weighed his options.

Walking out there now is a crap shoot. If he sees me first, I'm dead.

Waiting here is a waste of time, and he could slip through the cracks.

"Fuck it."

Hunter pushed the door open.

Chapter 73

Hunter moved into the atrium, each of his senses on edge. His legs ached, but he stayed crouched low and hugged walls, trees and fixtures. He listened for movement, footsteps or any sound revealing his prey. The sporadic eruption of gunfire in other parts of the complex complicated his hunt.

He crept down a pathway, past a restaurant called Zeppole and entered the center of the atrium. The amount of space to cover was daunting. The thick patches of trees and shrubbery intermixed with a winding river, bridges, multiple terraces and several standalone buildings, made him feel like he was searching through an entire village alone.

In the main pathway at the center of the complex, he found a cubby hole to crunch into. Pulled out his phone and called Billy.

"Hey, Cowboy." Sanders' voice was low and tense.

"Where are you?"

"Eighth floor, trying to see around a corner. I popped two of Mazanti's guys down on six. A third one bolted and I've been on his tail ever since. I think I've got him trapped."

Hunter did some quick math. Reyes had taken out one of Mazanti's guys, and, based on camera observation, the thugs had started out with eight.

"Try to get that situation resolved quickly. I'm playing cat and mouse with Frank in the ground floor village, and I need some help. Otherwise, we could be at it all night."

"Give me five minutes, and I'll head your way." Sanders clicked off.

Hunter stayed in his spot for a minute, analyzing the situation. There were a thousand possibilities, and none that stood out. A wave of exhaustion washed over him. For a moment, it was all he could do to not pass out.

In all the excitement, he'd forgotten to take his medication.

He shook his head and refocused. Another barrage of gunfire exploded from the upper floors.

His mind flashed to Reyes, and then to Sanders. Worry crept through him, the fate of his men was on his shoulders. His phone buzzed.

"I'm on my way." Sanders' voice was full of adrenaline. "Mazanti's down another man. Maybe the others will bug out."

"Let's hope. I'm headed to the lobby. Meet me near the valet. I want to get reinforcements and go at this logically. Zeke's team has all the exits covered, so he's not getting out of the building."

*   *   *   *

By the time Sanders made it to the lobby, Hunter had recruited four Grapevine patrolmen and three Grayson Security Guards and had them gathered in a circle.

"Okay, here's the plan." Hunter nodded to Sanders as he joined the group. "I want three teams. Two Grapevine PD and one hotel security will take the east atrium. Two Grapevine PD and one hotel security will take the west atrium. One hotel security, Billy and I will take the center atrium."

He waited as the teams formed. "I want hotel security officers to be in constant contact with the command center via radio. Your role is to be our navigators. The command center has the cameras and you know the building." He looked at the Grapevine patrolman. "Be methodical. Look in every nook and cranny." He looked around the group and made eye contact with each of them. "Most importantly, be careful. This guy is responsible for a string of dead bodies, and he's trapped like a wild dog. He won't hesitate to shoot if he thinks there's a way out."

Heads nodded. Each man checked his firearm and they moved out to their assigned areas.

Hunter looked at Billy. "Enough bullshit. Let's get this son of a bitch."

Hunter and Sanders led the way, leapfrogging each other as they moved down the main pathway. The layered levels, uneven topography and the heavy landscaping made it impossible to see much more than twenty feet ahead at ground level. Anything beyond that was around a curve or obscured by landscaping.

Even though night had fallen outside with the stars twinkling above the glass ceiling, inside the building might as well have been high noon.

"Detective!" The security guard slapped the ground to get Hunter's attention.

Hunter crouched over toward the guard. "What do you have?"

"Command says they saw someone dart into Texan Station."

"Where is that?"

"Up the path to your left about seventy-five feet."

Hunter nodded and resumed his lead position. He pushed forward quickly. Sanders and the security guard rushed to keep up. Hunter wasn't exactly sure where he was going. He just hugged the side of the path and moved from one cover spot to the next.

As he rounded a long bend, his eyes caught a flash of movement and he ducked behind a decorative concrete garbage can. The explosion of gunfire sounded like it was right in front of him. The bullets impacted the concrete tearing craters into the sides and showering Hunter with small bits of concrete shrapnel.

He had no line of sight on Frank. He willed himself not to move. As the sound subsided, he heard footsteps running away. He took one quick peek around the corner and bolted after the sound of the steps.

"He's heading toward the Bell Tower." The security guard's voice seemed to be a mile behind Hunter.

The Bell Tower was up to his right.

"Billy, flank left." He didn't wait for a response. He ducked off the path and tore through bushes and trees.

After about twenty feet of thrashing through shrubbery, he spilled out onto another path. Shots once again exploded and ricocheted off the concrete near his feet. He jumped behind a stone wall.

Footsteps charged off once again. His pulse pounded between his ears louder than his heaving breath. There was no time to settle himself. He launched once again toward the footsteps.

As he ran towards the Bell Tower, he had no idea where Billy or the security guard had gone. Hopefully, they heard the sounds and circled toward the other side of the Bell Tower.

Bushes shuffled twenty feet ahead of him down the path.

He pushed his legs to pump faster as he awkwardly ran, his Glock held out in front, trying to maintain some semblance of a firing position.

Rounding a curve, the back of someone's head ducked into a small bar near the base of the Bell Tower. The building was an open air, adobe structure with tall tables and barstools beyond the doors.

Hunter paused to catch his breath. For the first time in this game of cat and mouse, he felt like he had the advantage. He knew where Frank was, but Frank was blind to him.

He grabbed his phone and started to punch to call Billy. He had to gather his focus as he realized his left hand shook to the point he could hardly hit the button.

Billy answered in a whisper. "Hey, Cowboy, you got eyes on him?"

"He's in the little bar at the base of the Bell Tower. Can you approach from the south?"

"Exactly where I am."

"Let him know you're coming. Flush him back out my way. I'm waiting for him."

"Roger that."

Hunter approached the entrance Frank had used and positioned himself off to the left of the door where he couldn't be seen.

Sanders clomped down the path toward the front of the bar, the noise crystal clear, followed quickly by Frank's feet scurrying across the rock floor directly toward him.

The door burst open. Frank barreled through the door and out from the awning. He never saw Hunter until he was fully exposed.

"Freeze, Frank! Police! Don't move."

Frank stopped as if he'd hit a brick wall. He raised his hands, his pistol pointed up.

Hunter stood less than three feet away, his Glock aimed at

Frank's chest.

Both men froze in place, the seconds drawing out with each heartbeat.

Hunter's Glock jiggled and shook uncontrollably.

In unison, both men looked at Hunter's Glock. Shaking.

For a moment, Frank's face registered hope. As if he thought he could make a break.

Before Frank had a chance to make a bad decision, Sanders burst through the door with his gun targeted at Frank's head.

"Drop the weapon, Frank. Hands behind your head."

Frank complied. His gun clattered to the ground at his side.

Billy moved to cuff him.

Hunter let out a deep breath, his ears pounding.

Billy looked over Hunter's still shaking hands.

"You okay, Cowboy?"

He holstered his Glock as all the energy drained from his body at once. He ran his hand through his hair. His fingers trembled against his scalp.

"I'm fine." He pointed to a bench. "Just need to sit a moment."

Sanders didn't respond. He just stared at Hunter, his concerned expression clear he wasn't buying it.

Hunter shook his head.

"We'll talk later. Read this prick his rights and get him out of here."

Chapter 74

"Hey, Cowboy." Jimmy Reyes sang in a weak voice. He smiled through his glassy eyes. "What are you doing here?" He giggled and looked around. "What am I doing here?"

It was almost six in the morning. Reyes had come out of surgery an hour earlier and the anesthesia was still wearing off.

"Oh, boy." Hunter smiled. "I'll let the doctor explain that to you. We're just glad to see you awake. It's been a long night."

Before he could say anything else, the door popped open and a whir of energy blew into the room. Dr. Conway Johnson stepped across the room while looking at a clipboard. "Detective Reyes, how are you feel—" He stopped when he saw Hunter. "You're back?"

Hunter shrugged.

"Do you come with a warning label? It appears hanging out with you is kind of dangerous."

"It's been a tough couple weeks."

"Seems so." The doctor turned his attention to Jimmy. "Detective Reyes, you are one incredibly lucky man. You managed to get shot in the torso without doing serious damage to any major organs."

"I got shot?" Reyes' sing song voice registered concern.

Dr. Johnson smiled. "Yes, you got shot. Why don't I let your friend fill you in on those details. I'll come back in a bit. Try to get some rest." He pointed at Hunter. "Keep it short."

He was gone as fast as he'd come and Hunter spent the next few minutes trying to explain. Though he doubted the man would remember any of the conversation. Reyes spent that time reaching for imaginary butterflies.

* * * *

"This is starting to become a bad habit Detective. I've had to clean up after you more times in the last two weeks than I have in the last two years. My patience is wearing out." Lieutenant Sprabary directed Hunter to sit.

On the drive from the Grayson to John Peter Smith, Hunter had confided in Sanders and had told him about the diagnosis and all that had led up to it. Billy was understandably shocked, but, as expected, was supportive. He was concerned about what it meant to Hunter's career. So was Hunter.

Now, the Lieutenant was expecting a full debrief on everything that led to the arrest of Francis Lorenzo Conte, as well as the arrests and deaths of the other members of the Mazanti organization. Hunter was prepared to give him a full report.

Based on what had happened during the arrest, Hunter also knew that his debrief would have to include a discussion about his health. Any possibility that he could keep his diagnosis a secret, had flown out the window when he couldn't keep his pistol from bouncing around like a jumping bean.

"Yes sir, I'm sorry abo—"

Sprabary cut him off with an arched eyebrow. "Other than turning one of the biggest local tourist attractions around into a huge crime scene, shooting up several organized crime thugs, getting one security guard killed and another detective shot, how was your day yesterday?"

He swallowed the lump in his throat. "I've had better."

Sprabary nodded. "On the bright side, I understand Jimmy is out of surgery and out of the woods. And Francis Conte is in custody."

"Yes. Additionally, the video shows all four of the Mazanti fatalities fired on us first. We also arrested two other Mazanti guys. Detective Thompson from OCD spent most of the night interrogating them and believes, since they were there under direct orders to find and kill Conte, we have enough evidence to arrest Alfred Mazanti on a conspiracy to commit murder charge along with accessory to murder."

Sprabary frowned. "You really think we can make that stick?"

"Maybe not. But it's solid enough to put cuffs on him and make his life miserable for the foreseeable future. Detective Thompson and I are heading over to Mazanti's place later this morning to escort him to the station."

Sprabary nodded. "Works for me. Maybe the Grayson Resort can sue his ass for damages since the place will essentially be shut down for a couple days. Not to mention the countless refunds they'll have to issue."

He leaned back. "Why don't you walk me through the last few days. How did we get here?"

Hunter recapped the details about teaming up with Mazanti's tech team to find Conte, how Mazanti received the information first, and how the Grayson Resort became a shooting gallery.

Sprabary shook his head and gestured toward the door. "Sounds like you've got a hell of a lot of paperwork to complete."

"Yes, sir." Hunter nodded, but didn't get up.

"Is there something else, detective?"

"Yes, sir." Hunter paused, looked down at his hands, and took a deep breath. "I have a bit of a situation, and I need to inform you. Because it may... No. It *will* impact my ability to do the job."

Sprabary leaned forward, and folded his arms on his desk. "What's going on Jake?"

As he had done with Stacy and Billy, Hunter started with describing the struggles and symptoms he'd experienced the last year. He finished with the diagnosis that to him already seemed like a lifetime ago, but in reality was only ten days prior.

When he finished talking, he looked up.

Sprabary's face was pale. He looked stricken. The silence hung for a moment before Sprabary regained his composure.

"My God, Jake, I'm so sorry. Are they sure?"

Hunter nodded. "Yeah. They're sure."

His boss leaned back, the chair creaking with the weight.

"First, on a personal note, if there's anything I can do, name it. You'll have it."

Hunter smiled. "Thanks, but it's really not at that point yet."

Sprabary nodded. "Of course. I'm sorry... I just... Never mind." He paused and took a deep breath. "Jake, I have no idea what this means from a work standpoint, but as your lieutenant, I'm required to report this to HR."

"Yeah, I know."

"It's not just that." Sprabary blinked several times and cleared his throat. "I'm required to put you on administrative leave until the situation is evaluated. I—"

Hunter stopped him. "Lieutenant, I know. I expected that when I walked in here today." He paused. "I do have one request. I want to finish this case. By arresting Mazanti."

"Jake, um..."

"I'll have Thompson and Billy with me. They'll do everything except put the cuffs on him."

Sprabary sat for a moment, then looked at his watch. "You're arresting him this morning, right?"

"Yes, sir. Within the hour."

"I see on my calendar right after lunch, you're scheduled to debrief me on the case and any other relevant personal news you might have, right?

Hunter tilted his head. "Yes, sir."

"I look forward to our meeting this afternoon. Can't wait to hear the details on how you found Francis Conte, and how you got enough on Mazanti to book him."

Hunter stood and stepped toward the door. He stopped in the doorway and turned back to Sprabary.

"Thank you."

Chapter 75

"Check it out. We're back in the Explorer." Sanders smiled as he and Hunter climbed into Hunter's SUV. "No more nasty FWPD sedan."

"Yep. After our visit with Alfred, next stop is buying a new phone and getting that part of my life back together." Hunter shook his head as he pulled out of the station parking lot and headed west on Fourth Street. "I had no idea someone could hack your life that way."

"Yeah, he made it look so easy. Can you imagine if he'd gotten away? He could've tormented us for the rest of our lives, from anywhere in the world."

They both shook their heads and let the heater kick on to warm the car. The morning had broken with a brisk breeze and clouds threatening rain. As Fourth Street curved and became Macon, just before turning west on Seventh, Billy broke the silence.

"So, did you tell Sprabary?"

"Yeah." Hunter nodded, but kept his focus on the road.

"And?"

"Arresting Mazanti will be my final act before I go on administrative leave. He's obligated to report it to HR by the end of the day."

"Any idea what's going to happen?"

"You know what's going to happen, Billy." His voice was raw. "You saw what happened when we arrested Frank. They can't let that happen again."

"First, no one but you and I know what happened. Second, you said yourself you hadn't taken your meds." Sanders turned his body toward him in the car, his voice stern. "I'm your partner and I have no concerns. That ought to count for something."

A sad smile crossed Hunter's face. "Thanks Billy, but we both know Alfred Mazanti will be the last scumbag I'll ever cuff."

Billy shook his head and looked out the passenger window. "That just sucks, man. It's not fair."

They pulled into the parking garage of Mazanti's building, and found a spot.

Hunter switched off the engine and they both sat there for a few seconds.

"Life's not fair, but in the grand scheme of things, it could be a hell of a lot worse." He paused. "Look, I'll be fine. You'll be fine. We had a hell of run." He smiled. "Now, let's go cuff a mob boss."

*   *   *   *

Detective Thompson's broad smile greeted them in the lobby. "I'm so excited." He shook each detective's hand, then lowered his voice. "You guys are my lucky charm. Do you know how long we've been investigating Mazanti?"

Neither detective responded.

"Decades. Not once have we had enough to book him. Not once." He fidgeted to the point of spasms. "Now we've got him on conspiracy to commit murder. How cool is that?" He stepped toward the elevator. "Let's go get this scumbag."

"Hold on." Hunter pulled him over to the side. "Let's have a plan first. There was enough shooting yesterday. I want this to be calm and easy."

Thompson nodded. "Gotcha."

Hunter pulled paperwork from his jacket. "We've got an arrest warrant and a search warrant. There's two patrol units in the parking lot on standby. Since his right hand man, Carlos, took a bullet yesterday, we don't know who will meet us at the door. Let's keep it simple. We hand these to whoever answers the door and walk right past them. Billy will secure them if needed."

Thompson nodded again. "Sounds like a plan."

*   *   *   *

"Can I help you?" A guy who looked like Carlos' brother greeted the detectives on the top floor.

As planned, Hunter handed him the paperwork and stepped past him. "We're here for Alfred Mazanti."

"Wait, you can't—"

Sanders stepped forward and went nose-to-nose with the man.

"That warrant says we can."

Thompson was on his heels as Hunter walked quickly into the heart of the residence. He spotted Mazanti on the balcony, took a few quick strides, opened the door and stepped out.

Mazanti looked irritated, but smiled. "Detective, are you back to enjoy my view again?"

"Nope. I'm here to ruin your day. Stand up and turn around. You're under arrest." Hunter held his cuffs in his hand.

"What the fuck? You're kidding. You've got nothing."

"I won't ask again."

For emphasis, Thompson pulled back his jacket and rested his hand on the grip of his pistol.

Mazanti eyed his hand, put down his magazine and slowly stood. "Whatever. I'll be out by dinner."

Hunter clicked the cuffs in place.

"Alfred Mazanti, you're under arrest for conspiracy to commit murder. You have the right to remain silent..." His voice cracked slightly as the reality of his last arrest set in.

"I didn't know you cared about me so much." Mazanti snickered.

Hunter cleared his throat. "Anything you say can and will be used against you in a court of law. You have the right to an attorney. If you can't afford one, one will be provided to you. Do you understand your rights?"

"Sure. Whatever." Mazanti shrugged.

Hunter turned to Thompson. "Get him out of here."

As Thompson escorted Mazanti to the elevator, Hunter absorbed the view . The clouds had darkened and rain just started to spit against the glass. The weight of it all felt like he wore a lead suit. Dragging him down, and his career right along with it.

MURDER BY PROXY

"Whose are these?" The booking officer held up the handcuffs while Mazanti was fingerprinted and photographed.

Hunter held out his hand. "Mine."

The officer handed them over. "Nice collar, detective."

Hunter stared at the metal restraints in his palm for a moment before putting them in his pocket. He looked at Sanders. "You can take it from here. Call me if you need me."

Sanders nodded.

Hunter took the stairs and walked into the empty conference room. He looked around the room at the whiteboard, the maps, the tables covered with documents. Chairs sat haphazardly around the table. The silence pressed down on him in the same room where they'd solved countless investigations.

Where do I go from here?

He stepped over to the windows and looked out. Waited for something to hit him, to guide him to his next move.

He extracted his cell phone and dialed.

"Colt Barkley. We bag 'em. You tag 'em."

Hunter smiled, but his voice was serious. "How are you doing?"

"I'm healing up."

"Have you heard anything about Kenzi and the other girl?"

"Yeah. I got a call from the congressman when I got home from the hospital Sunday. She's in a medical rehab facility to detox and begin the healing process. The family was ecstatic to have her home."

Hunter nodded to himself. "Great to hear. How's unemployment treating you?"

"Too busy to know. My phone hasn't stopped ringing since yesterday. Who knew there were so many people needing security and investigation services?"

"If you've got a minute, I might be able to help with that."

Colt paused. "Cowboy, you sure as hell know how to get my attention. What's going on?"

·   Hunter once again launched into his story. While it was never

337

easy to tell even after his third explanation, he was getting used to it. The words came a little smoother. After a few minutes, Hunter wrapped it up succinctly.

"So, the net-net is you're not the only one who's unemployed."

A long moment of silence filled the phone.

Eventually, Barkley spoke in the most serious tone he'd ever heard.

"Your employment status isn't an issue. There's plenty for us to do. My concern is you. How are you doing?"

"I'm good, Colt. This is a long-term thing. My day-to-day functioning is fine, and should be for the foreseeable future."

"Okay." Barkley's smile came through crystal clear in his voice. "I guess the only real question is do we call it Barkley Hunter Investigations or Hunter Barkley Investigations?"

* * * *

"Well, hello, stranger." Stacy's voice danced through the phone.

"Sorry for ghosting you. It's been a busy few days." Hunter sat in his truck in a store's parking lot.

"Catch me up. I hear Frank's in jail and Jimmy's in the hospital."

Hunter nodded as if she could see him. "Yes on both accounts. But can I suggest we have dinner tonight? We've got an awful lot to talk about, and I'd prefer to see your face, sit with you, and enjoy a glass of wine when we do."

"That works for me. Why don't I meet you at your place around six?"

"Perfect. Can't wait." Hunter hung up and slid his phone back in his pocket.

The clouds from this morning had dissipated, and rays of deep yellow sunshine peeked through.

He took a deep breath. Through the windshield, the storefront stared back at him. The black and gold awnings fluttered in the breeze. The store manager was waiting for him inside, and already knew what he was looking for.

After a moment, he climbed out of his truck, walked up the

sidewalk and through the door.

The well-dressed woman looked up and smiled. "You must be Detective Hunter. Welcome to Haltom's Jewelers. I've set aside a wonderful assortment for you to peruse."

Afterword

As a novelist, it's almost impossible to write about a character, topic or scene without letting a certain amount of your own personality, worldview or opinions seep onto the page. While I have purposely gone out of my way to not craft any characters after myself, there is a little of me in all of them.

In this particular installment, I bent that rule a little more than I usually do. While I still didn't write any characters based on me, I did choose to challenge Hunter with a situation with which I am deeply familiar.

Parkinson's Disease is an incurable, progressively degenerative, neurological disorder which is usually diagnosed in patients in their late 50's or older. It manifests in a wide range of symptoms, most notably tremors (hands shaking), muscle rigidity and impaired movement. While manageable through medication, exercise, diet and physical therapy, as the description above indicates, there is no cure and the symptoms continue to degrade your physical capabilities throughout the rest of your life.

In September of 2019, after almost three years of struggling, and suspecting something was wrong, I was formally diagnosed with Parkinson's. I am very fortunate to have been diagnosed early and to have world class medical care. If there is such a thing as an optimistic outlook when you're talking about an incurable, degenerative, neurological disease, mine is. I'm almost five years into my Parkinson's journey and my ability to function normally on a day to day basis has not been significantly impaired. I have no idea of the path the disease will take in my case, but I remain positive and hopeful.

As I've done with my other novels, I've chosen to highlight an issue or topic so that, in addition to hopefully entertain, the book can also educate, enlighten and inform about that topic. In this case, I wanted to pull back the curtain on Parkinson's so the reader might gain a better understanding of the disease and the challenges a Parkinson's patient faces in their daily life.

The other topic I chose to highlight is the world of cybercrime. While I am by no means an expert on these topics, I've worked in the Information Technology world for nearly thirty years. I've also researched the topic enough that all the hacking techniques described in the book are very real and happen every day.

While cyber criminals may not use their skills and tools to manipulate someone into committing murder, they do use them to harass, manipulate and defraud innocent victims.

Our legislators are woefully uninformed on these topics, and therefore our laws are antiquated and often useless. Law enforcement is also well behind the technology curve.

Because of the nature of the internet, the criminals preying on innocent victims are often committing these acts from remote locations that fall out of the jurisdictions of US Law Enforcement.

There is no easy answer. The real defense is vigilance and awareness, and really strong passwords.

Acknowledgements

There is much more to writing a novel than coming up with an idea and typing it onto the page. It's a process that, either directly or indirectly, involves many people.

As always, the patience and support provided by my wife Greta and my two daughters, Caitlin and Aubrey, is priceless. I appreciate and love each of you.

I'd like to acknowledge Nicole Perlroth. Her wonderful book, This Is How They Tell Me The World Ends, was an amazing source of knowledge regarding cyber crime and computer hacking.

Once the final words are typed on the first draft, there are several folks who help carry the final product over the finish line. Beta readers and proof readers help shape and tighten the manuscript. Thanks to John Warnock, Marti Giffin, and Hank Wiechman for your time and your input.

Finally, it wouldn't be a Detective Jake Hunter novel without the amazing editing skills of Susan Sheehey. Thanks as always for helping to make the final product readable.

Thanks also to my readers for regularly reaching out and motivating me to get my hands on the keyboard. Your enjoyment is what it's all about.

Made in the USA
Columbia, SC
05 January 2022

53621510R00205